C000057503

P S Y C H
INVESTIGATION EPISODES
EPISODE ONE

KEVIN WEINBERG

First published in the United States by Ragz Books 2012

This edition published by Sehn Books 2015

Copyright © 2015 by Kevin Weinberg

The moral right of the author has been asserted.

All characters in this publication are fictitious and any resemblance to real persons, living or dead is purely coincidental.

All rights reserved.

Except as permitted under the U.S. Copyright Act of 1976, and the United Kingdom Copyright Act of 1956 and 1988. No part of this publication may be reproduced, distributed or transmitted in any form or by any means, or stored in a database or retrieval system without the prior written permission of the publisher, nor be otherwise circulated in any form of binding or cover other than that in which it is published and without a similar condition including this condition being imposed on the subsequent purchaser.

Published in United States by Sehn Books

Illustration by Daqri Combs

OTHER BOOKS BY KEVIN WEINBERG

In the Psych Investigation Episodes series
PSYCH INVESTIGATION EPISODES: Episode II
PSYCH INVESTIGATION EPISODES: Episode III
PSYCH INVESTIGATION EPISODES: Episode IV
PSYCH INVESTIGATION EPISODES: Episode V
PSYCH INVESTIGATION EPISODES: Foxes I

In the Questing Sucks! series
QUESTING SUCKS!
QUESTING SUCKS! Book II

Coming Soon:
PSYCH INVESTIGATION EPISODES: Episode VI

Questing Sucks! Book III
Spell Book

Acknowledgements

This reprint was made possible due to the support of the fans who asked for it.

In truth, I never imagined I'd end up working so hard to get out another paperback. And so, I dedicate this paperback to you.

Without you, there would be no Jack, and there would be no Foxes.

Chapter 1: Problems at School

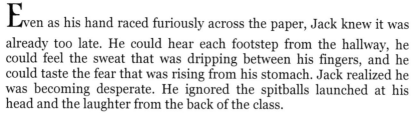

Even as his hand raced furiously across the paper, Jack knew it was already too late. He could hear each footstep from the hallway, he could feel the sweat that was dripping between his fingers, and he could taste the fear that was rising from his stomach. Jack realized he was becoming desperate. He ignored the spitballs launched at his head and the laughter from the back of the class.

"Why do you even try, Harris?" shouted a student.

Jack sat in his usual wooden desk, surrounded by his classmates, and he was overjoyed that his teacher always came late. Since the beginning of the school year, their teacher had made it a habit to arrive ten minutes late. None of the students ever minded, of course, and on this particular Monday morning, Jack Harris thanked his lucky stars for it.

In front of him were two pieces of loose-leaf paper. One was a neat, organized, and most importantly, correct, homework sheet. With each answer placed carefully on the red line, it resembled a work of art. Written at the top was the name *Adam Baker*.

The second piece of paper, although mostly illegible and appearing rushed, contained the same correct answers as the first. The left side of the page numbered one through twelve. The only problem was that the teacher had assigned *twenty* math problems to solve.

Well, I really screwed myself this time.

If Jack failed the class, he'd be forced to attend summer school, which would be catastrophic. What could be worse than school in the summer? To Jack, that was a violation of human rights.

"Time's up. Give it back," his friend, Adam, whispered. "Just hand in what you have before we *both* get caught."

"Please," Jack begged. "You know if I miss another assignment he's gonna fail me."

"Oh, well in that case ... still not my problem."

The classroom door swung open. Thirty-two students turned to face the teacher as Adam snatched the assignment from Jack's desk.

Jack's only hope was that the teacher would let him slide for missing a few questions. It was true they'd been given a week to complete the assignment. It was also true that this was one of the easier ones. But in Jack's mind, no part of this awful situation was his own fault. After all, how did the teacher expect him to complete his homework, especially when a *House* marathon was airing that week? Jack hated putting in effort, and he hated it even more when he had better things to do, like watching television and eating popcorn.

Jack shifted forward in his seat, wiping sweat from his face with the palm of his hand. He brushed aside his messy black hair that fell just short of his eyes. He looked enviously at his friend Adam, whose brilliant blond hair and stylish glasses amplified his look of intelligence. Adam was calm and collected as usual, alert, with his eyes directed at the teacher in the front of the room.

"Good morning, class," Mr. Munson said. He laid his briefcase down on the teacher's desk. Opening the folder, he took out the day's attendance sheet.

Despite the late-night movies, television shows, and snacks that had occupied Jack's life for the past week, he really had intended to finish the assignment. In fact, he had gone so far as to plan out precisely when he was going to complete it. Jack figured if it was assigned on a Monday and due the following Monday, then Sunday at midnight would be the perfect point in time to get started. Needless to say, it didn't work out quite the way he had planned it.

When the time had come on Sunday night, Jack no longer felt up for the task of doing math. After a glass of soda and a quick shower, he crawled into bed muttering "to hell with it" before rolling over and falling asleep. Well, that wasn't exactly true, either. He *should* have gone to sleep. Instead, he'd sprung out of bed and spent the next four hours reading *Bleach*. Damn internet, once it had you it was like the Matrix.

"Well," Jack said, "no one can say I didn't try."

Adam rolled his eyes. "Will you just calm down?"

"I am calm!" Jack responded just a few too many decibels above a whisper. Mr. Munson stopped calling surnames beginning with the letter *G*. He removed his gaze from the attendance sheet and his eyes fluttered around the room, searching for the source of the distracting noise.

"Excuse me, Mr. Harris. Do you have something you would like to share with the rest of the class?"

Jack pointed a finger at himself and gave a questioning look. "Do you mean me? I didn't say anything, Mr. Munson. Are you sure it was from my direction?"

Mr. Munson stood from his chair, his face contorting into a scowl. To interrupt him during attendance was one thing, to lie about it was unforgivable.

"Well now, what do *you* think, Mr. Harris?"

Jack needed an excuse, and he needed one quickly. He was never very good with words, but this time, he had an idea.

"Umm, I don't know. Maybe one of the students is a ventriloquist and he's trying to frame me. I saw this one thing on CNN about that, and wow, let me tell you—once you've seen what these ventriloquist people can do, you wanna be able to do it yourself. Like, you wouldn't even believe the—"

"Are you trying to make a fool out of me, Mr. Harris? Do you think I can't recognize the sound of your incessant yak?" The other classmates turned to watch, and Jack knew they were eager to hear more yelling. If there was one thing they all had in common, it was that they loved to see Jack Harris get into trouble.

"Well, I, umm ... what does incessant mean again? That's the one that means *not* stopping, right?" This set the class further into giddy chaos. Someone threw a paper ball, which bounced off Jack's head with a thud.

"Everyone be quiet this instant!" the teacher yelled. "Richard, if you throw another object in my class, I will have you removed. Jason, I can discipline him on my own, thank you. Keep your comments to yourself. And Mr. Harris, don't interrupt me when I'm taking attendance."

An invisible belt tightened around Jack's stomach. Shame and embarrassment spread over him like a blanket. "I'm really sorry. It won't happen again."

"Yeah, it better not. You kids need to learn that Mr. Munson doesn't take crap from anyone. Especially not you, Mr. Harris. Oh, and by the way, how did you manage to score a 'seven' on the last test? I graded it out of two hundred."

More laughter came from the class, and Jack wanted to crawl under his desk and hide from the humiliation. To make matters worse, Mr. Munson was lying! Jack's grade was a nine, not a seven. It would have been a fifteen, too, but the evil teacher had marked him wrong on a question he'd answered correctly. At least, Jack was pretty sure he'd answered it right.

Of course I did, Jack reassured himself. *Two plus 'X' equals 'Z.' Everyone knows that!*

Jack cringed while he waited for the laughter to die down. The worst part was that Melissa, the girl he had his thinly-veiled crush on, had laughed harder than everyone. She sat two seats in front of him. Her golden hair dangled from her shoulder and ran over the back of her seat. She had beautiful blue eyes and a warm smile. Jack's heart beat faster at the sight of her.

"Before we start today, I'm checking your homework, which I really hope you all completed. It is, after all, fifteen percent of your grade." The teacher hummed and wiggled his finger. "It all adds up, it all adds up."

Adam sighed. "I suppose we've got no choice here. Alright, look, just give me your paper. I can copy your handwriting pretty well, and I'll finish these last few before he gets to us, okay? But this is the last time, Jack. I swear it. And don't even give me that look."

Jack had to cover his mouth to stop himself from bubbling with excitement. He waited until Mr. Munson faced away before sliding over his pen and paper.

As usual, it was an incredible sight to behold, for not only was Adam writing at a lightning-quick speed, but he was making his handwriting appear identical to Jack's. For the next few moments, Adam's hand skipped and danced over Jack's paper, at a speed that made Jack wonder how he wasn't burning a hole through it.

"Okay, it's done."

"Wait, already?"

"Yeah, it was easy. Just make sure you—"

Adam stopped short and his eyes widened. He bit the corner of his lip.

"Adam, is something wrong?" Jack asked. He didn't understand what could have stopped Adam mid-sentence. A few seconds went by before Adam turned and inhaled, meeting Jack's eyes.

"Jack."

"Yeah, what's up?"

"Do you remember when I told you to copy my homework exactly as it appeared?"

"Yup. I wrote it just as you said—number for number, word for word."

"Well, when I said that, I thought you understood what I meant by 'copy exactly'."

Now Jack was confused. What was Adam talking about? Why did he look so angry?

"Do you see *this*?" Adam slid the homework back over to Jack, pointing to a spot at the top of the paper. "Do you see what *that* is?"

Jack gasped. His eyes were ready to pop out of their sockets. Nerves rushed into his stomach, and his pain grew exponentially.

"When I told you to copy my paper, I assumed you wouldn't put *my* name on the top of yours too!" Adam's tone was a whispered scream. "Why are you such an idiot? How did you manage to copy my name as well? Tell me, Jack, is this news to you? You know, that you're supposed to put your own damned name on your own damned paper? And to make it worse, you wrote it in pen."

Jack wanted to close his eyes and pass out. Now, both he *and* Adam were in jeopardy. "Adam, I—"

"Don't even speak," Adam said, cutting him off. "Sometimes you amaze even me with your stupidity. We'll just have to find another way out of this."

Jack felt another violent pinch in his stomach, the fiercest yet, causing him to steady himself with a trembling palm on his wooden desk. "Aww man, my stomach is killing me."

4

Jack could tell by the wrinkles forming under Adam's eyes that his friend was taking notice of his pained condition. "What's going on with you today?"

"It's nothing," Jack said. "I just, well, I'm nervous is all."

"Alright, just take it easy. No sense having a fit over this."

Adam's words were ineffective. Jack barely heard them. He was too busy following Mr. Munson with his eyes, watching each step as the teacher neared their desk. Jack's arms trembled, his pain intensifying. A hot, prickly sensation ran across his spine, and Jack twitched, knocking his pen and notebook to the floor.

"Hey, seriously, man, are you okay?"

Why is my stomach hurting so much?

The pain multiplied. His stomach felt as if it were being sliced open. Jack had missed many assignments before, but why was this one so important? He couldn't understand it. All he could do was watch in silence as Mr. Munson came closer and closer to his desk. Everything was going wildly out of control. His head started to fog up. The room was spinning, each rotation adding another notch of pain. He closed his eyes, wondering what was happening to him.

Then, as if he'd fallen out of reality, there was pure silence. Jack could no longer hear the sound of Adam's voice, he could no longer hear the sound of Mr. Munson checking papers, and with a start, when Jack opened his eyes, he realized he could no longer see the two, either. Everything had gone black. All at once, his vision had been stripped from him, and the entire world had been submerged into darkness. Nothing filled his vision, nothing filled his mind, and nothing filled his ears. He was senseless.

Jack tried to look around the room, but he could see nothing. The spinning had stopped, and thankfully, all at once the pain in his stomach faded. Everything was quiet.

It was then that Jack came to realize the assignment didn't matter to him. In fact, even his own well-being didn't matter to him. He was calm, and yet something else—Jack felt his mind open like a door sealed shut for hundreds of years. For the first time in his life, everything became crystal clear. A simple truth emerged. It was a truth that was so obvious, so apparent, and so pure. It was a simple fact, a simple reality made bright.

If the damned assignment didn't exist, it wouldn't even matter if I did it.

Jack didn't know why the words had so much meaning to them. Obviously, if there had never been an assignment to finish, he would not have had to complete it, but what did *that* matter? There *was* an assignment, and yet he had *not* completed it. And there was nothing he could do to change that, right?

But what if I could?

Jack filled with excitement. What if he could change it? What if there was still something he could do to fix everything? Something had clicked in his mind, something he couldn't explain.

In that instant, sound returned to him, as well as sight. The class was once again noisy and chattering away while waiting their turn to have their homework checked. Jack surveyed the room. He could once again see the gum-filled desks, the blackboard, and the freshly-cleaned tile floors. He could see something else, too. There was wild amazement in Adam's eyes.

"Adam, what's wrong?" Jack asked. His voice was calm and serene.

Adam's expression held an air of disbelief. "Something is dangerously wrong here. It's like … It's like someone poured drops into your eyes when I wasn't looking. Your eyes are dilated."

"My eyes are what, Adam?"

"Jack, don't move." Adam rose from his seat and turned to face the teacher. "Mr. Munson!" he called. "We have an emergency." The class turned to face Adam, all probably eager to find out what was happening.

"Well, it had better be, for you to disturb me during a homework check."

"Mr. Munson, it's Jack, he—"

An ear-piercing scream from the back of the room cut Adam off. Everyone turned to look at the redheaded girl who jumped from her desk, knocking over her chair in the process.

"*What in the hell?*" she yelped. "Oh my god, there's a freaking fire. M-my … my desk is on f-fire!"

Burning on top of the girl's desk, in bright yellow flames, were her notebook, her homework assignment, and her binder. Dozens of students crowded around, pointing and shoving each other for a better view.

Mr. Munson, wasting no time, grabbed the fire extinguisher off the wall and sprinted to the back of the classroom, where he unleashed it on the burned papers. What had once been an organized desk was now nothing more than a charred piece of wood, covered with burnt, unreadable papers turning to ashes. Thick black plumes of smoke trailed from the wrecked desk, filling the classroom with an acrid smell.

Mr. Munson looked down at the fire extinguisher and then back up at the class. "Somebody better explain to me what just happened. If I find that anyone was playing with matches, you can bet that your entire high school career is—"

There was another scream, this time from the middle of the room. The boy who had been throwing paper balls at Jack leapt from his burning desk and fell backward. Every paper on top of it was now shooting flames.

"Oh, for the love of God, what is happening now?" Mr. Munson darted to the middle of the room, fire extinguisher in hand. He wasted no time hosing down yet another desk.

He wasn't half finished putting the flames out when two more students cried out, one from the front of the room and one from the back, each with their desk on fire. Mr. Munson, now in a complete state of confusion, sprinted back and forth between the three fires, trying to put little bits out at a time, as if he was somehow holding each at bay. Students panicked. Shouts of terror filled the classroom.

One by one, the papers, homework assignments, and notebooks erupted in flames all around the classroom. Eventually the class became too shocked to speak, settling instead for barely audible whimpers. Adam and Jack stood up in unison as their desks ignited. The smell of smoke was thick in the air, and as if on cue, the sprinklers above activated, showering the room with cold water.

The bright yellow flames continued until every last desk—including the teacher's—had been set alight. Mr. Munson's mouth fell open while he watched the impossible take place. Between his drenched hair and horrified expression, Jack found the sight of him comical.

"Everyone out of the classroom—now!" Mr. Munson opened the door and evacuated the room. He might not have known what was going on, but Jack knew that now wasn't the time for the teacher to worry about it. His first priority was the safety of the students.

Everyone on the third floor tried to catch a glimpse of the fire before being led out of the school. That is, everyone except Jack, who was shaking his head in confusion, marveling at the coincidence that had just taken place. He felt a bit groggy, and he had the feeling that he'd forgotten something very important, but he pushed the thought out of his mind, grateful for his sudden change in luck.

Whatever had just happened, Jack was saved, though at the expense of his entire classroom. He swore that from then on he would hand in all his assignments on time.

Oh, who am I kidding?

Chapter 2: A Bit of a Situation

"So, another child has been murdered?" Paro asked his team, his tone filled with regret. He inhaled, calming his nerves and steadying his shaking hands.

"Yes," Sarah answered, "and this one is just as bad as the rest."

Paro looked around at his team, each of them sitting at the round glass table in their newly-renovated staging room. Computers and lights blinked and flashed different colors, temporarily brightening the dimly-lit room and indicating various status updates. They had some of the most advanced technology on the planet at their disposal, but it came to them at a steep price.

To his left sat Sarah Blighter, a beautiful, slim woman with black hair tied neatly into a ponytail. She was in charge of gathering intelligence, and her brilliant mind made her right for the job. She passed the report around to Paro and the other two members of the team.

To Paro's right, sliding the paper off the table and into his massive hands, Kazou Takashi grunted. He was a muscular Japanese man whom Paro had recruited two years earlier. He tracked a finger along the report Sarah handed him and shook his head. Kazou had short black hair and several deep scars running across his face. He looked like a warrior, a man who had seen the depths of hell and lived to speak of it.

Paro sensed a grin burning into the side of his face, and he turned to glare at Michael Reed. He sat casually back in his leather chair with his legs propped on the table. Of all present, Michael had been with Paro's team the longest.

Despite all the years Paro had worked with Michael, he found him to be quite a troublesome individual. Michael's inability to take anything seriously, his utter lack of professionalism and playful mannerisms, were a never-ending distraction that often drove Paro to the edge of madness.

Paro's identity was unknown to the team. Not only his birth name, but where he was from, how he got there and any other information about him.

"So, tell me, people. What do we know?" Paro wasn't surprised when Sarah was the first to speak.

"The child's name was Jonathan Herbert. One of ours found him this morning in an abandoned baseball field outside Anker Town.

It's too early to know for sure, but from what I can see he was probably murdered in the same way as the others." She picked up the remote resting on her lap and projected the images onto the screen.

"As you can see," she continued, "much in the same way as the other children, our victim had his heart removed from his chest, punctured through his body, and then exited through his mouth."

Paro remained silent while he watched Sarah shift through the disturbing photos of Jonathan Herbert's last moments. Kazou was the next to speak.

"And just to confirm with you," he said in crisp, unaccented English. "There were no cuts or external damage anywhere on the victim?" Kazou had a surprisingly gentle voice, in spite of his scarred face and massive physique.

"That's right. Because there was no cutting, and because the victim apparently 'coughed' up his own heart, there is little doubt that a Psych is responsible. The only question left is which kind? Who or what is responsible?"

The team pondered quietly for a moment. Michael was first to break the silence. "Well hey, isn't it obvious, fellas? The murderer has gotta be a Telekinetic. I mean, since his heart was ripped through his body and all."

"It's not as simple as that," Kazou said. "Sure, an unusually strong Telekinetic Psych could have that kind of destructive power, but Psychs from that line can only move what they can see. How would this killer be able to dislodge someone's heart? It doesn't make any sense."

Michael grinned. "I'm more concerned with how Sarah is dislodging *my* heart, with that sexy smile of hers." He made an exaggerated gesture of blowing a kiss in the air. Sarah shook her head. Paro knew she was used to Michael's annoying remarks.

"Unless, he was an Unrestricted," Sarah said, prompting the entire team to once again shift in their seats. She mentioned the one thing the others preferred to be left unsaid.

Kazou leaned forward in his chair. "You can't be serious. As rare a breed as we regular Psychs are, the chances of someone having the ability to control all the lines are one in a million. In fact, with the exception of Paro here, I don't know anyone who was born with such a talent."

Paro, who had been listening in silence, decided to involve himself in the argument. "I agree with Kazou. The chances of the killer being an Unrestricted are slim to none, but there's another possibility we're overlooking. What if there was more than one killer?"

"I see what you're saying, Paro," Kazou said. "If there were two killers, and one was a Telepath, that would certainly make things easier to accept. I've heard some of them are not limited to seeing just inside the mind, but throughout the entire body. With a very powerful

Telepath, he or she could project the images directly into the mind of a Telekinetic, and then it would be quite simple for him or her to …"

"Exactly," Paro said. He folded his hands under his chin. He could see by the look on his team's faces that they were taking a moment to think of the dangerous possibility of two Psychs murdering people together. It was not a welcome thought.

A knock came from the door. A tall man entered and whispered something into Paro's ear, handing him a file before leaving.

"We seem to have some new information that may pertain to this case. There have been some … interesting developments that may lead us to be correct about our killer, or killers, being students."

The three other members of the team exhaled. In the past, some of the bloodiest and most horrifying murders turned out to be the work of mere children.

"Odd," Paro said. "It seems there was an attack today in a classroom with a probable link to a Psych."

In one motion, the team turned their heads towards Paro. Sarah exhaled, Kazou tensed, and Michael took his feet off the table and sat up straight.

Sarah exclaimed, "Was anyone hurt?"

"And who were they attacking?" Kazou asked.

"Well, according to the report no one was injured, and it seems the attacker was after …" Paro paused. He double-checked the file. Was he reading the proper information? He checked once more before continuing to speak. "It appears the attacker was after everybody's homework."

Michael scratched his nose while Sarah tilted her head like a curious puppy, prompting Paro to recheck the file yet again. He passed it around the room so his team could see for themselves.

"Do you think the attacker is one of the suspects we're looking for?" Sarah asked.

"I'm not sure. There's certainly the possibility, but I believe it unlikely. Think about it. Up until now, the murders have been conducted secretively. There's been little evidence to work with. Why would such a person give away his or her location, especially over something so trivial?"

Kazou rubbed his chin. "Well, Paro, what are the chances of more than one unregistered Psych being in the same area? Personally, I think whoever is in that class is taunting us, daring us to find them. What if our killer is growing overconfident or bored?"

"That's something we'll consider," Paro said. "But for the time being, we'll need a list of everyone in that class, along with full academic records. It's very possible we're simply dealing with some overzealous brat. But, at any rate, let's at least find out who this kid is and take him or her into custody. I'd prefer to know for sure."

"Sure, boss," Kazou said.

"Sarah, I want you at the Herbert crime scene. See if you can find anything they happened to miss the first time around, or anything else that might lead us to something of value. Michael and Kazou will go with you. After all of you have given it a final check, meet me at this Elms High. Even if this fire is an unrelated incident, I can't have some newbie Psych that just discovered their abilities running loose and starting fires." Paro looked around the room. "And everyone, please, be careful. If it turns out our killer and this kid is one in the same, we could be dealing with one of our most vicious criminals yet. Take every precaution to ensure your own safety."

The three members of his team nodded their acceptance. They rose from their seats and left Paro behind in the dim room.

His team was not unique—there were many like it around the world, all part of a government sanctioned organization designed to deal with the growing number of Psychs in recent times. Well funded and well trained, they were responsible for their own kind.

Each member of his team was a Psych. Not that there weren't many "normal" people assisting in Psych matters, but the people who ran things wanted to keep as little information as possible from leaking out. The world was not yet ready for Paro's kind, and he didn't think it ever would be.

The purpose of his team was to manage juvenile Psychs, their behavior, health and everything that fell in between. While others would scoff at their tasks and perhaps laugh it off as the easiest of the jobs, Paro knew the difficulty firsthand. On more than one occasion, they had gone after some of the deadliest killers in the organization's history. It amazed Paro how people so young could act so violently. But in a way, he understood them. Many were abused, brought into the world without loving parents, and realizing their incredible abilities, they lashed out with violence.

Paro sighed. He was a handsome man, with short black hair and dark eyes. He looked older than a man in his mid-twenties. He was muscular, though not quite to the degree of Kazou. Paro maintained a solid physique, though he wasn't as persistent in his training as he was a few years earlier. He sat up in his chair, giving the photos on the screen another glance. They caused him to wince.

Thankfully, the majority of their cases weren't murders or acts of violence. Typically, Paro's team dealt with youths discovering their abilities and acting out. There were thefts, of course, pranks and other sorts of mischief, but it was usually a matter of finding the kids and scaring them, and then freeing them on the promise of improved behavior—and their silence.

A few minutes went by, and the assistant returned, this time carrying another file containing the list of students, their ages and full academic records. Paro frowned at the man.

"No photo IDs?"

"Sorry about that, but this was all we could get. You're going to have to go down there yourself if you want to see the kids."

Paro nodded. "I was going there anyway. I'll see what I can find. Thanks, Dennis."

Chapter 3: More Problems at School

"**L**ook at her, Adam. She's so hot."

Adam listened to Jack ramble and stare longingly at Melissa. The students were crowded together in the school's football field, waiting while the firefighters extinguished the flames in the third-floor classroom.

"I have to ask her out! I mean, after that trauma we all just went through, I might have a shot this time."

Adam leaned on a fence near the bleachers, uninterested in Jack's attempt to find love. "Never mind that," he said. "That fire in the classroom—how did you do it?"

Jack paused a moment. "Hey, wait a minute. Now I know I'm not exactly an honors student here, but you don't really think I'd start a fire just to save myself from an *F*? And besides, I don't even bring matches to school. You know I don't smoke."

"That's not what I meant. Come on, you know exactly what I'm talking about." Adam opened his mouth to continue speaking—and then paused. Was it possible Jack really didn't know? Adam wasn't sure what he was accusing Jack of, either. One minute they were sitting in a normal classroom, and then, within the next four minutes every desk in the room was on fire.

At first, he thought it the work of some prankster. Perhaps someone had placed gasoline on the students' desks before class? No, that was impossible. Everyone would have smelled or noticed it.

I know what I saw. His pupils were dilated. Jack was acting very unusual.

Adam had been close friends with Jack since long before entering the tenth grade, and he was positive that his friend wouldn't lie to him.

But what happened?

"It's like I'm telling you. Your pupils were dilated, and then moments later the fires started. It was beyond insane."

Jack shrugged. "You must be mistaken, Adam. I don't recall any weird eyesight problems. You know what? It was probably just passing indigestion. Besides, the teachers already said the fire was due to like umm, a weird anomaly with the sun, or something. At least, I think that's what they said. I've never been any good with sun-stuff."

The neat lines the school had placed the students in dissolved. Students wandered off towards all ends of the field. Melissa stood on the grass near the other end of the bleachers, huddled together with two of her friends, the three of them chatting away.

"She's right there," Jack said. "I think I'm actually gonna do it this time. I'm serious. I'm feeling really lucky today."

"Look, you need to forget about that. I mean, let's face it, Jack. You're just going to humiliate yourself. Besides, we have more important things to talk about."

"Well, we can talk about whatever you want later. I'm going over there!"

Adam watched his carefree friend march over to Melissa. He decided to follow Jack, if for no other reason than pure amusement. If Jack refused to discuss Adam's theories now, he would drop them for the time being.

Melissa had transferred to Elms High during the beginning of the term, becoming immensely popular in a short period of time, although Adam didn't care much for her. She was pretentious, overly snappy, and she dressed like a woman in her late thirties. Melissa and her friends turned as they heard Adam and Jack approach.

"Hot day out today, isn't it?" Jack remarked casually to the girls. Adam took a seat on the bleachers and waited for the show to begin.

"Hey, I know you," Melissa said. "You're that kid that sits in the back, the one that's always getting yelled at by the teacher. I remember, because last week the teacher was yelling that you've missed every single assignment this term. You're Jack Harris, right?" The two girls behind Melissa giggled. Even Adam, who was normally indifferent to such comments, let out a chuckle from where he observed on the wooden bleachers.

In a sadistic sort of way, it amused Adam to watch his friend struggle to find a reply. Most people would quit while they were ahead, but not Jack. No, he wouldn't be satisfied until he made a complete fool of himself.

"Well, I guess you could say that's me," Jack said. "But come on, homework is a waste of time. Anyway, how about that fire in class today, eh? It was scary, right?"

Melissa glanced at Jack with a puzzled expression. "I think that's pretty obvious. Personally, I can say I've never seen anything like it. A girl has to learn to accept a lot of things in life, but having her desk turn into an inferno for no apparent reason, well, that's not one of them. So, is there something that you wanted, Jack?"

Adam refrained from snorting with laughter as he watched his friend try and muster the courage to move forward. Melissa's tone wasn't unfriendly, but it certainly wasn't warm. Adam felt the oncoming embarrassment in place of Jack, as he had done so many times before.

"Well, you know, I just kind of wanted to say hi, and all. I saw you standing here and I thought hey, another classmate, maybe we could talk about that crazy fire, and you know, some other stuff."

Melissa yawned and scratched dirt from under her nails as if nothing Jack said mattered to her. "It was really weird," she said. "Another mystery of life, I guess."

"You know, I actually didn't do the homework last week, and as bad as a fire is and all, I'm actually kinda glad. Now that everyone's homework has been burnt to a crisp, Mr. Munson's kind of out of luck, isn't he?"

Melissa cocked an eyebrow and then walked to the bleachers with her two friends. She took a seat before continuing to speak. "Well, some of us, Jack, actually worked pretty hard on that assignment, and won't be glad if we have to do it over again."

Jack tensed, probably realizing he'd said the wrong thing. He let out a breath and took a seat next to Melissa. She gave no indication it bothered her.

"Well, at least we're not in class for the time being."

"I suppose if you're someone who hates school that would be something to smile about." She paused. "What do you really want, Jack?"

"Well," Jack began, "Melissa, I really like you, and I have since the very first time I saw you. Now I know that I'm not exactly smart, and I know that I'm lazy, but if you gave me a chance I know I would make you happy."

Adam thought he'd fall off the bleachers. He couldn't believe the bluntness with which Jack asked Melissa out. Not only was it poorly executed, but coming from Jack, it sounded unreal.

Melissa also noted the awful attempt. She and her friends looked at each other and shook their heads.

"I'm sorry, Jack, but that's going to be a 'no'. You're a nice guy and all, but." Melissa paused for a moment. "To put it nicely, you're a mess. And as a friend, let me tell you—a girl wants a guy with at least some sense of fashion. Get a haircut, put on some muscle, and gain some ambition."

Jack's mouth fell open. He looked as if his heart had been ripped out of him and then detonated with explosives. He tilted his head down towards the grass and avoided meeting Melissa's eyes. It was cruel, but it was life. Adam was only moments from going to console his friend when Melissa shocked everyone by putting down her books and placing an arm around Jack's shoulders.

Her impassive voice softened. "Look, how about this? You seem like such a nice guy. You're not like all the other macho-brained idiots around here, and I could use a good friend like you. Why don't you let me help you with this math? I know you're struggling with it, and I'm actually pretty good. Let me tutor you."

Jack looked up from the ground, surprise forming wrinkles over his features. Adam was glad Melissa decided to spare his feelings.

"*You* want to tutor *me*?"

"Sure, why not? You could certainly use the help, and since I moved here recently I don't have a lot of guy friends." She winked at him.

Melissa and her two friends stood from the bleachers. She took one step forward then stopped mid-stride. "Oh, and by the way. We're starting tonight, so be ready for me around eight. I'll come to your place."

Adam thought he could hear the sound of his friend's heart beating faster. "You're what? Tonight!"

Melissa laughed. "Yes, Jack. Give me your address. The teacher is probably going to make us redo the assignment in record time, so ... you kind of need to learn this stuff as soon as possible."

Jack rustled around his pockets in a fanatical craze, and Adam knew he didn't have paper to write down his number. When Jack came up short he pouted, giving Adam a pleading, desperate look.

"Yeah, yeah, I know," Adam said. "This is why you should come to school prepared." Adam reached into his backpack, and then passed Jack a pen and a yellow Post-It. Jack scribbled something that might have been English, but upon closer inspection resembled ancient Egyptian hieroglyphics.

Melissa saluted them. "I'll see you boys around later." She walked gracefully away with her two friends.

"Did you see that, Adam? She's coming over tonight. I told you I was lucky today. She's going to be tutoring me. The most gorgeous girl in school is coming over to my house." Jack wore a grin, and Adam couldn't help but return a smile of his own. "Adam! Let's do our victory bump."

"No way, Jack."

"Aww, come on."

"Jack, there's no way in hell I'm bumping fists with you while shouting, 'wonder twin powers activate.'"

Adam didn't know what could've possessed Melissa to try tutoring Jack. That in itself was a lost cause. Adam knew because he had tried. He had tried on *several* occasions, he recalled bitterly. At any rate, he appreciated the kindhearted response.

"Can we please go back to what we were talking about before?"

Jack sighed. "Fine, fine, whatever."

Adam thought of a way to return to the odd conversation. He hoped for the life of him he was correct in his assessment of Jack. If the fires turned out to be the work of some freak, scientifically-explained accident, then Adam would feel stupid for months.

"Right before the fires started, moments before it was our turn to have our homework checked—what were you doing?"

"I already told you. I wasn't doing anything. You were there, remember? We were sitting down waiting to be yelled at, and the desks just started lighting on fire. If you seriously think that I somehow pulled out a firework or something, you're crazier than I am."

Adam rubbed his eyes. Clearly, his friend didn't understand what he was implying. Adam needed to explain that he suspected him of doing it mentally. Adam wasn't sure where his suspicions came from, yet he couldn't shake the constant nagging in the back of his mind that something was very wrong.

Adam was about to speak, but he closed his mouth, catching movement out of the corner of his eye. Two classmates marched over to the bleachers, halting in front of Adam and Jack. Adam knew by the scowls on their faces that the two punks meant trouble.

Adam recognized one as Richard Davins. He'd been the one throwing paper balls at Jack earlier. The other one, Adam didn't recognize. Both were giants. With each step, muscles popped out of their tank tops. Oh, they meant trouble alright.

"Wow, Jack," Richard said. I've seen some pretty stupid people in my day, but you've gotta be pretty far up that list to ask Melissa out on a date." Richard's lackey snickered like the good little minion he was. "We saw the whole thing. Pathetic, Jack. Really, really, pathetic."

Jack's face drained of color. Whenever he came across Richard, the behemoth-sized boy couldn't resist creating trouble, and it was obvious that Richard enjoyed it.

"You did a real good job, didn't you? Getting Melissa to pity you like that."

"What do you mean, pity me?" Jack asked. "We're friends and she's tutoring me. That's all there is to it, I swear."

"You know, I don't get it, Harris. I mean, did you honestly believe that a pathetic loser like yourself could even be friends with someone like Melissa, let alone date her?"

Jack held up a finger and tried to reply, but Richard cut him off. "Tell me, Jack, did you really think in that unbelievably stupid brain of yours that you had some kind of a shot? Have you lost your mind?" Other students approached, and Adam knew by their wicked grins and eager strides that they were each hoping to see a fight break out.

Adam turned to Richard. "No, I'm sure she's much better off with you, Dick. After all, I'm sure she would go together much more wonderfully with a misguided Jock whose only scholastic achievement was learning how to tie his own damned shoelaces."

Dozens of students arrived to catch the comment, laughing madly at the remark. They turned to look at the one who had said it. Adam closed the chemistry book he'd been reading and readjusted the glasses falling low over his eyes.

"Did you say something to me, nerd?" Richard glared at Adam while punching his open hand.

"Did I say anything to whom?" Adam asked. "I hear a voice, but I don't see anyone. Oh, that's right. My vision automatically filters out idiots. It's a defense mechanism, you see. I would lose my mind if I had to gaze upon brain-dead imbeciles all day."

Thirty students pointed and laughed at Richard. In a battle of words, someone with Richard's meager intellect had little chance of defeating Adam.

Rage formed lines on his pit-bullish face. Adam knew he'd provoked Richard, but Adam was feeling pretty angry too. It was true he had expected Jack to receive some kind of ridicule, but this was absurd.

"Do you have a death wish, punk?" Richard said. He flexed his muscles, accentuating them to impress the crowd.

In hindsight, I may have just made a big mistake.

Adam glanced at Jack. His friend was in his own little world, looking at the ground in silence. Then Adam turned back to meet Richard's eyes. If the larger classmate decided to make things physical, Adam doubted he would be able to do much against him.

"What are you looking at?" Richard asked. He peeked at the crowd each time he spoke. Adam knew his type. Richard needed to ensure his actions were met with approval.

What an idiot.

Jack roused as if coming out of a trance and stood beside Adam. "What's your problem with us anyway, Richard?"

Richard sneered at Jack. "I just plain don't like you, or your nosy little nerd friend, for that matter."

Adam sighed. "Well, I can assure you we don't like you either, which is why the simplest solution would be for us to not speak at all. Think of how much of this nonsense we could avoid."

Adam never understood why Richard bothered with them. If Richard hated Jack and himself as much as he claimed, why not just ignore each other completely? It was a part of human nature Adam couldn't grasp.

"Do something about it then, I'm standing right here," Richard said, missing Adam's point entirely. He spread his arms wide in an inviting gesture, once again looking towards the crowd. They were growing hungry for action. Richard gave Adam a preemptive shove that sent him backward and onto the grass, prompting the spectators to go wild.

"*Fight! Fight! Fight!*" they roared.

Adam jumped back to his feet. At this point, a fight was unavoidable. As poor a fighter as Jack was, Adam hoped they'd have a chance if they both went at Richard together. That, of course, was assuming the friend Richard brought along stayed out of it.

"Fine, if you want a fight, then I'll give you a fight," Jack said to Adam's surprise. "But not here. How about tomorrow at the entrance of the school, one hour before class starts?" Melissa was now among the spectators, which explained Jack's sudden change of demeanor. He obviously wanted to impress her.

"What's wrong with right here? Are you so afraid that you're trying to put it off?"

"No," Jack responded. "Look around. Security is everywhere. As a matter of fact, some are already on the way here."

Richard shrugged. "Whatever, it's your funeral. Just make sure you show up tomorrow, because if you don't, I will break every bone in your body."

Despite Jack's bravado, Adam knew very well that on the inside he was morbidly frightened. He was lazy and hated exerting himself. If ever someone was less suited to fighting, Adam would like to meet them.

Three men in the school's blue security uniforms arrived a few moments later, flashlights and walkie-talkies dangling from the sides of their belts. "Is there a problem?" a tall one asked, looking in Richard's direction.

"Not at all, sir, I was just having a chat with my friend here." Within a few moments the disappointed crowd broke up, leaving Adam and Jack alone on the bleachers.

"Oh God, this is horrible. I can't fight! What am I gonna do? I only acted brave because Melissa was watching."

Adam looked up towards the sky. A single cloud challenged the bright sun's rays, providing them with a few moments of shade from the onslaught of heat.

"We'll figure something out. I can't fathom why you decided to feed into him and take on his ridiculous challenge. In fact, the easiest thing to do now is to just not show up. Then he'll have just wasted his time."

Jack nodded. Adam had earned his full trust over the years. If he said it was pointless, then he was positive Jack would listen. Sure, he might experience some shame if he didn't show up, but anything was better than getting his teeth knocked out. Besides, at the very, least Jack now had something to look forward to.

Chapter 4: It Takes Three

Andy opened his eyes with a start and gasped for air. Where was he? He looked around the room, and two faces filled his vision as his eyes came into focus. Both people were dressed in black. One was a tall, slender, and handsome young man. He had dark hair and a genuine-looking smile that would've served well to cover his intentions had Andy not known what lay beneath.

Andy was new to the group, so he didn't know the man's name or the name of the woman with him. She appeared to be as young as the man, perhaps no older than eighteen. Her red hair flowed down her small face, causing shadows to create an illusion of dancing strings in the scant light.

"We welcome you to our little club, Brother Andy," the young man said. His mature voice was at odds with his youthful face. His innocent smile was disturbing, but not quite as disturbing as the girl's. Her grin carried madness, a deeply etched insanity that chilled Andy to the bone.

"For the time being, you shall refer to me simply as Ruin, and you shall refer to my sister here as Requiem." They were odd names, but Andy didn't press the point.

Andy looked around the room. It was some type of disused bomb shelter, dark, with row upon row of empty wine racks. He sat in a wooden chair with his feet resting on the gravel floor. The room was noticeably quiet—the only sound was the soft echo of their voices.

Andy had no recollection of how he'd gotten there. This was not the first time they had met, and it probably wouldn't be the last, either. The pair of them had approached Andy that morning and asked if he was finally ready. After Andy had nodded yes, he'd lost track of time.

"Do you know why you are here, Andy? Why you have come to us?"

Andy inhaled and pushed back his fear. He had been reluctant to join them. It was the most dangerous commitment he had ever had to make. Yet he knew he had no choice. In the end, society made the decision for him.

"I am here because of my right, the one that God has given me. I am here because the three of us, as well as those that will join, will reshape the world." Andy looked around at the unchanged faces of the two. Did he say the proper words?

Requiem was the first to speak. She slowly licked her bottom lip. Her madness did little to betray her beauty. "Excellent answer, Darling."

Ruin nodded. "But before you can join us in changing the world, before you can possess the greatness we offer, you must first be cleansed." Ruin's smile grew until his teeth were visible.

"It is almost dark," he continued. "Tonight, you must kill three people. Any three you wish. Bring to us something personal from each, and your admittance will be complete."

A shudder spread throughout Andy's spine. "Please, anything but that. I don't know if I can just kill people."

Requiem sighed and met his eyes. "What is the first tenet, Darling? What did we teach you above all other things?"

Andy's eyes fluttered around the room before answering. "That we, as superior beings, have the God-given right to take life from any we please."

"Correct. So why, then, does this disturb you?"

Andy thought for a moment. He didn't want to kill anyone. He wanted to change the world, for sure, and he knew this would be asked of him, but now that it was all on the table, it wasn't as easy as he thought it would be.

"Because, well ... shouldn't we kill people that deserve to die? I thought that maybe you would have a list of our enemies, or something."

"Ah, but the people who deserve to die are the ones you pick," Ruin said. "You have these abilities because you are great. Your strength gives you the right to choose."

Requiem placed a hand on Andy's knee. "Ah, my poor baby, you still don't get it, do you? It is *because* you want them dead that they deserve to die." A look of something resembling sadness crossed her fiercely beautiful face. "These gifts we have allow us to make choices that others cannot. And one of these choices can be made at this very moment. Are you a frightened sixteen-year-old boy? Or are you a great man, capable of great things? We will leave you to think on it, but I do hope you think quickly, Darling."

Andy was entranced by the soft, soothing sound of her voice. Even with her madness, he felt an instant attraction towards her.

"I understand."

"I knew you would, Darling. I knew you would."

Ruin and Requiem stood up from their chairs then climbed the dirt-filled steps to the door.

"When night falls, go and accomplish your task," Ruin said. There was a surprising touch of sympathy in his voice. "And know this. What we're asking you to do, we're not asking out of cruelty. This kind of business was difficult at first for us, as well. But while you're out there fighting your guilt and having second thoughts, try and remember how everyone in your life has treated you. We understand. We understand more than anyone. Andy, you will be our brother now, and we will be the only family you need. But first, you have to prove to us, you have to really prove to us, that you will do anything to change this wicked world we live in. And for that, it takes three."

Andy heard the creaking door open and close, leaving him alone in the dark room. One hour, that was when he would begin.

Andy climbed the shelter's steps, gravel crunching under his foot as he walked. Popping open the door, he stepped into the warm night.

I'm going to kill people.

He stopped short. The thought penetrated his mind like a dagger.

I'm going to kill people.

Andy tried to force it from his mind, to turn off his brain and continue on. But despite his best efforts, the words repeatedly entered his head. He could no more control them than he could his own crippling fear.

I'm going to kill people. This ... this is really happening. What do they mean by "I have to cleanse my soul?" Who am I supposed to kill? Richard from school, he makes my life miserable. Yes, him for sure. But how do I pick two others? How can I simply kill people who have never wronged me?

The shelter led out into an abandoned construction site. Old broken vehicles, unusable wood, and other junk lay in pieces on the gravel. The area was completely desolate, making the site the perfect— if not a little creepy—place for a meeting ground.

Lost in thought, he walked aimlessly, anxious to leave behind the scent of burnt wood. The quiet of night amplified the crunch of gravel underfoot, the only audible sound.

After a quarter-mile of walking, he left the site behind him, returning to town and the comfort of light. The town of Elms was a residential area, with houses along most streets and parks at the ends of many blocks. The first thing Andy noticed was the pleasant scent of freshly mown grass.

As typical of larger towns, it had its own school district, plenty of shops, community centers, and a usually reliable transit service. To his left, Andy spotted a bus stop across the intersection of Oak Street and Cedar Road. He walked over to it and examined the small writing on the bottom of the sign.

Fifteen minutes until the next bus, but it goes in the opposite direction of my house.

Andy shook his head. He might as well take it. He had no clear goal—wherever the bus dropped him off would be as good a place as any.

A few minutes passed, and then the dark street brightened with the headlights of an oncoming vehicle. With a screeching halt, the bus stopped in front of Andy. He gave a curt nod to the driver then chucked whatever spare change he had in his pocket into the meter before heading to the back.

It was late, so there weren't many people. To the front of the bus, a mother sat with an infant on her lap, bouncing and hushing him. Three college-aged kids mumbled amongst themselves in the rear, with thick textbooks on their laps and backpacks casually slung over their shoulders. Andy walked to the middle of the bus and took a seat across from an elderly woman staring absently out of a window.

He struggled to clear his mind but to no avail. He was aware that each person on the bus, each living soul, could have his or her life stripped away as if it were nothing. It was a disgusting, tainted feeling of empowerment.

Andy knew he had the power to end life, to deprive someone of their most basic right. But now that he had been commanded to do so, now that he would bloody his hands, Andy couldn't help but feel the weight of it all on his shoulders.

Any one of these people—with a single thought, I could end them.

He released a breath he was unaware he'd been holding. He had to take life. It was not optional but demanded of him. Andy's mind whirled in thought, his rational mind conflicting with his emotions. He knew the longer he delayed the harder it would become, and that if he waited too long, he would lose the will to go through with it. Each second saw a reinforcement of his reluctance, a growing distaste for the night's dirty work.

"It's such a warm night tonight, isn't it?" a soft voice said.

Andy turned to look at the elderly lady sitting across from him, a kind smile upon her face, her silver hair dangling over her eyes. Andy returned the smile. "It is," he said.

"I'm off to see my grandson. Tomorrow is his birthday, and I bought something very special for him." She smiled. "His name is Tommy and he turns four." Her face beamed with pride. She cradled a box on her lap—a remote-controlled helicopter.

"Wow, that's nice of you, taking the bus this late at night to bring him a present. You must be one very special grandma."

The woman nodded. "Well, I love my little Tommy. He's my son's child, but he's still my boy. Whenever I come over, he runs to the door and yells 'Grandma!' He's such a little angel."

"He sounds like one. I'm actually heading home myself. I got held up in afterschool club activities, so I'm gonna be a bit late tonight. Here's to hoping Mom doesn't have a fit. I'm Andy, by the way."

The woman giggled. "I'm Grace, and my, it is lovely to meet you, young man."

"The pleasure is mine, Grace."

Andy made idle chat with the woman for several minutes, until eventually she leaned over and pulled the yellow cord above the window to call for a stop.

"Again, it was a pleasure meeting you, Andy. I get off here, and I can hardly wait to see my little Tommy."

The woman stood with a shaking leg and held the back of her seat for support. She grabbed her walking cane and slowly made her way to the front of the bus with the gift under her arm. Without realizing he was doing so, Andy followed.

"I get off here too. My house isn't far from this stop."

Despite her wrinkled face, Andy could imagine she had been quite beautiful when she was younger. With a quick "thank you" to the driver, he stepped with her into the warm, but temperate night.

"My son lives two blocks from here, over on Powell court," she said.

"Wow, really? I live only a bit after that. Hey, I'll walk with you."

At that moment, as the sounds of their feet clicking against the sidewalk echoed in the night, Andy knew she would be the first. An ocean of guilt washed over him, and he fought not to be drowned underneath it. If he could just get it done, then he could worry about the consequences later. But if he faltered now, he would catch the next bus home and never work up the will to do it again. Not to mention there was no telling what the two creeps who ordered the killings would do if they found out.

"When I was a little girl, I used to love taking walks at night. But these days with my arthritis it gets to be just a little too painful."

"That can't have been very long ago," Andy said. "You don't look a day over thirty." Grace laughed louder than Andy would have expected from such a small woman.

"Oh, don't you go flattering me now. I'm not ashamed of my age."

They turned left at the end of a narrow street onto a slightly wider one. Neat, ordered houses with freshly trimmed grass lined each side. Most had swimming pools and some had hot tubs, as well.

They were getting closer to the home, and Andy was running out of time. But with each step he took, he felt more despair. He wished he didn't have to do this, and he tried to remind himself that he still had a choice. He could call the police and explain everything to them. He could beg for forgiveness and put all this nasty business behind him.

But would they believe a word he said? That there were people with these staggering abilities who could read minds and ... change things? Andy was one of them, and even *he* wasn't sure he believed it.

The woman paused. "What's the matter, young man? Why are you crying all of a sudden? Don't tell me some girl broke your heart at school."

Andy hadn't realized that his tears began to flow, but with small sobs, he knew he couldn't contain them.

"I'm so sorry. I'm so very sorry."

"I don't understand. What do you mean 'you're sorry'?" The compassion in her eyes added another layer to Andy's guilt. Without realizing it, Andy's sobs turned into whimpers.

"They treat me so horribly. Every day they treat me like I am trash, like I am dirt. The pushing, the bullying, it never ends. I made a deal with the devil and now I can't go back. I won't be able to go back!"

"I ... I don't understand. Is there someone I can call, ah, your mother, perhaps? Why don't you come inside? My son's home is just on the next block, and I'm sure whatever's bothering you I can—"

The woman panted. "Dear me, it's become hot all of a sudden, hasn't it?" She wiped her face with her sleeve.

Andy extended his arm, palm open. The woman's eyes flashed with confusion. For a few seconds, she met his tearful gaze, and then came the screams.

"Something is wrong with me, with my face. My face is burning!"

She wiped away another trickle of sweat, only this time, her sleeve took with it a small strip of flesh, leaving behind a pink bloodied trail that ran across her forehead. Her screams intensified. Andy ignored them, focusing on the energy gathering within him.

"Young man!" she screamed. "Please, call for help. Something is happening to me!"

Andy heard her cries, felt them rip at his soul, but he pushed them aside. Her skin softened and then in pieces, small at first, fell from her face, revealing the dark red tissue underneath. Soon her screams became wails. She clawed at her face, furthering the damage, each swipe removing larger clumps of bloodied skin. Neighboring houses turned on their porch lights, no doubt curious about the commotion. Andy hurried the process.

He watched in horror as the last bits of flesh fell away from her face, revealing a terrible sight. It resembled something out of a horror film. Soon, even her screams were hushed, as her lips melted from her face.

As her last moan escaped her, and her lifeless body fell to the floor, Andy realized that his tears had dried. This was it—he had done it, and regardless of whatever pain he felt, Andy knew the next two would come easier, especially Richard.

Richard. The name echoed in his mind, replacing guilt with anger. He would die a dog's death, far worse than the old woman's. All of this was his fault, his responsibility. He forced Andy's hand. He was the underlying cause of Andy's misery.

Several people emerged on their porches, and Andy bent down to retrieve the box. He ripped it open and took the toy helicopter. With the toy firmly in hand, he turned to flee the block. No one could've seen his face, and even if they had, Andy hadn't laid a single hand on the woman. There would be no evidence.

For five minutes he ran at a full sprint, until two blocks later he reached the corner of the street and doubled over, panting for breath. His emotions were a mess. He felt guilt, anger, terror, but oddly enough, also a creeping exaltation.

Struggling to catch his breath, Andy jumped when he felt a hand slide along his shoulder. He spun around and almost shrieked. It took a moment to register the girl in front of him. His mind scrambled to form words.

"You ... What are you doing here?"

The madness was evident. Even a small child would feel unease by looking into those dark, yet hauntingly beautiful eyes.

"One," Requiem said. She held out her hand. As if automated, Andy placed the toy in her soft palm. She turned around and walked back into the night.

Too startled to follow or call after her, Andy stood with a blank look on his face. Had she followed him? She hadn't been on the bus, and he hadn't seen her during the walk. She was the type to stand out.

When did she ...?

He forced the thought from his mind. Maybe one day he would come to understand the two and perhaps shed some light on their secrets. But anything beyond his immediate mission was out of his control. He could only do as instructed, or suffer the consequences.

He gathered his strength and continued on. Richard would, *must*, be next. Andy had earned this.

"Incredible," Paro said. He surveyed the room around him. The smell of smoke was thick in the air. Burnt desks and papers scattered about. The chalkboard had turned purple from the heat. "It's amazing no one was hurt. This is far more damage than I expected."

Paro could see he was not the only one surprised. Michael, usually cocky and self-absorbed, stood in silence. The room was destroyed, perhaps never again usable. The walls were ruined from the heat and the soaking they had received from the firefighters. Though horrific, Paro had to admit the destruction was impressive.

Sarah shook her head. "What does this tell us, Paro? Do you think this is the work of a mischievous kid?"

"I doubt it, Sarah. This was done by a Psych with experience and exceptional power. To be able to bring about this much destruction untrained, I can only assume it has to be one of the suspects we're after, the Telekinetic, most likely. To cause this much friction, though. We're dealing with someone very dangerous."

Paro swallowed before continuing. "And being that it was done in this particular class worries me, as I'm sure it worries you all, too. The best we can do now is go through each name on the list, carefully and thoroughly, and see if we can find anyone who might be worth looking into. This punk is taunting us, daring us to find him or her."

Kazou flipped through the pages of a file, pausing a moment to examine a name. "What about this kid? Richard Davins. He's a known bully, frequently suspended, even has a criminal record."

"Doesn't seem likely. I've actually looked into him already, and he's not a good match. Think about it. Here's a kid who regularly vents his frustrations by torturing the people around him. Every whim or desire he acts out without regard for consequences. No, we're looking for someone a bit more reserved, someone harboring years of rage. Whoever's doing this isn't likely to be the emotional sort. They probably have excellent control over their emotions and an even temper."

Michael, apparently recovered from his lapse of disbelief, wore a toothy grin. "That hot little biology teacher we passed looked totally suspicious. Hey, I bet she knows something. I should go ... investigate."

With a massive crack, the sound of smashing wood resounded in the classroom, as Paro's fist split a burned desk in two. "Be serious, damn you. Lives are at stake here."

"Easy now, Paro—anything odd you do will have to be explained," Sarah said.

Paro calmed down at the sight of her smile, ashamed at the sudden display of his temper. The desk collapsed with Paro's use of inhuman strength. "Just say it was weakened by the fire."

Sarah walked toward the rear of the room. She looked at the spot where math posters used to hang, only to see charred paper containing a blackened, incoherent slew of numbers.

"No matter how you look at it, this was a fortunate event. For one, no one was hurt. Now, for the first time in months, we have a lead on one or both of our killers. We have finally narrowed it down.

Be thankful for their arrogance, because there are now thirty-two names in front of us, instead of thirty-two thousand."

Paro nodded. "But still, Sarah, these kinds of things put us all at risk. It's not easy to cover up. If this continues, then people *will* start to ask questions. At any rate, we'll each have to look into these kids, at least as many as we can without drawing suspicion. I'm sure we've all got our own guesses as to which one or two are worth looking into. Pick who you think most likely and find out what you can."

"In that case, I'll look into this Richard." Kazou looked to Paro for permission, and Paro returned a nod.

One way or another, all of this would come to an end. The fool that was taunting them would regret every life stolen. In the end, they were always caught, and nothing would change that now. There would be hell to pay.

Chapter 5: Code Red

A small draft of air entered the house as Jack whirled in, slamming the door shut behind him. He threw his bag on the kitchen table and sprinted up the stairs. Reaching the top, he paused a moment and tried to catch his breath.

Jack would have been home hours ago, but Adam had made that quite difficult, nearly hauling Jack back to his house and pestering him with his ridiculous questions and theories. Now it was after dark, and Melissa would arrive shortly to tutor him. She would be there within the hour, leaving him little time to prepare.

"Mom, where are you?" he called. She wasn't downstairs, and she wasn't in the basement. The pool of light under her bedroom door and the vacuum-sounding hum were the only indications Jack needed. He dashed the few feet from the foot of the stairs to her bedroom door.

"Hey, Mom, are you in there? I could really use some help right now."

"Just a second, hun, I'm drying my hair."

Jack tapped his foot while the seconds whittled away. After a minute that felt like ten, the door opened to reveal a blonde, short-haired woman with an amused expression on her face.

She was in her mid-forties, short, and she carried herself with an air of resolve. She was a pretty woman, kind, and fun loving. For most of Jack's life, his father had been away on business of some kind or another, seldom finding the time to visit and not for long on those occasions. Most people thought Jack's parents were divorced, but his mother was very much in love with his father. It wasn't a typical relationship.

"Now, tell me what it is that's got you all worked up. And why are you out of breath?"

Panting, Jack held up a finger, taking a second to catch his breath.

"Mom, listen, I need you to help me take down all my posters and wall scrolls."

Alana blinked in confusion while Jack danced around and moaned.

"What do you mean? Why do you need to take down all that stuff? And why all of a sudden?"

"I can explain as we go, Mom, but we really need to get this done. There's no time. Oh yeah, and grab some of Dad's old sports posters and stuff and help me throw them up. I don't even care which ones, just grab any of them. Except golf, definitely no golf posters. Wait, does he even have golf posters? Ah man, why did Adam hold me up for so long?"

Jack tried to explain as much as he could, but his mother's confusion slowed everything down.

"Even the Naruto poster?"

"Yes, Mom, *especially* that one. God help me if she sees that."

Alana grinned. "She?"

Jack knew right away he'd said too much. His mother wouldn't be able to resist giving him a hard time. She had a playful nature, which at times deviated into outright harassment for the sake of amusement.

With a hearty chuckle, she said, "Who is this 'she,' Jack? Are you bringing home a girlfriend?"

Jack felt his cheeks grow hot. "She's just a friend, Ma. She's tutoring me at math, and that's all."

"She's just a friend, huh? I thought Adam tutored you at math."

"Well, she's better at it!"

Jack knew his mother was toying with him, trying her best to make him squirm.

"Does this girl have a name?"

Jack soured as even more time spilled away. "Her name's Melissa. She's a girl in my class and she said she'd help me learn the math. I figured why not? So she's just a friend and that's all there is to it, Mom, so don't ask any dumb questions or embarrass me when she gets here. And stop looking like you're enjoying this."

Alana inhaled and made an exaggerated expression of shock, as if Jack's words were cruel and unfounded. One of concern quickly replaced it.

"Jack, I got a call that there was a fire in your class today. What happened? Were you scared? I was worried, but they said no one was hurt."

Aww man, now she's gonna wanna talk about some dumb fire.

"Mom, we don't have time for idle chat. Hey, do you still have Dad's old football poster? You know, the one of that player, umm, Iverson Allenson or something?" Jack recalled seeing it up a few years back.

"I think you mean basketball, sweetie, and it was Allen Iverson. You really need to watch more sports. It's not normal for someone your age to be this clueless when it comes to man-stuff. Heck, I'm your Mom and I know more than you."

Jack grunted. He did not have time for a sports lecture from Mrs. Know-It-All.

"Whatever. Do you have anything I can put up that doesn't make me look geeky?"

Alana frowned. Jack braced himself. He knew she was not one to let her disapproval go unvoiced.

"Now why should you be ashamed of the person you are? I think you're overreacting and blowing all of this way out of proportion. If you're trying to impress a girl and you hide who you are, don't you think she'll find out eventually, anyway?"

"What? Of course not! Dad used to tell me it's a man's job to lie to a woman."

"Oh? Did he, now?" For a moment, Jack thought he saw her face darken.

"At least help me get rid of my playing cards. We can move them into the den for a little while until she leaves. If she sees my collection she's gonna laugh at me. Just make sure you don't—"

"I know," Alana said, cutting him off. "Don't touch the 'Black Lotus'."

"That's right, Ma, never ever mishandle my beta edition 'Black Lotus'. It's my most precious treasure. For no Mana, it gives me three, not two, but *three* Mana of any color until the end of my turn. No one but me can handle 'The Lotus'."

"Jack, honey, don't you think you're just a bit too young to be telling *me* how to handle a 'lotus'?"

"No, why would I be? You don't even know anything about Magic the—" Jack stopped short. "Oh, wait, oh, OH MOM, come on." Jack felt his face flush with embarrassment. Alana erupted with thunderous laughter.

"Look, hun, you're not changing anything. I'll be damned if I'm raising a coward who needs to hide behind false images of himself. Just be yourself. The way you always talk about this girl to Adam over the phone—and yes, I can overhear your conversations, don't give me that look—I know you really like this one. But trust me, you're a great person, and I promise you that you alone are enough for any girl, and always will be."

Jack didn't know how to respond. He felt his eyes grow moist at the confidence his mother had in him.

"Thanks, Mom. I just hope I have enough time to prepare before she gets here."

As if on cue, loud chimes rang over the intercom, announcing a visitor.

"Ah, that's the door. Well? Go answer it, Jack."

In the time between heartbeats, Jack went from calm and collected to nervous and frantic.

"I don't know if I'm ready for this! What if I say the wrong thing? What if you embarrass me by accident? What if I trip and fall on my face, and then I have to go to the hospital, cause like, I'd be bleeding from falling?"

"Man up, Jack, and get the door. Or I will." The playful-yet-sinister look returned to her eyes.

Jack ran down the stairs in pairs of two and then paused in front of the door. Reflexively, he patted his shirt and the sides of his black jeans. He tugged to straighten out each end. With a deep breath, he opened the door.

Standing in the frame was the goddess he'd come to fawn over. Her delicate golden hair rested gently on the back of her pink tank top. She wore tight-fitting jeans, and her arms were crossed, cradling math books, extra pencils and a bundle of loose-leaf paper.

"Hey, sorry I'm late. I got a bit held up on the way over here. Are you just going to stand there or let me in?"

Jack tried to form words, he really did, but nothing seemed to come out. Instead, he forced his feet to move. He stood aside and waved his arms toward him in an inviting gesture.

Melissa entered the home and followed Jack into the kitchen. She set down her books and turned her gaze on him.

How can anything be this pretty? It doesn't even make sense.

Jack forced saliva into his mouth and spoke. "Can I get you something to drink, Melissa?"

"Just water—I'm trying to watch my weight. The last thing I need is soda or more carbs."

Gliding down the staircase behind them, Alana Harris carried a look of pure amusement as she examined Melissa like a hawk searching for prey.

"You must be the Melissa my son has told me so much about."

"Only good things, I hope."

Alana gave Jack a wink that he prayed to all known deities went unobserved by Melissa.

"Well, we might as well get started. We've got a lot to cover, and you're pretty far behind. Where's your room?"

"This way," Jack croaked.

"This is impossible. No human brain can comprehend this stuff. It's completely and utterly impossible."

All thoughts of happiness, joy and even apprehension had been thrown out the window in favor of total frustration.

"Oh, stop being such a baby and actually look at the problem. Okay, look. The integral of 'two x squared, from zero to four.' Just like all the other problems, we just need to add 'n plus one' exponent and divide by 'n plus one'."

Jack inhaled. "Melissa, I understand what you're saying, but all I see here is a 'two' and an 'x.' Where is this 'n' thing? If I didn't know any better, I'd say you're making this up as you go along."

Melissa chuckled. "Oh, come on, you asked me the same question just before. The 'n' value is what we call the degree of the exponent. In this example, it's two, because we have an 'x squared'."

Jack looked at the loose-leaf paper and stared at it with the intensity of a burning star.

"Okay. I think I see what you're saying. Basically, what you're trying to tell me is that this garbage is beyond what the human mind is capable of solving, no sane person can do it and we should just give up because no one would ever need or want to know this stuff."

"Yep! I think you finally solved the enigma. The real way of winning is not to play!"

Jack scratched his head. "Stop teasing me. I'm really trying here."

He flinched as Melissa ruffled his hair. "Hey, you're actually making progress," she said. "Don't feel down. I mean, look, you managed to finally get derivatives ... even if it did take us all night."

Jack smiled as the reality of his situation dawned on him. He was in the company of a beautiful woman who wanted to help him, and he had made her proud. Melissa laughed and playfully punched him on the arm.

"What are you smiling about?"

When she laughs she's so beautiful. Well, even when she doesn't she is, but especially then, when her smile lights up her face.

The sound of his mother's voice snapped him out of his reverie.

"Jack, Melissa, dinner's ready. Come down!"

Melissa followed him down the steps to the warm smell of a pot roast. Initially, Melissa had insisted she wasn't hungry and that Alana shouldn't go through the trouble of cooking a big dinner on her behalf. But Jack's mother was stubborn, and "no" was not being taken for an answer.

As usual, the food was delicious. Jack's Mom was quite the cook. She had prepared a plump pot roast with well-seasoned mashed potatoes and her homemade iced tea with just the right amount of sweetness.

Jack was amazed by how much Melissa ate, asking for both seconds and thirds. His father had once told him that a girl who wasn't afraid to eat was a keeper. In a moment of clarity, he wondered if he would ever be able to make Melissa his girlfriend, someone who seemed so clearly out of his league.

So much for her avoiding carbs, Jack mused.

., how do you like living in our humble little town? ut from New York and transferred to Jack's school ." Jack flushed with embarrassment as his mother between mouthfuls of pork.

lid something Jack would never have expected of a a response back the same way, almost appearing to t with his mother.

I whike-iwt," she barked while chomping on her potatoes. w... a humongous and painful looking gulp she continued. "But I do miss the big city."

"I've been to the old N.Y.C a few times with my husband when he wasn't away on work. It's quite a place there, very noisy, though."

Jack's mother and Melissa continued the idle chat while they ate with the kitchen TV playing reruns in the background. For dessert they had apple-pie and coffee, with Melissa politely asking for tea. Alana smiled and was happy to oblige.

For nearly an hour, they laughed and discussed current events, even the fire from earlier in the day. Jack and Melissa each took turns describing it from their perspectives, agreeing on certain parts and laughing at others.

"And the teacher's hair was a mess! He was drenched from the sprinklers. I don't think I've ever seen him so mad."

A moment of quiet overtook the room. The television playing in the background paused.

"We interrupt this program to bring you breaking news."

Jack put down his fork and turned around.

"Local One has more." The screen flashed, and the picture resumed with a tall Hispanic reporter centered on the screen. He had the *Local One* microphone held close to his mouth, and his eyes were wide with shock.

"This is Michael Alvarez of Local One, reporting live from Maple Hill. What started off as a warm, peaceful summer day has ended in a tragedy of unspeakable proportions. Richard Davins, age sixteen, along with his mother Roberta Davins, age forty-four, and two Seven year old sisters, Casey and Brianna, were found brutally massacred in their home just a few hours earlier."

"Very little is known at this point, including the means of murder, leads on who is responsible, or why this even occurred in the first place. What has been a peaceful community for over twenty years is now the site of one of the most brutal killings any of the officers on the scene have ever born witness to. We haven't been able to get a look, but judging by the officers' faces, it's pretty bad, folks."

Behind the reporter, dozens of police, medical and forensic personnel were visible, scurrying from task to task while the reporter spoke from behind the yellow tape.

"RICHARD, ROBERTA! Please ... Oh God, please let me see them!"

Cries of pure anguish echoed from behind the reporter, as the father of the victims struggled to get through the police.

"My family, my babies, my sweet little girls. And my son! I want to see them. *LET ME SEE THEM!*"

Jack remained motionless at the dinner table, as did his mother and Melissa. To his own surprise, he was the first to speak. Despite his voice being cold and dispassionate, there was a heat behind it. There was a burning fire that spoke volumes more than the words themselves.

"This is horrible. How could someone do this to another person? How can we live in a world where this is allowed?"

Jack stood up from his chair, his arms hanging loose from his sides while Melissa and his Mom watched with puzzled expressions. He turned away from them.

"This morning I hated Richard, his name brought me anger. But this, no, he didn't deserve this. What in this entire world could possibly possess a person to inflict this on another?"

As if unsure of how to proceed, Alana stood up and placed a comforting hand on Jack's shoulder.

"Jack, you knew this boy from school? I understand this can be pretty harsh news, but sit back down, sweetie, we can talk about it. Sometimes really bad things happen to good people. You're old enough to know this."

"Know it? Yeah, of course I do. But accept it? No way."

"Jack, why are you acting so strange all of a sudden? This can't be the first time you've seen a murder on the news. I know you knew this boy, but you're not acting like yourself."

Melissa, who until this point had remained quiet, stood next to Alana. Her expression was the oddest in the room—it was a mix of outrage and shock, only it covered her from forehead to chin.

"Jack, turn around," Melissa said. "It's kinda weird having you turn your back to us for this long."

Jack spun around. Melissa and Alana recoiled in surprise. Alana gasped, and Melissa's jaw dropped.

"Jack, your eyes! What's wrong with them?" Alana seemed frightened. She ran over and cupped his face.

"Why are your eyes dilated?"

Jack felt dizzy for a moment. He shook his head to clear his mind then looked around the room, confused.

"Sorry about that. I was lost in thought for a moment."

"Jack," Melissa said, "why don't we go for a walk? It's a beautiful night, and it'll be just you and me. What do you say?"

Jack went instantly from impassive coolness to pure delight. "Sounds great! I'll grab my phone and wallet." He picked them up from the table in the next room. When he returned, his mother appeared to be deep in thought while Melissa stood by the entrance to the door in silence. Neither of them made eye contact.

"Mom, I'll be back in a bit, thanks for dinner."

"Wait a minute, Jack," she said.

"What's up, Mom? If you're worried about us running in to the killer from the news, don't worry. I doubt he'd be out there with all the cops and what not looking for him."

Alana's lips formed into a pout, which she held for a few moments, until suddenly a wave of understanding seemed to cross over her. Her eyes opened wider than Jack had ever seen them and she turned her gaze on Melissa.

"Melissa, it was truly lovely meeting you, and I thank you for all your help, but my son may *not* go for a walk with you."

"I beg your pardon, Mrs. Harris, but I don't see why not."

Alana walked over to Melissa, and Jack's mind hammered him with confusion. What was going on?

"I really don't think that Jack should go out right now. You saw what just happened on the news, and I think it would be best to stay indoors. You're welcome to stay as well if you wish."

Melissa's face seemed to register some kind of understanding, and her eyes hardened. "Well, I have a feeling we'll be fine. And I think you and I both want him to go for that walk with me."

Jack couldn't put his finger on what was happening, but for some reason both ladies were glaring at each other.

"Do I, now?"

"Yes, you really do."

"And if I object?"

"You don't want to."

"And you can promise my son won't be hurt? You can guarantee it?"

"I swear it on all that is important to me. This may be hard to believe, but I actually really like Jack."

Jack didn't know if at this point it was more advisable to be confused or flattered.

"I guess he should go for that walk with you, then," Alana said. Jack wasn't sure, but for a moment he thought he saw a tear flash in her eyes.

What the hell are they on about?

"I can tell my son has feelings for you. Treat him right."

Melissa nodded.

"Whoa, Mom. Embarrass me some more, why don't you?" Jack felt blood enter his face in such a rush that he wondered how some still managed to travel through his veins.

"Jack, let's go already, come on. It's a beautiful night."

"Requiem, you're sure it's the Harris boy?" Ruin sat cross-legged in the shelter, an expression of delight on his face. His sister's still contained the madness, as it always did, but this time, it contained something else. Pleasure. She wore this expression only at times when she was confident she had solved a problem. It gave her such feelings of elation.

"When I know, I know, Darling. You should understand that about me by now. It's that Harris boy. Oh, I will love turning this one. Ah! I can see it now. This one's different than Brother Andy. He's pure. But he'll be turned. I want to see it! I want to see it so badly it hurts! The innocence fall away from him, as he kills and takes his birth right. Ruin, oh, Ruin, I want to see it right this instant! I am unable to wait any longer.

"Now, sister, you know the value of patience. First we have to make him ours and convince him. The killings must be done of his own volition."

Requiem moaned. "Then let us take him, let us take him now! It's the waiting that hurts more than anything."

Ruin sighed. "As you wish, let's make our move."

Chapter 6: A Ball in Motion

"Unacceptable," Paro said. "They've gone too far this time."

Kazou watched the way his team-leader struggled to contain the seething hatred from leaking into his voice. Glancing down, he saw the way Paro interlocked his fingers, attempting to steady his shaking hands.

"Easy now, Paro," Kazou said. He placed a hand on Paro's shoulder and shot nervous glances at Sarah and Michael. It went unsaid that the least productive thing that could happen at a time like this was for Paro to explode with rage and possibly take down the building around him.

It was no secret that Paro was very powerful, the depths of which even he didn't possess a clue about. Kazou estimated that, at the very least, Paro alone had the power to destroy a small army. He had met many Psychs since he began working for Paro's team, but none of them came within a fraction of his ability.

"Don't tell me to be 'easy'," Paro growled. "Look at this, Kazou. Look at what they have done here. They even killed the little girls."

The once well decorated home was now covered in blood and tissue. It was to such an extent that Forensics had issues determining where one body started and another ended.

The blood covered the walls, floor, and in some cases even the ceiling. The victims appeared to have been shredded, their skin peeled from their bodies with evidence suggesting painful, agonizing deaths. From what Forensics had pieced together, the mother had crawled several feet before dying, dragging clumps of skin along the floor with her.

"I've got no choice," Paro said. "I don't care if we're dealing with children anymore. In fact, my feelings on this no longer matter. We're out of options here. I have to put out the kill order. The Operations division will handle this from here on."

As if her life depended on it, Sarah, in a blinding flash snapped her head around at Paro and roared at him. "What did I just hear you say? Hey!"

Sarah had wept upon entering the scene, whereas Michael had said nothing, forgoing his normal one-liners, but Sarah had been hit hard. Kazou hadn't been on the team long, but in the time he had, he couldn't recall having ever dealt with a murder on this scale. Even still, Sarah had composed herself and done her job. At least until Paro's remark.

"Take it back right now, Paro. Take it the hell back."

Sarah glared at him and planted her feet into the ground. Kazou couldn't believe what he was hearing. The usually soft-voiced Sarah was snarling and growling demands.

"You know I can't do that, Sarah, even if I wanted to. This is over our heads now. Look around you. Look at what's been done here. Don't you think I'd like to solve this without loss of life? That's no longer possible. We're out of options here. And trust me—the gravity of what I must do is not lost on me. I promise you."

Kazou, although upset by the decision, did not voice any protest. He knew it was necessary. For Paro to even be considering it, let alone following through, meant it was nothing short of vital.

The Psych-Ops were divided into two broad categories— Investigative and Operative. The job of the Investigative teams was to inspect, arrest, and handle the vast majority of crimes. They weren't fighters or killers, and the use of force was intended to be kept as minimal as possible.

The Operative teams, on the other hand, had only one simple job. They tracked and they killed, nothing more. They received a target, the list of crimes, and all information found by the investigative team that pursued it. From then on, they did not rest until their target was found and eliminated. But if only that were all, Kazou could have rested easy with the decision, yet it didn't end there.

For one, the Operative teams did not have the authority of negotiation. Once a target was found, he was eliminated despite any pleas, begs, or even offers of surrender. A target may, and in the past have gone as far as, spreading their hands wide above their head, going to their knees and assuming a position of surrender. For an Op. team this was nothing more than an easy kill.

Once issued, a kill order was irremovable. There were only two conditions by which a person may escape death. The first was if they somehow contacted the Investigative team that pursued them and negotiated their surrender or turned themselves in. That, of course, relied on the team making it in time to secure the arrest, as even in the event of surrender no time would be bought for the target. In fact, if a bloodthirsty Op. team followed an investigative team in route of pursuing a surrendering target, they would be well within their legal rights to tail the team and kill the target upon arrival.

The only other way to escape death was to never be caught. Large bounties would be placed on the targets' heads, and the target would then have to live their life knowing they were being hunted.

Among Psych-Operatives, there was no love lost between the Investigative and Operative branches. It would be more accurate to say there was a form of hate. The Investigative teams despised and looked upon Op. Psychs with disgust. Those choosing to enter the Investigative branch did so because they believed in stopping crime and enforcing justice, not blind murder. If asked, any member of the Investigative branch—including the members of Paro's team—would all agree on one thing—*the Operations branch should not exist.*

It was for all these reasons, Kazou knew, that Sarah was now trembling with anger. She was standing close enough to Paro that her nose could poke him in the eye, and she began jabbing him in the stomach with a finger.

"Can't or won't, Paro? It's not our way to throw people under the bus, especially children. How can you stand there and order the execution of ... of children? How dare you look me in the eyes and tell me you have no choice? There's always a choice. We're not killers—we are a force of justice. I don't care if you're the leader of this team, and I don't care if you can lock me away for disobeying you. I joined this team so that I could be one of the few people in this world that does what's right. And this isn't. Children aren't sentenced to death, they are rehabilitated. Isn't that what we're all about? Isn't that the reason we work in the Juvenile department in the first place?"

Paro recoiled as if hit by a train, and Kazou knew how he must have been feeling. Without a doubt, Paro was revolted by what he felt he had to do and deeply ashamed of it. Kazou was sure that they all were. But what could be expected?

"Sarah, I—"

"I don't want to hear it, Paro. Place that kill order and I'm off this team. I will not be part of another excuse for those ... *animals* to murder yet another victim, let alone a child."

"Same goes for me." It was the first thing Michael had said since arriving on the scene. His voice was different from normal. Every last trace of his usual sense of humor had vanished."

"Paro, we've been through a lot as a team. Hell, we've seen firsthand what children are capable of more times than I reckon I'd like to remember. We've tracked and captured more than I can count. But one thing has never changed—the reason we do what we do. You keep telling us to take a look around us, and ya know what, buddy? I have been. What I see is someone who's really messed up and needs help. What I see is the reason I joined this team. If you take out that cell of yours and call the Op. teams, well, I'll finish this on my own—sanctioned or not."

Silence took the team over for a while, seconds that seemed to stretch for hours. During this time, Kazou stared blankly at the myriad of officers, profilers, and forensics teams shuffling in and out of the house. More than a few stopped to stare at the four of them, no doubt wondering what their big secret was, and why all authority was deferred to them. Paro shook his head and turned to face his team.

"I'm sorry everyone. You're right. Sarah, Michael, I was acting in the heat of the moment. We need to continue our investigation and find out who is responsible for this. I can't believe I almost ordered the deaths of kids. Thank you for making me see the error of my ways."

I thought you were right, Paro. I still do. What does that make me?

Kazou shook the thoughts from his mind. Contemplation was not a luxury he could afford.

"Is there *anything* here that can help us?" Kazou asked. "Why has the M.O of the killers changed? They targeted children, followed soon after by an old woman and now an entire family? This doesn't make any sense."

"Ah, actually I think it might." Michael cast his eyes downward at the sea of blood staining the carpeted floor. Kazou had never seen him like this. He was showing a level of professionalism that Kazou didn't expect from the man. Even more off-putting, Kazou wasn't sure if he actually preferred it that way.

"I know you guys are gonna try and call me crazy and say I'm just commin' up with wild theories and stuff, but umm, hear me out for a second, kay? I know I'm normally the dumb one here, but there's something that's been bothering me about all this. We all keep saying that it would be an incredible rarity for more than one or two Psychs to be in the same school. But what if there was?"

Paro's eyebrows rose. "Interesting, what is it you're thinking?"

"Well, it's like this. Supposin' for a sec here that the kid who did the fire wasn't involved in the old killins' right? What would the real ones do?"

Sarah gasped. "My god, they would recruit him. It would make perfect sense if you think about the killing spree that went on tonight. Everything from the old woman to what happened here, good God it was an initiation!"

"Yeah, ya see that's what I'm thinking. They probably found him somehow and made him do some of this stuff. And it's got me thinking, right? That if he went from an old woman straight to here, he was buildin' up to it, ya know? It's like he or she had a choice to do whatever they wanted, and it ended up with this. No one told the killer what they had to do. They figured it out all by themselves."

"Damn," Paro said. "I think we have a very serious problem." The three of them looked at Paro, worry on their faces. "The forensics team said that special attention was paid to Richard, that the other killings were done as a result of the first and that his was prolonged and personal. Among the students in the class of the fire-incident, wasn't there one who the school reported as having a feud with Richard? Someone who would fit the description of harboring rage, perhaps someone often bullied?"

Kazou felt a sickening despair. "I was so sure it was the now deceased Richard that I never even considered ... Oh, god." Kazou struggled to contain himself.

"I thought for sure it was that Adam boy," Sarah said.

Paro slowly took his cell phone out of his pocket. "*She* was right. We didn't listen to her, but she was right. We can't panic. It may not be too late. She's got an overwhelming tendency to deal with things by herself, but in the end it was my fault for letting her go off alone."

Sarah's eyes sparkled with the beginning of tears. "Paro, tell us the truth. Is she with him right now?"

"Yes. She has good intuition. She told us she had a feeling about that Jack Harris, but I looked at his profile and it didn't seem possible. She begged me to let her investigate the lead on her own. I told her she was wasting her time but to do what she felt was necessary. She ... she's with him right now. Alright, we need to calm down. We need to get organized and—Michael, wait! Where are you going? Hey! We need to stop and think for a minute!"

"Like hell I'm gonna let one of our own get picked off like some animal. She's just a kid. Damn you Paro, damn you to hell! I told you she was too young to join a team, but you didn't listen to me. I ain't gonna let her die like that family in here."

Michael dashed out of the house, running like a madman, prompting the officers nearby to throw a questioning glance at Paro.

"We need to go after him!" Paro yelled.

"Okay, I'm just gonna right come out and say it—there's no way Spider-man would win in a fight against Wolverine. For one, let's talk powers. Spider-man has great reflexes, and yeah, he can dodge quite a few hits, but he can't dish out any damage, you see? Wolverine has been hit by buses. At the very least, if the two ever fought, I'd say it would come to a stand-still. See, Spider-man could just run away or hide on a ceiling or something, and Wolverine wouldn't be able to do anything about it. That is, of course ..."

Could I have really been wrong about him?

Jack had been rambling on about the "X-mans" or the "Spidermans" or some kind of nonsense since they left the house fifteen minutes earlier. Mostly, she knew, because he was nervous being alone in her presence, and needed some way to break the silence.

It did make her feel guilty to take advantage of him and trick him this way. She had even led him on a little, but she needed to get close. She needed to be sure. He wasn't a bad guy. In fact, with his sloppy hair and playful personality, he was kind of cute.

That he was a Psych was no longer up for debate. It didn't matter what Paro said about the odds of there being a third Psych—well, a fourth, really—in her school. The empathy he showed when the murders were announced, the sadness she could feel within him—he couldn't have done it. Besides, he'd been home with his mother the entire night, waiting for her to show up.

The fire, though, that was him. Whether he did it on purpose or not was irrelevant. She was in that room. She wasn't a Telepath, but she didn't have to be one to know he was responsible.

When it was happening, she had immediately put up her guard. Never in her life had she been so frightened. But later, when he'd approached her in the courtyard and started speaking with her, it seemed to all fall into place. A monstrous killer wouldn't set a classroom on fire just because he missed a homework, but Jack was a simple-minded boy, and intentional or not, that was the kind of thing she'd expect from him.

As she walked over the soft grass three blocks from his home, through a park with a majestic water fountain carved from stone, she felt the building remorse. She was going to break his heart. Even if he didn't commit the murders, he still had to be tagged and released. He'd committed a crime, and unwittingly or not, he had to be brought in. She knew it shouldn't matter to her what he thought of her, but she couldn't help but wonder if Jack would hate her when he learned the truth. More so, she wondered if he was even capable of hate.

"Which is why if they ever made a sequel to Episode VI, they would obviously have to find all new actors."

Melissa smiled. "You think so, Jack? I actually haven't seen those movies."

Jack looked as if he'd been punched in the face. "What! You mean you haven't seen Star Wars yet? Oh man, Melissa, you have got to come over and watch them. I've got them on VHS, DVD, and now Blu-Ray. We could make a thing of it! I know, first we'll watch the originals, and then the special edition. Then, we can watch the new trilogy. Wait, actually we should watch the new trilogy first, since it's in chronological order and then you could ... Wait, that's a bad idea too. I don't want your first Star Wars experience to be soiled by 'Phantom.' Okay, here's what we'll do, we'll—"

"Jack, stop for a minute. I need to talk to you."

"Oh? What's up, Melissa?"

They took seats on a low to the ground section of the giant water fountain. She enjoyed the moist, delicate wind that caressed her skin as it cooled off from the fountain behind her.

"This isn't going to be easy for me to say, but there's some things you need to know." She tried to think of how to tell him what she must. She needed a delicate way to explain to him why he might not be able to return home for a few nights.

As she opened her mouth to speak, the phone in her pocket went off. "Just a sec, Jack." She raised the phone to her ear. "This is Melissa."

"*Melissa, thank god you're okay. It's Paro. Are you with the Harris kid?*"

"Umm, yeah, he's right here. It's as I thought, but there's not much to worry about. He's exactly what we thought him to originally be. No link whatsoever."

"*No, you're wrong. Listen, we found out some stuff.*"

Melissa tensed as Paro spoke. She shook her head instinctively as she listened to his theory.

"No, that's not possible," she said. She turned to Jack. "Jack, you were with your mother all day, right? I mean, after you got home from school?"

Jack looked puzzled. He definitely had no idea what the phone call was about or who she was speaking to. "Umm, no, I didn't get home until about a half-hour before you showed up. I was busy doing some stuff with a friend."

For the second time that day, she felt the cold touch of fear.

"*Melissa, we're already on our way. Just keep him there and don't do anything stupid.*"

"Wait a minute, Paro. You're wrong about this. I've gotten to know him ... It can't be."

"*You should know by now that anything can be. It might even be possible he doesn't realize what he has done. Who can tell what is inside the mind of a killer? But what we do know at this point is that we have every reason to believe he is either an initiate of the original killers or solely responsible himself.*"

Melissa looked over to Jack, who was now oblivious to the conversation. He seemed to be preoccupied reading some kind of black-and-white comic book on his phone.

"It's almost impossible to believe."

"*It often is. Just hang tight, and don't let him leave. We'll be there within five minutes. And Melissa, thank God you're okay. We were worried sick about you. Just hold on and be safe.*"

Melissa gulped as she hung up the phone. So, this was the monster they were looking for? Without realizing it, her fear turned to anger.

Don't worry, Paro, she thought to herself. *He's not going anywhere. Not unless it's over my dead body.*

Chapter 7: Ambushed

Jack watched Melissa flip her phone shut and turn his way. She looked a bit off. Just a few moments earlier, her eyes held comforting warmth, yet now they held a strong sense of caution. Had the friend she spoke to earlier told her of some disturbing news?

"Is everything okay, Melissa?" Jack asked.

It was like she'd seen a ghost, and Jack felt concerned. They were still sitting on the corner of the park's giant fountain, bathing in the gentle breeze from the wind bouncing off the water.

"Everything's fine. It was just my Mom asking me if I remembered to turn off the stove. I'm not really sure if I did or not, so I got a bit nervous. But thinking back, I'm pretty sure I did."

Jack had the overwhelming sense that something had changed about her in the last few minutes, but he decided to drop it for the time being.

"Where do you wanna go now? Do you want to head back, or should we walk somewhere else?"

Melissa twitched at the question. "I think we should stay here for a few more minutes. It's really comforting near the fountain."

Jack shrugged and leaned back against the stone. At first, he had been nervous, but now he was relaxing and enjoying her company. There was something special about her, something that drew him to her like a magnet.

"You know, Melissa, you're a really great person. You helped me with my math without asking for anything in return, and then you hang out with a loser like me when I'm sure there's a zillion other guys that would die for your company. I really appreciate it all."

Melissa shook her head and sighed. Jack couldn't understand why she looked so bummed.

Did my remark make her uncomfortable? Was I too forward? I just blew it, didn't I? Damn it all! I totally just freaked her out. Okay, calm down, Jack, we can recover from this. I just need to change the conversation. What is it that girls like more than anything? Is it flowers? There's gotta be something I can talk about to connect with her. Think Jack, think! Girls, what do they like? Oh, wait! I know. Why didn't I think of this before?

"So, Melissa, how about that Twilight? You know, I gotta say, all the other guys in school are all like 'Twilight is so stupid, and vampires aren't like that.' But you know what? I think vampires *should* get all sparkly and glittery when they're in the sun. In fact, I like that better than normal vampires. Cause like, if I were a vampire, I'd save a ton of money on art supplies. Who needs CVS, right? When you can just shave and have enough glitter to last you a lifetime!"

Hah! That oughta do it.

Melissa remained silent and motionless, save for flipping open her phone and checking the time every few seconds. Jack's confusion doubled. Where had he gone wrong? She didn't appear to be upset with him. Rather, she seemed lost in thought. She rested her elbows on her knees and her head on top of her palms. Her golden hair dangled back and forth like the swing of a pendulum in sway with the cool breeze.

Thinking of the time, Jack wondered what it was. He reached into the left pocket of his black jeans. The bright screen cast surprisingly far shadows in the darkness as Jack glanced downward.

Whoa, it's almost midnight.

Being alone with Melissa was nothing short of a dream come true. Were it up to him, Jack would spend an eternity resting next to her on a warm, beautiful night, as the whispering breeze rustled the leaves and blew upwards into the trees. But his mother was expecting him home soon, and he didn't want her to worry.

"Melissa, I can't tell you just how much fun it was to hang out with you tonight, but I've *really* gotta get going. You don't know my mom. If I'm home even a minute later than I promised, she worries herself sick. I don't know what your friend said on the phone that's got ya all worried, but I promise whatever it is, I'll talk about it with you tomorrow. Adam says I can sometimes be a good guy to talk to when something's bothering you, so don't ever look to anyone else, okay? It's the least I can do."

Jack dusted off his pants and began to rise. Without warning, Melissa, as if snapping out of a trance, shot upward from the fountain and grabbed Jack by the elbow. Her eyes held a dangerous glare.

"Jack, wait! What are a few more minutes?" Hearing this, Jack beamed with delight.

Whoa, she's totally into me! She doesn't even want me to leave.

"You have no idea how much I'd love to stay, Melissa, but I really, really need to get going. My mom's crazy when it comes to being home on time. I'm sixteen and she treats me like I'm ten. Don't worry, I'm free all week, so we can hang out any time you want."

Jack knew he should be more concerned with her worrisome glances, but he was too happy at seeing how disappointed she was at him leaving.

"Come on, what's the worst that can happen if you're five minutes late?"

She was definitely making this hard for him. Every last fiber of his being wanted to stay with her and drink in her majestic blue eyes. But if he angered his mother, the consequences would be vast and far-reaching. No, he *really* had to go.

"You're killing me here, but I just can't. In fact, as it is if I don't sprint I won't make it home in time, and then Mom is gonna take away my Xbox."

(Monday, June Fourth 11:47PM -> Jack's Heart Rate: 95 BPM)

"So, you're really just going to leave me? Without even a goodbye kiss?"

(Monday, June Fourth 11:48PM -> Jack's Heart Rate: 1,402,182,154 BPM)

Did I just hear that right?

"I'm sorry, Melissa, what was that?"

Melissa released his arm and instead playfully tugged on his shirt, pulling him close. Jack's mind reeled in surprise. Instinctively he hoped, no, he prayed that his mother had signed him up for a donor list, because the way his heart was hammering in his chest, it was going to burst out of him.

It was only a millisecond, but the time it took to go from arm's length to a distance close enough to be mesmerized by her enchanting eyes felt like an eternity. He could feel the soft touch of her long hair on his forehead. She had the scent of cherries, and her perfect features were the only sight that filled his vision.

This close, he could feel her chest pressed against his body, aflame with white-hot passion. His emotions transitioned at a maddening speed. From nervous, to excited, to exalted, to a feeling of bliss so pure it could remove the dark from the murkiest swamp.

Her breath was sweet as she pulled him in, her powerful arms wrapping around his neck. Her lips came into view, moving ever closer to his. His heart beat faster, faster ...

When their lips connected, fireworks brighter than a thousand suns lit off with glamour to the sound of a million beating drums. A pure joy and sensation of ecstasy far beyond that which he had ever known possible blossomed and coursed throughout his heart. Not even an eternity burning in the fires of the deepest layer of hell could make him forget this moment.

The sweet-cinnamon taste of her lips covered his and any thought of returning home vanished. The kiss seemed to last a lifetime, a perfect moment repeated on a loop throughout the infinitum. It was powerful, like a concrete floor slamming into the back of his head.

Wait, what?

The pain was so great that Jack didn't feel the boot on his throat blocking his airway, and the fuzzy feeling almost distorted the furious roaring words that Melissa shouted, in a booming, angry, and commanding voice from lips that moments ago were so passionate and filled with lust.

"MOVE A MUSCLE, EVEN A MUSCLE AND I'LL END YOU HERE AND NOW."

Jack blinked, trying to clear his mind. He was on his back, his ears ringing, pain shooting in and out from under his eyes. The impact of the fall had disoriented him—he struggled to make sense of something, anything.

His inability to breathe came to him as a sudden burst of recognition. With a gasp, he gripped his arms at the boot slamming down on his throat.

"I said, don't move! Stop struggling this instant or so help me god I will kill you."

The confusion was so strong that it hurt. Jack's brain scrambled to find some kind of answer. He had kissed her, he was sure, but then something had happened. She had lifted him off his feet and tossed him on the ground as if he were an infant.

Jack's body cried to him for oxygen. "Wh—" he struggled to speak. The words came out between raspy half-breaths. "Wh-why?"

"Is that what your victims asked you, you sick freak? Did they ask to know why? Did you even bother to tell them the reason they had to die?"

Is this a dream?

Jack fought frantically to remove the leg pinning him. The strength of it was not natural. It carried the force of a tree trunk. It was as if an SUV parked on top of him. How was this even possible?

"Understand one thing, Jack. As of now, you are under arrest. I'd like to bring you in without having to resort to further violence, but if I feel so much as an inkling of threat coming from you, I won't hesitate to crush your windpipe and end you where you lie. Others will be here any moment to take you with them. Cooperate until then, and I can promise you'll live."

At once, she lifted the boot from Jack's throat, and he looked up at the girl he had kissed. Her face revealed an anger so terrible, so fiery, that Jack wondered how it could be contained within a single person.

"Me—" he tried to speak. He choked and coughed as his body attempted to reclaim the lost oxygen.

"Melissa, is this a game or a joke?"

Jack didn't think it was possible, but somehow her anger seemed to multiply. She bent down and did the unthinkable. With a single rowing-pull of her arm, she grabbed Jack by the scruff of his neck and lifted him. Not just to his feet, but off them, leaving him dangling in midair like a key on a chain.

"Does this look like a joke? You know what the real joke is? It's that scum like you are allowed to live in this world."

She released him, and he fell to his knees. The confusion reached such a level that Jack was no longer sure he even cared what was happening. Survival was the only thing that remotely mattered to him.

On his knees, he looked up at the woman of his dreams, now the woman of his nightmares. Thoughts bounced back and forth between the corners of his mind. His brain scrambled for any kind of explanation, likely or otherwise, and the pain from being thrown to the ground made the confusion worse.

Melissa walked behind him and nudged him forward. He fell on his chest with an *"oohf."* Then, he felt her hands overlapping his as they were bound and tied.

"What's happening to me?" Jack asked.

He was still in a daze. He felt her hands tie his own with a thick cord.

"I've pictured this quite a few times, but this is definitely *not* one of ways I always imagined you tying me up." Jack was no longer sure what words he was spouting. Spots danced before his eyes while dizziness overtook him.

Melissa grunted as she sealed the knot on his hands. "You know, I wasn't supposed to do anything until my team arrived, but you were trying to go running off. I couldn't just let you leave."

Jack tried to crawl away on his stomach, but Melissa sighed and took a seat on his back, holding him in place.

"I guess I'll just sit here until they arrive. I've got to say, you really disappointed me. I thought you'd be tougher. But then again, only a pathetic slob would do what you did to all those people. God, you sicken me."

A few minutes passed, and Jack's head cleared while the dizziness faded. His confusion remained, but at the very least, he felt slightly more grounded in reality and aware of his situation.

"Melissa, please, just tell me what's going on."

She made no attempt to respond, content to simply sit on his back and leave him on the ground. She didn't speak a word, until moments later, the sound of nearby feet gliding through grass resounded from a few yards away.

"It's about time!" she called.

"My, my, my. Oh what, oh what do we have here?" a man's voice asked. The shadows of two dark silhouettes could be made out from a nearby brush. Jack didn't recognize either voice, but he was too distracted by his current situation to care who they were.

"Ruin, Darling, do you have any idea why that horse of a woman is sitting on my prey?"

"Not even a clue, my dearest Requiem. Perhaps this is some kind of new sex game?"

Two figures exited from the brush. One was a tall, languid-looking man. He was handsome, with neatly trimmed hair and a kind, sincere face, though Jack suspected it was all a front. The other was one of the most striking women Jack had ever seen. She almost ranked up to Melissa, but her face was what disturbed Jack. Her smile was wicked, and her expression was one of pure, unfiltered madness.

Jack felt a weight lift as Melissa got off Jack's back. "Who the hell are you two? What's happening here is none of your concern, and I seriously advise you to turn around and leave."

"Do you hear that, Darling? This creature is making demands of us. Shall I kill it?"

Melissa's face darkened. "What did you just say to me?"

The woman called Requiem ignored her. Instead, she shifted her gaze directly towards Jack. Her face lit up with delight, and she clapped her hands.

"That's him, brother, that's him! He's the one I want, the one the other boy told us about. Why is he tied up? Did the pig do this to our new brother?"

Jack wasn't sure, but assuming no dogs were around, he heard Melissa literally growl in response.

"Your new brother? What does that mean? Who are you two?"

Requiem laughed. "Hah! Oh, look at this, Ruin, look! It's still trying to converse with me. I'll deal with it later."

Jack felt a foreign sensation on his wrists, and then, as if by magic, his bonds were cut, freeing his hands. With a trembling palm, he pushed himself off the ground and slowly stood to his feet. Melissa looked over, panic now on her face as Jack stood freed before her.

"Okay, everyone. I'm not even gonna try, pretend, or better yet even ask to know who you guys are." Jack dusted off his pants and shirt with a shaking hand. "But I think I finally understand what's going on here. Actually, I'm sure of it." Jack felt his confusion fade a little as the pieces finally came together.

"I have somehow activated a portal to a parallel dimension, where Melissa is as strong as a troll, and everyone has names that start with *R.*"

Requiem put a gloved palm to her face and laughed with delight. "Oh, look at him, Ruin, look at him! He's a funny boy. Our new brother is a very funny one. Oh, this is so lovely!"

Melissa turned to Jack. Her face had gone cold, but raw anger seeped through her expression. "What do you mean by that, Jack?"

"Well, Melissa, if you'd been paying attention—see what I did there? You're always saying I don't pay attention but now you're the one who isn't—you'd have heard that both their names start with the letter *R.*"

"Not about that!" she screamed back at him. "About you having no clue who these two people are."

Jack scratched his head. "Nope, not ringing a bell. I haven't seen these guys anywhere."

Requiem clapped her hands yet again with delight. "Oh, Jack, you'll come to know us as family soon enough. We're your liberators, the ones who will allow you to step forward and take your birth right and yes, even shake the very heavens!"

Jack, still trembling from Melissa's roughhousing, limped forward past Melissa to stare directly at the two weirdoes.

"I," he began, "have absolutely no idea what any of what you just said means!"

Now, even Ruin joined in the laughter.

"Oh, Ruin," Requiem said, "I love this one already. I can't wait to have him." Her face changed, the madness growing but now a perverse lust seeped through her haunting eyes. "I'll wait no longer."

Melissa took two steps forward to stand beside Jack. It was apparent from her expression that she was trying to piece together the situation. The park wasn't very large compared to others, but it did have the basics. They were in the front, near the swings and jungle gym, and a few feet behind them sat a large fountain, and just beyond that a grassy playing field.

"I don't know what's going on here any better than Jack here seems to, but may I please ask you two a question? For some reason, I have a feeling you're crazy enough to actually answer it. First of all, are you two the ones who have been killing the children around this town? Specifically, Jonathan Herbert, age sixteen, Pepe Alguerra, age fourteen, and Don O'Rielly age ... ten."

Jack looked at Melissa and noticed the way she twitched as she spoke, as if it were taking all of her willpower just to contain her fury. She seemed to be bubbling with rage on the inside, yet despite such tremendous hate she kept her voice to a conversational level.

"Secondly, did you recruit Jack Harris to commit the murder of the entire Davins family, including all but the father?"

What is she on about now?

Ruin stepped forward. "Now why would we refuse such a question? We would never be ashamed of our work. Yes, we committed those works of art as you have described. Why wouldn't we? It's our right to choose who lives or dies. And as for your second question, I might as well say yes, for while the names may be different, eventually our Jack Harris here shall do the same. But to answer your question more specifically, we did *not* order the murder of the Davins family. We ordered three murders, if you can really call them murders, as a murder by definition is an unjust killing, which, ours were most certainly *not*."

"But I digress, we only asked for three. Our Brother chose to add a few more, filling us with such pride, I might add. We hope that after we retrieve Mr. Harris we can feel the same pride over *his* accomplishments."

Melissa's shoulder tensed, and her hands turned to fists. "Thank you. That was all I needed to know." She turned her head to face Requiem. "And as for you, Mrs. Crazy-eyed skank. I am not an 'it', I am not a 'horse', and I most certainly am not a 'pig.' But I'm going to enjoy making you say *oink*."

In a blinding display of speed so incredible that Jack barely managed to see it, Melissa dashed towards the two. With a swift motion, she brought her fist down on top of them. Nimbly, the two leapt out of the way, and with a thundering *boom,* her fist smashed into the cement, cracking through it and spraying debris as if struck by a grenade. Jack blinked and wondered if he was watching a movie. He had never seen anything even close to what he had just witnessed. It was as if Melissa was some kind of superhero.

"Well now, she's like us, is she?" Ruin said. "No matter, it looks like all she can do is break things," He pointed his index finger at her, and Jack watched as an invisible force swept her off her feet and sent her crashing into the blue fixture of a nearby jungle gym.

Jack was stunned. His eyes darted from the pothole she had somehow made in the ground then back to Melissa. She was panting and rising to her feet.

"I didn't expect you to be this strong." She charged at the two yet again, and this time, she only made it a few steps before her body took a nose dive into the ground, as if an invisible truck had fallen on her.

Jack was speechless. He didn't know what was going on—he didn't know how to react.

"Hey, Harris-boy, want to see something cool?" Ruin asked. He carried himself with an air of confidence, yet his smile and relaxed posture only added to the overall menace.

"We're going to literally rip her heart out. She was bullying you just before, no? I think you're going to enjoy this."

Rip her heart out?

Were they serious? Jack was never a deep thinker. Throughout his life, he had never been one to examine things closely, accepting most stuff on face value. He had just seen the love of his life pound a hole into the ground, get thrown through the air and back again. Jack guessed that most people would stop and think, "*Can this be happening? Is this real?*" Not Jack, however.

For almost every living person on the planet, when faced with the revelation that human beings possessed these kinds of abilities, it alone would be enough to send them into mental turmoil for weeks.

They would contemplate, they would question. But to Jack, what was, simply was. It was another part of life that had to be accepted.

In a single moment, Jack came to accept something that would take others weeks, months, or even years. He realized in a fraction of a second what might even leave some insane. That this was how life was, and how it would be from now on. This was the way the world worked.

"Are you really going to do that to her?" Jack looked at Melissa. She was pinned down by something, yet her eyes showed defiance. Whatever invisible force had bound her, she kicked her legs and struggled against it.

Requiem smiled. "Of course we are, and I do hope you enjoy it. I promise I'll make it slow so you can watch."

Melissa struggled but to no avail. "Don't expect me to beg or plead. I won't even scream."

A wave of urgency shimmered down Jack's spine.

They're going to kill her!

For the first time, in many, many years, Jack felt the cold touch of anger. It was a foreign emotion, something that revolted him and instilled him with nausea. But he felt it nonetheless.

They're going to kill my Melissa. They're going to rip her heart out and make me watch!

Melissa, as if lifted by a rising noose, tilted her head upward and floated above the ground. Despite her convictions, she screamed. She must have known what was coming.

"Say 'Ah' for the doctor, love," Requiem teased. "This one is going to be a pleasure to ... Hey, do you feel that, Ruin?"

"Feel what? You know I'm not good with sensing things, sister."

"The Harris-kid, his emotions—they're gone. I can only feel emptiness."

"Hmm, what's he up to anyway? He's just standing there. Hey, what's wrong with his eyes?"

Jack walked at a sedate pace towards the two. All of his passion, fear, rage, it had vanished. Somehow, in the back of his mind, he remembered feeling this way before, but he couldn't place it. A single thought emerged within him, a single reality made bright.

I would never allow Melissa to be harmed.

The phrase at once meant both something and nothing—it was both understandable and inconceivable. Yet he understood it, while at the same time it remained a mystery.

He squinted at Melissa. *How did I not see it before?*

It was around her neck, the projection from the tall man to her, such a trivial, simple thing. It was much like a child's knot of a shoelace—if he would only just give it a small tug ...

Melissa fell to the floor, gasping for breath. Ruin's eyes widened in surprise, as did Requiem's.

"Incredible!" Ruin said. "That's never happened to me before. How did you do that?"

Jack spoke. His voice was calm, his emotions nonexistent. He passively looked at Requiem. Seeing her maddened face, he felt nothing.

"I don't believe we've met. My name is Jack Harris. I'm sixteen years old, and I attend Elms High. My favorite movie is 'Back to the Future', and I love popcorn. Oh, and could you please do me a favor and leave?"

Ruin opened his mouth to respond and then cried out as he was lifted a dozen feet into the air and sent soaring through the brush where he'd first appeared. Melissa, now in a crouched position nearby, looked on with amazement.

"Brother!" Requiem shouted. "You monster, what have you do—"

"Goodbye," Jack said with a soft, uncaring voice. She looked like she had more to say, but Jack didn't give her the chance. She too was hit with the same force. An invisible wall slammed into her, flinging her back a dozen paces. There was a crash as she collided with a tree-trunk, and she cried out in pain.

"Now I'm the one that wants to know what's going on." It was Melissa's voice. Looking over, Jack saw she was back on her feet. She was clutching her left side.

"Where did you learn to do that?" she asked.

"Do what?" Jack had the feeling he'd forgotten something important, but at the very least, he was glad to see Melissa was unharmed.

"Don't you remember? You just sent those two guys flying."

Jack shrugged. "Not really."

Melissa ignored the reply. "Listen, I think they're getting back up. Can you do that again? If you can hold them still for just a second, I can knock them out cold."

"Are you crazy? You want me to hold them down? They've got like, powers and stuff. How would you like me to fight against them?"

"Jack, who do you think just knocked them off their feet? It was you."

"That's impossible, Melissa. I don't even know how to fight."

Jack and Melissa watched in horror as the two rose back to their feet. They did not look happy. Worse, they looked more or less unharmed.

"That was not nice, Brother." Requiem said. "You're going to learn to be nice to your sister or you'll be punished."

Ruin nodded. "After we kill the woman, I'm going to break in the new guy. He's going to learn not to raise a hand to his new family."

"I'm not your family!" Jack was going to make sure Melissa explained everything to him when this was over. She looked like she knew what all this was about.

"Can you really not do that again?" Now there was a sound of morbid fear in her voice, and Jack wondered if the two crazies were going to resume where they left off. Would they re-grab her by the neck again and try to slice out her heart?

"I don't even know what I'm supposed to have done."

The two approached, confirming Jack's earlier fears. They were very much unharmed. To make matters worse, they seemed to be enjoying themselves.

"That was a really impressive burst from the Harris-kid, wouldn't you say, Requiem?" Ruin licked his upper lip.

Requiem nodded. "Did you see the way he tried to protect his pig-faced lady friend? Oh, I want him even more now! I can't wait to see him weep over his first kill. Maybe he'll cry himself to sleep like our new brother."

New brother? What's a 'new brother'?

The two approached, and Melissa stepped protectively in front of Jack with her hands balled into fists.

"Jack, I'm sorry if I hurt you earlier, but I was so sure that you were this 'brother' they keep going on about."

"I still have no idea what any of this is about, but it's okay. I forgive you."

Ruin was now only a footstep away from them, and Jack could see that behind his smile, there was a deep sadness, but it was downplayed by an overwhelming evil. Requiem stood to his side. There was no sadness in her, just a bottomless pit of madness and despair.

"Oh, Ruin, how sweet. Maybe we should just leave them alone after all?"

"Don't tease them, sister. Let's kill the girl and take the Harris-boy."

Melissa did not wait idly for her death. Again, she charged forward, and again she collided into an unseen barrier. Her fist was stopped mid-punch, and she struggled against a force that Jack had no understanding of.

"You're nothing, child," Ruin said. "You're a lifetime too early to take me on."

Melissa looked up into the murderous, smiling face that would send her to the death, and Jack realized he was powerless to do anything to help her.

"What about me? Am I too early?"

Ruin howled in pain as an enormous fist crashed into his temple, bringing him to his knees. Blood dripped from his nose and mouth as a kick met him in his jaw, sending him scrambling backward.

Standing before them, with a look of outrage on his face, was a large, muscular Japanese man. Tears fell from Melissa's eyes. "Kazou, you came! You finally came!"

Ruin, losing all composure, screamed at what Jack suspected was the top of his lungs. "*Another one comes to die! I've had enough of this. I will kill you all and take the Harris-boy.*"

Kazou went in for a second attack but stopped in his tracks the moment Requiem placed a hand on his shoulder.

"Did you forget about me? I'm a Telepath, Darling. Right now, you should be losing your will to go on, and fatigue should be filling your muscles."

Kazou grunted and struggled, but it seemed to be useless. He halted in his tracks and showed no indication of moving again anytime soon.

"Do it now, Ruin."

Jack stared in horror as a four-foot bar of metal from the jungle gym snapped free of its hinges and sped straight towards the Japanese man. Jack was no metal-scientist, but he didn't have to be one to know that at the rate it was traveling it would surely kill the man.

Maybe I should be a metal-scientist. At least then, I'd get free metal.

"Kazou, no!" Melissa yelled. She struggled to break free but was still pinned by whatever force Ruin had used against her.

From somewhere out of sight, an even faster piece of a metal, which on closer inspection appeared to be a lead pipe, collided with the first broken piece of jungle gym, and in a shower of sparks both fell lifelessly to the ground.

"Well, well, I reckon things have finally gotten interesting around here. Hey, who is that hotty? She available?" Standing on top of the giant fountain, a man in a cowboy hat waved at the Japanese man.

Where did these guys come from? Jack wondered. *And how many of them are metal-scientists?*

Ruin and Requiem looked around frantically. The odds were no longer in their favor. With an exhausted grunt, Melissa ripped free of whatever constraints had been holding her and stood up. The Japanese man, too, seemed to be recovering.

Ruin took a few steps back and frowned. "Requiem, we need to leave. We can get the Harris-boy another time."

The man in the cowboy hat jumped down from the fountain, a distance of at least ten feet, and yet he landed with ease. "Like hell I'm letting them get away." Both the broken piece of jungle gym and the lead pipe glided along the grass, over Melissa's broken concrete and into each hand of the man as if pulled by a hidden string. "I'll bash them over the head until they see stars."

Ruin and Requiem turned to flee, and the man chased after them.

"Michael, stop this instant!" There was yet another new voice. Jack looked over his shoulder and saw a man with short black hair approach with a woman by his side. They both appeared to be in their mid-twenties.

"We have injured. Do *not* pursue."

Michael spat and dropped the two pieces of metal. Appearing to regain himself, he faced Melissa, almost diving to her side.

"You okay, sweetie?"

"Yeah." She winced as she spoke.

Jack decided to slip away while he had the chance. He got as far as stepping on the nearest twig. The man they called Michael set his gaze upon him.

"And what about you?"

"Umm, I'm just the local metal-scientist. I'm not involved in whatever's going on here, so if you'll please just excuse me, I'll be on my way."

Michael, the Japanese man, and the two newcomers all shot a look of amazement at Jack and then in unison turned to face Melissa.

"You guys, meet Jack Harris. You know, the boy I've been telling you all about?"

As all five people converged on him, one thought stuck out in Jack's mind.

Well, at least I remembered to TiVo the new episode of Dexter.

Chapter 8: I Don't Wanna

"Just relax, Jack. You're making this so much more difficult than it really has to be."

It was a struggle for Paro to keep frustration out of his voice. The Harris-kid was impossible to deal with, and while Paro was known for a great many things, patience did not number among them.

Jack retreated a few steps and had his back to the now broken jungle gym. Kazou and Michael had backed off as a gesture of goodwill, while Sarah and Melissa tried to speak to him gently in an attempt to calm him down.

"I don't care what you guys are. Honestly, I don't. I won't say anything to anyone. I'm too lazy to even bother. But there's no way I'm going anywhere with you people."

He's gonna make this hard for us, isn't he?

"Jack, listen to me. In this world, there are laws, and there are rules. Often people break them without even knowing they exist, but the penalty is nonetheless enforced. Whether you're involved or not, you may have valuable information that can save lives. More than that, you have to answer for some other things as well—namely an incident in your school that took place earlier this morning."

Paro winced as Jack lifted up his chin in defiance, an age-inappropriate gesture expected of a four-year-old.

"I don't know what any of that means. Why don't you guys tell me what's been going on around here. I wanna know why Melissa beat me up, and then just when I was feeling better two weird, crazy people came and said all kinds of weird stuff. Then they tried to beat me up again. Then everyone started punching each other and things started flying, and then more weird stuff was said. Oh, I also wanna know why they called me 'brother.' Wait a minute." Jack paused and his mouth gaped. "Are they my illegitimate ...? But surely mom would have told me. Ah Jeeze, they're my siblings, aren't they?"

Paro tried to be a tolerant man, he really did. But his glass wall of patience cracked, and he gritted his teeth. Sarah wanted to do this diplomatically, but Paro—and Melissa, from the looks of things— would rather knock him over the side of the head and be done with it.

"We're trying to explain that to you, hun," Sarah said. "But every time we try, you take another step back and ignore us."

She was the closest to him, only a few feet away. Sarah was the only person Jack didn't retreat from, and it didn't surprise Paro. Sarah was among the kindest people he'd ever met. She was empathetic, understanding, and patient with everyone. Even the stress-inducing actions of the Harris-kid had little effect on her. Paro knew he chose right when he picked her for his Telepath.

If only it were possible for a Telepath to rip data from a person's mind without damaging them, Paro's life not only now, but for many years, would have been much easier. Unfortunately, the use of telepathy to extract data from a suspect ranked highly on the list of taboo practices. One minor misstep and the suspect could end up comatose.

Paro cleared his throat. "Listen to me, Jack, and listen to me well. After that little fire you started in class, if I wanted to, I could haul you into a lockup where you wouldn't see the light of day for a half-dozen years. You're lucky that all I want is information about the murders."

Paro was lying, of course. It was a first time offense by an unregistered Psych. But still, he didn't mind using fear to get his way. Not with everything at stake.

Paro's comment seemed to agitate Jack. The boy bounced on his feet and frowned.

Good, let him be afraid. Maybe he'll finally cooperate.

"Here we go with the fire again. I am *so damn sick of hearing about that fire!* All day long, everyone's all like, 'Hey, Jack, how did you do the fire?' Or, 'You're under arrest for starting fires.' Or, 'I was so worried, Jack! I heard there was a fire today'."

Jack stomped the ground. "Leave me alone about that stupid fire! I had nothing to do with it. Even if I wanted to I couldn't. I never once in my entire life brought matches to school."

Paro grunted. So, now he was going to try to deny it?

"As we have been trying to explain to you all along, you're like one of us. You have both the ability and power to create a fire, perhaps even something much worse, the extent of which I don't even know. That's what we're trying to find out. You can play innocent all you want, but even on the off chance you didn't do it on purpose, you're still responsible."

Jack seemed to be lost in thought for a moment, because it was the first time he stood still since they had arrived, and he was no longer jittering. He looked over to where Sarah and Melissa were slowly approaching. In an instant, his eyes widened in delight, and he grinned at Paro.

He pushed himself off from where he leaned against the jungle gym and pointed a finger at Melissa. "Ah hah! I got it! Wow, this all makes sense now. *She did it!* Yup, it was definitely her. It was Melissa's fault. Just look at her, playing all innocent and stuff. She's totally responsible and she knows it. I bet she's only blaming it on me so she won't get into trouble."

Melissa snarled and looked ready to pop a blood vessel. "Why you little—"

"Calm down, Melissa." Sarah grabbed Melissa's shoulders. Melissa was rolling up her sleeve with her hands balled into fists and outrage covering her face.

"Melissa couldn't have done it," Paro said. "She's neither a Telekinetic nor is she a Manipulator. She wouldn't have been able to set a room on fire."

"Oh yeah? Well, I don't know what that means, but what if she used a *scroll of enchanting* and that changed her ability?"

"A scroll of what?" Paro looked around at his team. "What's he on about now? What's this 'scroll of enchanting' he's ranting about? Anybody have a clue?" Michael and Sarah looked at each other then shrugged.

Kazou cleared his throat. "I don't know," he said. "But it sounds like some kind of spell-thing."

Spell-thing? Don't tell me he ...

"Okay, hold up a minute now, hold up. Jack," Paro began, "do you mean to tell me you thought from everything that happened today that ... we were using *magic*?"

"Well, I was actually gonna say Sorcery, but why split hairs, right?"

Paro shook his head as a powerful sense of both realization and surprise dawned on him.

I'm arguing with a complete imbecile. I can't believe it. Here I am, standing in the middle of a children's playground, arguing with an absolute moron. This is the most demeaning thing I have ever done. Shame on me!

"Okay, that's it. You're coming with us right now. I've had enough of this. Get over here, you little runt." Paro took a step forward.

"Like hell!" Jack attempted to dart away, but before he could make it two yards, Melissa dashed from behind him and tackled him to the ground.

"Not again, Melissa!"

She pulled him to his feet and smiled at him. From what Paro had gathered, Melissa had roughed Jack up a bit when she suspected his involvement in the murders. This time, she didn't hurt him. In fact, she had something of a playful aspect to her.

"Come on, Jack. I've said this before, and I'll say it again. Stop being such a baby. Paro, what do we do with him?"

Paro sighed. "The Heli won't be here for another few hours, but I know a good place we can chat in the meantime. Let's bring him to the van. Jack, are you going to walk, or do I need to drag you?"

For the love of God, I hope he doesn't continue to make this difficult for us.

Jack had a sour look on his face. He crossed his arms and turned his head away. "You might as well drag me. I'm not listening to a word you sorcerers have to say."

Paro opened his mouth to speak but stopped when he noticed Michael. He had a devilish grin on his face. Michael strutted over to where Melissa held Jack.

"Actually, you're gonna cooperate with us in full, buddy. You're gonna do every last thing we say, and do you know why? Do you know why you're gonna cooperate?"

"Why's that?" Jack asked.

"Because if you don't, then you'll never get to see Melissa in her tight gym uniform when she works out back at H.Q."

Melissa's eyebrows rose to the top of her face. She shot a deadly glare at Michael, who grinned like a madman. Her eyes promised payback and revenge.

Jack tapped Paro on the shoulder. "Hey, you said your name is Paro, right? I've been thinking about it, and I think some seriously dangerous stuff might be going on here. I've decided on second thought to come with you. I think I might be able to help."

Paro watched as Sarah turned away from everyone so she could laugh silently into her arms. Kazou joined her, pretending he had to sneeze.

Melissa tightened her grip on Jack's shoulder, causing him to grunt in pain. "Keep moving, buster, or I'll throw you back to the ground."

It took the sound of his own voice for Paro to realize that he too was laughing.

Damn that Harris kid.

Chapter 9: As If Pulled By a Thread

The sporadic and uneven crackle of foot on gravel was the only indication Andy needed to realize something was wrong. It was a slow, dragging sound, instead of the usual one-two of feet descending steps.

The door creaked open, and the sight of Ruin limping and supported by his sister greeted Andy. Ruin's nose was broken, and his mouth had a trail of blood streaking over his lips. Yet, despite the injury, he seemed amused.

"Well now *that* was unexpected," he said.

Requiem, on the other hand, looked downright furious. Her eyes were sharper than usual, shining with all the madness and chaos of a black hole.

"I will kill that Pig-faced brat. I will show you her lungs, yes, and you shall rip them like paper. But only enough to make it painful to breathe. I will take my time with her. Oh, yes! That one will suffer an agonizing death. No place on this earth will keep her safe from me. I will destroy her!"

Andy had no idea what happened and found it hard to care. He was still sitting in the corner of the room with his knees tucked into his stomach. His eyes stung from the hours he'd spent crying. He was physically exhausted, but sleep would not come.

"Are you still crying, Brother Andy? Don't tell me you've been bawling here all night. It's morning already, you know? What if your mother reports you missing? You need to man up and go home before you arouse suspicion."

Andy tried to turn away from Ruin, but his head wouldn't move. It was as if an invisible hand held it in place.

That's right. He's a Telekinetic, and he's different from me.

"You weren't there. None of you were! I just wanted Richard. I didn't think anyone else was awake. They saw what I did, and then they screamed and reached for their phone. I didn't know what to do, honestly, I didn't. Will God ever forgive me? I keep thinking to myself over and over how things could've been different. Sometimes I even doze off, and in my dreams, none of this ever happened. But it did. I massacred them. I butchered them. I am disgusting! *I am the worst!*"

Ruin and Requiem looked at each other for a moment and then simultaneously burst into a laughing frenzy. Andy felt destroyed, too exhausted to care what it was they found so humorous.

"Oh, Andy, Darling, lighten up. My brother and I have been thinking of a new name for you. How about, 'Andy, the Family-Slayer?'"

The hysterical, laughing fit continued.

"I actually preferred, 'Andy, the Ruthless'," Ruin said, "but my sister's was better."

If the two weren't so much more powerful than he was, Andy would have killed them on the spot. He had vomited twice since returning to the shelter, not bothering to clean it, but neither of them paid it any mind.

Several times over the long night, Andy had contemplated suicide. More so, he had even come close to attempting it. But he was weak. Despite his desire, he couldn't bring himself to go through with it. All he wanted was to start over, to return to his life and forget that any of this had ever happened.

"What happened to you two tonight?" Andy asked.

Their laughing stopped instantly, and their eyes took on a more sinister look.

"There are others like us. More than we expected. They intervened with our capture of the Harris-boy."

At this, for the first time in almost twenty-four hours, Andy's attention diverted to something other than his crimes.

"Intervened? What do you mean? That doesn't make any sense."

Requiem licked her lips. "Apparently, Darling, there's others like us that can do what we can. Only, I suspect they're somehow affiliated with the government or police, because they seemed to have it out for us."

Ruin nodded. "We are not positive, but if this is the case then they are our gravest enemies. It is our God-given right to kill those who we please. Those with strength can make or break laws, but they are *not* subject to them." He scowled as he spoke. It was the first time Andy had ever seen Ruin angry. It was hard to believe.

"These fools," Ruin continued, "they dare try to use their powers to enforce ... rules! On us! I'll personally see to the execution of each one of them. No one has the right to take our freedom, not unless they are stronger than we are. And I promise you they aren't. Had you been there with us, Andy, we would have devoured them completely. I need you to get out of this pathetic state you're in and join us in exterminating these rodents."

Despite all of Andy's terror and sorrow, his grief and his misery, his nightmare and his pain, up until now, there had still been a glimmer of hope. Even with the unbearable torment and realization that he had utterly and completely ruined the hopes and dreams of an entire lineage, there had been one small, almost unrecognizable escape from despair. In the farthest reaches of his mind, Andy knew that due to the nature of his crimes he wouldn't be suspected. After all, he killed without laying a finger on his victims. If he wanted to, he could simply start over and never hear of his atrocities again.

Now that was gone, and all that remained inside of Andy was misery. So, there *were* people who could track these powers? If he'd had even a morsel of suspicion, he never would have gone through with any of it. He could have called the police, or he could have reached out for help. Ruin and Requiem had told him he was unique, but now he knew otherwise.

I'm done. I'll be executed, my mother shamed, my life snatched away from me. Do I even deserve any better?

"I know what you're thinking, Darling, and it's not because I'm a Telepath," Requiem said. Ruin simply nodded.

She walked over to him in the corner of the dark bomb shelter. Gravel crunched underfoot as she crouched down in front of him. With her red hair and her fierce eyes, her beauty somehow managed to overshadow her madness.

"Do not lose hope. There is no going back, but we can still move forward. We have broken no laws because *we are the law*. I've seen this 'Harris-boy'. Once we have him, nothing will stop us. I think you can help us. You claimed to know him."

Andy shook his head. "You might as well forget about Jack. Even if Jack is *like* us, he'll never *be* us. In fact, he'll never be like anyone. Sometimes I wonder if he's even human."

Ruin rubbed under his chin. "I noticed something was off about him as well," he said. "Andy, tell us everything you know about Jack Harris, starting with your relationship. Are you two friends?"

"Kind of," Andy said. "It's very difficult to say. Jack seems to think we are, but I mostly avoid him. He's one of the few people abused at school more than I am, and he reaches out to me—not for help or pity or anything, I think he just doesn't like seeing me alone. He has this friend of his, umm ... Adam. So despite it all, he always has someone to talk with. I mostly keep to myself, and I think he feels bad for me."

Ruin nodded. "Interesting. You say he is abused at school?"

Andy shook his head just thinking about it. "You have no idea. It's a miracle he hasn't gone on a rampage, abilities or otherwise. What that kid's gone through makes my life seem like heaven by comparison. I don't even know where to start with Jack."

Requiem and Ruin slid over two metal chairs, which scratched against the gravel floor.

"Well, tell us what you can," Requiem said.

"I live about two miles from him, so we've gone to the same school since about the third grade. Since then, I've seen some of the worst things humanity can offer brought upon him. If it was just being beaten up or spat on, or even shut inside of a locker for a few hours, he'd be no different from me. But with him, they took it beyond that."

Andy inhaled. "In the early sixth grade, he found an abandoned baby rabbit outside the schoolyard. For weeks, he nursed the thing and brought it with him to school. The teachers didn't seem to mind, which was weird. I guess they thought it was cute."

"He carried it with him for almost two months, caring for it, playing with it. When bullies would come near him he'd hide it, and they'd threaten to beat him if he didn't give it to them. Let's just say he got quite a few beatings. But one day, as a 'joke,' this kid Jeremy Sanders gets hold of some rat poison. He breaks into Jack's locker, replaces the food, and within a day the little thing dies."

Requiem stood from her chair and picked it up, tossing it into the corner. The chair crashed against the wall and landed on the floor with a thud.

"Those bastards! *How dare they?*"

Andy was confused. So now Requiem was a compassionate person? Insane people made no sense.

Noting his confusion, Ruin spoke, "Andy, we already consider Jack to be our brother. The rabbit was his *thing*. If he wanted it to live, then damnit it *lives*. That is our way. It was his choice, and it was violated by trash like this Jeremy. But please, continue, what happened next?"

Andy tried to ignore the remark and continued. "Well, it didn't take long for Jack to find out who did it. It was also the first time I'd ever seen him angry about something. Normally, he just ignored the torture, but this time, he went up to this Jeremy kid, who mind you, was quite a bit larger than Jack."

"So anyway, Jack knocked this guy to the floor with one hit. I've never seen that kind of power from anyone. Oh man, you should have seen the surprise on this kid's face when little old Jack sent him to the ground. Jack jumped on top of him, right? And he made like he was going to punch him again. I remember because he pulled back his fist like he was ready to go all out on this guy."

Ruin laughed. "And you say he can't be made to see our side of things?"

"Wait, Ruin, there's more. Just when Jack was about to start pounding this kid into oblivion, the kid started screaming, 'Wait, please! Don't hurt me. I'm sorry, please!' And then Jack just ... stopped. He didn't even think about it. The moment Jack heard his voice he just stopped, got off the kid, and told him he forgave him."

Andy continued, "You see? This is why he'll never join us. He's not like other people."

Requiem's lip pulled back, distorting what was normally a beautiful face. Her eyes, too, seemed crossed, and her tongue lolled out the side of her mouth like a hungry animal.

"Oh, I want him so badly. I need to be alone for some time, my sweets. I can barely contain myself, and I don't wish to hurt my two dear brothers. This Jack Harris, he will ... he *must* be mine. I will have him slaughter his family. No, better, I shall make him kill *children!* I need to be alone. You two, get out of here—now!"

A chill went down Andy's spine as understanding dawned on him. *She's excited by the thought of destroying innocence? It seems the greater the innocence, the higher the pleasure. Who is she?*

If asked, most would say there are three types of people in this world—the sane, the mad, and those who know they are mad. But seeing Requiem, Andy came to realize there was a fourth.

Those who know they are mad and loving it.

Chapter 10: Hunters

Cemmera Wilson, Division Captain and team leader of Op. team four-H, smiled as she felt the excitement grow.

"Give me the analysis, Santos."

Santos looked towards the ground and appeared to be deep in focus. He was a fat, weird-looking fellow with mushroom-shaped hair and large cheekbones, but none of that mattered to Cemmera. Santos could be as fat and ugly as he wanted, as long as he did his job properly.

"It's the two we're looking for, no doubt about it. They're both Teleys and they're both scared out their wits. They have a feeling we're closing in on them, and they're about to lose it."

"Do they sense you?" she asked.

"Not at all. They're amateurs, untrained."

Cemmera nodded. This was good.

They were crouched out of sight and huddled behind a filthy stretch of wall that lined a storage facility in Midtown Manhattan. All five were bundled in bulletproof T.A.C jackets, Comm radios, 9mm. firearms, and non-constrictive helmet gear.

As usual, Manhattan roared with activity. Cars sped to and from work, restaurants, and a few other less respectable places. Positioned over a sewer grate, the stench annoyed Cemmera, but she pushed it from her mind and focused on the entry point.

"Can everyone here make the jump? It's only a two-story window." Cemmera beamed with approval as one by one, her team-members nodded. It was only about a fifteen foot jump to the window, and her team was well-trained. Even a Telepath could make the jump with proper training.

Cemmera motioned with her hands, and in one fluid motion, the team bolted upright from their crouch and followed Cemmera. She sprinted from behind the dusty wall towards the left end of the complex. The second-story window was low enough to the ground that the wall behind them hid them from any onlookers.

With a grunt, Cemmera kicked off the ground and leapt, grabbing hold of the base of the window. Concentrating, she focused on the chemical structure of the glass. As a Manipulator with almost two decades of practice, the chemical composition of glass could be manipulated as easily as a piece of bread in a toaster.

Silently, the glass faded away into sand, and she entered the building. One by one, her team members leaped, grabbing a hold and pulling themselves in behind her. Once inside, Cemmera signaled weapons-free, and the men removed their guns from their holsters.

"Santos, location," she said.

Santos looked down again—it was his gesture of gathering Intel. It was different for every Telepath, but they all had some noticeable quirk when they were concentrating. "Just down the hall and to the left. They have ah, let me see here now. Any deeper and they'll feel the probe."

A small drop of sweat fell from his forehead as he concentrated. "Okay, they have weapons. They're carrying Colt M1s and sufficient ammo to take down a small army."

Cemmera nodded. "Alright, we'll put our Kinetics up front and our Brute in the middle."

Neil Witherson, her team's sole Reinforcer, grunted at the derogatory term. More than anything else, Reinforcers hated to be called a 'Brute'. Cemmera knew he wouldn't voice any protest during a mission, but he'd approach her about it later, for sure.

Cemmera rubbed her gloved hands together. "On three we go."

One.

Here it was. This was the reason most joined the Op. department. She knew she was not alone in feeling the rush, the excitement fill her belly—the giddy feeling of pleasure and empowerment she'd come to live for.

Two.

She licked her lips, with her fingers held tightly on the trigger of her weapon. Not that she would ever use it—very few did. It was less powerful than what she was capable of by herself.

Three.

This was it, her favorite part—watching her plan come to fruition. On cue, Neil balled his left hand into a fist and then slammed it into the door. With a tremendous crash, the door exploded off its hinges and flew into the room, startling the two frightened men huddled in the corner.

As Cemmera expected, they reached for their firearms. They were Telepaths, widely accepted as the weakest fighters among Psychs. Before they could raise their weapons halfway into a shooting position, the guns were ripped from their fingers and sent soaring across the room and into the hands of her Kinetics.

Cemmera smiled. She only loved two things in this world—the thrill of the hunt and the men she hunted with.

The two targets looked at each other in confusion before raising their hands into the air and dropping to their knees.

"We surrender!" one cried. "Don't shoot!" begged the other.

Cemmera shrugged. "Okay, I had the last few kills, so who wants this one?" Cemmera's men filled her with pride as each member of her team raised their hands like school children with an answer to their teacher's question. They were such good boys.

"Alright, you seem kind of agitated, Neil, so go ahead and smash 'em until their skulls look like jelly."

The two Telepaths gasped. "But wait, we said we surrender! Take us in, lock us up. Did you not hear us? We surrender!"

Neil walked closer to them, ignoring their pleas.

"Wait, please, I beg of you. I only cheated the casino to feed my family. I didn't mean any harm. I beg of you, please! For the love of God, don't kill me. I will do anything, I will plead guilty to any charge, just don't do this to me."

Cemmera knew that Neil liked to walk at a slow, sedate pace and draw out the killings.

"You boys are gonna learn that crime just does *not* pay," he hummed at them.

The sound of horror quickly transformed into one of pain, as Neil's massive fist met skull. The man had never even removed himself from a surrendering position. His cranium was smashed into nothingness.

The other man stood and attempted to flee, but only made it into a standing crouch. Neil kicked him in the throat, snapping his neck and killing him instantly.

The two men, who were full of life only moments before, were now crumpled in a heap on the floor. Life was entirely absent from once shining eyes.

"We got lucky on this one, boys," Cemmera said. "Those Carebear investigators almost brought these two in. They never let us have any fun."

All five of them shared a laugh.

God, I love my team.

Cemmera picked up her radio. "Hey, Mitch, guess what? I got your two Paths. Thanks for leaving that file on your computer. And don't sound appalled, of course I broke into your office. I was bored!"

The voice on the other end fired back with outrage. *"Damn you all, you Op. team animals. You're no better than they are! Those were good people. All they did wrong was cheat on a few casino games. They weren't murderers or thieves!"*

"Ah, but Mitch, cheating is thieving. Besides, I don't make the law. Once a Psych hits twenty-large, it's a Grand Larceny. Your boys had their chance, and they didn't catch 'em, we did—cry about it."

The returned explosion of anger-filled shouts annoyed Cemmera, so she closed her radio, prematurely ending the conversation.

"You love to tease the poor Carebears, don't you?" Santos asked, chuckling.

The men laughed with him. "I can't help it," Cemmera said. "It's just too easy. Besides, it's our job to make sure that the bad guys pay when the good guys show up, isn't it?"

The men gave Cemmera a pleading look, and she knew why. They all probably had the same thought on their mind—drinking to celebrate their kill. It was tradition.

"By the way, I've got a lead on some other great stuff to do. You boys are gonna love this one. I filed for another kill authorization without permission from an Investigation Team. They're gonna flip when we cut down their targets like we did to these sorry excuses for men."

Cemmera's men beamed with appreciation.

"Tell us more," Neil said. "I don't know how you manage to keep getting these kills authorized without consent."

Cemmera laughed. The only way to receive an authorization for a kill-order was to send in the Investigative files to the proper commander. The problem was that investigation teams were stubborn fools that refused to cooperate half the time. So, Cemmera stole what she could and bribed her way to the rest.

"We've got some serious murders going on over in Elms New Jersey. Nine dead, more will probably follow. Paro's got this one. Oh man, he's gonna lose it when we grab our targets."

"Wait a minute," Santos said. "Isn't Paro doing Juvie crimes now?"

"Yep, the suspects are kids. He's probably going soft on them, that Carebear. You know he used to be one of the baddest guys around, back when I started. He's a legend, that one. Unrestricted too, if you'll believe it."

Cemmera watched as she could visibly see the chill running down the men's spines. "Did you know he started when he was only fourteen?" she asked. "I'm not kidding, he made it rain blood. It's sad to see him go so soft."

Santos' face turned pale. "I'm worried. What if he comes after us for killing his targets?"

Cemmera gave him a friendly nudge. "Don't be ridiculous. Once we get authorized, there's nothing he can do about it. Let him be angry, the world is angry!"

"If you say so ..."

"Did you guys know that if you took *every* living animal out of the sea, then the water level of the ocean would go down?"

"Jack!" Paro snapped, "I'm going to tell you this one last time. Shut the hell up, or I will shut you up. We can speak when we get there."

"Jeeze, someone forgot to eat a Mentos today."

The van whizzed by on the North Roadway. Jack had no idea where they were headed, but he no longer cared, either. He took life on a thing-by-thing basis, but he did fear that his mother would worry about him.

Looking out of the window, he could see communities and neighborhoods pass by. He loved his suburban home. It was like a paradise of swimming pools, parks, and gardens. The beautiful sunrise cast exotic shadows along the trees and flowers.

I wonder where we're heading. God, this is so boring. Stupid Paro, telling me to be quiet.

Jack was sacrificing a great deal by wasting all his time with sorcerers.

Then they try and tell me that I'm a sorcerer too. Hah! If I were a sorcerer, I would summon a dragon-demon-thing with long black wings that breathed fire. Then I would ride it through the clouds.

Jack relaxed as the ride continued, until a dangerous, horrific thought came to his mind.

Oh no! This can't be ... how could I have let this happen?

"We need to stop the car right now!"

Kazou, Melissa, and Michael all turned to where Jack sat in the back. Their faces filled with alarm.

"What's wrong?" Kazou shouted. "Has something happened?"

Jack nodded. "Yeah, you guys. My Magic the Gathering tournament ... it starts in a few hours. We need to turn this thing around. Today's prize is the all new Plainswalker card."

With a grunt, Melissa slapped him on the back of the head. "Paro, can I gag him, please?"

"Be nice, Melissa," Sarah said.

Jack rubbed his head. Why was everyone so mean?

Chapter 11: My Name, Darling, IS REQUIEM

Requiem entered the small shop on the southern-end of Anker Town—not that she had a choice, it was the only one of its kind in this pathetic town—and looked frantically around her. There was no one in the room.

"Oh, Jason, counter-boy? Where in God's name have you run off to?"

Requiem didn't like to be kept waiting. She tapped her foot with impatience and rested her arm on the wooden countertop. All around her, cages buzzed with life. Some moved, some shook, and others sat still and silent.

She needed to see him. She always did after such a horrible dream. She had dreamt herself in an Amazonian jungle, on a hot, humid day. She had been chased by a giant pig with a human's face, or was it a giant human with a pig's face? The exactness of it she couldn't recall.

When I get my hands on that Pig-faced horse of a woman, I'm going to strangle her!

The dream was both the most humiliating and terrifying Requiem's brain had ever had the misfortune of conjuring. For miles she had run from it, listening to it oink, hearing it taunt her. She had even tried to shut down its mind with telepathy. But in her dream, her powers were ineffective, and it kept charging at her, and charging at her. She had woken screaming, sweating, and furious.

She heard a door creak behind her, and she turned to glance in its direction. A young man no older than twenty-four exited with a look of disappointment on his face. He was short, with curly-brown hair and deep blue eyes.

"Oh, it's you again, is it?"

Requiem was in too much of a rush. She needed to see him now! She would waste no time making small talk with this buffoon.

"Darling, release him—now! I can wait no longer."

The man sighed and lifted a key chain off his belt. The jangling keys were one of the only sounds in this quiet part of the shop.

He disappeared through another door behind Requiem and closed it. For seconds that felt like days, Requiem waited while her excitement grew. Finally, after an agonizing thirty seconds, the door creaked again. Requiem did not bother to let it finish opening. As soon as the door had been half-opened, in one swift motion, two beings charged at each other.

Requiem and the dog collided in the center of the room, and she wrapped her hands around its neck and sighed with delight. "Oh, Mr. Wellington! My sweet underling, how are you today?" she asked, planting kisses.

The dog wagged its tail, spinning, jumping, and licking with excitement. Requiem reached into her pocket to give him treats. She knew from the moment that Pig-girl had escaped that she needed to see Mr. Wellington. He would know how to make her feel better, in a way that no pathetic human life could.

"You know, miss. I gotta tell ya—I got a shop to run here. We sell pets, we don't store 'em, ya sure you can't take it home with you?"

Requiem kissed Mr. Wellington's nose and then looked up. She glared at the man, obviously from New York by the sound of his obnoxious accent.

"Silence, you insignificant worm and obey my orders! Have I not paid you for the storage? Have I not paid you for the animal as well? If I ever return and find out that you have either sold my underling to some disgusting human, or that you kicked him to the curb, then so help me god I shall rip your still-beating heart from your body. Do I make myself clear, *Darling*?"

The man eyed her skeptically but sighed then nodded. "You really shouldn't talk to people like that, you know? It's not polite."

Requiem ignored the fool and crouched back down to continue playing with Mr. Wellington. The golden retriever was still young, not even a year-old, but already he had reached close to his full size. His tongue lolled happily from the side of his mouth, and he stared intently into Requiem's eyes. She cupped his face with her smooth hands.

"Don't worry, Mr. Wellington. Once Ruin and I have found an appropriate lair, I'll remove you from this filthy place." Looking over her shoulder, she could see the man was back behind the counter and out of earshot.

"I know, Mr. Wellington, you want me to turn off his brain or send him into a coma. You're very smart—yes, that's a good Mr. Wellington—but I can't yet. We still need him. Once I get you out of here, I'll take care of him and bring you home."

She stood up and raised her voice. "Oh, Jason, counter-boy, I am in need of another service. Hurry yourself and attend to me this instant!"

The shopkeeper grumbled and walked back over to her. "Don't tell me you need me to store another animal. We sell 'em here, ya know?"

Requiem spat in his ugly face, causing him to recoil in shock. "Silence! You do not proceed to give *me* orders, fool. I require a rabbit, of the bunny sort."

The shopkeeper wiped the spittle from his chin and wisely decided to ignore the gesture. "Well, we've got few here. Take ya pick." He pointed to a pen a few feet to their left.

Inside, Requiem saw the things hopping around. There were five in total, all roughly around the same size and height. But yet, they weren't all the same, no two animals ever were. Only a fool assumed otherwise.

"Counter-boy, give me the one on the left. No, you fool, that's your right. It's no wonder you're selling rabbits! Yes, that one."

Requiem cradled it in her arms and smiled.

Oh! He'll love this one. From what our newest and dearest brother has told us, this should be just like he remembers it.

Requiem brought it to the counter. "That'll be thirty-five even, ya sure you don't want a cage for it?"

"That won't be required," Requiem responded.

"Alright, so thirty-five bucks it is."

Requiem extended her arm over the counter, much to the confusion of the shopkeeper. Gently, she flicked his forehead with her index finger. In response, the shopkeeper opened his drawer and pulled out a stack of twenty-dollar bills.

"Here's your change, and thank you for your business," he said Requiem snatched it from his filthy, animal-reeking fingers.

"Ya know, I notice you come in here a lot, and you never tell me ya name,"

"Ah, but I always do, Darling. My name is Requiem."

The van pulled up to the diner. The *Golden Pearl* was open around the clock and favored by the team. Paro parked in the lot and turned off the ignition.

"Alright, we're here. The helicopter will be here soon, but we should have enough time to talk. Kazou, it's your turn to sit something out. Roam the area. Make sure nothing is after us. I doubt they would be, but it's better to be safe than sorry. Everyone else, we're going inside."

Sarah and Michael yawned in unison and exited the van. Paro watched as Michael made small-talk with Sarah, recommending certain foods, beverages, and desserts.

Paro still couldn't believe someone like Jack existed. Right now, after seeing what certain humans were capable of, his world should have been shaken. He should've been in an almost comatose state of deep thought, wondering what it meant and trying to figure it all out. This is what was expected. Instead, he was asleep with his head resting on Melissa's shoulder.

"Don't get the wrong idea, Paro," she said with a sheepish look. "He's finally stopped going on about nonsense. I'm only doing this to keep him quiet."

Paro laughed. "Good job then, Melissa. Jack, wake up, we're here."

A moan of reluctance was the boy's only response.

"Hey, Jack, get up."

"No ..." the boy responded in between licking his lips. "Five more minutes, go away. I promise, only five more minutes.

Just when Paro was starting to calm down, his frustration peaked yet again.

What is wrong with this Harris-kid?

"I'll handle this, Paro," Melissa said. She slapped Jack on the back of the head, causing him to bolt upright in the seat.

"Ouch! What the hell? Who did that?" Jack rubbed his head and looked at the two of them accusingly.

"Sorry about that—there was a mosquito. I didn't want it to bite you."

"Oh, oh well, in that case ... thanks, I guess."

Jack followed Paro and Melissa into the restaurant. The *Golden Pearl* was a smaller place, with four round tables, seven booths, and a bar in the middle. It was empty this early in the morning. Its only visible occupants were the waiting staff, the bartender, and Michael huddled in the corner booth with Sarah. Paro took a seat next to Sarah while Melissa pushed Jack into the other end of the booth and sat next to him. Jack still appeared drowsy and showed no indication of fear or excitement. In his entire career, Paro had never seen anything even close to this kind of behavior.

Why is he no longer frightened of us? He even thinks we're some kind of magic beings, and yet he just wants to sleep and watch television?

A young waitress came by to take their orders.

"What will it be, ladies and gentlemen?" She was cheerful. She unclipped her writing pad and went around the table.

"I'll order the egg and onion omelet," Sarah said.

"For me, I'll just take French toast on rye." Melissa grinned. "I don't want white-bread because that stuff is *terrible* for you."

"What about you, sweetheart?"

"I don't suppose you're on the menu, darlin'?" Michael asked. The waitress blushed, and Melissa gave Michael an evil glare. Sarah turned her head away in disgust.

Michael puffed his cheeks in imitation of a small child. "Alright guys—don't give me that look. Okay, I'll take the same as Sarah here."

"I just want water," Paro said. "And you, Jack?"

All the drowsiness that had been in Jack's expression faded away in its entirety. He was flipping through the menu with a vigor that could only be called passionate.

"Oh, wow, do I want the strawberry pancakes, the chocolate chip ones, or the Breakfast Champions combo? Oh man," he said with excitement, "you guys have so much stuff! Choosing something is the biggest hardship I've been through all week."

At this, every single member of Paro's team, including Paro himself, dropped their jaws and widened their eyes. Luckily, they were quick to regain their composures.

"Well, I say try our chocolate pancakes, sweetie. They're our best seller."

"True, I do agree that they have a certain appeal," Jack responded, oblivious to his reason for being in the restaurant in the first place and soaking up valuable time.

"But let's just think about this for a minute, okay? Let's say I *do* get the chocolate chip pancakes. What if I take some home? In fact, I probably will, because they always give you too much. Here's the problem—for some reason, chocolate chip pancakes dry out faster than other ones. I don't know why, and they're never as good as they were before. Also, while usually the most delicious of pancakes, chocolate chip ones have a tendency to make me feel sick after eating them. I'm never sure if it was worth getting them in the first place. Now, let us discuss strawberry pancakes. If we highlight the pros and cons, I think you'd find—"

Melissa's shout was not actually a shout, but in fact more like a bat-like screech. *"He'll take the damn chocolate ones!"*

Paro said nothing. He couldn't. He wasn't trained for this. Nothing had prepared him to deal with someone like Jack. He only knew two things for certain. Number one, he was now sure that the Harris-kid had nothing to do with the murders, like Melissa had said. She was completely right about him. There was no way in heaven, hell, or earth that this kid was a murderer, excepting if he made you murder yourself. And secondly, Paro was no longer sure that he would care enough to bring him in even if he was a murderer. Sometimes work sucked.

Chapter 12: Serious Conversations Are a Sacred Thing

Jack sighed happily while he munched on another bite of the delicious chocolate chip pancakes. Melissa had been right. They were the perfect choice. With a gulp of milk, he looked around at the strange people surrounding him.

"Jack, before we begin," Paro said, pushing aside his plate and revealing a thick tan folder, "I think you should know who we are, what we are, and who *you* are. This should clear up a lot of the confusion you're feeling."

Jack nodded. It had been quite the strange night.

"You already know Melissa Sayre. To my right are Michael Reed and Sarah Blighter. The Japanese man from earlier is Kazou Takeshi, and myself." He grinned. "Just call me Paro."

Jack lowered his fork and waved. "Well, it's nice to meet you guys, but I'm not really sure why all this has been happening or umm, who those two people were that attacked me and Melissa, but I guess I can try to help out."

Jack didn't understand why, but Paro visibly relaxed, and he looked as if a burden had been lifted from his shoulders. He slid a folder across the table towards Jack, who pushed his plate to the side and opened it, frowning. Even just seeing a picture of school was enough to make him cringe. Thoughts of late assignments, future projects, and incomplete homework returned to him in a rush.

"Is this about that fire again?" Jack asked.

"Yes, it is, and very much so. Before we can assess the bigger problem, we need to first give you an idea of where all your involvement in this started."

Jack looked down at the pictures of the burned classroom, which was more than likely never usable again. It looked nothing like he remembered it. The once colorful math classroom was now nothing more than a box of charred items, none of which were recognizable. He supposed the tiny black lumps were desks.

"Jack, we are not the sorcerers you seem to think we are. We are known as Psychs. Everyone sitting at this table is actually a Psych, and yes, that's including you, Jack Harris There is a much longer scientific name for what we are, but even I can't remember it, so this is what we call ourselves."

Paro continued, "I don't know how long we've existed for—how long people like us have been around, I mean. As far as our history goes—if we're being truthful here—I don't know, nor have I ever really cared. The reason my team exists is because sometimes people born with our gifts take it upon themselves to commit atrocities. They use what they were born with to slaughter and take from others what they've no right to take. For instance, Richard Davins, a classmate of yours. Here, see for yourself. Our importance is easier shown than said."

Paro slid another file across the table and Jack opened it. In an instant, his cheer was gone. Jack recoiled at the gruesome image. For a moment, it was hard to breath. Jack had known this person. He had been walking and talking such a short time ago. Now, he was nothing more than a bloodied clump of gelatinous tissue, barely recognizable as a person, let alone a person with hopes, dreams, and aspirations. This was beyond awful. This was intolerable. A tear glided down the side of Jack's face.

Melissa looked at him sadly. Sarah leaned over the table and dabbed Jack's face with a soft cloth.

I didn't like Richard, but this ... why would someone do this to him?

"Do you understand now why we're needed, Jack? The police can't stop this, and even if they could, they still wouldn't be able to make a difference. That's assuming, of course, that they could understand all of it in the first place." Paro had a grim expression, and he maintained it while he shuffled through the files.

Jack nodded. "I get it, Paro. But I still don't see why you guys came after me."

Paro sat up straighter in the booth and folded his hands under his chin. "Richard wasn't the first boy from your class to be killed. There was another, earlier victim—yet still not the first. His name was Jonathan Herbert."

Jack leaned over and looked at the file. "But ... but I thought he was just absent. You mean they did this to him too? Why, Paro? He was a good guy. I swear it. He never hurt anyone. This can't be. No one would kill him for no reason like that."

Jack felt the loss deep in his heart. Jonathan wasn't a person Jack knew well, but it was still someone Jack knew. Thinking back, Jonathan had wanted to be an astronomer. In science class, he'd discuss the stars, even when the topic was biology. He had hopes, dreams, and loving parents that wanted to see them fulfilled. And now he was gone? He was no longer in this world? But for what, Jack wondered. What made it so his life had to be taken from him?

Jack forced his tears to a halt. "I still don't understand."

Paro sighed. "When the first boy was murdered from your class, we thought it had been a random killing because it matched the M.O. We see now, of course, that it was random and that we were correct. But at the time when the fire incident occurred, we had a growing suspicion that it might be the killers taunting us. We were sure of it when the second boy was murdered from the same class so soon after the fire. But it wasn't until now that we realize the fire was just a coincidence. It was something that you did to stop yourself from failing an assignment, which, by the way, we're going to need to have a word with you about. That is not acceptable behavior, and it won't be tolerated."

Jack shook his head. "I see what you're getting at, but I didn't do the fire-thing. Even if I'm a Psych like you guys, it doesn't matter— I wouldn't do something like that. It's too dangerous, and someone could have gotten hurt."

Paro nodded. "I believe you, which leads me to my next point. It is very rare for Psychs to use their abilities on accident, as we can almost always control them. Having spent just a few hours with you, I'm now positive that you didn't know what you were doing. But that's not a good thing. It makes you dangerous. It's for this reason, among several others, that you need to come with us and get a handle on this stuff. We can't have you walking down the streets setting people on fire."

Jack sighed. "But I don't even remember doing it, not even a little. Honest!"

"Tell me, Jack," Sarah said. She had been quiet for a while. She looked at him with soft eyes, and Jack felt a gentle presence brushing the corner of his mind.

"What was going through your mind yesterday morning? Don't be alarmed—I'm just helping you to relax and remember. I am not infiltrating your mind, simply stimulating it. Many have told me that it helps them to relax and remember things more clearly."

She was right. Jack felt pressure and tension release from his body.

"I was cheating, and I was gonna get caught. Oh, by the way, can you guys punish me for that too? Because if so, then I wasn't cheating, I was, umm ... receiving 'help'."

Sarah chuckled. "Just keep going. What next?"

"Okay, so anyway, I remember that much, but then something happened. I can't describe it. It's like, umm, I don't know how to explain it. It's there but it's not. My stomach was hurting really bad, and ... I don't know! It's like the answer is there but it's just too hard to remember."

Sarah continued to stare at him with a warm, tranquil expression. "As long as you're thinking about it and keeping it on the forefront of your mind, I may be able to access it, this ... memory of yours. Yes, I see it now. You were sitting in your desk, and you started thinking to yourself. You were thinking—"

Sarah shouted and turned away from Jack, nearly leaping out of the booth, twitching and rubbing her face. She shook her head furiously. Michael and Paro turned to her.

"Sarah! What's wrong?" Michael put his hands on her shoulders. She was gripping her head with both hands, shaking her head as if trying to clear it of confusion. She turned to Paro, and her face reddened.

"Stop right there, Sarah," Paro said. "I can see it on your face. You're about to apologize. You have nothing to be sorry for. You are learning at a very fast rate, and these things don't always work at first. You'll be fine. It was just a normal mental shock. Don't beat yourself up every time you make a mistake. You're an excellent Telepath, and you know I mean that."

Sarah looked both ashamed and embarrassed. A wrinkle formed under her lip as she met Jack's eyes, and it reminded him of the same apologetic look he gave people when he did something wrong.

What in the hell was that about?

A moment of silence settled on them. The restaurant was empty, which was a shame because the food was fabulous. Jack figured it was probably because of the early morning hours. Most people wouldn't come in for breakfast until at least seven a.m.

The waitress returned a few moments later with the same smile on her face as earlier. "Can I get you guys anything else? Any refills, maybe some pie?"

"We're fine, thank you," Paro said.

He turned once again to face Jack. "So, where were we? Ah yes, the fire. You see, Jack, we had every reason to believe that—"

"That was so rude, Paro!" Jack pointed a finger at Paro and glared at him. He didn't understand why Paro returned a questioning look, because surely Paro knew what he had done wrong. When Paro continued to look confused, Jack moaned in frustration.

"You answered for all of us! I wanted some more milk and pie, and I bet we're all thinking to ourselves about how much of a jerk you are. Isn't that right, guys?"

Melissa elbowed Jack on the shoulder. "Jack, cut it out! We're having a serious discussion. No one here agrees with you—Michael, stop nodding or I'll hit you too. You *would* agree with him, damn Telekinetics—now, can we please get back to the important stuff?"

"Thank you, Melissa. And Jack, interrupt me again, and I'll show you why people used to call me a devil. Do-not-test-me."

Jack shuddered at the menace in Paro's eyes, but refused to look away. That pecan pie looked amazing, and it was Paro's fault that Jack didn't get to have any. Stupid Paro!

"Now, as for why we thought you were linked after the second killing. Michael, do you want to explain? It was your idea, after all. One which I still think might be partially correct."

Michael gave a sitting bow, much to the annoyance of all but Jack.

"So, Jack, I was thinking, right? The killings changed after the fire that these fellas over here are tryin'ta blame on ya, even though you probably didn't do it."

Melissa squeezed her hands into fists, but luckily, Sarah reached over and patted her on the shoulder, calming her down. Michael simply tipped the cowboy hat he wore, hanging just off the top of his thick, blond-hair.

"So as far as I reckoned, let's say you know a guy that does the same old thing every time, right? And he keeps on doing it and doing it, and then one day, it just changes completely after something else big happens. I was thinking—"

Jack inhaled as he filled with understanding. Now here was a man who made perfect sense. "That I had been recruited," Jack said, "even if I wasn't involved to begin with! Wow, everything about what you guys are doing makes sense now. Man, you and I are smart, Michael. I'm surprised you haven't already solved this thing on your own."

Melissa made a sound that half resembled a moan. "I could cry right now, Paro. Michael alone was bad enough. Now he has an apprentice."

Paro nodded his head in agreement.

"So then Paro, if you guys know I didn't do it on purpose, then I get why you want to take me in and what not, so I don't do it again. But what still doesn't make sense is what I can do to help with the killings?"

"Two things," Paro said. "One, the killers—from what Melissa told us on the way here they were determined to capture you at any cost. They feel some sort of connection to you or something. I don't understand just yet. We believe that if we set you out into the open, they'll come back looking to grab you."

"And two," he continued. "The recruitment theory is still our best lead. Even if they didn't recruit you, we have every reason to believe that they recruited *someone*. At first, the killings were done telekinetically, like how you started that fire—and get that smug look off your face. If you try to deny it once more, I will throw you out of a window—but back to what I was saying. The most recent killings were done using chemical manipulation. And I see the confusion on your face. Don't worry—we'll explain that side of things later. For now, just understand that the fire was caused by friction, which means only a Kinetic could have done it. Thus, we know you're not involved with them. But you may be able to lead us to whoever is."

Jack thought for a moment about Richard and then about Jonathan. What was Jack's life worth if he allowed these killings to continue while he had some way of stopping them? Jack didn't care about the danger to his own life. What had to be done was as simple as tying a knot. Actually, sometimes that could be kind of hard too, he realized.

He laughed. "Paro, I don't really understand most of what you just said, but if I can lead you to the guys who did it, I'd be happy to. Just not on Sundays, because True Blood is starting up again." Jack narrowed his eyes. "After what they have done, I'd do anything to see them caught."

For the first time since late last night when they had met, Jack saw Paro smile. "Good man."

The sound of a loud and whiny hum caused Jack to look over his shoulders. He jumped up in the booth and tried to nudge Melissa out of the way.

"You guys were serious? I get to go in an actual helicopter? This is amazing, wow! Is it just gonna like, land right outside?"

Melissa laughed. "You better believe it, Jack. We get to do a lot of things most people can't."

Michael and Sarah looked at each other and grinned.

"Wait, guys, can I fly it? I can use my Psychicho-sis-ness or whatever to control it, so I'll make sure we don't all die."

It was yet another in a day full of slaps, as Melissa playfully tapped him on the back of the head. "Literally over my dead body."

Chapter 13: H.Q

Astounding didn't begin to describe it. The sensation Jack felt as the helicopter descended to land in the wide parking lot was a cross between excitement and wonder.

Small glass bottles, dirt, and empty potato-chip bags were sent flying as a gust of wind hit the six of them. The helicopter touched down on the lot outside of the *Golden Pearl*. Jack attempted to charge into it like a dog fetching a bone, but Melissa grabbed the back of his shirt, halting him in place.

"Are you an idiot, Jack? Wait until the propeller stops spinning or you'll be cut in two halves." Jack ignored her.

Stupid Melissa, not knowing what she's talking about. How could a propeller cut me in half? That only happens in the movies.

"Window Seat!" Jack called out, ignoring the sighs of frustration around him. As soon as the pilot opened the side-door, the blue-suited man was forced to leap out of the way. Jack took a nose dive into the aircraft. This was a dream of his, one of many. He always wanted to ride in a helicopter, almost as badly as he wanted Buffy to return for another season.

The interior was just what Jack had expected, only better. This was the type where he could stick his legs out while they were flying, just like in those old Vietnam war movies. The piloting console was amazing, too, with buttons and lights and all kinds of other neat stuff. Jack wondered if everyone would be annoyed if he pushed a few just to see what they did. He decided against it. After all, the last thing Jack needed was Melissa getting on his case again just because of a teeny-tiny little helicopter crash.

One by one, the members of Paro's team entered and strapped themselves in around Jack. Melissa sat next to him, with Sarah taking a place beside her. On the other end Paro, Kazou, and Michael strapped in and passed around large headsets.

Jack placed one over his ears. "What are these for?"

"It's so you can hear us, Jack," Kazou said. "It gets pretty loud when we're flying, but we can communicate easily with these on."

"It's so cool, isn't it?" Michael asked. "I love flying in these things too."

The propeller resumed its loud whine as it spun faster and faster with each rotation. Jack could swear his heartbeat accelerated to match the thumping sound of the vehicle.

The first twenty seconds were pure bliss. The helicopter lifted off and slowly gained distance from the ground. Jack could see the *Golden Pearl,* the highway, and the trees around him become smaller while he reigned over it like a God.

The wind beat against him, ruffling his clothing. The helicopter was only a few hundred feet up, but Jack was still filled with pure joy. He tried to look in every direction at once. Flight was truly one of the most amazing and magnificent things that human beings had ever brought to this world.

As the helicopter lurched forward, Jack felt tears form in his eyes while he watched the small cars on the road. He wondered if they were looking up at him, wishing they too could soar over the skies. They were nothing more than little dots that whizzed by on the highway.

Paro said the flight would probably only be about forty-five minutes, so Jack tried to take in every detail and burn it into memory. He wiggled his feet, feeling the force of the wind push against them. He looked down as they flew over the residential areas.

Jack watched in a fascinated trance as he flew over swimming pools, rooftops, and kids playing basketball in front of their homes. Several people looked up at him and pointed.

"Hey, Jack, do you like it?" Michael asked.

"Oh, hell yeah! Can we go back to the diner and start over? I think I missed a few details along the way."

Melissa sighed into her headset. "You've just landed yourself one slap in debt, Jack."

"Don't listen to her," Michael chimed in. "She's just trying to kill the fun of flying."

"Yeah," Jack said, laughing. "Melissa hates fun. We should call her the 'Funinator' from now on."

At this, even Kazou seemed to join in, chuckling with Michael. A feminine growl came from the headset. "Two slaps."

The helicopter soared over New Jersey, until the land turned to water and they flew over the ocean. Jack delighted in the misty wind that hit his face. In the distance, he could spot the outline of Manhattan Island. This was beyond a doubt one of the coolest things he'd ever done. He looked at the water, only a few dozen feet below him, hoping to see a fish.

If Jack had been amazed early on, he nearly lost his ability to speak when they reached Manhattan. It was a dream world of tall buildings, cars, pedestrians shuffling across streets, and giant skyscrapers with flashing lights visible even during the day.

The helicopter set down on the landing pad of a giant, grey building. Jack had no idea what part of Manhattan this was, but he didn't care. All he wanted was to stay in the helicopter and redo the flight from scratch.

He unbuckled his restraints and jumped out, almost tripping and falling on his face. Melissa, Kazou, Michael, and Sarah followed close behind while Paro whispered something into the pilot's ears. He was the last to join them. Before Jack had time to take in his surroundings, he felt a pinching sensation burn across his face.

"That's for being stupid and calling me the 'Funinator'."

Jack rubbed his cheeks and stared menacingly at Melissa. Whatever, he wouldn't let her spoil his good mood. And she *was* a Funinator.

Paro led them off the landing pad and pressed the call button of an elevator opposite the helicopter. Within seconds, the doors opened, and Jack cheerily entered with the rest of the team. He was immediately intrigued by the myriad of buttons and labels. One said *Homicide,* while another said *Theft.*

Paro pressed the button labeled *Juvenile Crime* just above *Special Operations*, and the elevator lurched downward at a speed Jack hadn't been expecting, causing him to lose some of his balance and tumble into Melissa. The two made a light thud as they bumped into the corner of the fuzzy elevator wall.

"Whoops," Jack said.

Melissa pushed him off and scowled at him. "Be careful, Jack."

The elevator door opened, and Jack stepped out. He was greeted with an incredible sight. They were in a wide, tall room, with two sets of stairways leading up three floors. Hundreds of people answered phone calls while the buzz of conversation rang through the air.

There were vending machines and eating areas with large glass tables. Looking up, Jack could see massive windows that displayed beautiful views of Manhattan with neighboring buildings in the distance.

"Do all these people know about us?" Jack asked.

Sarah nodded. "Every single person here has taken an oath of secrecy and some are even Psychs themselves. This is where our team works. It's here that we handle all matters pertaining to you younger Psychs."

Paro put a hand on Jack's shoulder. He appeared to be in a decent mood for once.

"Jack, our department's pretty big, and we're not the only team that works here, either. There are a few of us. We've got quite a few amenities here. Food, a gym, sleeping rooms, a holding cell—cooperate with us and you won't have to see the last—and most importantly, our planning room. We'll be taking you there in just a bit, but why don't you get some rest? You were up all night with no chance to relax, so go ahead and sleep for a few hours."

Paro beckoned a small woman with a tiny headset and an earpiece attached to her face. "Margaret, come here, please."

The woman, Margaret, hurried over. "Yes, Paro?"

"Will you kindly show Jack to a room for a bit? I need to have a word with my team, and Mr. Harris here has been through quite a bit."

Jack felt like sticking his tongue out. "I'm not tired at all, Paro! I wanna see everything here, and then maybe Melissa and I can go see Phantom of the Opera. It's not every day I get to come to the big city."

Michael laughed and gave Jack a pat on the back. "It's too soon for that, bud. Just rest up and I promise you we'll have some fun later, okay? I'll make sure of it."

Reluctantly, Jack followed the woman past the rows upon rows of people speaking loudly into headsets and typing madly on computers. He followed her up the first flight of stairs, and Jack couldn't help but stop for a moment to take a glance out of the large, rectangular glass windows. Manhattan was beautiful, truly and surely. He could make out at least five other buildings this high up, and he wanted to visit each one of them.

Margaret opened up another door and led Jack into a hallway with doors on each side. Halfway down, she stopped to open yet another door, this one leading into a small, hotel-sized room. It had a bathroom, a bed, and a fridge.

"This is where you'll be staying for a bit, Jack. If you need anything else, please let me know."

She closed the door behind him, and Jack resisted the urge to follow her out. He decided to at least try and get some rest. He doubted he would be able to sleep with so much excitement still on his mind. He wanted to replay each moment of the helicopter ride in his head.

Jack lay down on the bed, and although it was comfortable, he seriously doubted he would get any rest.

Within four seconds, he was snoring.

Melissa closed the door to the planning room, struggling to contain her anger. She had decided not to undermine Paro in front of Jack—she respected Paro too much to go that far. But now that they were alone as a team, she would let him have it.

The team didn't require any data on screen at the moment, so the room was well-lit and cool. Melissa took a seat on her leather chair next to Kazou and Michael, leaving Paro and Sarah on the other side of the round table.

"Melissa, I can see you're angry," Paro began, "but you must know that what I'm doing—"

"Save it, Paro!" Melissa didn't care how much he hated being interrupted. This time, he'd gone too far.

"You're going to get Jack killed. Did you even stop for a minute to think about what you've just set in motion?"

Paro sighed, apparently willing to let Melissa slide for the disrespect. "Melissa, don't think I haven't thought about this carefully. This is our first chance to find who is responsible for the travesties that have been committed. Can we really afford to let this opportunity slip away?"

Michael, Kazou, and Sarah said nothing. They knew better than to get in the middle of a Melissa-Paro feud. Melissa liked Paro the best on the team, and usually the two got along wonderfully. But when they clashed, they *really* clashed.

"This is an innocent's life we're playing with, damnit. You didn't spend as much time with Jack as I did. He's not like anyone else I've ever met, Psych or otherwise. We can't throw him to these animals. He's not some piece of meat to be devoured. What if he dies? What if they kill him?"

Paro's face remained unchanged. "We have no reason to believe he's in any danger. From what you've told us, the two rogue Psychs you ran into wanted him pretty badly." Paro shook his head. "They won't kill him."

Melissa couldn't help herself. She picked up a water-filled glass in front of her and threw it into the wall behind Paro, shattering the cup and leaving a dark, wet spot on the white surface.

"*How can you possibly know that, Paro?*" she screamed at him. "You're the one who's always telling us we can't assume to know what's going on in the minds of people this deranged. How can you know they simply won't walk up to him when we least expect it and murder him like all the others?"

She felt embarrassed for her sudden display of outrage. Even Michael didn't offer a quip in response.

Jack, she thought to herself. *I can't bear the thought of him being killed like the others. No, I won't let that happen.*

Her emotions were still a mess from when she kissed him. Feelings, thoughts, they were all scrambled and didn't make any sense. He was immature, he was sometimes an idiot, but he looked at her like she was the most wonderful thing in the world. When she kissed him ...

She forced the thought from her mind, trying to seal it behind a mental-door made with the densest metal.

"Are you finished?" Paro asked. He stood up from his chair and retrieved a broom and pail, then spent the next few moments cleaning up the glass.

"Melissa," he said with a sweep, "I know that on some level you must like this boy—and quiet—do not think to interrupt me again. This is the first chance we've had to finally solve all of this and put an end to these massacres. If you've learned anything about me from your time here, you should've learned that I do *not* take these things lightly."

Paro emptied the broken glass into the trashcan in the corner of the room.

"When I say I will succeed at something, I do." He walked to where Melissa was sitting and knelt on the floor to look directly into her eyes. His gaze was not his typical. He held a fierce look to his face, a tightness that promised death to whoever dared to gaze for too long. Melissa couldn't help but feel a pinch of fear.

"I will not let Jack Harris die. And, he *will* help us catch the men and women responsible for these killings. If you've got any further objections, we can step outside. I'm not the type to report my own team-members for disobedience. No, I handle it myself. Do we have an understanding?"

Melissa choked on her pride and nodded. Paro smiled and returned to his seat.

"Now," Paro said, "we need to work on stabilizing the Harris-kid. This isn't going to be easy. It's rare enough for a Psych to not to be able to control himself, but it's even more complicated when that same Psych is Jack Harris. So, here's what we're going to do. We're going to get the kid just comfortable enough with his abilities, at least to the point where we don't have to worry about repeat incidents, and then we're going to set him loose. Melissa, since you go to his school, you are to stay with him at all times. You want to make sure he's safe, yes? Well, here's your chance to do it. We'll be within a half-mile of you at all times, if not closer."

Melissa nodded yet again. This was good. Now at least matters were in her own hands, and she could do what she must to keep Jack safe, provided he listened to her. And she would make *sure* he listened, she thought with a grin.

I'll teach him to show me respect! Calling me the 'Funinator' in front of everyone, oh, I'll have him barking on command.

Sarah broke the short moment of silence. "So, should we register him now?"

Paro nodded. "Yeah, we'll need to take a small sample of his blood. It's already beyond a doubt that he's a Telekinetic, but we still need him to test-positive and get him in the records. His mother will need to be informed and sworn to secrecy. For this, at least, we can go about our normal routine."

Melissa laughed. "Alana isn't going to like this."

Paro's eyes widened in the biggest display of shock Melissa had ever seen on him. "Melissa, I'm sorry. What did you say?"

"Umm, I said Alana, his mom—she's not going to like this news."

"Jack's mother, her name is *Alana Harris?*"

Kazou and Sarah looked at each other for a moment before Sarah craned her neck to face Paro. "Yeah, didn't you read the file, Paro?" she asked.

Paro sat back in his chair, motionless and silent, causing Melissa to become confused. From the looks of things, so was everyone else.

Finally, he spoke, "Harris is a pretty common name ... it's just a coincidence. It has to be." There was a sound of fear in his voice, and Melissa saw a trickle of sweat roll down his face.

"Paro, what's this about?" Kazou asked. He was never one to show much expression, but there was a certain curiosity to his look.

"Alana Harris, she'd know better than to have a kid and not report it. It's just me being irrational. It's a common name after all, and that's all that there is to it."

Kazou met Melissa's eyes and shrugged.

Paro's face took on a pleading look, and he shook his head. "No, the similarities, I just ... I'm an idiot, because I ... but then ..."

"Paro, you're rambling, bud," Michael said. "Wanna tell us what's going on here?"

Paro looked at his team. Melissa had no idea what had him so spooked.

Paro inhaled then said, "I think we might be in some trouble, is all. I mean, just, let's proceed as normal and forget I said anything."

The intercom on the center of the table rang. Paro reached over and flipped the red switch.

"Paro, there's a call for you from someone. They requested to speak to your team specifically."

Paro gulped. "Pass it through, please."

The room quieted at the sound of an enraged voice from the other end of the device. In the background, Melissa could hear heavy traffic, frustrated drivers, and roadwork. It added a sense of chaos to the thunderous voice.

"Paro, where is he!" the voice shouted in a high-pitched shriek.

Paro looked like he was ready to cry. "Easy now, Alana, I didn't know he was yours. Just give me a chance and I can explain everything, but please, calm down, for the love of God."

"Calm down? Calm down! I'm gonna beat you like you're sixteen again, Paro. Tell Jack mummy's coming. You better pray I

like your explanation, because I haven't been this angry in a long, long time."

Melissa wondered what was going on. It didn't make any sense for Alana to be calling, but the voice indeed belonged to Jack's mother.

Paro visibly tensed. "Look, this is an official investigation, and you can't just come barging in. You had no right to not report him. Keeping this a secret from us was a crime. Oh, and I'm not a child anymore, so don't treat me like one."

"Or what?" the voice mocked. "You'll throw another one of your 'temper tantrums.' I didn't deal with them when you were a kid, and I certainly won't deal with them now. You'll always be just a little boy to me Paro. Now, you better have Jack bundled up and ready to go home by the time I get there, or I'm going to whip you in front of your little friends."

Paro growled. "Listen to me, Alana, I'm a captain now, and you do not possess the authority to tell me what to do! Your precious little brat set a school on fire, and thanks to your criminal act of keeping him a secret, we didn't even know there was a Psych attending it in the first place. Now, you can turn that car around and go home, or I can press charges against you for not reporting Jack. It's your choice. Let's be reasonable here."

"Oh, I'll be reasonable alright! By the way, is that Melissa girl there?"

Melissa forced saliva into her mouth and answered, "Yes, Mrs. Harris."

"I wanted to tell you earlier, but I forgot. I love your shoes. I was thinking of getting a similar pair. But we'll talk about it when I get there. Alana out!"

Michael laughed, while the rest of the team remained silent, with the exception of Paro. He wore a scowl and curled hit bottom lip. With frightening growl, he grabbed the intercom off the table and threw it. It smashed into the same spot on the wall where Melissa's cup had hit only moments before.

Paro poured his anger into his voice as he shouted, "Goddamn Telekinetics! I'm so sick of them ... I'm so sick of all of them!"

It was a lot to take in, but Melissa learned that in this world, she had to adapt quickly. Paro held out his hands and inhaled, and his voice calmed. He looked around the room.

"That conversation meant nothing. Nothing has changed. Proceed as we planned, and let's get to work. We need to register Jack and work with him to get his abilities under control. Don't worry about anything you've just heard. Now, all of you—get out of my sight. If the Harris kid gives you any trouble, knock him over the head a few times until he cooperates."

Melissa waited until she was certain Paro couldn't see her and then smiled. She wasn't sure why, but she really liked Mrs. Harris.

Chapter 14: Jack Vs. Melissa—Round 1: FIGHT

J ack rubbed his eyes as he slowly got out of bed and responded to the knock on the door. He was still in a dreamy state, so walking in a straight line was a bit of a problem. He tumbled to the left and almost knocked over a lamp resting on a glass nightstand.

He turned on the light and opened the door. In an instant, he went from groggy to elated as he spotted Melissa in the doorframe. His elation diminished when he also spotted the rest of the team behind her, all but Paro. The four entered the room.

"Get any sleep?" Kazou asked.

"Yeah, a bit. Hey, where's Paro?"

The four of them shifted on their feet and for a moment avoided looking at him. Jack wondered if he said something wrong. Was it considered rude in the Psych-world to ask someone's location? Who knew, right?

Michael walked past Jack and sat on the bed in the corner of the room. "Jack, we've got quite a bit of stuff to do. And being that I'm the only Kinetic here, I reckon it's gonna be my job to show you the ropes."

"What ropes?"

"You know, using the power ya got. The one you were born with."

Jack shook his head in disappointment. Learning. Oh man, he hated learning things. Now it was like he had two schools or an extra class to take on the side.

"You don't look too excited, Jack. Did ya not hear me? I just said I'm gonna teach you how to use Telekinesis, ain't that like the coolest thing ever?"

Jack moaned, "Do we have to? I don't wanna learn stuff!"

Michael laughed, and Melissa grunted as she and Sarah entered the room. Melissa held a small metal box and directed Jack to sit at the little table in front of the bed. She opened the box and began setting up some kind of equipment.

Michael stood up and came to join the two. "Jack, look," he said.

He placed a tiny toy-soldier on the glass table. "Knock that over. I know you can do it. Ya just gotta try, bud. You should actually already know how, but it's just that you don't realize you do."

Jack looked at the thing. How was he supposed to knock it over? It made no sense. Melissa continued to set up her equipment while Jack stared at the toy, feeling like an idiot.

'Knock it over,' he tells me. How the heck can I do something like that?

"Are you sure there's not some special word or phrase I need to say?"

Sarah stood behind Jack and massaged his shoulders. "No, you just do it. I'm a Telepath, but even I could do something like that. We can't branch far out from the line that we were born with, but all Psychs can do some basic stuff—here, watch."

Sarah squinted, and the small figurine toppled on its side. She lifted it up and pointed. "Now you try."

Jack looked at it again. How was he supposed to know how to knock it over? Why couldn't they just give him an instruction manual or something? The small figurine was the stationary type, with an oval-green platform on the bottom. Jack hated these when he was younger. He hated all action figures that couldn't be moved. Who wanted to play with a toy that had no flexibility?

Move! Move!

Jack focused on the object. His eyes honed in on its tiny plastic face.

Move, damn you. Move!

Jack sighed. "It's not working."

Sarah gave him a pat on the back. She seemed like she had infinite patience. Melissa watched but said nothing as she put on a pair of latex medical gloves.

"Try again, sweetie," Sarah said. "This time, don't try willing it with thought. You were screaming, 'Move, damn you' so loud in your head that every Path in this building probably heard it. It's more like a muscle, like, how you wave your arms or jump up and down. Try to think of it that way."

A muscle?

"But I don't feel anything. Unless you're talking about that stinging, unpleasant one, but everyone has that, don't they?"

"Haha! Jack, you're hilarious, bud," Michael said. "That's exactly what we're talking about. Don't tell me all your life you felt that odd, different part of you, and you thought everyone was that way?"

Jack was shocked. "You mean not everyone has that 'inner thing' in them? I don't know what to call it. That like, weird thing that you feel from your chest to your eyes."

"Nope, just us. That's the one. First, you have to ... draw from it. It's hard to explain unless you've done it."

Jack couldn't believe this. All his life he had ten fingers, ten toes, and that 'thing' that he could feel. He thought everyone did!

"So what do I do, Michael?" Jack asked.

"Well, like I said, first ya gotta draw on it. Go ahead. You should already know what to do."

Jack closed his eyes and searched for that sensation, that feeling of something else. He felt it, and with a deep breath, he drew from it. Then he screamed, jumping out of his chair and waving his arms around frantically. Sarah leapt backward as Jack fell to the floor writhing in discomfort.

Kazou and Michael both laughed at him while Sarah gave them disapproving glares.

"What the hell was that?" Jack yelled. "Oh God, that felt ... terrible."

"That's called the sensitivity, Jack," Michael said between chuckles. "You get that when you first start out. Don't worry, I promise you it goes away after time."

Jack didn't care if it went away after the third time. He was *never* doing that again. It was by far the most unpleasant and disturbing sensation he had ever felt. It was both disgusting and uncomfortable. It wasn't pain, as in the sense of being injured or pulling a muscle. It was more like an extreme feeling of unease.

"Jack, talk to us," Sarah said. She helped him back to his feet. With a trembling hand, Jack picked up the knocked over chair and sat back down at the table.

"It was like ... Well, here's the best way I can describe it. You ever try and 'scratch' your eye when it's itchy and the lid keeps closing? It was like trying to force yourself to be able to touch your own eye, but at the same time, it felt like throwing up. It was awful! I'm never doing that again. It just feels ... wrong. I feel like it's going to be really bad if I do it. Like it's going to hurt or kill me."

Michael gave Jack a friendly punch on the arm. "It's like that for all of us at first, Jack, but the only way to make it go away is to keep doing it. Now, try again."

Jack was petrified. He didn't want to try again. It was the most sickening thing he'd ever experienced. It was actually *worse* than trying to touch your eye while making yourself vomit. It was even worse than the Airbender movie.

Melissa finished whatever she was doing, and with the gloves on her hands, she grabbed Jack's arm.

"Jack, hold still, I need to draw some blood."

"With a needle?"

"Durr, what else?"

I'm going to get a needle?

94

"Jack, get back here!" Melissa shouted. "And stop laughing and help, Michael. Restrain him or pin him to a wall, but do something other than stand there laughing like an idiot."

"I can't," Michael said. He looked like he was struggling to form words. "I ca—I can't." Tears were streaking down his eyes while he laughed at Melissa's frustration. She was going to break Jack's face when she caught him. Ignoring Michael, she bolted out into the hallway after Jack while Kazou and Sarah stared wide-eyed like morons.

"Jack, you get back here right now! Or so help me God—"

"Shut up, Melissa!" he screamed back at her. "I'm not going anywhere near you with that medieval torture device in your hand. That's not a needle—I saw that thing. It's a freaking sword."

Unbelievable, she thought to herself. *A tiny little needle triggered his fight-or-flight response?*

She ran out of the hallway which had the doors on both ends and entered into the wide second-floor opening of the Juvenile department. Secretaries, assistants, and even other Psychs all turned to stare as Jack whirled past them, followed by Melissa in close pursuit. She realized she must look ridiculous—a sixteen-year-old high-school girl chasing after a boy while wearing latex gloves and carrying a medical needle.

She stopped in front of an older secretary's desk. The silver-haired woman looked up at her in confusion as Melissa grabbed a stack of files in a brown paper envelope from the desk. "Sorry, gotta borrow this for a second."

She flung it at Jack. It spun twice in the air before hitting him on the back of the head, causing him to stumble, but unfortunately not to fall. Jack kept on running. He zipped down the staircase, descending two steps at a time.

Melissa followed after him. She paused, reaching the small banister overlooking the lower floor. Drawing power into herself, she leaped over it and landed softly on her feet in front of Jack. Now she was mad—she was going to enjoy this.

"Just for that, Jack, I'm going to draw an extra vial. No, two extra vials. Then I'm going to pump it back into your system just so I can draw it again!"

Melissa noticed the crowd that was forming around her, but she didn't care. There were now over two dozen people surrounding them in a circle, with Paro and the rest of the team joining in. Everyone had their eyes on her and Jack, yet none seemed to intervene. Damn Psychs and their curiosity.

Jack didn't care what Melissa's intentions were. He was *not* about to have that jousting pole rupture his heart. There was no way that thing was touching his skin—no way in hell. He didn't know why so many people were looking at him, either. Couldn't they just mind their own business?

Now that he and Melissa were surrounded, Jack had nowhere to run. What could he do in this situation? What was the right choice to make? Melissa walked slowly towards him with a sadistic glee on her face. She was going to torture him.

"Melissa, don't make me hurt you!" Jack warned.

She laughed. "Try it! You couldn't beat me if your life depended on it. Now, sit still and take your *'medicine'.*" She pronounced the word venomously.

Jack had never fought a girl before, but with the size of that needle, it truly was life or death. He knew now that he had to knock her over, much like he had tried to do with the toy-soldier. Then he could run past her and make it to safety.

He reached into the part of himself that he hated, that place that made him feel sick. He wanted to double over and pass out. The feeling was so damned uncomfortable. Jack grinded his teeth as he opened himself up to it.

The moment the power started pouring in, Jack knew he'd die if he didn't stem it. The power raced into him, almost like poking a tiny hole on the bottom of a submarine—it slipped through the tiniest of cracks. He only allowed himself to remain open for the smallest fraction of a second. Any longer, and somehow Jack knew he'd be blown-away by the storm forming inside his mind.

Melissa grabbed his arm and tried to steal his blood. Jack had no idea how to use the little bit of power that had trickled in, so he acted on reflex alone, guessing. With an audible crackle, Melissa cried out as she was sent ten feet back, like a fly being swatted by an invisible hand. She landed on her butt, and a look of surprise appeared on her face.

Her surprise quickly turned to ferocity as she narrowed her eyes. "Oh, you're going to pay for that, Jack."

Before Jack understood what was happening, Melissa was charging at him, and it was only then that Jack realized he was in a fight—him, Jack Harris, in an actual fight with another actual person, and in something that wasn't Street Fighter or Tekken. This had never happened before. He always wondered what it would be like to be in a real fight, and now he was going to find out.

Jack wasn't sure how he pushed her back the first time, but he tried it again. He still had enough of the power to make a second attempt. It was as if his brain was a computer with thousands of buttons, levers, and triggers—simply learning them wasn't enough, because they were constantly shifting and moving. He didn't know which was which, and with nothing else to go on, Jack reached into his mind and grabbed at one randomly.

He guessed right because an instant later, he felt the exertion of his own energy projected into Melissa. But this time, she was only slowed to a standstill instead of flung across the room.

How come it didn't work? I don't get it— I'm sure I did it right.

Melissa shook it off and continued to charge. She slammed into him, and Jack was knocked to the ground. Once again, he bit his tongue while drawing the power into himself. Then he searched for that same trigger. It was moving around wildly in his mind—he needed to focus.

He grabbed the trigger mentally and forced power into it. With a grunt, he hurled the force at Melissa, and she was again sent flying, lifting off him as if thrown. She flipped once in the air and landed on the balls of her feet with a click against the ceramic tile. Who knew she could do something like that?

"Whoa, awesome! You're so cool, Melissa."

She smiled. "It's so damned hard to stay mad at you, Jack, but we're not done here. You picked this fight, and now we're finishing it."

Jack nodded. "It's my first real fight, you know? Hey, umm, Melissa—you're ... you're *doomed*. I've waited years to use that word."

"You're something else, you know that?"

Melissa rushed at him yet again. Despite the awful feeling, Jack allowed himself another small drop of power. This time, Melissa seemed to be going in for an actual fistfight. She balled her hands into fists and swung at Jack.

Years of being bullied and hit, pushed and prodded, were for the first time in Jack's life paying off. He knew what he had to do. Jack ducked under her overhand blow, and for the briefest of moments came to an understanding. Jack had always been told not to hit girls, so he didn't, but then again, he never really hit anyone. Melissa, though, was as strong as she was beautiful. Jack realized that it would be more offensive to treat her like a princess than it would be to beat her like a guy.

Jack countered, throwing his fist at her with all his strength. Her left arm was still extended from her missed punch, and Jack remained crouched down from having ducked under it. He pivoted, and his fist collided with her abdomen, forcing her a step back. His hand ached as if he'd slammed it against a rock.

"So, you want me to step up my game then, do you, Jack?"

This is not gonna be good.

Melissa went in for another volley of attacks. Once again, the years of pummeling Jack had taken allowed him to be somewhat evasive. He ducked under one swing, going off nothing but reflex, then Melissa spun, attacking with a backhanded swipe.

Jack kicked off his front foot and dashed backwards, dodging by a centimeter. Melissa didn't give him the opportunity to recover. She closed the distance and jabbed Jack in the face before he could react.

He felt the impact as it sent him backward, and this time, it was he who landed on his rump. He shook his head to clear the dizziness that followed.

Melissa grinned. "That all you got, Big-Shot?" For some reason, Jack had the notion she was enjoying this.

A trickle of blood squirted from Jack's nose. He wiped it on his sleeve and stood up. He didn't realize it until then, but over a hundred people were now cheering and shouting encouragement to the both of them. Michael seemed to be taking bets, and Paro was studying the bout like a referee. Psychs were weird people.

The makeshift arena was actually kind of cool. All around him, the large glass windows let in bright sunlight, and he could still see all of Manhattan from where he stood.

Paro held out a hand and motioned for them to pause. "Jack," he said. He walked between the two of them with a massive grin covering his face. "You lose this fight, and you cooperate with us in full. You win, and Melissa here goes on a date with you. Oh, and I'll personally buy you every video game ever made."

Melissa didn't seem bothered by this. She simply grinned. "I'm okay with that, Paro. But I'll make it even more interesting. Land just one punch on me, Jack, and I'll go on a date with you, but you still have to beat me if you want Paro's reward."

Jack nodded. "You're on."

He wiped his nose once more for good measure and prepared himself to square off with Melissa again. For a moment, he almost didn't hear the voice calling to him in the background.

"She's a Reinforcer, Jack! Keep your distance and don't let her get anywhere near you. Mummy loves you!"

Jack felt like he was going to die of shock. He turned around, and sure enough, the front-most spectator was his own mother.

"Mom! What are you doing here?"

Paro too, looked as if he had seen a ghost. He backed away from Jack and Melissa and strolled over to her. "Alana, when did you—"

She shushed him. "We'll figure this out after, Paro. You of all people should know I can't miss something as fun as this. It's almost enough to make me forget how mad I am at you. Oh, by the way, look at how cute my little boy looks, fighting and making bets that he can't possibly win! He reminds me of a younger you, Paro. Oh, look at him! *Go Jack! Go Jack!*"

Jack watched as Paro shook his head in disbelief. "Damn Telekinetics," he muttered.

"What is *she* doing here?" Jack asked Melissa.

"Jack, there's a lot you still have to learn. I'm sure this is very shocking to you, and I'll understand if you need to wrap your head around this for a bit, but your Mom—naturally—is like one of us."

"That's not what I meant, Melissa. I mean what is she doing here without my Dunkaroos? She knows I love that snack more than anything. If she was gonna drive all the way over here, she could have at least brought me something good to eat."

Melissa tilted back her head and laughed. "Does anything surprise you, Jack?"

"Of course stuff does. I had no idea that Sookie was actually a fairy. I almost passed out when that was revealed."

"I see, so it's only stupid stuff that shocks you. Whatever, you've had enough of a break. Let's end this."

Before Jack could reply, Melissa dashed at him. Jack allowed himself another droplet of power, and he fought off the terrible sensation rising from his stomach. He hurled it at her, slowing her down but not stopping her completely. He knew she wasn't fighting at her best—he'd seen her pound a hole into the ground. But the deal didn't say she had to be.

Jack followed up his blast by charging at Melissa head-on. He collided with her, and the combination of his Kinetic force and his own charge was enough to knock Melissa to the ground. Pain exploded in Jack's body as he made contact. Melissa was now as rough as iron, even tougher than before. He fell down along with her.

Lying on the floor, Jack took a moment to notice that now every single person in the department was watching, screaming, and yelling out encouragements. He felt like he was at a rock concert.

Jack got to his feet, but Melissa was quicker. She kneed him the chest. It felt like being hit with a tire-iron. He landed on his back with the wind knocked out of him. Before he could stand, she jumped on top of him, sitting on his chest with her right hand clutching his throat.

"Give up?" Her eyes didn't hold any menace, just a playful grin and a look of determination.

Jack realized that he would yet again be forced to resort to that disgusting draw of power. This time, he left the 'door' open for a millisecond longer. He almost regretted it, as even in that tiny bit of time, it felt like he'd never be able to shut it again. It was risky. Jack knew somehow on an instinctual level that if he left it open for too long, power would flood into him until he exploded and wouldn't be able to stop it.

Jack scrambled around in his mind. He had been lucky the last few times, but now he was starting to get the hang of things. It wasn't easy to locate, but it was becoming easier each time. It was that trigger, that pathway, the one that sent things that were near to him farther away. He reached for it ...

Melissa was sent soaring off of him. She landed on the ceramic floor and rolled across it. After three rolls, she clutched at the ground and halted, pushing off her arms and flipping back to her feet.

"That was way stronger than before, how did you ...?"

Jack followed it up with yet another burst, and again she was flung backwards and knocked to the floor. But like the other times, she was quick to get back to her feet, so Jack sent a third burst her way. And this time, it had no effect. Melissa didn't even appear to be fazed by it.

Sarah whispered something into Paro's ear, and he nodded.

"You two!" he shouted. "No more powerful than what you were using before—that's an order."

Melissa stuck out her tongue, but she nodded. "Alright, fine. You hear that, Jack?"

Jack thought he understood. "Yeah, I heard."

Jack didn't mind. If he understood Paro's meaning, then it was actually a good thing. Jack didn't want to have to reach that deep again. He feared losing control of himself.

Off to his right, he saw a childish glee in his mother's eyes. She was screaming louder than anyone else was while she chanted his name. She looked so proud.

Jack gritted his teeth as he once again replenished the small droplet of power. He didn't know what Michael was talking about—this wasn't becoming any less unpleasant. Although Jack did feel it was slightly different this time. He felt a bit ... weak. It was as if he hadn't eaten in a while despite not being hungry. He wasn't physically exhausted, like the way you get when you run too much or do too much exercise, but in a way, he felt drained.

Melissa looked at him as if reading his thoughts. "You newbie Psychs have no stamina. I can already see it in your face. You're going to collapse any minute. Just give up now, Jack. You've already lost."

"No way in hell! It's not over yet. Come on, I'm ready."

Melissa approached cautiously this time. By now she was obviously aware of Jack's ability to fling her backwards. Jack reflected on the fight—it appeared she had some way of resisting what he could do. He wondered if he should try one of the other things he felt in his mind, but he decided against it. Somehow, he knew that there were just some strings that he wasn't ready to pull on.

With the caution of a boxer, she squared in on him. She started with jabs that had no chance of making contact, but slowly she backed him into a corner by a nearby window. Jack realized that at the rate things were going, he didn't have the slightest chance of winning. All he needed was to land one hit, make contact just once, and then at the very least he could take the girl of his dreams out on a date.

Melissa faked with her right then sprang off her left, dashing at Jack. It was at this point he knew he had two options—dodge and prolong the fight, or risk it all and maybe win part of the bet.

Surprise was the only thing Jack could see on Melissa's face, as he too dashed to meet her assault. With his remaining power, Jack reached for that familiar feeling, that trigger, and launched the last of it at Melissa. It didn't do much, but she was slowed just enough so that Jack's fist made contact with her hard-as-steel face at the same moment she did the same to him.

Jack's punch had no effect, but hers knocked him off his feet. Jack lay there with the wind knocked out of him and a smile on his face. He had hit her!

It was hard for him to move. He was exhausted. He tried to get up but to no avail. Melissa walked away and returned a moment later. She once again took a seat on his chest, and Jack's eyes lit up in fear when he saw what was in her hands.

"No!" Jack screamed, terror in his heart. "For God's sake, Melissa. It's like the size of a car antenna."

Jack closed his eyes and hoped it wouldn't hurt too much. To his utter humiliation, the crowd applauded and laughed.

Chapter 15: One-Way Ticket.

"Look, please try and understand, Alana. It's like I've been saying—I had no idea he was yours. How could I possibly know something like that? You should know better than anyone why we're supposed to report these things. Tell me, what if Jack would have killed someone?"

For the first time in the last fifteen minutes, Paro felt that his point had finally been made, indicative by the twinge of guilt he saw creep into Alana's youthful face. The years had been kind to her. Paro hoped he still looked that young at forty-five.

Alana had been willing to put off this discussion yesterday, and Paro owed her the chance to be heard out. She had spent the last few nights in a room parallel to Jack's, where she and Michael had tried to teach him little bits of things here and there. He was learning slowly, but he was still making some progress.

"Jack would never do something like that, Paro. You've only known him for a little over two days, and even you must already be sure of it."

They were in the planning room, alone. Paro had sent everyone on one errand or another, and he was glad to see that the situation was being diffused. Not long after Jack's humiliating defeat, Alana had ripped the planning room door right off the hinges and sent it hurling at him. She had even brought a basket full of pots, pans, and other painful objects that he had been forced to deal with. She was rarely angered, but as Paro so vividly recalled, when her temper was sparked it was even worse than Paro's usual sporadic outbursts. Luckily, she'd only damaged the door and not the equipment in the room. It was easily repaired.

She hadn't been willing to let things rest, but Paro had managed to convince her to at least give him until early the next morning to work everything out. So, here she was.

"I am sure of it. I'm sure that he'd never willingly hurt another person. But, Alana, this kid didn't know what he was doing. Even an environmentalist can step on a bug and never know it happened. Look, I respect you, more than you will ever know. I'll never forget how you yanked me by the ear and took me away from that Op. team. Not a day goes by that I don't feel grateful to be a force for helping people rather than slaughtering them."

Paro shuddered as he remembered some of his older, more violent days. He was only Jack's age when he started with the Psych-Operatives. He never knew what it was Alana had seen in him then, but she beat him to a pulp and dragged him away from that team. It was years until he was able to properly thank her.

If Paro wanted, he could bring her up on so many charges for the last few days alone—let alone for not reporting her child—that she'd spend years in one of the facilities. But Paro had never been the "reporting" type. If he could deal with a situation, then he dealt with it. From the bottom of his heart, Paro felt that only the truly wicked needed to be locked away.

"You know why I couldn't report him, Paro. Why I still think this is a bad idea." She walked away from Paro. He was sitting casually in his leather chair. Turning away from him, she lowered her voice to a distant whisper.

"Sebastian still hasn't found him."

Paro shook his head, dismayed to have this brought up again. "We can't bring him home, Alana. Not yet. Sebastian can take care of himself, and besides, he knew very well what he was getting into when he decided to take on an Unrestricted."

Paro knew why she turned around—she didn't want him to see her tears.

"He comes home maybe once every few years, Paro," she sobbed. "Jack barely knows him. How long has it been now? He's been chasing this man since before you were even part of the organization, so you couldn't possibly understand. If that man ever came to the discovery of Sebastian's child, if he found out about Jack ... Do you have any idea what I would do if something happened to my baby?"

"I do understand, Alana. But you've actually endangered him more by not telling me about him. And not just himself, but you've put at risk everyone around him that could have been hurt by his abilities."

Alana sobbed into her sleeve. Wiping her eyes with the cuff of her black shirt, she whipped around and faced Paro. It was as if not a single moment of sadness had just crossed her eyes. She resumed her typical playful expression.

"Anyway, you've got him registered now, yes? I assume that means I can take him home? He's missing school today, and I'd like to have him back for tomorrow's classes. The longer he stays here, the more he's going to think he's allowed to ditch school. Let me tell you, Jack does not like going to his classes. I have to fight with him some mornings to get him out of bed."

Paro laughed. "Trust me when I say that I believe you completely. I've only known him a short while, but I already think I know how his mind works. Of everything that I have said to him, of all the shocking revelations I've made, I think the one thing that'll remain on the top of his mind, even above all other things, is that I told him he'd be here for a few more days. Seeing that fight with Melissa, I can tell he's got a pretty good idea of what all this is about, and I don't need to keep him here any longer. But I can only imagine how disappointed he's going to be when he finds out he'll be back in school on Friday, bright and early in the morning."

Alana joined Paro in smiling and walked over to playfully ruffle his dark hair. "Well, ya definitely got that right, Paro. He probably thought this would drag on and last him until next week. That's definitely the way he thinks."

A knock on the door snapped them both to attention, and Paro stood up to open it. "Melissa, please, come in."

Melissa entered, wearing the same devilish grin Paro was used to seeing on Michael. "Hey, Mrs. Harris, it's nice to see you again so soon. Sorry about lying to you the other night, I didn't exactly have much of a choice at the time."

Alana waved her hand at the remark. "Don't worry, hun. It's perfectly fine. I'm happy to see you too. My son has a crush on you something fierce, but don't tell him I said that, because he'd lose it."

Melissa blushed and ignored the comment. "Anyway, Alana, do you think you could give me a ride back today? I don't feel like waiting on the team, and they're going to be held up for a while."

Ok, Paro thought. *Here we go. This part is critical. We need to keep her close to Jack.*

Alana's face lit up. "Oh, of course! It will be lovely to have you. I'd be glad to give you a ride home. There's more than enough room in my minivan, and we can have some girl-talk. Just give my son a slap on the back of the head if he tries to interrupt us in one of his many God-awful superhero rants. Did he ever try that with you?"

Melissa beamed with the shared experience. "Oh, like thirty times, Mrs. Harris."

"Please, call me Alana."

"Okay then, Alana. So, where was I? Oh yeah, you've got no idea. He spent twenty minutes trying to teach me about some war that took place with spider-man or something. Anyone know what I'm talking about? I think it was, 'A Crisis on Earth' or something ridiculous. Paro?"

Paro shook his head—he didn't have a clue.

"It's actually kind of cute, Alana. He's even got these cards that have like, strengths and stuff and he fights other people's cards. It's amazing what some boys are into."

Alana nearly doubled over with laughter. "Oh yeah, that's his 'Magic the Gathering' game. You don't know how much money he gets me to spend on those silly little pieces of cardboard. And it's confusing, too. He tried to show it to me once. He was all like, 'Hey,

Ma! You can't summon that one. It's a four-four flying trampling beast-thingy.' I've got no idea what he's talking about when he and Adam are up to that nonsense. Oh, and that's going to be an issue too. We've gotta make sure he keeps his mouth shut."

Listening to them speak of such, Paro felt a small pinch of anxiety. Jack was among the least-capable liars Paro could envision. In fact, Paro wouldn't believe that Jack was capable of fibbing his way out of Jury Duty. But Jack had given his word that he wouldn't mention anything about their current case to his mother, and Alana had no reason to be suspicious. As long as Jack kept his mouth shut— which was the dangerous part—they'd be fine. Jack was quite the troublesome individual, but despite it all, Paro believed that deep down Jack wanted to end these killings as much as he himself did. Paro was certain the boy would make a real effort to prevent anything from slipping, and due to his easily distracted nature, he'd probably forget what all of this was about the first time a song he liked played on the radio.

"Alana, I think its best you take them home soon," Paro said.

Alana looked over to Paro. She had a mischievous, sly glint in her eyes.

"It's Friday, yes? It's not even six a.m. yet. If we leave now and beat the traffic, I might be able to get Jack back to school in time for at least half a day of classes. Oh boy, I'm almost looking forward to seeing the look on his face when we tell him. Does that make me a bad mother?"

In unison, Melissa and Paro shrugged. They looked at each other for a short moment, and then they both burst out laughing. "Melissa and I feel the same way, so we're just as bad as you."

Paro picked up the repaired intercom off his desk—he was going to enjoy this. "Margaret, wake up the Harris-kid and send him in, please."

For nearly ten full minutes, the three of them struggled, exerting their utmost will-power to keep from laughing hysterically. The result was that they stood with tight-lips in silence. By the eleventh minute, the first of Jack's shouts could be heard as the sounds of his loud voice neared them.

"I hate you! I'm so damned tired, just one more hour. Please, just one more hour, that's all I want. Fine, then just five more minutes. Get off me, Ahh! Let me go back to bed. I need sleep. I'll die unless you give me three more minutes. I thought you were my friend, Margaret. You're mean. You lied to me. You said that if I needed anything, I just had to ask. Well, I need sleep! Let me go back. Just one more minute, JUST ONE MORE MINUTE!"

The door slammed open, and Margret entered with a fierce look of frustration on her elderly face. Paro wasn't positive, but she seemed to have double the wrinkles on her poor face than she did the last time Paro had seen her.

"This one is your problem now. I dragged him here, so now you deal with him. I recommend horse tranquilizer for this one."

From what Alana had told Paro, the only time Jack was ever truly angered was when he wasn't allowed to sleep. Jack scratched his head, and rubbed his sandy eyes. The boy looked positively miserable. His usually messy hair was even more so, and he had sleep-lines on his face. It was comical how miserable and angry he looked.

Paro cleared his throat. "Jack, good news, you're going home, and guess what? You've got ten minutes to take a shower and get dressed. You know why? Because your mom wants you to make at least half or more of the school day. Isn't that great, Jack? You can make it in time for school after all!"

Never in Paro's life had he appreciated or liked being yelled at. In fact, it numbered highly on the list of things he most despised. But for the first time in his (granted) short life, he felt it was more than worth it in exchange for the explosion of misery and torment from the Harris-kid.

"Whaaaaaaaaaaaaaaaaaaaaat? School? Are you kidding me, Paro? NO! I've got like, magic now. What good is school anymore? You can't do this to me, damnit!"

Paro couldn't help it. It had been years since he laughed this hard. Melissa looked like she was having an issue simply remaining on her feet, and Alana had already fallen off hers.

"I can handle it from here, Paro," Alana said between deep breaths. "Let's go, mister, and we're not stopping home for anything. Straight to school with you!"

Jack looked like he had just been told the world was ending. Paro had never seen a look of such discontent and misery on someone's face, especially over something so stupid.

"I'm not going anywhere!" Jack protested.

Melissa glowered at him. "Oh yes you are! I've got a test today, buster, and you're not making me miss it. So I can either drag you with me and your mom, or you can hurry up, 'cause if we don't leave now we won't make it in time for school. And don't even think of using that as an excuse to take your sweet time."

Now Jack look confused. "But ... it's only a short flight. What's the big deal?"

Jack was not going to like what Paro had to say next. He was careful not to mention anything about the killings in front of Alana.

"Jack, the helicopter is only for emergencies and extraction. We needed to bring you here quickly, and we didn't have time to waste. We don't just bust out a chopper every time someone needs to travel back and forth between Manhattan. Do you know how expensive that is? Gas prices have skyrocketed."

"So, let me get this straight, you guys. I have to go to school *today*, and I don't even get to parachute into class like I've always dreamed of doing? You guys suck, all of you. Leave me alone."

Jack stormed off, and Melissa chased after him.

"You suck more!" she yelled on his heels, reminding Paro that despite her maturity, she was still just a kid.

"Kids," Alana said.

"Indeed."

"Why?" the dying man asked.

What a dumb question. The only why that anyone should ever ask is *why* people ask *why*. Ruin didn't have to answer these rodents. It was his choice, and he had made it. He had decided that this person's right to live had been revoked. It was Ruin's choice to make—his decision. There didn't need to be a *why*. People annoyed him sometimes.

"Darling, let's give him a free appendix removal," Requiem purred. She placed a soft hand on Ruin's face, covering his eyes and letting him see as she did. Within moments, his sister's Telepathy projected the images into his mind. He could see capillaries and the man's inner workings.

The fool's screams were intense. Blood dripped from his mouth while he was torn from the inside-out. Luckily, no one would be around the park area this early in the morning, so they could have as much fun with the man as they wanted.

They didn't bother to find out his name, and why would they? They were bored and this looked like something fun to do at the time. Besides, Ruin didn't like bald people. They reminded him of someone he despised.

The bald, middle-aged man shuffled side to side, rolling on the ground and clutching his stomach. "P-please," he begged, "no more."

"I am growing bored with this, Dearest Brother. Can we end him and look for someone else to play with?"

Ruin frowned. "Sister, he's first starting to show us how loud he can yell. Do you really want to stop now?"

Requiem had been acting off these last few days. This was usually her favorite part. With a shrug, he turned to face his sister. "Oh, very well, but I want to do it myself this time. I've never tried it."

"But what about the evidence, Darling?"

"Forget the evidence—who can stop us?"

Ruin pulled a small knife from the side of his loose-fitting jeans and crouched down in front of the wailing man. With his left hand, he lifted up the man's head, tilting up his neck as much as it would go.

"I know how to make him stop screaming," he joked.

Slowly, so as to enjoy each moment, Ruin ran the blade deeply across the man's throat. He didn't expect the blood to gush all over him the way it did, but he had to admit it was actually kind of cool. The man's screams diminished into half-hearted gurgles, as if he were choking or drowning in water. As the light left his eyes, Ruin rose back to his feet and turned towards his sister.

"More fun than I thought it would be," he said.

"Dear me, brother, but you're covered in blood. You need to get rid of those clothes and clean yourself up. You look like you've been swimming in a pool of the stuff."

Ruin shrugged. All in all, it wasn't as fun as their usual method, but it was still a unique experience. Maybe he should have Andy try it sometime? Thinking of which, he hoped their new brother was holding up well. They were going to need him to help catch the Harris-kid and kill all the other fools.

Chapter 16: Integration by Substitution

If luck existed in this world, then Jack had none of it. As his mother soared by on the East Parkway, Jack realized he'd not only make it in time for half his classes, but more than likely the entire day's worth.

He did have to admit, though, driving through Manhattan from the ground was almost as awesome as flying over it. Mom and Melissa had distracted him by pointing out buildings and weird-looking stores. Some blocks had as many as forty to fifty different shops. It was incredible. His mom promised she'd bring him back here during the summer break. But they wouldn't fly there, which Jack found disappointing.

His mom's van was relaxing, spacious, and Jack had no problem catching a bit more sleep as they drove through the boring parts after leaving the city. He'd have slept even if he wasn't tired, what with the ridiculous conversation Melissa was having with his mom in the front seat.

In a way, it was hard to believe. It was almost like the two had been meeting for weeks and had been working tirelessly on creating *the most* boring conversation that had ever been conversed in all of human history. Alana and Melissa went back and forth discussing matters so trivial and unimportant that at first Jack thought they were joking around and creating satire. At one point, while fading in and out of sleep, Jack had actually heard the two discussing bags, of all things, from some place called "Juicy Couture" or something like that. Why any human being would want to carry on a conversation about storage compartments was beyond Jack's ability to comprehend.

Jack had tried several times during the ride to bring up more important, vital matters. He'd tried to discuss things such as the release date on the upcoming James Bond movie, or whether or not Hunters were finally getting nerfed in the next big patch. Melissa had reached over the front seat to give him a tap on the head and a threatening glare. His mom laughed at it all too—whose side was she on, anyway?

Jack woke when the car slowed and pulled up into the school lot. He groaned. The worst part of school was actually entering it. It was still awful throughout the day, but it was at its peak-awfulness when it was first beginning, and he took those dreadful first steps into the building. Why did his area of New Jersey have to be so damned close to New York City? This was the first time in Jack's life where that had ever been a bad thing.

So, after all that, I end up back here again anyway. I don't get it. If I really started that fire, couldn't they at LEAST throw me in prison for a few years?

"Jack, come on," Melissa commanded.

Jack moaned and purged himself of drowsiness. Before he could leap out the back of the van, his mom, with the reflexes of a ninja, grabbed him and pulled him close for a kiss on the cheek.

"Jack, I knew all this nonsense would happen someday, but you know what? I'm glad it's finally all out of the way. You've had a bunch of excitement these last few days, I'm sure. But now life is going to return to its normal routine. This is just something we live with, and I promise you that on most days you'll forget you even have any of the abilities you do."

Jack sighed. "But Mom, why don't we just—"

Alana cut him off before he could even finish speaking. "I know what you're going to say—it's what every new Psych thinks. But using your power for personal gain is not only very much illegal, but it's highly immoral. If you want to make money and be successful you need work to hard like everyone else."

Jack shook his head. "That is *not* what I was gonna say, Mom. I was gonna say why don't we talk more about this at home. I just found out about all this shocking stuff, and I've got so many questions. My world has been shaken. I don't know if I'm mentally capable of going back to school just yet."

Melissa and Alana laughed together. Alana ruffled Jack's hair. "If you were anyone else in this world, I'd believe that, sweetie. I'd take you home right now and help you cope with it, all of it. I'd answer your questions and hope that someday you can wrap your head around this insanity. But you're you, Jack. Let's be completely honest here—you're already thinking about playing video games after school. In a way, I'm glad that you're you, because as a mother I know you don't have to live with all these torturous feelings and questions. For years and years, I wondered what I'd say to you if you ever found out what I was—the things I'd try and do to make you understand."

Alana sighed. "And then that day finally came. I showed up to H.Q and you knew at once what I was, and who I was. For a split second, I was worried what you'd think about me, wondering what all this meant to you and how your life would be changed, but within twenty seconds of finding out the truth, you already started focusing on something else. That's who you are, and that's why you're so special. I don't know anyone else like that, Psych or otherwise. Now quit trying to bail out of school. I drove like an animal to get you here on time."

Melissa yanked Jack out of the van, and together they walked towards the school building, stopping to wave once more at Alana before turning around.

"She's right, ya know."

"Hmm?" Jack buzzed. "Right about what?"

"You're really not like anyone else."

Jack shrugged—he didn't see it. The two entered the courtyard to the tall, three-story building. Well, tall for where he lived. Nothing could compete with New York City. He'd only just returned from it and already everything seemed like a dream.

School, as expected, didn't change at all in the few days he had been absent. It was a semi-disorganized mess. The students waited inside the courtyard until seven a.m. sharp, when the doors would open and they'd be allowed to go in.

In some places, there were circular cliques of friends, some exclusively guys and others solely girls, and a few were mixed. Several played stupid games like hacky-sack. Jack felt that any game you couldn't win was stupid. Would that technically make him stupid for the massive time he put into World of Warcraft?

Many people walked around aimlessly, stopping to chat with friends before moving along. It was the group closest to the west-end of the courtyard that attracted Jack's attention. Sitting on the small bench was an odd mix of people. One was a hairy boy, resembling more of an animal than a man—Stephen Menar, rival to Jack Harris. Across from him on the shabby bench sat Antonio Delgado, an even greater rival. From the looks of things, the battle had already begun.

Jack didn't so much as sprint as attempt to leap over to them. He was stopped mid-stride and wondered what force was tugging on the back of his shirt.

"Where the hell do you think you're going?" Melissa said with a snarl.

"Melissa, what gives?"

She released the back of his shirt and poked his chest. "You're not to leave my sight for even a minute. I thought we went over all of this. I'm in a kind mood today, so I'll allow you to do whatever it is you were going to do. Just walk slowly, and keep close."

Jack didn't know if he should've been happy or not, but for some reason he had the odd feeling that Melissa was going to make his life a living hell. Luckily, his father had taught him how to handle this situation when Jack was growing up in one of their few late-night conversations when he wasn't away on business.

"Woman, I need me some space."

Slap!

Okay, Jack noted. That approach didn't work. Rubbing the handprint forming on his cheek he led Melissa to the bench filled with the eight people society had labeled misfits. He felt into the pocket of his dark jeans, making sure the *true* source of his power was present. Forget all that Psych nonsense.

"Gentlemen," Jack said, "the master has arrived."

Four people leapt up from the table with excitement on their faces. Antonio slowly approached Jack. "So, Jack, you've finally come to die, have you? I wondered why you didn't show up the last few days. I'm sorry to do this to you, buddy, but your time is up."

Antonio reached into his own pocket. What happened next was almost too fast to follow. In a high-pitched shout, Melissa called out, "*Jack, get down!*"

She pushed Jack to the ground and then lunged at Antonio, grabbing his free hand before it could leave his pocket. The boy howled in pain as Melissa twisted his arm around his back and pushed him face into the bench.

"Melissa, what the hell are you doing?"

All the boys at the table laughed as Antonio wailed in pain. "Is this how you fight now, Jack? Have you no honor? In Mexico, you would never be allowed to play again for this kind of treachery."

"Wait, don't tell me ..." Melissa released the boy and turned towards Jack, who was getting back on his feet. He had to think of something quick.

"Sorry about that, Antonio. I'm trying to teach her the rules of the game, and she thought a counter was a physical assault."

Melissa blushed a deep shade of red, and all around the table, the eight boys laughed at her. Antonio once again reached into his pocket to reveal the stack of playing cards.

"Class is going to start soon, so let's make this quick, Harris."

Jack only managed to play half a game before the doors opened. The exaggerated moan came not only from the bench, but from people all around them. Like a league of zombies in route to a corpse, the students of Elms high shuffled in the doors and headed to their first class of the day.

Even as his hand raced furiously across the paper, Jack knew it was already too late. He could hear each footstep from the hallway, he could feel the sweat that was dripping between his fingers, and he could taste the fear that was rising from his stomach. Jack realized he was becoming desperate. He ignored the spitballs launched at his head and the laughter from the back of the class.

Jack sat in his usual wooden desk, surrounded by his classmates, and he was overjoyed that his teacher always came late. Since the beginning of the school year, their teacher had made it a habit to arrive ten minutes late. None of the students ever minded, of course, and on this particular Friday morning, Jack Harris thanked his lucky stars for it.

Adam, his impatient friend who sat next to him, shifted his eyes toward Jack. "Seriously, Jack, again? Sometimes I wonder if this happens every week because I coddle you."

Jack frowned at him. "This time I really couldn't do my homework, Adam. I was really, really busy. Man, you have no idea how nervous I am right now. Just give me a little more time."

"Fine, but hurry up. You really need to learn how to better yourself, Jack. I can only imagine how much stress you're causing yourself by doing this each week. And don't put my name on your paper again. Oh crap, you already did. Are you kidding me, Jack? Are you freaking kidding me?"

Jack felt close to his breaking point. Sweat dripped down his forehead. He tensed, and he felt a nervous pinch in his stomach. As if to settle the issue, Melissa glided out of her desk and walked swiftly over to the two of them. She ripped the assignment from Jack's fingers.

"There's no way in hell we're going through *this* again, Jack. Stop enabling him, Adam. This is exactly why he never learns." She shoved the assignment back in Adam's face.

Melissa returned to her seat, now only two desks away from them. She was using the excuse that it was hard for her to see the board from her previous angle. Mr. Munson wouldn't object because Melissa was his favorite student.

"She's really been on your case since she started tutoring you. Where have you been the last few days?" Adam asked.

"So much has happened that you wouldn't believe."

Melissa swung around in her desk and shot Jack a warning glare, as if overhearing their whispered discussion. Jack winked and ran a finger across his lips, sealing them. Adam simply shrugged and looked back down at his assignment.

"Good morning, class," Mr. Munson exclaimed as he kicked open the door. "You're all in luck, because today we get to learn about 'Integration by U-Substitution.' Can Munson get a what-what?"

As usual, only Melissa and the math geeks in the front row actually bothered to chant it back to him. Adam looked like he was tempted but thought the better of it.

"Are you telling me we're the first to find this?" Cemmera asked, a smile forming on her lips. If Paro's team didn't know about this then she'd get her kill for sure. It was a rarity for an Op. team to stumble upon a murder without the Investigative team having knowledge of it.

"I don't think even the police know," Santos said. "From what we found in his wallet, his name is Harry O'Donnell, age forty-two. He's an accountant and has no living family."

"Very good, very good. This didn't happen that long ago, so we're getting close. Neil, see if you and Santos can't manage to track these guys. Just make sure if you find 'em, you don't kill them without me. You two," she said, pointing at her two Kinetics, "you're with me. There's someone I want to look into—name is Jack Harris."

Neil looked confused. "But Cemmera, I just got the updated file on his registration today. He's not linked to any of this."

Cemmera licked her lips. "I don't believe that for one second. In fact, if you look at the evidence I was able to steal, you'd see that he's the most probable suspect at this point. Paro never should have left the Op. department. He's got no talent as an investigator. We'll grab the Harris kid and beat him until he confesses. Then, we'll kill him. It's that simple, works all the time."

Cemmera had no idea how the Carebears were able to miss something so critical. The fire coinciding at the same time as the murders—it was too much of a coincidence. Were they blind?

"We weren't able to get every document, Cemmera. What if there's more to this that we don't know?" Santos shifted on his feet.

"Santos, buddy, just relax. It's like adding one and one. You've seen the evidence. This is one of our guys. I can't wait to hear him scream in pain as he apologizes for the wrong he's done. Oh, and by the way, this kill is mine. You boys had the last few."

Cemmera felt like drinking—she always did when filled with the thrill of a hunt. So, this Jack Harris managed to slip through the cracks, did he? Have no fear, Cemmera Wilson was here! Her team looked at her like she was a lunatic while she stood over the dead body, laughing hysterically. Noting her team's reaction, she ceased immediately.

There was an awkward four seconds of silence, and then all four of them cracked up.

I love my team.

Chapter 17: History

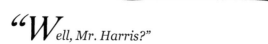

"*W*ell, Mr. Harris?*"

For a moment Jack thought he heard another person's voice, but he was probably mistaken. Why would there be a voice here besides hers?

"Jack," Melissa said seductively. She was in her finest form. She had on her usual tight jeans, white top, and black boots. She ran her hand down the back of his neck, caressing his skin and making him shudder. Jack's heart beat faster at the touch.

"Melissa, we shouldn't," Jack said. He knew he wanted this, but at the same time, he knew it was wrong, all of it. This was not the way things should be—it was forbidden. But staring into her beautiful eyes while her golden hair flowed in the soft breeze, he was barely able to control himself.

"Why not, Jack?" She crawled on top of him, pushing him down onto the soft grass.

"Because, Melissa. It is not the Jedi way."

All of a sudden, storm troopers came, and Jack unsheathed his Lightsaber with a crackling hiss. Then she took out her own Lightsaber, and together they fought off the waves and waves of storm troopers.

One storm trooper approached Jack and demanded that he surrender. "Well, Mr. Harris?" the storm trooper asked. "Do you know the answer to question four on the worksheet?"

Wait, what?

With a deep and sudden breath, Jack's eyes popped open. "I'm not surrendering!" he yelled at what he thought was an imperial storm trooper.

"That's very noble of you, Mr. Harris. But class participation is ten percent of your grade. Were you sleeping in my class again?"

"Umm, no Mrs. Titherson, of course not."

"Then why were your eyes closed?"

"I was, umm, dream-thinking?"

Mrs. Titherson ignored the offhand remark and continued. "I see. Anyway, question four, Mr. Harris. Your answer, please?"

Time to roll the dice, Jack thought.

"Is it seven?"

At this, Mrs. Titherson placed the worksheet she was holding back on top of the teacher's desk. She removed her glasses, taking a full twenty seconds to stand in the front of the room and clean them. Placing the glasses with care back on her old, wrinkled face, and adjusting them to fit her needs, Mrs. Titherson picked the worksheet back up from her desk and looked down at it.

"The answer to, 'Describe the treaty of Versailles', Mr. Harris, is seven?"

"Umm, eight?"

The woman showed no emotion. Instead, she simply picked up her grading book and made a mark. Jack knew what that meant, and it wasn't a good thing.

Well, it wasn't a fair question anyway, Jack justified to himself.

Of all the classes Jack had to take, history was by far the most boring, even if it was the least difficult. But Jack tried to cheer himself up. Next period was lunch, and it was the only class he wasn't currently failing. Oh, who was he kidding? If it were possible, he'd probably also fail lunch.

When the bell finally rang, Jack made sure he was the first student out of the door. It wasn't hard, because the rest of the class was still asleep at that point. They would need at least half a minute to snap themselves awake and gather their things together. Struggling to make his way through the hall, Jack went to meet up with Adam. He'd be getting out of Biology class, only two doors down.

Navigating through the school was never easy, as the hallways were teeming with students. People shoved, pushed, and did whatever they could to get past the crowds shuffling from class to class, but Jack had no desire to rush.

He met Adam in the center of the hallway. "What's wrong, Jack? Why do you look so down?"

"Because, I am. I scored a negative four on my history test. I thought the lowest you could get was a zero, but I guess I was wrong, which means I'm bad at math *and* history."

"Let me see," Adam said. He grabbed the paper from Jack's hands.

"I don't understand why I got question number fourteen wrong," Jack said.

Adam pulled the paper closer to his face and examined it. Jack wondered if it was hard to concentrate with the massive hum of chattering voices coming from every direction as the students hurried to their next class.

"Hmm, the question asks, 'Do you agree with the United States having a strong central government? If so, explain why.' Here's the problem, Jack. You just wrote the word *no.*"

"Yeah, cause it only asks you to explain why if you write yes! But what I don't get is why Mrs. Titherson gave me a negative four."

"It actually says it right here, Jack. There's a note at the bottom. It says, 'Dear Mr. Harris, for sucking this badly at history, you deserve even less than nothing. Study more.' And there's also a picture of a sad face."

"Can she do that?"

Adam sighed. "Forget it, Jack. Let's go grab some food."

The two began walking. They were heading towards the end of the second-floor hallway, to the door leading into one of the school's many staircases. On both sides of the hallway were bulletins, school news, and meaningless diagrams on subjects most people had zero interest in. Or, in Jack's case, negative four interest in.

"Adam, there's so much you need to know. But now that we've got some alone time, I need to tell you some stuff. It might not be easy to believe, but you'll just have to trust that I'd never lie to you and that I'm not crazy."

"Go ahead," Adam said. His voice was neutral, but inside, Jack knew that he was probably battling impatience and an abnormal curiosity.

"So, after I left your house on Monday, I went home to meet Melissa for tutoring, right? And then—"

"Hey guys," Melissa said, appearing from literally out of nowhere. She gave Jack a pat on the back. "What'cha talking about?"

Adam and Jack answered at the same time.

"History," Adam said.

"Naruto," Jack said.

"The history of Naruto, he means," Adam corrected.

"That the one with the ninjas?"

The three walked together down the narrow staircase, pushing open a door leading to yet another set. The lunchroom was located in the basement, a wise choice on the part of the school. During the end of the school year, when summer was rearing its head, it was the only place that didn't feel like the center of an oven—the one spot to escape the boiling temperatures of the upper floors. Melissa followed Jack and Adam into the lunchroom.

"Let's get on line," Jack said.

Adam squinted at him. "On line? Have you been spending time in New York or something? It's, 'Get in line'."

Jack frowned at Officer Grammar. The three of them got *on* line behind the already long train of students waiting for food. Melissa, as she had been doing since the beginning of the day, was still snapping her head from left to right, scanning the room for any sign of trouble. Jack was starting to think she was taking things too seriously.

The line moved at a crawl while Adam and Melissa made nonsensical small talk. Jack wasn't in the mood to have any conversations other than the one he'd been about to have with Adam. If he could just lose Melissa for a few minutes, he'd be able to tell Adam everything, and his friend would know what to do—he always did. Sometimes Jack wondered if Adam was even human. His intelligence was something to fear.

"What'll it be?" the lunch lady asked.

Adam gave Jack a look of warning. "Don't start."

Jack tried his best to make a good choice, he really did, but he was getting fed up with the lackluster culinary options. It was almost cruel that the school expected the students to eat this stuff.

Jack smiled. "Janice, is there literally nothing else on the menu today?"

The woman looked ready to rip the hair out of her head. "Harris, the few days you were absent were the best days I've had in years. Just pick something, would ya? You're holding up the line again."

"Well, it's not my fault," Jack argued. "I have to pick between a circular piece of re-heated 'pizza' and a peanut butter sandwich. Oh, and the pizza never tastes like real pizza."

"Your point? Don't blame me for that, Harris. I don't make this stuff."

"Well maybe that's the problem. What kind of lunch-lady doesn't make lunch, Janice? You've lost your passion for this business. Chef Ramsay would not stand for this."

"Just pick something already, Harris!"

Jack walked away with his mediocre lunch, followed closely by Adam and Melissa. The lunchroom was probably the largest room in the school, with wide white tables and vending machines in every corner. The three took a seat in the back, at one of the few tables that still had any room. Too many people had lunch fifth period, so it was no surprise that every day it was crowded.

"So, Melissa. You and Jack seem to have become good friends lately, anything going on there?"

Jack almost spit out the first bite of his food. Was Adam nuts? Was he trying to embarrass Jack into Oblivion? Or Skyrim?

"That's our business. Wouldn't you just love to find out?"

She didn't say no! Jack thought triumphantly. *Well, she didn't say yes, either. I'll have to pull out all the moves on her when I take her on that date she owes me.*

Thinking of which, Jack had quite a few possibilities in mind. There was the arcade, bowling, the movies, and plenty of other good choices. He couldn't wait to have Melissa all to himself for a day. And to think, all he had to do was punch her in the face. After all the years that Jack had been struggling with women, in the end, all it took was to try and knock one out.

"I'll be right back," Jack said. He picked up his lunch and crossed to the table at the opposite end of the room. He sat down and dropped his plate on the table, then tried to have a chat with its sole occupant.

"You again," the boy across from Jack said, "I'm fine being alone, you know?"

"No, you're not, Andy. We're friends, aren't we? Come sit with us over at our table. There's plenty of room, and it has be lonely sitting here all by yourself every day."

Andy looked even more bitter than usual. His face was withered and held a pale sickness. There were bags under his eyes, as if red from hours of crying. He looked tired, beaten, and worn. It really bothered Jack.

There's gotta be something I can do.

"Andy, cheer up. Want me to come over today?"

"Do I even have a choice?" he groaned. "You stop by whenever you feel like it, and my mom just lets you in without asking me."

Jack laughed. "I'll bring over some anime, and we'll have fun. Hey, is something wrong? I mean like, seriously wrong? You really don't look well."

Andy looked into Jack's eyes. He had been glancing around the room, but now his gaze fell fully upon Jack.

"What is a life worth?" The question came out of nowhere. Jack had no idea how to answer it.

"What is my life worth, Jack? What makes me have a right to live?"

"Ah ... well, because you're you, Andy. What other reason is there?"

For the slightest of moments, Andy smiled. It was replaced soon after with a sullen look.

"I knew you'd have an answer like that. Hey, do you think we could talk later? In private, I mean. There's something I really need to talk to you about. It's not easy for me to say."

"Umm, sure, whatever ... I mean, yeah, of course."

"After lunch, meet me in the third floor bathroom. Make sure you come alone. And Jack," he whispered, "try to keep an open mind."

Paro was deep in thought. His elbows rested on the glass table in their planning room. He had promised Melissa they would be within half a mile at all times, and yet he was still here working. He needed to finish up and get back.

He tried to find some connection, some reasoning behind the killings. He had seen their faces, both of them. It was only for a brief moment, but between Melissa's descriptions and his own view of the two, he had a pretty good picture. Yet, he still didn't have the slightest idea of who or what he was dealing with. There was a knock on the door.

"Come in," Paro yelled behind him.

Paro jumped out of his seat when he saw the tears in Sarah's eyes. She was clutching a small white paper and trembling. Paro had never seen her this upset before. Even with all that they had seen, Paro had never witnessed such a look of pure anguish on her face. Small strands of her black hair were moist from contact with her sobbing eyes. They were red, and the way she craned her neck told Paro that she was having trouble looking at him.

Paro forced himself to contain his growing alarm. But what was wrong? He glided over and gently lifted up her head, making her meet his gaze. "Sarah, please, calm down. Tell me what's wrong."

She opened her mouth to speak, but released her words between pants and sobs. "It-It-It's Jack, Paro."

Paro held his breath, fear beginning to creep into his bones. Had something happened? He had assumed they would be fine alone until at least the end of the school day. Were they attacked in the middle of class? Paro forced the thoughts from his mind, ripping them from his brain.

"Did something happen?" Paro asked, forcing his voice to remain calm.

"No," she said. She buried her face into his shoulder. His shirt became moist with her tears. "But he's a good person. I only knew him for a little while but I liked him. He's innocent and kind. I don't want them to take him away! He'll never see the light of day again. It's not fair!"

"Calm down. Please, Sarah. I have no idea what you're talking about. Who is taking Jack away? Why would they?"

"Paro," she sobbed, unfolding the small piece of paper. "He's an Unrestricted."

Chapter 18: Unrestricted

Paro tried to control the turmoil he felt within his heart, the flurry of unrelenting emotions. How could this happen? Of all the people in the world to befall this tragedy, why did it have to be the Harris-kid?

No one spoke, least of all Michael. He wasn't his normal self. There was no crooked grin to be found on his face, no sly, amused look or overly relaxed posture. He didn't even wear that ridiculous cowboy hat of his. No, he simply sat with his eyes to the floor, filled with a look of regret.

Someone needed to break the silence, but Paro didn't want that to be him. They all knew what had to be done, but none wanted the responsibility. Jack Harris was like no other person in the world, and Paro could not bear to think of what needed to come next.

"Someone has to say it," Kazou said. Paro could sense relief in his team-members that someone had broken the silence. "I like the Harris-kid," he continued, "but we don't get to make the rules, none of us do. He has to be sent away. Right now we have a responsibility. This case, these murders, we have to put all of it aside. An Unrestricted takes priority over all other things, and right now there's one walking free."

Paro had never seen Michael angry. He had seen him annoyed, frustrated, and agitated, but as a light fixture was torn free from the wall and sent crashing to the floor, Paro didn't need anything else to go on to know that Michael was pissed.

"How could this have happened?" he shouted. "I thought he was a Telekinetic. He acted like one, and he had the abilities of one—there must be a mistake, Paro! We need to redo the test."

What Paro said next was borderline treason, but the law be damned. "None of you are supposed to know anything about Unrestricteds, except for the fact that we exist. But I have come to trust all of you with more than just my life, which is something that when I was younger I never would have dreamed possible. Now, you all already know that Psychs are born with an affinity, every last one of us. For most, it's like our heart—there is just one, and it defines us. But for people like Jack and I, it is like a favored hand. Jack has a natural affinity for Telekinesis, much like a person who is right-handed. But that doesn't mean he's limited to it."

"We can't do this," Sarah said. "This is wrong. All of this is just wrong, and you know it." Sarah did not look Paro in the eyes while she spoke. "Jack Harris is a sweet boy. Think of what his life will be like if we send him away and make him live in one of those awful facilities for the rest of his life."

"I know, Sarah. Believe me, I know. But you've already sent in his blood. There's no way I can fake it with someone else's." Paro's team shot him a look of surprise, and he knew why. To even suggest doing something so illegal was in itself a crime. A very, very serious crime.

"Damn, Paro, this kid's not dangerous!" Michael's voice, though a shout, had a pleading tone. "And even if he could be dangerous, he never will be. I had to beg him just to learn a few simple things. He's never gonna bother to be destructive or anything else like that. There's gotta be something we can do."

Paro stood from his leather chair then walked to the back of the room and turned away from his team. He couldn't bear to see the look of disgust on their faces—the looks aimed at him.

"I can't make a case for that, Michael. It's already been documented that he started the fire in his classroom by accident. Had I known in advance, I might have been able to alter that as well. But the facts are the facts, and the higher ups fear few things more than an Unrestricted that can't control himself."

"But that was then, Paro! He's not like that anymore. We showed him how to—"

"Quiet, Michael. Don't you think this is hard for me too? Because of this organizations ridiculous rules, we now have to refocus valuable time from stopping a pair of homicidal maniacs to ruining the life of an innocent child."

Sarah slammed her fists against the glass table, almost shattering it. She too, was showing signs of aggression that Paro had rarely seen from her.

"Then we'll hide him," she said. "We'll put him somewhere safe, some place they'll never find him."

Paro smiled. Sarah was such a courageous, caring person. "I can't believe you just said that, Sarah. If anyone in this room ever reported you, the consequences would be dire."

"But we're not like the other teams," Michael insisted. "I trust everyone in here with my life as well. We're more than just colleagues."

Sarah and Kazou nodded. "I don't mind putting my life on the line if it's for someone like Jack," Kazou said.

Paro sighed. What they were attempting was so far on the other side of the law, that if they were ever caught—and they probably would be eventually—more than likely an Op. team would be dispatched with no opportunity for surrender.

Looking around, Paro had never felt so much pride in his life. He was truly honored to have gathered these people. They all had their faults, sure, but in this world, there was no one he cared more about than the people sitting around him.

"You guys," he said. "Are you sure you understand the risks? If we grab the Harris-kid and we get caught—and believe me, we'll be the first suspects—are you all willing to pay the price?"

They all nodded without a moment's hesitation, and for the first time in a tiring life, Paro actually had to resist the urge to weep. "Very well then, we'll take the Harris-kid somewhere safe. We'll protect him from what lies ahead."

"Well said, well said!" shouted a voice from behind Paro. The door to the planning room swung open, and Paro filled with alarm as he swung his head to see who'd entered. His heart almost stopped, his palms began to sweat. Sarah almost fainted, and Michael's jaw dropped. Kazou remained motionless, but even in his eyes the fear was unmistakable. Did the man standing in the doorframe hear their conversation? If he did, then their only chance would be to try and kill him immediately. It wouldn't matter, though, Paro realized.

I think I just got my entire team killed.

A tall black man entered the room. There was a smirk on his face and an almost oppressive aura. He didn't say a word as he closed the door behind him and took a seat, as if he were just another member of the team.

Sarah and Michael remained frozen. Once again, Kazou broke the silence.

"Ge-General Moore," he whispered.

Paro rarely felt the touch of fear, but when he did, it was a sickening feeling. Sitting before them, with a casual and relaxed smirk, was General Deven Moore, considered the greatest and most powerful Telepath in the known world.

He was a very tall man, muscular, with the tattoo of the General's insignia embedded on the shoulder over his dark skin. He had the build expected of a Reinforcer like Kazou, yet he was far from it. He had short buzzed hair and a clean-shaven face. Despite his powerful body, a single glance into his eyes revealed a deep, complex intelligence.

"You're thinking to yourselves, if you all attack me at once, perhaps only half of you will die, yes?"

Paro almost lost it. His heart beat faster as the man somehow managed to gaze at everyone at once while in actuality looking at no one in particular. The feeling of oppression was so powerful that Paro felt weak in his knees despite being seated, and he had the urgent desire to flee.

"I see none of you are making a move against me. I could tell the moment I walked in here that if I attacked a single one of you, you'd all die protecting each other. This is good."

The man smiled, and all at once, the feeling of oppression was gone. The sensation of impending death was replaced immediately by a purity and brightness so vivid that it was almost too much to contain. For the first time since entering the room, the man allowed his true self to be shown. There was greatness there, a hopeful feeling of inspiration so powerful that the team was almost blown away by it. The man's smile was genuine—Paro was certain of it. The general had falsely created the feeling of oppression, but now that he allowed it to fade, he was showing his true self.

Paro blinked to ensure his eyes did not deceive him. Here the man was, sitting in their very planning room—one of the Psych Generals, part of the most feared, yet also most respected group of men and women. The highest rank one could obtain as a Psych.

"Are you going to kill us, General Moore?" Paro asked, trying desperately to keep his voice steady.

General Deven Moore stretched his arms and relaxed in the seat he occupied, but his eyes turned hard. He sat up straighter and took a moment to look at each one of them. "No," he whispered.

He stood up from the chair and paced around the room. "Jack Harris, Unrestricted Psych, age sixteen. He is one of the luckiest boys alive. Why? *Because I saw the file first.*"

He continued to walk around the room while he spoke. Every time he passed a member of Paro's team, he would stop momentarily to give one of them an evaluating look, before moving on to the next.

"He needs people like you," the general said. "If I were any other general, he'd be on his way to one of the facilities as we speak, and you would all be dead."

Paro tried to form some semblance of understanding, some idea of what was going on. "So you're not going to send him away?"

"Unrestricteds are not permitted to walk free. That law has been in place since before any of you were even born. It seems foolish, but it is not without purpose. But this Jack Harris, I think he deserves, at the very least, a chance to live a happy life. So, Paro, kindly write up a notice of employment. Jack Harris is to become a member of your team."

As soon as the last word was spoken, the only sound that could be heard was one large gasp, as all four present members of Paro's team looked around at each other in awe.

Paro shook his head. "But he hasn't gone to the camp! How can we sign him up if he hasn't received any training? All juvenile applicants have to go to the training camp. It's practically written in stone."

"So, now you know why I am here." Moore's face brightened. "I am a general, and I can do whatever I want. So, here's the deal—I will sign the forms, and it will be done. Boot camp starts up again in a few weeks, and you fellows just need to make sure he gets there, and I'll take care of the rest. For now, consider him accepted."

"Why would you do this for us?" Paro asked. "Why would you do this for Jack?"

General Moore shrugged. "Because everyone in this world deserves a chance, Paro. And make sure you don't tell anyone I said that, either! Generals are supposed to be impartial. I can't have anyone think I'm favoring the Investigation department, now can I?"

Paro remained seated in astonishment. Generals were not supposed to take sides in the ongoing feud between Investigations and Operations departments. The Op. teams recruited from the facilities and occasionally willing participants from the training camps. Investigations received most of their members from the camps as well, and on rare occasions elsewhere, but for a general to take the Harris-kid out of their domain and give him a chance at a life—it was a violation of their impartiality.

"We won't speak a word of this," Michael said. His face held a look of gratitude that Paro had not seen on him before. It was almost a look of worship. It made sense, though. Michael already considered the kid to be an apprentice of his in some ways.

"I'm going tell you fellows a little secret, something you're really not supposed to know. When a Psych becomes a general, he or she must swear under oath to forgo all beliefs, feelings, and prior opinions, and work only at improving the overall schematic of our organization. But it never happens this way. We investigators will always be what we were, and so it remains the same for the dogs over in the Op. teams. I'm telling you this so that you can trust me as well. Much like the risk you were willing to take, by me simply saying these words, I put my own life in danger."

In an instant, Paro understood the man and even came to revere him. So, at one point General Moore was just like them? Paro forgot his place for a moment and reached over to shake the man's hand. At the last second, he realized what a massive breach of protocol and formality that was. The General seemed oblivious to rules, and grasped Paro's hand in a firm shake.

"Paro, you're an Unrestricted as well, so I know you don't want to see Jack end up as some soulless killing machine. Take care of him, but if there are *any* problems at all, be sure to report them to me immediately. I'm willing to give the boy a chance, but you alone should know what kind of destructive power someone like him could possess. If anything happens, anything at all, I trust in you to report it to me without hesitation."

Paro nodded and the man took his leave. He paused at the door and saluted before exiting.

"Well," Michael said, "I sure hope the kid doesn't mind waking up early most mornings."

With Deven Moore gone from the room, a single thought entered Paro's mind.

Maybe I should have let him just kill us.

Chapter 19: There's Always a Way

No matter how hard Jack tried, he couldn't get Melissa to give him a moment away from her. He wanted to tell Adam everything, yet no matter what he did, he couldn't seem to get more than a few feet of distance.

Part of it, he knew, was because she wanted to ensure that Jack kept his mouth shut, which was absurd—Jack was great at keeping quiet! But more so, from the way she darted her eyes like she was crossing a crowded intersection, she clearly feared an attack, even in the middle of school. Jack thought she was being ridiculous. From what he remembered about the two weirdoes from the other night, they'd stick out like a sore thumb. They wouldn't just show up like Melissa seemed to believe they would.

Melissa followed Jack through a narrow hallway on the first floor. There were classes in session on both sides, as teachers, male and female, old and young, struggled valiantly to teach students pointless things, like art history. Jack wondered why anyone would care about the history of art.

Already Jack was receiving wide-eyed stares from everyone they passed, but it wasn't surprising. After all, what else could be expected? Jack, the wimpiest and most bullied kid in school, was walking hand-in-hand with a knockout like Melissa. With a devilish grin, Jack realized he didn't mind some of the jealous stares. He wondered if Melissa would become angry or embarrassed, but so far she didn't seem to care what people thought of her.

Adam had ditched them a few hallways back while on his way to the library to study or something.

Studying, Jack thought. *What a boring thing to do.*

Jack had promised to meet Andy in the first floor bathroom after lunch. Something was really bothering him, and Jack was not content to sit idly by and let him suffer. Melissa was just going to have to give him some space.

The hallway was finally quiet—the click of their feet tapping against marble floor was the only audible sound.

"Hey, Melissa," Jack said, "I need to use the bathroom."

"Okay, let's go."

Jack choked on his own breath. "But it's right here." He pointed. "There's nowhere to 'go' other than inside."

"Exactly," she said, "let's go inside."

Jack felt blood rush to his face. "To-together?" he gasped.

"I'll stand outside the stall. Jeeze, will you quit being such a baby?"

Jack couldn't believe what he was hearing. Melissa was going to waltz into the boy's bathroom like she belonged there? Even if he wasn't meeting Andy that would still be taking things too far.

"Ah ... I think I'll be fine on my own for a few minutes, and umm, just think what people would say about you if they see you following me in there."

Melissa grunted as if the thought had already been going through her mind. With a frown, she turned to Jack. "Fine, but make it quick. You're not taking any of this seriously enough. These people that want you are the ones who slaughtered Richard and his family. I'll be right outside, so make sure to yell if anything happens—and hurry up."

Jack laughed. What could possibly happen to him in a bathroom? Jack grimaced as he remembered how quite a lot could happen. The bathroom was home to some of Jack's most hideous and grueling bullying experiences. He shook his head as he freed himself of those dark memories.

Jack pushed open the swinging door and entered. As usual, his high school's bathroom, like most high schools, was the most disgusting and horrific place on the planet. It was almost as if—and probably was—intentionally made to be as gross as possible. Unspeakable things clung to the walls, and the stench was nothing short of nauseating.

Jack scanned the filthy bathroom—it appeared to be empty. He turned on one of the small, pressure-pressed sinks and washed his hands, waiting for something to happen. The sound of a stall being opened caused him to spin around behind him.

"Andy!" Jack said cheerfully. "You almost scared me to death."

Andy backed away and inhaled. "No! I wasn't trying to kill you."

Jack scratched his head. "Wait, what?"

Andy rubbed his eyes with his palms. "Never mind, I thought you said something else. I see, you said I almost scared you to death. Sorry, I misheard."

Jack had no idea what Andy was rambling about, and while he was no therapist, he didn't need to be one to see that Andy was in pure misery. Never had he seen someone so young look so old. It wasn't his physical features, but the way he carried himself. He looked worn, tired, frightened, and yet despite it all, there was a small glimmer of hope in his eyes.

"Jack, I need to tell you something. I need you to try your best not to freak out, run away, or yell to Melissa, who is probably outside the bathroom. She's there, isn't she?"

Jack nodded. "Okay, what's up?"

"Alright ... please remain calm and don't panic. What I am about to say is going to shock you, but you must trust me and not lose your cool. Jack, listen, I know what you are, and I am just like you. I can ... do things just like you can."

Jack laughed and shrugged. "Wow, that's so cool! Is that all? Hey, did you read the newest chapter of *One-Piece*?"

Andy looked as if his eyes were about to pop out of their sockets. For a brief moment his mouth opened then closed as if he were about to say something, but was instead shocked out of his wits. He stood motionless for a moment, and then again attempted to speak. This time, he succeeded.

"Did you not just hear what I said, Jack? I meant about the things you can do that others can't."

"Umm, yeah, I heard you. It's new to me too, but I guess some people can just do this stuff, right? No need to get all worked up about it. Don't tell me that's why you're all depressed-looking, Andy?"

Andy's eyes moistened, and Jack had no idea what for. He rubbed them with the back of his thumb and inhaled in sporadic, heavy breaths.

"You really are different, Jack. I knew it—everyone who knows you does. You're the greatest person in the world. I mean that."

Jack was confused. What was Andy going on about? He was acting really strange.

"Thanks, I guess."

"I need your help, man. I'll do anything if you'll help me. I'll give you everything I possess in this world. Hell, I'll even cut off my own arm and wrap it for you, if that's what it takes for you to help me out."

Jack reeled in surprise as Andy got to his knees with a pleading and desperate look in his eyes. Now tears fell freely down his face.

"Jack," he begged, "I'm a guy who will do anything in this world if you'd only help me. I'll give you anything—I'll *do*, anything. I'll even cut out my own liver for you. Just please, help me."

Jack felt the concern tug strongly on his heart. Andy was deeply troubled, and Jack would never refuse him. He grabbed Andy by the shoulder and lifted him off the floor, forcing him to meet his eyes. Jack was rarely so serious, but his mind turned only to thoughts of saving his friend from whatever caused him such misery.

"Tell me what's wrong, Andy. You said you'd do anything for me, right? I only ask one thing, and that's for you to tell me what's wrong in the first place."

Jack didn't think it was possible, but Andy's bawling increased. He lowered his voice to a whisper as the sadness fell from his cheeks and hit the floor with a small splash.

His voice was a barely audible whisper. He only said two words. "Ruin ... Requiem."

Jack's eyes widened in alarm—his emotions ran wild. At first, he thought he had misheard Andy, but that was impossible. Despite being a whisper, the words came out clear.

Jack hated taking things too seriously, but this was different. The words Andy had spoken, for innocent lives, literally meant the difference between life and death. Andy winced as Jack unintentionally increased his grip on Andy's shoulders, squeezing them tightly.

"What did you just say? Andy, where ... where have you heard these names?"

Andy took a moment to collect himself. His lips struggled to form words. Finally, he said, "How do you think I knew what you were? I'm their third wheel. I don't know how Requiem knew who you were, and I don't think I even care anymore, but Jack—they've ruined my life."

Jack released Andy and stepped back. "Andy, did ... did you kill those people? Did you kill Richard and his family?"

Andy wailed and slammed his fists against a sink. "No! But they're going to make me do worse. I don't know what to do anymore. They're more powerful than me, and I can't stand up to them. But they said that you work for some kind of police force or something. Jack, please, I don't want to go to jail. I don't want to die! I just want to go back to the way things were before. Please, I'm begging you. I will give you anything!"

Andy grasped Jack, hugging him around the waist. Tears dampened Jack's shirt while Andy clung to him for dear life.

Jack sighed. "Alright, I'll help you."

For a moment, Andy's face looked youthful again, and the withered lines smoothened as a glimmer of hope shone from his eyes.

"I don't want to go to jail, Jack. What do I do?"

Jack hummed to himself while he pondered the same. "I'll find out more. Okay, here's what we'll do. Right now, you should go home early. Tell the nurse you're sick and wait in your house. I'll see if I can work something out."

"Is it true?" Andy asked. "Do you really know these people? Are there really other people like us out there that stop these kinds of things?"

Jack closed his eyes and nodded. "Yeah, but I don't know what will happen to you. Just keep quiet and don't say anything to Melissa. Go home, stay there, and I'll come over tonight with an answer."

"Thank you! I will find some way in this world of repaying you, Jack. I just want this to be over."

"Don't worry. You don't need to repay me. Look, I need to leave before Melissa gets worried, okay? We'll talk soon."

Jack felt bad for leaving Andy by himself. He was still hysterical, shedding tears of relief. When Jack returned to the first-floor hallway, Melissa gave him a quizzical look and inclined her head.

"Took you quite a while in there. What were you doing?"

"Well, Melissa, since you asked, now you have to know. It all started with—"

Jack's words trailed off into mumbles as Melissa covered his mouth with her hand. "Sorry I asked."

Michael was really looking forward to seeing Jack's expression when they told him the news. "So, school gets out in five minutes, Paro. What do you want to do?"

Michael wondered how Paro felt about all this. At first, he seemed relieved, but now he looked frustrated. He must've known what a daunting task it would be to put someone like the Harris-kid on their team. In fact, everyone was up in arms, and Michael didn't understand why. He seemed like such a fun guy, that Jack Harris.

They were sitting in a black van parked outside of Elms High, at a distance close enough that if Sarah detected even the smallest of Psych ability, they'd be able to storm the place in under a minute.

Paro had even managed to acquire two full recon teams to survey the area around Jack's house and the area around his school. They weren't Psychs, but the twenty or so men hidden in the area would be more than enough to take down a pair of homicidal kids. Especially with the kind of firepower they were packing. But Michael, and probably the rest of the team, were hoping it wouldn't escalate that far.

"Anything?" Paro asked into the small black comm.

"Recon Team A reporting in, no sign of hostile Psychs, over."

"Recon Team B reporting in, no sign of hostile Psychs, over."

"Very well," Paro responded. "Keep your eyes peeled and let me know the moment anything changes."

Paro turned to face Michael. "We're going to have to bring this up with Jack as soon as he gets out of school."

"But what about his mom?" Michael asked. "She doesn't seem the type to go for something like this."

"That's why we aren't going to tell her right away," Paro said. "First, we're going to get this situation with the murders under control, and then we're going to break the news to her. She'll be hysterical, and I'm not in the mood to deal with that now."

"But won't she suspect something when you start meeting with Jack every day?"

Paro grinned. "Not at all, I've already taken care of that. She thinks we're just meeting with him as a follow-up to make sure he's keeping his Telekinesis under control. I've already told her we're picking him up from school today."

"That's so mean!" Sarah chimed in.

Kazou merely shrugged, and Michael continued to laugh. "Well, it's partly true, Sarah. I'm gonna be teaching the kid everything that I know, and I reckon if he's gonna be working for us he might as well learn to use the tools of the trade."

"Well, get ready to teach him, then," Kazou said, "because there he is."

A bell had rung, and students were pouring out of school by the droves. Jack was literally the first out the door, in what Michael figured was the only time he actually exerted himself. It seemed that to Jack, being the first one to go home was a race.

One of the first things Michael noticed was that Melissa did not seem happy. She was sprinting after him with her fist raised into the air. Even from this distance, it was obvious that Jack had snuck away from her. As the two neared the van, their voices were picked up on the high frequency audio. It was a high tech receiver capable of picking up audio even from a great distance.

"Jack, what did I say about leaving my sight?" Melissa shouted.

"You're not the boss of me! Ouch! Stop slapping me, Melissa. Ouuuch! Wow, just for that, I'm not letting you borrow my mom's season two collection of Glee."

Even the slap was picked up from the audio transmitter.

"You jerk, you already said you would, so you can't take that back now. We're watching it when I come over tonight."

"Whoa, you're coming over? That's sweet!"

"It's just for the mission, Jack, and don't you forget it."

Michael giggled like a schoolgirl and Paro shot him a reproachful look.

"Does anyone have any popcorn?" Michael asked.

Sarah laughed, and when Paro glared at her, she held out her palms and smiled. "It is kind of entertaining."

"The van's over here, idiot. Where are you going?"

"Oh, I thought you said they were parking by the left entrance."

"No, I said the right entrance. You don't listen to me when I talk to you. All day long you ignore everything I say."

"That is NOT true, Melissa. I only ignore the things that don't interest me."

Slap!

Paro grunted—it was a low, rumbling sound. "I can't believe we have a second Michael on the team now, especially when I didn't even want the first one."

Michael tipped his cowboy hat. "You'll thank us later!"

Chapter 20: Jack Harris a Psych Investigator?

It was very difficult to hear the man, being that he only spoke in short whispers. It was further complicated by the constant screech of jets passing low overhead. The airbase in Kuwait was always pretty active, with convoys and planes arriving and departing at frequent intervals.

It was hot too, which made Sebastian grumble every time the heavy wind blew scalding sand in his face. Sebastian pushed the torn brown letter across the small table. The man picked it up and examined it for only a moment before sliding it back across to him.

"You wish to find him, then?" he whispered.

Sebastian had to strain his ears every time the man spoke. He was covered from head to toe in cloth, revealing nothing more than his fierce eyes, which told a great deal about him. Though all his other features were masked, the complex and dark world that lay behind those haunting eyes were enough to send a shiver down Sebastian's spine.

"I've proved my worth, haven't I?" Sebastian asked. "All that's left is for you to give me the location."

Even concealed behind the brown cloth, Sebastian had the uncomfortable notion that the man was smiling. *"Check your left breast pocket, Mr. Harris."*

While Sebastian kept a straight face and allowed no sign of fear or emotion to seep through, he calmly reached into his shirt-pocket and felt a small paper folded inside.

When did he—Sebastian ripped the thought from his mind.

"Do you have ... any news?" the man whispered.

"Not much, but I do know those kids of yours are causing quite a stir. You ever going to trust me enough to tell me your real name?"

"But I have ... Mr. Harris. My name is Redemption."

"Suit yourself."

Jack was impressed by how much they had done in such a short time. Only two miles from his house, they had rented a large garage to act as a temporary base of operations. Laptops, equipment, and numerous personnel shuffled from activity to activity.

"How did you get all these people?" Jack asked.

Paro put an arm on his shoulder. "Well, murder is a very serious thing, Jack. And the more serious and numerous the crimes, then naturally the more resources we use in stopping them. Come, have a seat, we have a lot to talk about."

Sarah and Kazou were already sitting at the square table, shuffling through files and discussing notes. Melissa dragged him into a chair next to her, while Paro and Michael sat across from them. Sarah and Kazou stopped whatever it was they were doing the moment Jack sat down and eyed him with interest.

"So," Jack said, "I'm supposed to learn more about my whatever it is and then I can go home, right? But can we make it quick, please? It's Friday."

Jack didn't know why that tense look Paro sometimes wore appeared on his face. Jack had been cooperating just like he'd been asked. Michael gave Paro an odd, questioning look, and Paro returned a nod. The cowboy then turned to face Jack.

"Buddy," Michael began, "We got the results of your blood. You're not a Telekinetic like we thought. That's why we're all here today."

Jack shrugged. "Is that a bad thing?"

Michael stumbled for an answer, so Sarah took over. Melissa bounced on her chair in agitation, and she looked to be as confused as Jack, if not more so.

"It's not a bad thing, sweetie," Sarah said. "It's just not an easy thing."

Melissa tensed and lost her patience. "What is this about, guys? If Jack's not a Kinetic then what is he?"

"An Unrestricted," Paro said.

Jack flinched, because in reflex to the answer, Melissa grabbed his shoulder with the strength of a bull. "Ouch, Melissa! I thought I already paid my pain debt. This isn't fair. Now I owe you a slap."

"What do you mean he's an Unrestricted?" Melissa asked, ignoring Jack entirely. "How can that be possible?"

Jack had no idea why Melissa seemed to care more about this than he did, but from the time he had spent with these people, Jack had learned a few tricks to getting along with them better. Namely, just nod and pretend you knew what was going on. It amazed Jack how much that worked for him in life. It worked for him in school, and now with these people.

Jack tried to imitate Melissa's behavior. He stood up from his chair and threw his arms around in mock outrage. "What! How can I be an Unrestricted? Oh no and stuff. This is so bad. I can't believe it. I guess now we'll just have to do whatever it is we do now that I'm Unrestricted, right, Paro?"

Melissa dragged on Jack's arm and pulled him back into the chair with a scowl on her face. Jack didn't care—he knew he just nailed it. He was becoming a professional at pretending he was informed about things.

"Jack," Paro began, "do you remember what I taught you about Psychs? Recite it back to me, so I know you understand."

Jack grinned. He once again stood up and addressed the team sitting around the table. He knew the answer to something for once!

Jack cleared his throat theatrically. "There are four types of affinities people can be born with. Telekinesis, which is what you guys said I was, which lets me move stuff. Telepathic, like Sarah, which makes you do brain-stuff or whatever, and then there's Manipulators, which can ... manipulate stuff? You guys don't have one of those so I don't really know. Oh, and then there's Reinforcers, like Melissa, which makes you strong but also really mean and stupid."

Even the technicians at the end of the makeshift base of operations turned to look at the source of the popping crackle, as Melissa's slapping hand whirled across Jack's face. His cheek lit up in white-hot pain, and Michael started giggling uncontrollably. Kazou for some reason looked wounded.

Paro ignored the ordeal and continued. "An Unrestricted, Jack, is someone who is not born to any type. They still have something that is preferred, such is the case with you and Telekinesis, but they are not limited to simply the basics of the other affinities. They can do as they please, even combining several together in ways that are ... for better or worse, astounding."

Jack nodded. "Got it. That actually makes a lot of sense. So I can use things other than Teleke— aww, man does this mean I'm gonna have to learn even more stuff?"

Michael waved an arm. "No, Jack, we've already decided to treat ya as a Telekinetic. In fact, the people of our organization would rather prefer it if you didn't play around with any of the forces you got at your disposal."

"The problem, Jack," Paro said, "is that because of the inherent destruction that you're capable of causing, you're not allowed to simply walk away from us anymore. Because of this discovery, I'm afraid that from this point forward, you're going to have to become a member of our team. It's either that or a fate much worse, which I can promise you don't want."

Jack's mind reeled in shock. So he wasn't going to be done with all of this nonsense, after all?

"For how long?" Jack tried to keep his voice from cracking, but he was beginning to feel a creeping fear.

Sarah looked saddened "Forever, Jack. You can never be free."

Jack tried to find something to say back, some way to respond, but before he could so much as open his mouth he was distracted by Melissa's fists smashing into the table, causing it to shake.

"Like hell, Paro! Are you telling me that Jack's not going to be allowed to live his life just because of some formality?"

"Melissa, calm down! I've warned you about these outbursts." Paro stood up from his chair and pointed a threatening finger at her.

"This is more than just a formality—it is law. Do you even know what risks we were willing to take to keep Jack out of the facilities? We were willing to throw down our lives to stop that from happening."

"Yeah, but—"

"Melissa, it's okay." Melissa looked shocked as Jack put a comforting arm on her shoulder and stood up to face Paro.

"What did you just say about putting your life on the line?" Jack asked.

Paro sighed. "Normally they send Unrestricteds off to the facilities where they can be brainwashed and turned into killing machines. We all agreed that we would risk our lives to prevent that from happening. The end result was an agreement that you could still live a somewhat decent life by joining us instead."

Jack smiled at Paro. It was a pure and honest smile that Jack hoped would communicate his feelings of gratitude. "Thank you, Paro. You did something really great for me, and while I still don't understand everything, I'll join you guys. Thanks, all of you, for standing up for me."

Sarah wiped a tear from her eyes, and Michael simply put his feet on the table and smirked. Kazou nodded in silence.

Paro too seemed to be in good humor now. "That was much less painful than I thought it would be, Jack. Thank you for making this so much easier on us. And look, you'll get used to waking up at six a.m. Trust me, after the first week it's like you—"

"*What?*"Jack shouted. *"Six a.m.? I'm out of here!"*

Jack tried to flee, but Melissa grabbed him and held him in place. "Sit back down, you idiot! You'll get used to it, trust me."

Jack relaxed over the course of the next few minutes, while Paro and Michael for the zillionth time went over everything that had happened since the first murder, ending with the execution of the Davins' family. Occasionally, they asked Jack a question or two, which he once again answered to the best of his knowledge. Sometime during the middle of the team's discussion, Jack remembered there was something very important he had to ask.

"Can I ask you guys something?"

"What's up, Jack?" Michael answered.

"What's gonna happen to these people if we catch them alive? Like, let's say we were able to find out who their accomplice is and he agreed to cooperate. Would we be able to let him go free if he didn't mean to cause any harm?"

Paro looked at Jack with an expression of regret. "No, Jack, unfortunately not. Even if he or she is just an accomplice, they will probably spend the rest of their lives locked away for the massacres they aided in."

Jack struggled, trying with everything he was worth not to let any worry or anxiety show on his face. "But what if they really, really didn't mean it? Then could we make an exception?"

"I'm afraid not," Paro answered. "I don't know what awaits the two that you and Melissa fought in the park. But as for the accomplice, he or she will have a tremendous punishment waiting for them. But at the very least, they'll be alive. If we don't solve this problem soon, the Op. teams will step in and start piling up bodies."

"Op. teams?" Jack asked.

"They're a division of Psychs like we are, but they exist as a mirror to us. Their job is to kill what we can't catch." Paro spent the next few minutes explaining how the Psych departments worked.

Jack visibly shook at the explanation. So, there were teams that went around killing the criminals that Psychs like Paro couldn't catch? Jack couldn't believe something like that was permitted.

"Okay, just to make sure I got this. No matter what the situation is—if someone comes forward willing to cooperate and surrender, they still have go to jail for a long time?"

"Yes, Jack."

"May I please be excused? I know I'm supposed to get a ride home soon, but there's something nearby I really need to take care of. I need to pick up something at a grocery store that I promised I'd get for my mom. Is that okay?"

Sarah and Paro were studying him with an almost scientific gaze. Paro nodded. "Well, I guess if you're going to be on this team then we can at least treat you with the respect of a member. So yeah, go ahead. Just make sure you head home soon. There are still crazy people after you, don't forget."

"Thanks, Paro." He rose from the seat and grabbed his schoolbag.

"Wait," Melissa said, "have you forgotten once again that you're not supposed to leave my sight?"

Damn, Jack thought to himself. *I need to get to Andy's right away, but I can't bring her along with me.*

"Umm, can't I go by myself, for just a little bit, please? If I'm gonna be a member of the team, won't you have to trust me too, Melissa?"

Melissa growled at this. "Not at all, Jack. You're not going anywhere with—"

"Melissa, let him go!" Paro commanded.

"But Paro! He's—"

"I said, let him go."

Jack didn't know what was going on between the two, and he honestly didn't care, either. Based on what they had told him, Andy's life would be ruined forever if he got caught. Jack had promised to help Andy, and he didn't intend to break it. He'd head over to his house and get Andy as far away as possible from this place.

Jack sprinted out of the room, running faster than he had ever run in his life. The personnel around the garage-turned-base gave him odd looks as he soared by them.

Andy, hang tight, I'm coming.

Chapter 21: Turning Point

Jack ran as if his life depended on it, or rather, his friend's life. Andy's house wasn't very far from the garage that Paro's team—his team now—had rented out. It was only around three p.m. and the sun was still out in full force. Had it not been for such a sense of urgency, Jack might have actually enjoyed the run.

To his left was an open baseball field, with young children learning and practicing the game. To his right, Jack spotted fully-detached houses with gardens and large fountains dotting the landscape.

Jack's feet kicked up small pebbles and rocks as he raced his way down to the next block. He ran past a series of rather large homes. Swimming pools, hot-tubs, basketball hoops, you name it, Sparrow-Road was a higher income neighborhood. It was one of the most fascinating things about Elms New Jersey. Walking even one minute from a set of low income homes could bring you to a set of mansions. Finally, at the end of another block he came across the semi-detached home that Andy lived in. It wasn't bad for a middle income house, with two floors, a basement, and four bedrooms.

Jack had been there quite a few times, though never exactly invited. Andy was always alone, and while Jack had Adam, Andy didn't have anyone, so Jack came over every so often and hung out with him. Even if Andy told his mom he wanted to be alone, she still let Jack come see him. Hopefully, this time would be no different.

He walked over the white rocks that decorated the front lawn and rang the bell. It opened so quickly that Jack was convinced Andy'd been waiting on the other side for him the entire time.

"Jack," Andy said, his eyes lighting up. For the briefest moment as he was opening the door, he had that defeated, haggard look he'd worn as of late, but once his eyes registered the visitor, his boyish expression returned with full glamour.

"Come in." Andy waved Jack inside. His face darkened when Jack almost knocked him over trying to push him through the door.

"Andy, pack your things right now. We're leaving."

"Don't tell me ... please, Jack, don't tell me."

"I'm sorry, Andy, but we need to leave. I'll walk with you to the nearest train station. I have enough money to help you pay for a ticket. You need to go far ... as far as you can, and never show your face to anyone around here again."

Jack's heart burned for Andy. Tears slid across his friend's face and that same desperate look returned.

"Is there nothing else that can be done, Jack? Is there no deal or negotiation that can be made?"

Jack wanted so badly to be able to help Andy, but this was one thing he just couldn't do. No matter how hard Jack tried, he would never be able to stop Paro and the team from locking Andy away in a cell and tormenting him for the rest of his life.

"Andy, if you don't leave then those two will probably kill you, won't they? I know it won't be easy, but you can still have a life. I'll come find you some day, and I'll make sure that it won't be so bad, but right now you need to go. Pack your things and come with me—hurry!"

Andy scrambled out of the room and sprinted up the stairs. Jack could hear the thump on the second-floor above him as closets opened and closed, and drawers slammed shut. Finally, Andy came running back down the stairs with two small traveling bags. Jack's heart almost melted at the sight of pure grief and loss on his face.

"Th-this," he sobbed. "This is all I am now? These two bags, and then I'm all alone? I don't even have my mom now."

Never before, not through all the bullying, the years of torment, or the endless pain of loneliness had Jack felt so powerless.

Why can't I do anything? Jack wondered. *Why isn't there something else I can do?*

"I'm so sorry," Jack said, "but this is all we can do now. It's our only option. If we leave now we can make the next train. Come on." Jack had to almost drag Andy to get him out of the house.

Together the two walked away from the home. With each step, Andy's legs wobbled and he looked more and more like he was about to collapse. They walked slowly, much slower than Jack had wanted, but this would be the last time Andy saw the town he had grown up in. Jack supposed a few minutes wouldn't kill them.

Andy took in every sight, as if recording it all to memory. Jack felt his heart rip at the thought that Andy would never see his mother or father again and would be truly alone. But what other choice was there? It was either that or spending the rest of his life rotting away in some cell.

"Umm, Jack?" Andy asked. His voice sounded worn and exhausted. "Will you really come see me some time? I don't know anyone where I'm going. Heck, I don't even know *where* I'm going. Do you think you can sneak away and hang out with me some time?"

"Yeah," Jack lied. It was a painful lie, one that shredded him on the inside. Andy relaxed at the false promise, furthering Jack's guilt.

Despite the sedate pace, they arrived at the transit terminal well before the next train was scheduled to depart. Andy hesitated while following Jack in, forcing Jack to once again drag him.

The terminal was a two-story building, with the second-floor on the ground level that they entered on. Below them, and down a wide flight of stairs, was where the trains arrived and departed. There were waiting benches, vending machines, and newsstands, although most seemed to be empty, probably because of the off-peak hours. Looking around, there wasn't much activity going on. A few people waited patiently on the benches while a sole cashier waited for any customers.

"One ticket to Tampa, please," Jack said, stepping in the empty line. He nearly stuck his tongue out when he heard the price but thought the better of it. Eighty dollars? Were they selling tickets or the train itself?

Jack led Andy down the wide staircase, and together they took a seat on one of the many unoccupied benches. Andy tensed and then began to shake and twitch. He looked like a wreck, with tears still falling down his eyes. Even his legs started to tremble. He was traumatized.

For a very serious moment, Jack wondered if he was making the right decision. Andy did not look at all like he was going to be okay, like he was going to be able to someday recover. The confusion and indecision was almost painful to Jack, as once again he tried to think of some way, any way, that things could be different. But it all came down to this. Andy's only chance was to leave and never return.

"I'm going to miss school," Andy whispered. "And my mom. And my dogs, too. I love them so much."

Jack didn't respond. He did not know what words to say, if there even were any. Was there anything in this entire world that Jack could say at this point to make things better?

No, this is all that can be done, and I'm doing it. There's nothing else. No words, no gestures, nothing.

Jack forced a reassuring smile. "Do you want something from the vending machine?"

"No," Andy said with a sniffle.

"If there's anything you need, just let me know. The train should be here in half an hour."

Jack tried to make more conversation, but Andy was now trembling, shaking, and sobbing himself into silence. After a few moments of remaining motionless, Andy looked into Jack's eyes. Something was off, and Jack became alarmed. Andy's face was bright red, distorted, and full of depthless misery.

"Do you really think I'm going to be okay?"

"Yeah, you're gonna be just fine."

"Hey!" said a familiar voice. "I hope you two aren't going anywhere far. I mean, we've got finals coming up on Monday."

A gripping and horrifying panic rushed into Jack, and coursed through his veins at the sound of the feminine voice behind him. Melissa walked casually over and took a seat in-between him and Andy.

"Me-Melissa," Jack croaked, "what are you doing here?"

Melissa opened a bag of potato chips, and with a relaxed sigh, she devoured each one in a loud crunch. She was even dressed more casually than earlier, too. She wore tight blue jeans and a white tank top. Her golden hair glided down the back of her head. Yawning, she stretched her arms to get in a more comfortable position between them. It amazed Jack that no matter where she went or in what situation, she was always gorgeous.

Melissa shrugged. "Not much, I was in the area. Hey, Andy, what are you doing here? Didn't expect to see you around."

She must suspect something!

The thought breached Jack's mind like a sword ripping through flesh.

Why else would she be here? Andy knows what she is, he ... he needs to stay quiet.

Even a complete stranger could see the look of absolute terror and fright as Andy's mouth gaped and his eyebrows rose. He inhaled sharply and with his right hand, he squeezed Jack's leg.

"Nothing really," Andy answered. "I'm just hanging out with Jack. How are you, Melissa?"

"I'm just fine," she said cheerfully. "Here, want one?"

Andy declined the offer of chips and turned his head away to face forward. The train would arrive in just twenty more minutes, and Jack prayed that things would hold up until them.

"So, Melissa, do you normally come to hang out at train stations?" Jack asked.

"I could ask the same of you."

"I'm just here seeing a friend off. Andy's gonna visit his grandparents, and I had some free time. Hey, Melissa, aren't you coming over tonight? Let's go home now and watch some TV."

"Nah, I'll stay here and hang out with Andy for a bit." She gave him a playful nudge on the shoulder. "I don't think we ever really speak much."

Andy's face paled, and Jack feared he was only a moment from either passing out or throwing up, perhaps both. Jack was running out of ideas.

"Are you sure?" Jack asked. "I mean, I'm gonna leave. Do you really wanna stay here by yourself? Let's go together."

"No, I'm fine," she refused yet again.

Does she know? Jack thought frantically. *How could she? How could she even possibly suspect.*

Suddenly the realization dawned on Jack, and even he trembled.

They knew there was another Psych in the school! And because I originally met the profile, they suspected that it might be a friend of mine. When I stormed out of there earlier I must have looked really afraid or something ... Oh God, I did this! I bolted out of there like such an idiot. Melissa must have gotten suspicious and followed me here. But how much does she know?

"Melissa, I really think we should be going. There's no reason for us to be here. What do you say? Let's leave Andy in peace."

Jack shot Melissa his fiercest look, but the one returned by Melissa trumped his and made him lean back in his seat.

"I'll leave when I want—isn't that right, Andy?"

Just stay calm, Andy! Don't let her think something's wrong. Stay calm!

"Hey, Andy, are you alright?" Melissa asked. There was genuine concern in her voice. "You're shaking like you've got a fever. Here..." She placed her palm against his forehead. "Hmm, no fever, is something bothering you?"

Andy trembled even more, and the look of concern on Melissa's face didn't seem to help.

Jack cleared his throat and tried to change the subject. "Sooo, Andy, how about those relatives, huh? You excited to see them?"

"Y-y," he stammered, "Y-y-y—"

This was not good. Andy couldn't even speak—he was losing it. There would be no fooling Melissa, and playing this game was getting them nowhere. She definitely knew what was going on. There could be no more doubt about it.

"Please, Melissa, you don't understand. Just leave," Jack begged.

"Don't understand what, Jack? Why are you acting so strange?"

She was toying with him now. It was too much for Jack to handle. He wasn't good with words. He wasn't good with playing mind games, either. The situation was sliding out of his control faster than he could manage. All he wanted was to save his friend. All he wanted was for his friend to have some chance at living his life. All of these things raced through his mind, as tears began to glide down his face. He didn't want this to happen to his friend!

Before he realized he was doing so, Jack grabbed Melissa and hugged her, pulling her close. She didn't pull away. Instead, she surprised him by returning the hug, letting him cry into her chest.

"I know," she whispered in his ear. *"I know it can be really hard."*

"Please, Melissa, I'm begging you," he cried into her. "Don't do this, please. You don't understand."

"*No,*" she said in a soothing voice. "*I really do understand. I know it hurts, Jack, just shh. Please, say no more.*"

"You don't have to do this." Jack felt the tears as they dampened her shirt, but she paid it no mind.

"*I do, Jack. Please forgive me.*"

"How did you know?"

She ruffled his messy hair and smiled at him. "*Because anyone can read you like a book, Jack. Why do you think they let you go off alone? When you charged out like that, Sarah picked up your fear and worry like you were a pair of speakers playing explosive sound effects. She can do that, you know? And it's not hard to put two and two together.*"

"Are they here?" Jack pulled away and wiped his face, embarrassed for his display of emotions.

Melissa nodded.

"Jack, what's going on with you two?" Andy seemed to be recovering his voice. A look of panic spread across his face. "You know what? I'm an idiot! I just remembered that I wasn't supposed to visit until next week. I'll see you guys around. I'm heading home."

Andy tried to rise, but not before Melissa grabbed his arm. A look of fury and terror radiated off of him as he met Melissa's gaze.

"Let me go, Melissa! What the hell do you think you're doing?"

"Andy," she whispered, "you know who I am, don't you? I can see it on your face."

Andy tried to pull away and his voice filled with desperation. "No! Let me go—get your hands off me!"

Jack tried to look away. He tried to ignore what he was seeing. It felt as if his heart were being ripped in two.

"I don't enjoy doing this to you, but if you struggle, I'll hurt you. Look around you, there is no way out."

It took Jack a minute to realize what Melissa was talking about, but when he saw it, he wondered how he and Andy had missed it in the first place. All around them, the people on the benches, the janitors, even the ticket salesmen—they had all been replaced by men and women in disguise. Every one of them was beginning to converge on Andy, about twenty in total. They opened their bags and removed massive assault rifles, and with a tremendous roar surrounded the frightened boy.

"*Don't move, don't move! On the ground—now!*"

Andy wailed. It was a cry of pure anguish and terror, as twenty assault rifles were leveled at him. All around the room the men and women spread out, covering the perimeter and blocking all exits. They didn't seem willing to take any chances.

"One move and you're dead," came a voice from behind them. Jack spun around to see Paro, flanked by the rest of the team.

"Excellent work, Agent Harris. I know it's never easy the first time, but you'll get used to it."

Andy's eyes widened in surprise and betrayal. "Y-you were in on this, Jack? You ... you betrayed me? Why, Jack? I trusted you! You were the only friend I had in this world! At least tell me why?"

Jack cried again. "No, you don't understand, Andy. They followed me. I didn't mean to do it, I swear."

"*I hate you, Jack, I hate you!*"

Melissa kicked out Andy's legs and knocked him to the ground.

"*Melissa!*" Sarah screamed. "*Watch out, there's activity!*"

There was a murderous scream from behind Melissa, as the nearest recon officer clutched his throat and the skin bubbled around his neck. In one of the most horrific things Jack had ever seen, the officer collapsed, and the area around his neck became nothing more than a gelatinous, bloody mess.

Andy looked at Melissa. A sickened grin formed on his face. "You're dead, Melissa!"

Things moved really fast. Jack was knocked out of the way by an invisible force while the same force pulled Melissa away from Andy, sending her hurtling into Jack. He was sure Michael had done it. Paro sped past the two, charging at a speed that transcended human capability. He grabbed Andy by the throat, lifting him into the air and causing him to gasp under the pressure of Paro's squeezing hand. Then Paro ran forward while dragging Andy along with him, before slamming the boy against the wall, pinning him to it.

Small puffs of smoke started appearing inches from Paro's face, as if an invisible match was continually being lit and then put out around him.

"That won't work on me, kid. You may as well cut that nonsense out right now. As it is, I might just kill you to save me some time and trouble. After all, you did just kill one of my men. Look at them. They want nothing more than to lodge a bullet in your brain for what you just did."

Jack pushed himself off the floor and looked in disbelief at the body of the officer that moments ago was a living, breathing human being. The rifle was still in his hand, and his face was distorted, nothing more than red mush.

"Andy ... did he?" Jack struggled to form words. "Did Andy just kill that man?"

Sarah rushed over and tried to cover Jack's eyes, but he pushed her away. "Answer me, damnit! Did Andy just kill that man? Melissa, answer me!"

Jack had never used such an angry, commanding tone with her before. Yet she obliged and answered him. "I'm sorry, Jack, it was my fault. I wasn't fast enough, I—"

Jack stormed past her before she could finish speaking and came to stand beside Paro. Andy's terror was replaced by a thunderous hate. He groaned, struggled, and ripped at Paro's fingers. Paro had him pinned against the wall, hand extended, grip tight on the boy's throat.

"*Jack,*" he croaked, "*please, kill them, kill them all! You're like me ... you know what we have to go through every day. Do it! Help me, kill them!*"

Jack couldn't believe what he was hearing. Andy was actually asking him to murder people.

"First tell me something, Andy." Jack was surprised that Paro was allowing him to have this conversation. He seemed content to simply hold the boy in place while Jack had his words.

"Did you kill Richard's family? Tell me the truth and I'll help you. But please, Andy, I need to know. You told me you didn't kill them."

"*I'm ... sorry, Jack,*" he croaked. "*But you know he deserved it, all of them did. I did what I had to, for what they did to us at school. I did it for us, Jack. I did it for us! I went there, and I—*"

Jack didn't feel the explosion of rage until after the words were out of this mouth.

"*SHUT THE HELL UP!*"

Jack trembled, he actually trembled with anger. This was a terrible feeling, a horrible feeling. It was sickening, but he couldn't control it. He looked at Andy and poured the hate into his voice.

"You killed little children, Andy! Little girls, seven year-old angels, whose only wrong doing in life was to have met you! You killed his mother, you killed all of them! How could you ... tell me, how could you!"

"*Jack, I had the right!*" his voice was raspy. Paro didn't seem to be easing up on him. "*You don't understand—I had the right!*"

Jack wanted to vomit. "The right? The hell do you mean you had the right? No one has the right to do what you did!"

Jack's trembling increased even more. His stomach began to hurt, and he dropped to one knee. Michael and Sarah dashed over to him. "Jack, what's wrong? Hey, what's with your eyes? Do you see this, Sarah?"

"You mean that's not normal?" Melissa asked, rushing to them. "I thought it was just something some Psychs did, since I saw Jack do it once before."

Even Paro glanced behind him, surprise on his face. "Hey, Sarah, is Jack okay? What's wrong with his eyes? Why are they dilated?"

Jack tuned out their nonsense. A simple thought emerged within him, a simple reality made bright.

Andy is mine.

Jack remembered being this way before, and somehow he knew he would forget yet again. But the thought brought him no emotion, nothing did. For some reason, when he was like this, nothing bothered him. There was no sadness, hate, or anger. There wasn't even fear. There was just him, and his thoughts. And the things he wanted to do.

Jack got back to his feet. It would have amazed him, if he could feel amazement, just how much simpler life was when you couldn't feel emotion. In a way, he wished it could stay like this.

"He's mine," Jack said in a commanding tone.

Melissa came to stand next to Jack, unsure what was going on. She had seen him like this once before, but only now was she finding out that this was abnormal behavior. She hadn't been a Psych long enough to know everything about them.

Paro looked at him with ponderous eyes. "What do you mean, 'he's yours,' Jack? What's going on? Are you feeling okay?"

Melissa felt the first bite of fear. Jack didn't seem to be himself at all. In fact, he seemed to be nothing even remotely like his normal self. He was detached, cool, and he didn't seem to be listening to any of them.

"Paro, step away," he commanded.

"Harris, don't presume to—"

Paro was cut off as a force slammed into him, and Melissa saw him brace himself. The force caused him to step back and drop Andy to the floor. His eyes lit up in shock, and he looked at Jack.

"Did you just try to throw me?" Paro asked.

Melissa had no idea what was going on, but she had the overwhelming sense that whatever it was, it wasn't good.

"Jack, get back here. Hey, what are you doing? Put him down!"

Now it was Jack that held Andy by the throat, only he didn't use his hands. The boy was telekinetically pinned, and he looked at Jack with pleading, desperate eyes.

"You think you know death, do you Andy?" Jack's voice was conversational, lacking any discernible emotion. "Well, how about I show you what death really looks like?"

There was a shriek from behind them. Sarah's voice called out with a dire sense of urgency. *"I'm detecting Psych movement, massive amounts. At least ten! All with hostile intent."*

Paro turned away from Jack, but Melissa didn't budge. Upon hearing Sarah's warning, the nineteen living recon officers raised their weapons and stood at full alert, their guns clicking as they turned off their safeties.

"Sarah, are you kidding me? Are you certain there are ten Psychs heading our way? And all of them with hostile intent? I've never been very good with Telepathy. I need to know exactly what you're feeling."

Melissa turned her head around while still remaining near Jack and Andy. Sarah was shivering with her head downcast and off to one side—it was her gesture of gathering data.

"No, I was wrong. It's about fifteen now, and they're all Telepaths, like me."

Kazou and Michael had a grim look of death in their eyes, one that was beginning to form in Melissa's as well. Fifteen Telepaths working together could kill them all. But none of this made any sense.

"You must be mistaken," Paro said. "Where would fifteen Telepaths come from, and why would they be hostile? Please, Sarah, you must double check and make sure."

"I am, Paro. And it's at *least* fifteen! Maybe even more. I don't know where this army of Psychs has come from, but they're heading right for us. Paro ... are we going to die?" She began to weep.

One of the recon officers ripped off his helmet and threw it to the ground. "Not while we're here, missy. Men!" he shouted, addressing both the men and the women of the two squads. "Are we dying here?"

"No!" came the unanimous roar.

They lifted their weapons and waited for the enemy. Paro surprised Melissa by grabbing her shoulder.

"I've got no idea what's going on," he said. "But if it comes down to a fight, make sure you run away. Take Jack, and get the hell out of here."

"But Paro," she whimpered.

"That's an order."

At once, a stench hit them, an abhorrent, loathsome, reek of decay, which overpowered every other sense. The stench of death was so strong that two of the officers vomited.

Dark shadowy silhouettes could be made out from the upper stairway, where one of the officers standing guard screamed in the distance. The shadows came closer and closer. When Melissa, and all those on the first level were finally able to see what approached, every last one of them, even Paro, howled in terror.

No! Melissa thought to herself. *This isn't, this can't, this is not happening!*

What awaited them was literally something out of a nightmare. Slowly, at a crackling, slithering walk, ten decaying skeletons emerged from the staircase. Some had swords in hand, others had knives. They had dark red eyes, and blood smeared from their feet, leaving red trails as they walked closer to the astonished recon officers.

"Don't shoot!" Paro ordered, but to no avail. The recon teams began opening fire as soon as they saw the creatures. Even the loud pop of their automatic weapons couldn't dull the sense of smell and the sight of pure horror.

Their weapons had no effect. The creatures shoved them aside and kept on moving. Sarah wailed, pleading with God to make the things go away. Even the staunch Kazou, the man who never showed fear, whimpered as the nightmarish beings approached them. Michael dropped to his knees and prayed, while Paro and Melissa stood as the only two unshaken.

Paro didn't say anything, he just watched motionless, his body trembling. Melissa's mind filled with an oppressive dread. It almost knocked her off her feet.

Sarah reached over to grab onto and hug Michael, pleading with him, *"Save me, please, Michael! I don't want to die! Please don't let it get me!"*

Michael held her close, tears pouring down his face. "We'll die together, Sarah. There's so much I never told you. So much I wanted to. I ..." He cut off as the things neared him.

The crackling sound of bones rubbing together, combined with the stench of death was too much for even Paro to handle. He fell to his knees, tears in his eyes. Melissa was more shocked at that than anything else that was happening. Paro had never cried before. Michael, who had known him longer than anyone else, had once told her that nothing made him tear up.

All around the room the officers, the team, everyone, they were all falling to the ground, trembling, hugging themselves and each other, screaming at the tops of their lungs and begging for mercy or divine intervention, or anything that would make these wicked things disappear.

The creatures spoke—they actually spoke!

"Annnnnddyyyyy," they chanted.

"Annnnnddyyyyy."

Melissa took a moment to gather the situation, struggling against the overwhelming desire to simply die, to lie down and never wake up, if only it meant peace from these creatures.

Why are they chanting Andy's name? Why would they ... Oh my god!

The realization and understanding almost knocked her off her feet. "Paro!" she screamed. "Paro, do you see what's happening here? Hey, Paro!"

Paro was on his knees, trembling, whimpering. Melissa forced her legs to move, she fought against the oppressive sense of death and slammed her fist into his face.

Paro's eyes snapped back to their normal fierce intensity, and he shook his head, looking around him. He looked at Melissa, his expression one of pure gratitude. "You just saved our lives, Melissa, thanks."

"*Sarah!*" Paro roared. "*It's an illusion, and you're a Telepath, fight against it! There are no other Psychs!*"

"*That's impossible,*" she called back. "*I can see them, I can smell and hear them, and I can even feel them! Not even fifty of the strongest Telepaths working together could do this. THIS IS REAL! WE'RE GOING TO DIE!*"

Paro grunted and looked behind him, to where the skeletons had passed him and Melissa and were heading towards Andy. All around the room, the team was now lying face down, crying and groaning. The recon officers were unconscious.

"It's Jack, isn't it?" Melissa asked, tears in her eyes. When Paro nodded she shook her head. "But how? How can one person do this?"

"To even think about that right now is suicide," Paro said. "All that matters is stopping him and not dying. He's killing us, Melissa! Jack is killing us. He's attacking our minds."

The skeletons approached the boy. Andy didn't seem to be breathing any longer. Blood was trickling down his open mouth and even from his eyes.

"*Anddyyyyyy,*" the creatures chuckled, converging on him. They now had human faces, each one bearing the face of a member of the Davin's family.

"*Jack!*" Melissa screamed, louder than she had ever screamed in her life. "*Stop this, now! You're killing us! Please, Jack! You're going to kill all of us!*"

Jack didn't seem to hear her. He was staring at Andy with a blank expression, while the boy seemed to be in a comatose state, bleeding from every orifice. Andy would die within a minute at the rate this was going, and the Recon officers would probably only last another five. If this wasn't stopped within ten minutes then every last person would be dead, besides Jack.

She couldn't let Andy die. Jack would never forgive himself. She had to stop him. She had to stop him before he did something that would ruin his life.

She tried to charge at Jack, but there was a barrier between them. It hurt her to merely touch it and was almost agonizing if the touch was prolonged. Melissa didn't care—it was life or death. With every last bit of power she commanded, she slammed her fist into it with a roar, shattering the defenses Jack had erected. She tackled him to the ground, and all at once, the room was quiet. The skeletons faded, the oppressive feeling was gone too, and all that was left was her lying on top of the weak and fragile-looking Jack.

He looked spent and exhausted, his eyes red from crying.

"Uh-oh, Melissa," he said. "What did you do this time?" He closed his eyes and passed out.

Chapter 22: Brute

Michael's head was fuzzy. The pain had lessened for sure, but his lower mouth was numb, like the feeling of Novocain after a cavity filling. The floor was cold and dusty, and his body ached. With a groan, he pushed himself up into a sitting position, wiping the drool off his mouth with one hand while he picked up his cowboy hat with the other. He shook his head and stood up on uneasy, jittering legs.

Kazou was already back on his feet, and Sarah sat on the floor cradling her knees to her chest, weeping. Paro and Melissa were still near Jack, with the kid's head resting on Melissa's lap. Sometime during the whole ordeal, all of the lights and electricity had gone out of the building, and despite the small windows around the terminal, it was still pretty dark on the lower floor.

Groans and murmurs came from around the room as the nineteen recon officers regained consciousness. Some wept upon awakening, while others picked up their guns, remained silent, and pulled themselves together then returned to work.

There was so much confusion that it almost hurt. Even if an omniscient being were standing by, one capable of correctly answering any question in the world, Michael would still be confused by its answers because he wouldn't know what to ask.

Pull it together.

Despite the gravity of the situation, Michael was surprised to find that his biggest worry wasn't about what had happened, but instead he was more concerned with what he'd said to Sarah. He'd been so sure he was going to die, so certain that his life would be coming to an end. He had almost confessed ...

Michael stretched his muscles and sighed. He loved women. Everyone knew that, and he'd never kept it a secret. He didn't discriminate, either. He loved big women, small women, White, Black, Hispanic, young, old, all of them—it didn't matter. But above them all, he loved Sarah. Michael loved her so much that every time he looked at her he felt a desperate longing and a deep pain in his chest. Sarah was the second member to join Paro's team after him. She was perfect in every way. So kind, so caring, and her smile shone brighter than a star's. But for some reason, he could never get the courage to tell her how he felt, which was the strangest thing. Michael confessed his love to a dozen women a week, most of them perfect strangers. But with her, he couldn't do it, because for Michael, rejection by Sarah would be unbearable.

Within five minutes, everyone was back on their feet. The officers once again had weapons in hand. They shot dirty looks at the unconscious Jack Harris and kept their distance. Michael shook his head in disbelief. People would've started dying in just another few seconds if Melissa hadn't intervened. Lives would have been lost.

The sight of Paro worried Michael. He stood as still as a statue, with his eyes closed. He appeared to be deep in thought, and the fact that he had nothing to say worried everyone, be it Psych or recon officer. Paro was the one everyone looked to when they needed to know what to do. He was their team-leader, and he also held the Psych rank of Captain.

"Sarah," Michael said, "we should go check on the Andy-kid."

Sarah's eyebrows rose and she looked around as if startled. "Ah ... ah yes."

Kazou followed Michael and Sarah to the back of the train terminal, where Andy was lying prone with his eyes still open, but clearly either dead or unconscious. Sarah knelt down and wiped trickles of blood from his eyes, mouth and nose.

The entire situation was awkward and uncomfortable. No one was speaking about what had happened, and Michael didn't think anyone would dare to. Paro didn't help things by remaining silent, either.

"This isn't good," Sarah said. She cupped the boy's face.

"Is he dead?" Michael tried his best to keep panic and worry out of his voice. After all, the boy was a murderer. He'd slaughtered an entire family. If he died, it wouldn't be the end of the world, but if it turned out that Jack was the one who'd killed him, then things would become quite a bit more complicated. Somehow Michael knew that Jack wouldn't recover from the grief of causing someone's death.

"I know what you're thinking," Sarah said, "and not because I'm a Path. For Jack's sake, we can't let Andy die. But Michael, I'm not going to lie to you ... this doesn't look good. I don't know if I can save him. He needs a very powerful Telepath to undo some of this damage. And even then, I think some of it might be permanent. But as of right now, he's comatose."

Michael's heart ached for Sarah. He could tell by the way her legs shook that she was trying her best not to break down again. She was such a caring and considerate soul.

Kazou coughed into his hand, and Michael turned to face him. "Let's not pretend what just happened, didn't." He closed his eyes and breathed deeply. It was always him that brought up the most painful thoughts, and Michael didn't envy him the job. "We need to talk about this. Pretending we're not below ground in a broken train terminal with a dead body and a comatose child isn't going to get us anywhere." Kazou's words stung Michael, but they were the truth.

Michael sighed. "I just don't know anymore. I don't know if any of this is real. Heck, I don't know if *I'm* even real anymore, fellas. What I just saw, whatever that was. I just ... I don't even have the words to explain it. What words, what sentences can I put together to describe how messed up this is, ya know? I don't even know why I'm babbling right now. What Jack just did has shaken my entire world. Nothing makes sense anymore."

"I know how you feel," Kazou said, his voice but a whisper.

Michael rubbed his eyes and looked at Sarah. "Didn't you tell me once that most Telepaths could only do this kind of stuff in a dream or something? I don't know much about you Paths, but I always thought that illusions—even if done by the most powerful Telepaths—could only be seen by the person they're being used on and that even then it's very limited."

Sarah nodded. "That's what I thought. When I was much younger and studying my affinity, three of the most powerful Telepaths created an illusion together, one that everyone in the study group was able to see. For just one second, the briefest moment in time, they made a three-leaved clover look like it was a four-leaf clover, and that was considered an incredible feat, because together, three of our strongest were able to make something that more than one person could see while awake. And even then it was only for the briefest of moments, like the time it takes the light to fade when you turn off a light-switch."

Michael was exhausted, tired, and confused. He looked over to Jack and sighed. "Then how, Sarah? How in the hell did what just happened, well, happen?"

Sarah trembled, clearly on the verge of tears. Her voice cracked as she spoke. "I don't know, Michael. I just don't know. I wondered at first if the illusion itself was an illusion. But that makes no sense. I guess the only explanation is that Jack is just that powerful."

Kazou visibly shook. A look of fierce sadness entered his eyes, as he too seemed ready to weep. "You two know what we must do then, yes?"

Sarah looked at Michael with a blank face, and then back at Kazou. What was he talking about?

"We have to report him," Kazou said. "Right now."

Sarah's mouth gaped, and Michael leaned in closer. Was he mishearing?

"The hell did you just say, Kazou?" Michael demanded. "I'm gonna pretend I didn't just hear that."

"Well you did. I'm sorry that you like the kid. I do too. But he's a monster."

Michael stepped forward and pointed a threatening finger at his team-member. "Are you nuts? Did you seriously just suggest we *report* one of our own? Have you totally, utterly, and completely lost yer mind!"

"Don't look at me like I'm some kind of animal, Michael. You saw what Jack did."

"And?"

"What do you mean, 'and'?"

"I mean, and so what? Okay, so Jack is stronger than we thought. What's your point?"

Kazou was never one to raise his voice or show much emotion, but now he squinted his eyes and put ferocity into his shout.

"And no one in this world should be allowed to exist with that much power!"

Michael clenched his teeth and lost his cool. "What gives you the right to say who gets to exist, Kazou? Who the hell do you think you are?"

"Look around you, fool! This kid almost sent all of us to the grave. He is a monster, a demon. I don't want to see him ever again!"

That was the last straw. Drawing power into himself, Michael ripped free a bolted-down wooden-bench in the distance and flung it full speed towards Kazou, who responded by slamming his fist into it, shattering it on impact. The bench exploded and sent woodchips scattering.

"You wanna go, buddy!" Michael yelled. "I'm right here, brute. That's right. You're nothing but a brute."

The recon officers remained frozen. They all turned to watch the two prepare to brawl. They normally tried to stay out of matters concerning Psych teams, especially internal conflicts.

Kazou puckered his lips and snarled. "You do *not* get to call me a brute, Kinetic-scum! I'll break your face and spit on the pieces."

"Enough!" Paro shouted. His eyes snapped open and he positioned himself between the two of them. "Kazou, it is not, and will *never* be your decision who I report. If you ever again attempt to supersede my authority, I'll show you a world of pain that even you won't be able to handle."

Michael grinned while he watched Paro scold Kazou. He stuck out his tongue at the buff Reinforcer, but he regretted it immediately. Paro whirled around and grabbed Michael by his shirt, forcing Michael to meet his wrathful gaze. Paro didn't look happy, and he was terrifying when he got like this. Michael gulped.

"And you!" he growled. "Do not ever let me hear you call one of my Reinforcers a 'brute' again, do you understand me? If I ever hear you refer to either Kazou or Melissa with that word, I'll personally allow them to teach you how that derogatory term got started. *Do you understand me?"*

Michael bit his lip to stop it from quivering. He nodded without making a sound. Paro released his shirt. "Good. Now, pack up, sedate the Harris-kid, and get back to H.Q. I don't want him waking up any time in the near future, not until I figure out what in the hell just happened."

The recon officers were already watching the fight, so they didn't need to be told separately. They starting packing up and making preparations to leave. Michael joined Kazou and Sarah while they assisted in moving Andy and Jack.

He felt bad about using the 'B-word' against Kazou, but he was outraged. There was so much to figure out, so much confusion. Things had gotten way out of control.

"I'm sorry, Kazou. I know how much Reinforcers hate that word."

"It's alright. It's not the first time we've clashed. I'm just glad we were stopped before things got too far out of hand."

Jack Harris, Michael thought while he climbed up the stairs to exit the terminal. *Nothing has been the same since you entered our lives.*

Chapter 23: No Shouting

The smell of freshly baked brownies wafted through the air, and the kitchen was warmed by the hot oven. Alana nodded in approval—everything was coming along great. Jack was going to love them. She closed the oven door and flipped off the internal light.

Through the corner of her eyes, she spotted the old cat-shaped clock sitting snugly on top of the wall by the kitchen entrance. She frowned.

Jack should really be getting home around now.

She forced the thoughts from her mind. There was no sense in getting paranoid over nothing. She was happy her boy was a Telekinetic like his momma. There was so much she was going to (forcefully) make him learn. The thought made her grin. She loved Jack more than anything in the world, but he was simply too fun to mess with.

She gave the brownies one last look before starting on dinner. Melissa would be coming over tonight, and she loved talking with the girl. Jack was definitely going to be annoyed. Alana would probably end up spending more time with Melissa than he would while the two of them engaged in girl-talk.

She sung out loud to herself while she prepared dinner.

Paro made sure he met each one of their eyes while he spoke. "I have one rule and one rule only. No one is to speak at a volume above the conversational level I am using right now. Every single one of you will get your say, I promise. But if anyone so much as raises their voice, or speaks with an angry or demeaning tone, I will dole out punishment on the spot. And you know me well enough to know I'm not bluffing."

Paro looked around the planning room. Each member of his team looked each other in the eye and nodded.

"Now," Paro began, "let me make it perfectly clear that no one here, not even myself, knows how Jack did what he did, why he did what he did, or even *what* it was that he actually did. I won't waste any more time discussing it. I am allowing us to discuss his fate as a group, because I feel that as a team, you have earned at least that much. Though the decision ultimately is mine, I'm weighing in everything you say. This, I promise."

"That feeling," Sarah said. Her eyes were down trodden, and she looked exhausted. "It was like when that general Deven Moore paid us a visit, only it was so much worse."

Melissa raised a questioning eyebrow, and Sarah filled her in. She had been in school during that frightening ordeal.

Of everyone on the team, she seemed to be taking this the worst. During the nightmarish event, Melissa had remained calm and really proved her worth. Had it not been for her actions, they'd all be dead. But now that the situation had calmed down, Melissa looked sick with worry.

Paro noticed that Michael was almost shaking with anticipation, so Paro nodded and allowed him to speak next.

"Look, fellas, I know we're worn and shaken up from what just happened. But let's remember who Jack is and what he is. I don't think he did what he did on purpose. Remember how he had no idea he started the fire? Well, I think it's kinda like that."

Kazou sighed. "I never for a moment thought he meant to do any of this."

"Then why do you—"

"Let me finish, Michael. The fact that I agree with you is not a good thing. Jack could've killed every one of us. You, me, all of us, we all came very close to lying in caskets while being lowered into the ground. I *am* sorry that I called him a demon earlier, but Michael, after what we all just saw, Jack Harris should never be allowed out in public again. What he did was so unbelievable that I'm no longer positive he's even a human being."

Melissa balled her hands into fists and gritted her teeth while she listened to Kazou speak, and Paro gave her a warning glance. He wasn't in the mood for her attitude.

Sarah shocked the room with what she said next. "I agree with Kazou. It would be irresponsible of us to allow that boy around people again. I'm the only one here with an affinity for Telepathy, so you don't know what I felt. You can't even begin to understand it."

Tears flowed down her delicate face. Paro's heart warmed whenever he took in Sarah. She was as kind as she was brilliant. Her black hair hung from a ponytail behind her head, and her soft cheeks brightened as she spoke.

With each passing day, Paro felt increasingly uneasy in her presence. He had promised himself he would never love, his work was too important for relationships. Yet every time he looked at her, he felt emotions he didn't know he still had.

For her to suggest turning in Jack, she must be really, really shaken up. Never, would the Sarah I know be willing to give up on someone.

"Jack is a good boy," she whimpered, "but I just don't know what to do anymore. If he's ever allowed in public, what will happen if he does that again, whatever it even was. Oh, God, I thought there were twenty or thirty Telepaths surrounding us. I know we're not supposed to bring it up, and I'm sorry, Paro, but no human being should've been able to do what he did."

"Only as far as we know," Melissa said. They all turned to her. She was finally breaking the silent state she'd been in since they flew the unconscious Jack and Andy back to H.Q.

The situation was beyond serious—it would be more accurate to call it dire or perhaps even cataclysmic. Yet despite the world-shaking events that had just taken place, Paro had only been able to think of how upset Jack would be if he knew he'd flown in a helicopter while he was asleep and didn't get to enjoy the ride. It maddened Paro just how much the boy had changed him in such a short time.

"The way I see it," Melissa continued, "we don't know much about the higher ranks, do we? Paro, I know you're not allowed to go into specific details, but can you at least confirm to us that when you attained the rank of Captain you were told secrets and other stuff that most of us are forbidden to know?"

Paro nodded. "That I can."

"So then, who knows how powerful some of the higher-up Psychs are? I know I'm still new to all this, but they never really show us what they're capable of. Maybe Jack just has the strength of a General. I mean, didn't you say this Deven Moore did something similar?"

Even Michael had to shake his head at that. "Only slightly, Melissa. Sure, the guy did something weird that made us feel like running away and whatnot, but he didn't conjure creatures of the night to murder us."

"Regardless, does that mean he couldn't?"

Paro had to admire Melissa's thought process. She was correct about the lack of information. Nobody had any real idea of just how powerful the Generals were. And while Deven Moore had created a similar oppressive feel, that didn't mean he was using all his power at the time. But still, Paro thought it unlikely that anyone in the world had ever done what Jack just had. The mere thought of it made him tremble.

"There's one thing you guys aren't taking into consideration," Michael said. "Sarah, if we report Jack, he won't be locked away for long and ya gotta know that. The Op. teams'll pick someone like him right up. You think what Jack did was dangerous now? What about when he's forced to use his abilities with the intent to kill?"

Kazou's eyes became dark. He cleared his throat. Now, there was a terrible look to his face, and Paro was almost afraid of what he'd say.

"I've been thinking that same thing ever since we left the train terminal. Life can be cruel, life can be harsh, but life is still life. Much like you, I can't bear the thought of Jack ending up as a killing machine, and we alone know the danger he possesses to this world. The boy is unconscious, at peace. I will be willing, if allowed, to do what *must* be done. We could put him to sleep. He'd never feel a thing. I know it would kill us inside, but—"

"*To hell with the rules!*" Melissa shouted in a high-pitched wail. She leapt out of her leather chair and jumped on top of the glass table then sprinted across and lunged at Kazou, knocking him out of his own chair and onto the floor. She pulled back her fist and crashed it down onto his face, sending blood spraying from his nose.

Paro was so shocked by what he was seeing that he froze for a moment. In that instant, Melissa picked Kazou off the floor and slammed him into the glass table, shattering it with a loud and deafening clatter. The large Japanese man was smashed clean through it and again landed on the floor.

He howled and grabbed her by the shirt with one hand, and with the other he slammed his fist into the side of her face, flinging her backward.

Melissa was sent crashing into a wall, knocking diagrams and bulletins to the floor, and Paro recovered from his shock immediately. There were few things certain in the world of Psychs, but if there was one thing that was almost guaranteed it was this—when two Reinforcers clashed, one almost always died.

Paro put his incredible disappointment in the two aside and drew a great deal of power into himself. He'd always had an affinity for Reinforcement, but upon learning he was an Unrestricted, he spent a great deal of time studying Telekinesis and Manipulation. Telepathy was the only affinity he seldom bothered with.

With a strength born of natural talent combined with years of practice, Paro narrowed his eyes and focused on the two. As if grabbed by invisible, powerful arms, the two were separated and flung to opposite ends of the room, crashing into walls with a loud bang and hanging against them like dartboards.

Michael and Sarah were sitting in their chairs wide-eyed. Their arms dangled in midair where just moments before they rested on the now shattered table.

"What did I just say, you foolish, silly brutes!" Paro snapped at them. "Oh, you don't like that word, do you? *Well maybe you shouldn't act like them!*"

The two turned and glared at Paro, furious at the derogatory term, but after a moment they simply looked ashamed, especially Melissa. Paro released the two, and they slid down the wall and landed on their rears. The door to the planning room slammed open, and five Psychs of various affinities rushed in with almost a dozen security officers in tow.

"Is everything alright in here, Captain?" asked the first woman to rush in. She was Amanda Pierce, Telekinetic and team-leader of her own. The people that followed her in were her members.

"Ah, everything is fine, just a little accident."

She eyed him with suspicion as she looked around the room at the broken table, the Japanese man with the broken nose, and the ruined bulletins and diagrams littering the floor.

"Two Reinforcers just went at it, didn't they?" she mused.

"Can we keep this quiet please, Amanda?"

She laughed. "You owe me a drink. Come on, guys, this isn't our problem."

She left the room and the security officers followed in suit. Paro waited until they were out of earshot before turning his eyes back to his two idiot Reinforcers.

"I'm disappointed in you both." Melissa and Kazou both got to their feet and dusted themselves off.

"Melissa, you started this fight. The table, the bulletins, everything is coming out of your pay. Kazou, for you to even suggest what you just did ... you're lucky I don't report *that*. Euthanizing a member of *my* team, are you out of your mind? Every day I wonder why you don't join the Op. teams. It seems that each day I'm finding more and more about this bloodlust you have, and as your team-leader, I'm wondering where I've failed you."

Kazou looked more than a little ashamed. A look of deep regret and humiliation came into his eyes, as the usually stone-faced Kazou shed a single tear of his own.

"*Gomennasai,*" he whispered. He bowed and closed his eyes, before turning around and leaving the room.

Damn, now I have to feel guilty, Paro thought.

He had been too hard on him, and now he was the one who should be ashamed, but what Kazou had suggested was not only inappropriate, it was among the most disgusting suggestions any member of his team had ever made on the topic of anything!

"I've decided," Paro said, and with his words, the team snapped alert. "Wake up the Harris-kid and fly him back before his mother throws a hissy fit. I'll call her and tell her we got held up or something. I'll make an excuse. We've got no other choice. Kazou was right about one thing, though—we can't let him become a killing machine. So, as a team we'll just have to fight through this. I don't know what that thing with his eyes was, but Melissa, if you ever see him do that again, knock him the hell out before he gets to so much as blink with them."

Despite having torn her clothes on the glass and having several scrapes and bruises, she seemed to beam with relief and happiness. "You got it, Paro! I'll wake him up now. Wait, what happens when you wake up someone who's sedated?"

"Five more minutes!" Jack pleaded, tossing and turning on some weird, bed-thing. Where was he? Whatever, he didn't care. He was too tired for it to matter where he was or what he was sleeping on.

"Jack, get up—now!" It was Melissa's voice. His eyes shot open and he looked around him. He was in some kind of hospital room, with a needle and IV-bag sticking out of his arm. Jack opened his mouth to scream, but Melissa covered it.

"Don't worry. We're taking that out now, just relax."

A man in a white coat walked over and removed the needle while Melissa held him down. "There we are, Mr. Harris. You're up and ready to go."

Melissa ruffled his messy hair, looking as beautiful as always, although she was scraped up like she'd just been in a fist fight.

"So, how do you feel, Jack?"

"Ah, you know, as good as can be expected given the current economic climate."

Melissa sighed. "Why do I even ask?"

"Where are we?" he asked.

"You're in H.Q, on the second lowest floor of our building, quite a bit below ground, actually. We keep our med-center and temporary holding areas here."

Jack wiped his eyes. His vision was slightly blurry. It was cold in the room, which really did look like one from a hospital. There was a sink, needles everywhere, and cabinets with medicine. The walls were all white and there was a medical smell to the place.

"How did I get here?"

For some reason, Melissa looked taken aback, but when she spoke, she sounded like she was reciting something from memory.

"Andy hit you over the head pretty hard and you blacked out. It's okay, though. We stopped him. He's in custody one floor below us."

So I couldn't save him. Jack filled with sadness.

"Anyway," Melissa said, her face brightening with cheer. "I've got some good news. We're going to fly you home. We don't want your mom to worry now, do we? I know you've been itching for another helicopter ride."

Jack's eyes widened at the news, and he couldn't help but smile. "What are we waiting for then, let's go!"

Chapter 24: Brother

Carla made sure the boy was secured as she closed the back door of the truck. All she wanted was to finish the job and get home to her son, but the damned captain was making it difficult for her.

"Like I just said, and will only say once more—you can interrogate him at the facility. The orders are to bring him there at once, and that's what I'm doing."

Carla didn't care that the man was a captain, and why would she? Her orders superseded his. But the man was being more than just a little stubborn. Carla was not a mean person, or even a pushy person, but when you're a mom in your mid-forties with parental responsibilities, you don't always have the time to waste discussing matters that have already been settled.

"Listen to me," the man said. "I need the information in this child's head. It could very well mean the difference between life and death for a great many people. You can have him after we've revived him *here* and gotten what we need from him."

"And you listen to *me*, Mr. Puro, or Paro, or whoever the hell you are," she growled in retort. "A Commander has already given the order to take him to facility-B. If you want, you can see him first thing in the morning. Now, if you'll excuse me, it's already past dark and he should've been there by now. Out of my way."

She didn't give the man a chance to respond. She was so sick of arguing with idiots. Carla double checked the locks and restraints then made sure the bed the boy lay on was secure. The last thing she needed was to explain to her superiors why their prisoner was rolling around the highway.

The transport van was large. It was wide in the back with room for up to fifteen to be seated comfortably. Although, at the moment there were only seven of them, with her being the only Psych. Truth be told, she didn't really need to be there—she never did, but it was all standard procedure. All criminal transports required at least seven recon officers and one Psych.

"Doug, we ready to go?" Carla asked the man sitting behind the wheel. All seven men were armed with standard assault rifles, dark blue T.A.C jackets, and non-constrictive helmets.

"Moving out, Carla," he said.

There were no windows except the driver's in the front, so a sudden lurch in her stomach was the only indication she had to know they were accelerating. Facility-B was located in the Harbor off Staten Island. Given current traffic conditions and expected construction sites, she estimated a travel time of two hours.

Carla looked over at the unconscious boy. She was tempted to close his eyes. The way he seemed to be almost starting at her, it was more than just a little creepy. They were wide-open, bloodshot, and had an unnerving look to them, as if they were saying that whatever had put him in a coma was something beyond terrifying.

Carla was not a member of the Investigative or Operations departments. She was offered a job in both, but she didn't feel either was right for her. Psychs like her didn't have a name—they were just workers. Her specialty—if it could *really* be called that—was in prisoner transport. In other words, she got to sleep in the back of slow moving vehicles while comatose murderers gave her creepy looks.

The ride seemed to drag on, as the occasional bump woke her from her doze. She wasn't really supposed to be sleeping, but in the close to twenty years she'd been doing this, the only action she ever saw was a few car accidents.

She tried to doze off again but noticed that something was a bit off. The bumping had stopped for almost two minutes, and she no longer felt the movement of the vehicle.

"Doug, why aren't we moving?" she asked.

"There's a young woman lying on the street up ahead. Carla, you have to see this."

Carla unbuckled her seatbelt and walked to the front of the van. It was dark, and for Manhattan, the street held surprisingly few people, although some still shuffled about. Ahead of them, she saw the girl.

She was on her stomach with her left arm stretched out in front of her and her right extended to the side. Her face was turned, and her cheek rested on the pavement. This part of Manhattan wasn't as dense on traffic as others, but it *was* still Manhattan. How did nobody see her?

"You three." She pointed to the nearest three officers. "Go see if she's okay."

"*Yes ma'am!*"

The three officers leaped out of the back of the vehicle and ran over to examine the girl.

"So, Doug, how's the wife?"

The man sighed. "Well, she's a wife, if that answers the question."

The two shared a laugh. "Dougie, how many years have you been married now? You've given me that same answer since we started. You must love her to death if you're still with her."

Doug smiled. "Well, of course I do. But it's just that lately I don't feel like we share the same interests anymore. For instance, just yesterday—"

The sound of a bloodcurdling scream cut him off.

Carla whipped her head around and looked out the front window. Her heart almost gave out, as she saw the three recon officers on the floor, wailing and coughing up blood.

"What in the hell?" Carla leaped out the back of the vehicle, and ran toward them. "You three, what happened? Are you okay?"

There was no response, though Carla didn't expect one. They were leaking blood so fast that it looked like their mouths were fountains. A deep puddle of the stuff formed around the blue-suited bodies. Carla forced herself to remain calm, or at least she tried to, but she wasn't doing a very good job of it.

The other four officers rushed to her side, and she signaled for Doug to remain in the vehicle. They had weapons out and loaded, but each one of them looked scared out of their wits. These men had never had to use their weapons, and they probably never thought they would.

Carla looked around and tried to get an idea of what'd happened, and immediately she noticed the girl they had spotted from the road was now nowhere to be seen.

"Did anyone see where she went?"

They were on a narrow street, with entrances to shabby-looking apartments on both sides. A few small restaurants lined the block, but on the whole, they were in a low-income residential area. A cat jumped over a trash can off to the side, giving them pointed looks before crawling on.

"Well?"

The men glanced around at each other, but no one offered a word in reply. Not that it mattered, for only a few seconds passed before Carla heard yet another scream, this time from the van.

"Doug!" she cried.

Doug's lifeless corpse smashed through the front window of the van and was sent hurtling at her, flying at a speed so fast that she barely had time to jump out of the way. She leaped, and the body collided with the officer standing behind her, knocking him to the ground.

She remained frozen, so did the only three officers still on their feet. One by one, her men were dropping like flies, and she didn't even know who their enemy was. Carla felt an acidic bubble of fear in her gut. She wondered if she was only moments away from the end of her life.

The van shook, and she knew that whatever was still inside it was coming out. The men leveled their guns and waited for their tormenters.

The two that came out, were two of the oddest people Carla had ever seen. One was a beautiful young woman, with exotic red hair and a look of madness so deeply embedded into her expression that Carla wondered if she was born with it.

The other was a laid-back, tall, black-haired young man. He didn't have the crazy-look like the other one did. In fact, he appeared genuinely happy, yet upon closer inspection there was sadness present too, beneath the carefree exterior.

Carla loved to watch movies. She watched so many movies, that their influence on her was apparent even in the way she spoke. Upon seeing these two, she was expected to offer them an opportunity to surrender, to turn themselves in. But from a lifetime of watching cheesy action flicks, coupled with a growing collection of dead recon officers, Carla wanted these two dead before her next breath. It was always the hesitation that got the characters in movies killed.

"Open fire, now!"

The three officers didn't need to be told twice. They clicked off their safeties and unloaded a volley of fire into the two approaching Psychs. The guns were loud, and the deafening roar of bullets actually made her feel safer in a way. The dark Manhattan alley lit up with grandeur as the flashing of three assault rifles pumped bullets into the distance.

The men emptied their clips, refusing to take their fingers off the trigger until every last bullet had left their guns. They were just as shaken up as Carla was. Even with the sound of gunfire she could still hear the empty shells clinging as they hit the ground.

When the men had ceased firing, and yet the two remained side-by-side completely unharmed, Carla struggled with everything she was made of to resist the urge to flee.

Calm down, girl, she told herself. *All this means is that one of them is a Kinetic. We don't need bullets to deal with them.*

Carla took no chances. She drew every last bit of power she was capable of grasping, and let it pour into herself. She was a Manipulator, the deadliest of all Psych affinities. She would melt their faces before they took another step.

Narrowing her eyes on the two, she threw everything she had at them. Kinetics might be able to stop bullets, but they couldn't stop this.

Carla gasped, as small puffs of smoke materialized a foot away from the man's face. Her attacks were being stopped by something.

Does that mean the other one is a Path?

Carla doubled her efforts. Even if one of them was a Telepath, if she overwhelmed their defenses and broke through whatever it was they were doing, she would make it out of this alive. She poured every last drop of power she had into her attack, and the smoke came closer and closer to the young man's face, now only a few inches away. Once her attack connected, it would be over. His facial tissue would melt and fall off his head, and he'd drop to the floor as dead as the men he'd just killed.

"Ruin, Darling, this one is trying to push me back? Why are we toying with it?"

"Because, sister, it is more fun if they think they have a chance."

Carla tried to ignore their banter. It was nothing more than a distracting tactic. She pushed even harder, sweating with the effort, as the smoke came closer, and closer, to the man's face. When it was within an inch, it stopped. It wouldn't budge even a drop farther. The young woman seemed to be panting with the exertion of keeping up their defense. It gave Carla an idea.

"Men, reload! Open another round of fire. They can't stop the bullets and my Manipulation at the same time!"

Understanding dawned on the faces of three remaining recon officers. They attempted to reload. Before a single one of them could finish, lampposts, sewer grates, and manhole covers— all of these objects ripped free from whatever was holding them in the surrounding area and soared at the recon officers.

Carla and one other officer ducked, but the other two were not so lucky. The officer standing to the left of her had just enough time to cry in surprise as the soaring piece of metal made contact with his skull, killing him, but at the very least he died in an instant.

The other officer was not so lucky. The pointed end of a lamppost skewered him. Carla tripled her efforts, trying so hard to break through their defenses that she screamed with the exertion. Her voice cried out in a loud bellow as she used all her power in an attempt to push that final inch.

Eventually her knees gave out and she fell to the floor. The Telepath was just too strong. She was exhausted and worn. She lay on her back, looking up at the night sky, as she half-listened to the screaming sounds of dying men around her. Eventually her vision of the starry sky was blocked. The young woman's twisted face hovered over her.

"Do you know what happens now, Darling?"

Carla cried, "Please! I don't know who you two are, just go away!"

"Come here, brother," she called to the young man. She put her hands over her brother's eyes and he smiled.

"Ohh," he said, "you have such a lovely heart, ma'am. I can see it beating. I can see the valves that are connected to it. Anatomy is so interesting, isn't it?"

Carla shrieked as the realization dawned on her. *The Telepath! Kinetic's can only move what they can see, so that woman ... she's showing him my insides.*

She shivered, her fear reaching a level of intensity that crippled her. "Please! Don't do this!" she screamed. "Somebody, anybody, help! Oh God, please, help! I don't want this ..."

The young woman licked her lips. "Oh, Ruin, Darling, I do love it when they scream. If only it were the pig-woman lying here and not this other cow."

The man, Ruin, laughed. "Oh, dearest Requiem, we'll have our chance. Let's just kill this creature and save our Brother. Hmm, you'd think with all the times we've done this I'd have an idea of how the human heart works. I still don't, it's amazing. Like, what happens if I cut that little valve thing, sister, do you see it? The one to the right of where you're showing me."

"I don't know, Darling, but there's a way to find out, isn't there?"

Before the pain, there was blood. Carla coughed up a stream of dark red blood, slowing into a small trickle gliding over her lips and splashing the floor, painting it the color of death.

Then came the pain. It was the most unbearable, intense, and overwhelming sensation of agony. It exploded in her, so powerful and horrible that it blocked every other sense. Sight, sound, smell, none of these things existed for her. There was just the pain.

She couldn't even form words anymore, but that didn't stop her from trying. Each whimper ended in vomiting more blood. She wanted to die—she wanted nothing more than for it to be over. Tears fell but no one seemed to care. Her whole existence was one of torment. She looked pleadingly at the Kinetic who took great pleasure at tearing her from the inside.

"*Mphm,*"

She tried to speak, but yet again, she only caused another stream of blood to shoot out, landing on the man's shoe.

"What happens if I cut this one?"

Mom, Dad, I love you both so much, she thought as she turned her head to the sky. *Please, if you're up there, please take care of Justin. It hurts, Mom, it hurts so badly. Please, Mom, please...*

She felt it again—the sensation of something inside her being sliced. This time all she could manage was a moan. She wiggled back and forth on the ground and grabbed her chest, trying to hold and comfort herself. It didn't matter. There was no longer anything that could be done. Somehow, the pain continued to increase, making her wonder just how much a person could feel.

How was her son going to brave the world without her? Or her sister, who needed payments on her medical bills? She tried to look to the sky again, but her head would no longer move, it hung lifelessly to the side. She could still feel all the pain, but now she was paralyzed, unable to move a single muscle.

Eventually the pain dulled, and for that, she was grateful. She was finally dying. She almost wanted to laugh at how ridiculous it was to feel good about that.

As the light left her eyes, and the world turned to darkness, she wondered what, if anything would come next.

Chapter 25: Jack Harris, the Woman-Hunter

Tonight's the night, Jack thought with delight as the warm water hit his back. Grabbing the shampoo behind him, he squeezed a glob into his hand and lathered it into his messy black hair. It was like he was being given a second chance. Tonight, Melissa was not only here for dinner, but she was ... it was almost too much for Jack to even think it.

She was sleeping over!

Jack tried to remind himself that this was all for the sake of catching the two remaining murderers and also for his own safety. Melissa had told Alana that her parents were out of town and that she didn't want to be alone. Without even a moment's hesitation, Jack's mom had set out to prepare the guest room.

Speaking of my mom, Jack thought. *I really need to put a stop to whatever it is that's going on with them.*

Melissa and his mom were becoming way too much like friends. He suspected it was because neither of them had many their own age. The two acted like they were long-time friends whenever they saw each other, and Jack was going to need to put a cork in that right away.

When they'd gotten off the helicopter—the ride was just as awesome as the first one—Alana picked them up at some empty-field they'd landed in. Paro explained to Alana that Jack needed to use certain equipment in H.Q to aid in his learning, which was actually true. Before they left H.Q, Michael had made him wear some kind of helmet-thing he said was meant for newer Psychs, telling Jack that it helped diminish some of that sickening, uncomfortable feeling of drawing power. Jack had been surprised when it actually worked, but even then, it was still the worst sensation in the world.

Alana made it clear to Paro that as long as Jack didn't get home too late, he could take Jack wherever he wanted, and so once again Jack was forced to play along with yet another in a series of lies to his mom. It really grated him. Jack hated lying. Not only wasn't he any good at lying, but even when he was able to get away with one it made him feel dirty.

Jack ran his hands through his hair, scrubbing out the day's grime, shaking his head as he delighted in the warm water. He went to reach for the soap—and stopped. For a brief moment a thought came to his mind, a memory, only to leave in the same quick flash in which it arrived.

Andy, Jack thought. *Did I do something terrible to you? Why do I feel like I did?*

Jack forced the thought from his mind, stepping out of the shower and drying himself off. He dressed in a hurry—he needed to be fast. At that very moment, Melissa was downstairs chatting away with his mom, and he didn't want them saying anything embarrassing about him behind his back.

Even with his need to make haste, Jack knew that he couldn't just go charging downstairs. He needed tactical support. He needed the one person in the entire world who could finally help him get the girl of his dreams.

Despite the fact that he was in a windowless bathroom, Jack still looked around the small room, making sure he wasn't being watched. He crouched down and opened a drawer under his sink and retrieved a small device, placing it inside his ear.

"Sexy, this is Stud, do you copy?"

"Stud, this is Sexy, loud and clear, over."

Jack grinned. He shouldn't have stolen the device, he knew it was wrong, but this was the only way he was going to win Melissa over. He needed Intel and tactical support. He didn't like the ridiculous names, but he was forced to agree to them or risk not receiving any aid.

"Sexy, are you sure I should start by asking how her day was? Because I was there for most of it, and I don't think it was all that good, over."

"I reckon you might be right about that, Stud. But ya gotta understand how the ladies think. They want a guy that's gonna show some interest in them, ya know? Okay, I know, tell her how nice her nails look. She had them done a few days ago, over."

Jack's eyes lit up. "Whoa! I never would have thought of that! I never even noticed, over."

"We guys never do, over."

The device was so tiny that neither of them would see it in his ear. Technology really was amazing these days, and Jack was glad for it. Operation Women-Hunt would succeed, Jack would see to it. This was his chance. This was the moment he'd been waiting for.

Jack crept at a careful and slow pace towards the top of the stairs. He peered over it, out of sight of the two women below him. His mother and Melissa were engaged in some fiery debate about the best shop in the mall.

"Sexy, they're engaged in some form of debate, do I interrupt? Over."

"Don't speak the first word, Stud. You need to walk in and ignore both of them. Pretend you don't even see them. Then, when they address you first, make contact, over."

Jack nodded, knowing that "Sexy" could actually see the situation too. Somehow, the device gave him a visual as well. Some stuff was just so amazing. Jack didn't bother wondering how it all worked, but he was still grateful that it did.

He crept down the stairs at a casual walk, entering the kitchen and taking care not to give the two ladies so much as a single glance. He opened the fridge and leaned in to grab the carton of milk. He stopped.

"Not today, Stud," Sexy began, "you're a bad-boy now. We need something a bit more dangerous if we want to impress Melissa."

Jack reached for the bottle of *Patron Café* his mom kept in the lowest fridge-shelf and took it out. He closed the refrigerator and spun around, walking over to the table and taking a seat across from where Melissa and Alana were sitting. They stopped speaking and gave him an odd look, but said nothing.

Jack took a plastic cup off the stack in the middle of the table and looked down on it in confusion. After a few seconds of remaining motionless, Sexy came to the rescue.

"Oh! I see what's going on, Stud. You don't know how much to pour. I forgot you've never had alcohol before. Okay, fill it up about one-third the way, and that should be good enough. The stuff is powerful though, so watch out."

Jack continued to remain motionless. The voice on the other end sighed. "One-third is the same as saying, 'imagine if you could divide the cup into three pieces', each piece is one-third. Come on, Stud, even I know that much."

Jack ignored the slight feeling of bitterness he felt as he poured a small amount of the liquid into the plastic cup.

He thinks he's so smart and perfect just because he knows fractions, Jack thought, annoyed.

Jack refocused himself on the task at hand, making himself forget the annoyance at the demeaning tone that Sexy had used with him.

"Umm, sweetie?" Alana said. She and Melissa raised an eyebrow at each other. "Why are you pouring yourself alcohol?"

"Yeah," Melissa added. "What gives?"

Jack took a deep breath and prepared himself. The voice in his ear chimed in as well.

"It's now or never, Stud. Just do it exactly like we rehearsed. You'll be fine, bud."

Jack reached into the pocket of his black jeans with a shaking, nervous hand, and took out a pair of black sunglasses. Placing it over his face, he forced himself to wear his most confident and cocky grin, as he met Melissa's gaze.

"Because, honey, I need to get my freak on," Jack said, draining the black liquid in one massive gulp.

Wow, this doesn't taste that bad, it's actually not bad at ...

Jack had to use every drop of willpower not to spit out the burning black liquid. It was awful, it was painful, and it was among the worst things he'd ever tasted!

Oh dear god, he thought. *This is awful! Keep it together, Jack. Keep it together!*

Jack didn't think his internal struggle showed on his face, so he was probably still in the green. He got up and put the bottle away and returned to sit down at the table.

"So, Melissa, did you get your nails done? They look lovely, I mean, they're just so incredible."

Melissa gave Jack a suspicious, inquiring look. She turned to Alana, who seemed to be doing the same. For a brief moment, a look of amusement entered Melissa's expression, but it was replaced soon after by a grin.

"So, Jack, what's with the glasses? What's with the drinking?" Melissa asked.

Jack repeated out loud what the voice was telling him. "Babe, sometimes I like to play on the dangerous side of things. I'd show you, but I don't think you could handle it. Some people are just too hot to handle, sweetheart, and you just stumbled on one."

"Oh yea, is that right?" Melissa gave Alana a wink and stood up from the table. She walked over to where Jack was sitting and came to stand in front of him. Jack's heart beat faster as he wondered what she was up to.

She put her hands on his shoulders and pushed both him and his chair out a bit, so that it was no longer under the table. Jack croaked out loud as she sat on his lap, facing him.

IS THIS HAPPENING? Jack was screaming on the inside.

She ran her hands along his face. She lifted up his sunglasses and made him meet her beautiful, blue eyes. She ruffled his hair and moved her hands to hold the side of his face. Melissa tilted his head to the side, and before Jack could stop her, in one quick swipe she plucked the Comm-unit out of his ear.

"I can explain!" Jack cried, his voice high-pitched and broken.

Melissa got off Jack, and Alana burst out laughing. Melissa joined in soon after. "Did you know, Mrs. Harris?" she said in between laughing fits.

"Oh yeah, that was painfully obvious."

Jack sat paralyzed with shame. Melissa raised her palm to her mouth with the small device resting inside her hand. "Nice try,

Michael. I wonder what Paro's going to think when he finds out you and Jack stole expensive technology for such a stupid reason."

Even from where Jack was sitting, he could hear the voice shouting out of the other end, in a fake Russian accent. *"Is no Michael, girl, my name is a Vlad."*

Melissa put the device in her pocket and silenced the voice, causing Alana to burst out into another fit of laughter. They looked at Jack, a look of both disappointment and amusement in each of their eyes.

"Really, Jack? How dumb do you think I am, trying to seduce me with such stupid lines?"

Jack stood up and blushed. "That's not what happened, Melissa, I was only—"

For some reason Jack lost his balance and almost tripped over his char. "I was-was only, umm, what was I saying?"

"Haha! Look, Melissa, our little Jack is drunk."

Jack yelled at the two. "You-you don't know what it is ... what it is you're trying to know!" Jack wondered if his words made any sense. After a moment in thought, he realized they did. Melissa pulled him in and gave him a playful kiss on the cheek. "Try something a little more creative next time, Jack." She returned to her seat next to Alana.

Jack went to sit down and instead fell to the floor, landing with a thud on his bottom.

Oh yeah, he remembered. *The chair was over there.*

"So, this is where the Harris-kid lives, is it? Not bad, not bad at all." Cemmera scanned the house with hungry eyes. It was almost time for her to have some fun.

Her team took turns looking through the binoculars outside the only window in the back of the truck. The home looked like a cute place to live, in a decent and quiet neighborhood. Neil and Santos discussed the entry plan while the two Telekinetics remained silent.

"Santos, give me a read." Cemmera looked over to him. He disengaged his chatter with Neil and turned his face to the ground, gathering data.

"As far as I can see there are three in the house and all of them are Psychs. Looks like we got a Reinforcer, a Kinetic, and a ... that's odd. I can't tell what the Harris-kid is. This hasn't happened before. I mean, it feels like he's," Santos paused. "It feels like he's *nothing*. But that doesn't make any sense either."

Cemmera grunted. "We already know he's a Telekinetic— don't worry about it."

Santos was unlike most other Telepaths, in fact, most of her team members were unlike any other. Cemmera demanded greatness and strength. She made sure that each member of her team could pull their weight in any situation.

Few Telepaths could tell a Psych's affinity simply from sensing them. It was one of the reasons she allowed Santos on the team, despite only possessing a mediocre amount of power.

"As you say, Captain." Santos resumed peering through the back-window of the van.

"Cemmera, I really think we're about to make a very big mistake here," Neil said. He had a look of worry on his face, which Santos mirrored. The two Kinetic twins had blank expressions, which was pretty typical of them. Daniel and Joseph Remos rarely had much to say, often following along and agreeing with whatever Cemmera wanted. It was always Neil and Santos that gave her trouble.

"I agree with Neil, Cemmera," Santos said. "If the most updated report is to be believed—and I believe it is—Jack Harris is now an official member of our organization, and we already know that Melissa Sayre, age sixteen, Reinforcer, is a member as well. Cemmera, if we attack them, we might be signing our own kill-orders."

Cemmera trembled with anger. Nothing bothered her more than when her team was being stupid or acting like cowards. And right now, they were doing both.

"Listen up, you idiots! It's our responsibility to make sure that criminals like Jack Harris don't get to roam this Earth. You've all seen the evidence, and I know you've all seen the probable links. Once we force the Harris-kid to confess, he'll be within our jurisdiction to eliminate. And as far as the two with him go, well, we'll offer them the chance to surrender. If they give us a hard time, then we are well within our rights to execute them as well on the grounds of aiding and abetting. You two are really starting to drive me nuts. I mean, come on already guys! Will you just wake up and look at the evidence for crying out loud? Our investigation clearly shows that—"

"Investigation?" Neil interrupted. "Cemmera, with all due respect, it is *not* our job to investigate. We are operations. We just get the kill-order and act on it. We're taking things into our own hands, things which we don't even have the right to. Furthermore, even if we did, we still don't have nearly enough evidence to say for certain that Jack Harris is linked or involved in any way with the killings."

Cemmera tossed Neil a petrifying glare. His eyes lit up in fear as he realized what he had just done. "Neil, did you just interrupt me?"

Neil held out his hands in a surrendering gesture. "I'm very sorry, Cemmera. Please, forgive me."

"Your arm, now."

"Please, I promise it will never happen again, I was only caught up in the heat of the —"

"Your arm, Neil. Now!"

With a whimper, Neil rolled up his sleeve, revealing numerous dark red scars leading from his wrist to his shoulder. He made his way over towards Cemmera and sat down in front of her, his eyes closed.

When Cemmera's boys misbehaved, they were punished. That was the way it was, and that was the way it had to be.

"Open your eyes, Neil. I want you to see it. Don't aggravate me further, or I'll give you two punishments instead of one."

Neil opened his eyes and watched in horror as Cemmera prepared to add a sixth scar to his growing collection. Cemmera had an idea of what it must feel like to be on the receiving end of one of her punishments. It only made them so much more fun to administer.

Grabbing Neil's arm with her right hand, she raised her left pointer finger and gently stroked his arm up and down, from wrist to shoulder. She liked to tease them first, never letting them know when it was going to begin. Her finger glided along his wrist and back up again, causing Neil to wince each time in anticipation. Cemmera figured it was the worst part of the entire punishment, never knowing when the pain was going to start.

Finally, after thirty seconds—which probably felt more like an hour to Neil—she began. Starting from his wrist, she slowly ran her finger across his skin, leaving behind a bubbling, smoking, trail of red-scarred flesh. They never did bleed—the wound was cauterized in an instant.

Neil whined like a wounded animal, causing Cemmera to feel a sense of pride. There was no higher indication of a person's strength than their ability to make a brute cry. Looking into his eyes, Cemmera could see that Neil was just on the verge of tears. She leaned over and bit his ear, while her finger slid the last of the distance, completing his sixth punishment. It was then that the middle-aged brute wept, sniffing and trying his best to hold back the tears.

Pathetic, Cemmera thought.

"Listen up, boys, because I'm only going to say this once. Be ready to move out on a moment's notice. As soon as I give the signal, we move in. For now, we're going to wait here and see how things play out. Does everyone understand?"

They all nodded, even the wounded Neil. Well, he wasn't *really* wounded, at least not physically. Cemmera smiled. She needed to make a kill so bad that it hurt.

Long live the hunt!

Chapter 26: Time to Move

Those creatures, would their nightmarish faces ever fade from memory? Andy would give anything, if for only a few moments he could be at peace, away from those things with the human faces. Why? Why did they want him so badly? Why couldn't they just stay dead?

Andy wondered if perhaps he himself was dead. Was this dark place hell? Was this eternity, a never ending remembrance of the people he killed, of the skeletal creatures that reeked of death and decay?

"I think he's coming back."

There was a voice. It sounded familiar to Andy, like someone he knew. Was it Jack? No, this was a darker voice, yet at the same time carefree and cheery.

"Darling, I think it's working. Oh, Andy, can you hear us?"

So, I am alive, Andy thought.

His eyes shot open. His head was resting in Requiem's lap in the back of a large van with a broken window. He tried to sit up, but he had trouble moving. With the little bit of strength he possessed, he inclined his head up to Requiem. Even through the deep pits of madness that were her torturous eyes, there was a note of relief. She smiled.

"Ah! Ruin, it worked. I have cured him."

"Excellent, dearest sister, perhaps now we can finally get on with things."

Andy wasn't sure what was going on, but he had some idea. The last thing he remembered was running away with Jack. He was ... he was betrayed, Andy remembered with a frown. Jack had attacked him with something, something that shouldn't have existed in the real world. He shook as the memories returned to him in a flood.

The look of concern in both their eyes bothered him. Did they not know? Did they not know that he tried to betray them and run away?

"Why ... why did you save me?" Andy's voice was raspy. It was difficult for him to speak.

The two looked astounded by the question, as if it was the most ridiculous thing that anyone had ever asked them.

"What do you mean 'why', Darling? You're our Brother. We would die a hundred times for you."

Andy didn't think that he could still feel surprise, not with everything that had happened to him. But at that moment, it came rushing into him. Were they being serious? There didn't seem to be even the slightest hint of mockery in their expressions. They looked at him like he was a wounded loved one who had just been through a massive surgery, only to narrowly survive.

"I don't understand. Do you two ... actually care about me?"

For a moment it looked like Requiem was going to shed a tear. *"Of course we do!"* she shouted at him.

Now Andy felt a tremendous guilt. He was so frightened of these two, so terrified of the price of displeasing them that he never considered for a moment that they might actually care for him. He was so certain that if he stuck around long enough they would eventually grow bored and kill him. That was what he had thought of them, but yet, they had just risked their lives to save him. Sitting up, he could see the damage they had inflicted to retrieve him. Dead bodies littered the street just ahead of them, corpses that looked kind of like SWAT officers. Immediately Andy recognized them as having the same uniforms as the ones that had apprehended him.

He looked at his two saviors. "I never thought ... I never thought there were people in this world that loved me. I was so sure that you two were going to kill me off someday that I betrayed you. I don't deserve you both. I am so very sorry, but you have to know the truth. I went to Jack Harris and I asked him to help. I was going to escape. I was going to run far away and never look back. Do you see? I am not worthy of your care."

Ruin took a seat next to Andy and pulled him into a hug, his sister joining in. "Andy, families make mistakes, don't they? I told you once that when you became our brother, we would be the only family you needed. For feeling so alone, it was truly our fault. We should have been there for you more. We were too hard on you, and for that my Sister and I are very sorry. How about we forget all that has happened, and work on moving forward? What do you say, Andy?"

Andy, for the first time since the night he had murdered Richard, felt a great pain removed from his heart. "I'm so sorry for everything I did. I understand now that you two were just trying to help me all this time. I freaked out, I panicked, but at the last minute, I think I'd have made you two proud."

Now Requiem's eyes lit with an amused glint. "Oh? And why is that, Andy?"

"Because at the very end, when I was sure they were going to capture me, I finally understood your message. I killed one of them, you know? An officer just like the ones you guys killed outside. I screamed at them, all of them, that this was our right. I finally understood what you were trying to teach me. I acted upon my right! They should all burn for trying to take that away."

Pride seeped through the expressions of both Ruin and Requiem. "Yes, Brother," Ruin said. "Now you really do get it. Eventually the Harris-boy will too."

At this, Andy flared in outrage. "Who, Jack? He can't be part of this family, you guys! I want him dead. He betrayed me! I want you two to rip his damned heart out and feed it to him! *I want to hear him cry out in pain and—*"

Requiem slapped Andy, cutting him off. "Silence, fool! You do *not* speak that way of our brother. How would you like it if someone cut out *your* heart and made *you* cry out in pain? The nerve of some people!"

Andy shook his head. They were never going to convince Jack to join them. Even if Andy didn't feel a seething hatred towards his former friend, his opinion would be the same—Jack would never join them. In his lonely and sad life, Andy had finally found other people that cared for him, and now they were going to get themselves killed or worse, and all for what? So they could chase after some dream?

"You have a better chance of winning the lottery, guys. You'll never get Jack to go along with any of this."

"You thought the same thing about yourself, did you not, Brother Andy? Now look at you. I can see it in your face. You finally understand the comfort of family and the things we're going to accomplish together. I am sure that no matter how stubborn the Harris-boy is, he too will come to love us as his own. Of this, I am certain."

Not if I kill him first, Andy thought, concealing a devilish grin.

"So, what do we do now?" Andy asked.

"Now that you're up and about, Darling, we're going to head over to the Harris-boy's home. We've been putting this off for far too long. Tonight, I'll finally have him. Oh, I want him so badly it hurts!"

Ruin gave Andy a pat on the shoulder before standing up and heading to the front of the vehicle. Andy hoped it was safe to drive something with a hole in the front window and glass sticking out. As if reading his thoughts, Ruin snapped his fingers, and the remaining glass broke away from the vehicle, leaving nothing but an open front.

"Don't worry yourself, Andy," Ruin said. "I'm sure that Jack Harris can be made to see our ways."

"Ya know, I'm really starting to think that Will Schuester is a Psych," Jack said. He chomped down on the popcorn while he watched the TV from the living room couch.

"And what makes you say that?" Melissa snatched the bowl away from Jack before he could react, and started munching down on *his* popcorn.

"Well, did you notice that no matter where in the world a fight takes place, he seems to just show up out of nowhere before the first punch gets thrown? It's like, how does he know that they're going to fight, and always manage to make it on time? I'm telling you, Melissa, he's a Telepath."

She laughed and passed Alana the bowl. The three of them were sitting relaxed in the living room with the lights off, on Alana's wide, black leather couch. Jack really wanted to watch *Chuck*, but Alana and Melissa vetoed him and decided to go for *Glee* instead.

Jack got up from the couch and snatched the popcorn out of his mom's hands, and before she could react, he ran and jumped back down on the couch. "Make your own, Mom."

"Sweetie," she said with a grin. "Now that you know the truth about me, I'm not afraid to do *this*."

The bowl flew out of Jack's hands, soaring to the other end of the couch and back into Alana's lap.

That's so unfair, Jack thought. *No one steals my popcorn!*

Jack had made a promise to Michael that he would try and draw on his power at least twice a day. He'd said that within a few months the horrible feeling would decrease, and after a year or two, go away entirely.

Jack reached for that unique part of him, and with an audible groan, allowed himself the smallest trickle of power, before sealing himself off. It was the worst feeling. It made him want to roll around on the ground and scream.

It had been a while since Jack had attempted to do anything with his power, so he tried to remember how to grab at things. His mind felt like a room with a billion buttons, before shifting into strings, changing ever more into triggers. To make things worse, they moved, and shifted, changing constantly. He could always find the one that sent near things far away, the one that everyone called a "burst." Once he had done it enough times, it became easier and easier to locate.

The one Jack tried to find was the one that let him grab things and freely move them around. He searched for it, struggling to sort through the endless maze of triggers that were his mind. It took a second for him to realize it, but now Melissa and his mom were paying more attention to him than they were the T.V.

"You can do it, sweetie," she encouraged.

Jack felt a little frustrated, realizing that the only reason his Mom had nabbed the popcorn in the first place was to encourage him to sharpen his skills. Melissa had told his mother—even though he had begged her not to—that Jack was refusing to practice. Oh well, he had already gotten this far.

Jack reached for that familiar trigger, the one that he had only used twice before under the guidance of Michael—and he activated it ...

He must have activated the wrong trigger, because pain exploded in his mind. He fell to the floor with his hands on his head, moaning. He rolled on the ground as pictures and images filled his mind.

"*Jack!*" both his mother and Melissa called to him, jumping off the couch and kneeling beside him on the carpet. They held him down, yelling his name, calling to him. Jack's mind filled with more images, more pictures, until they blended together to make a concept, something he could understand. His eyes widened in alert.

Jack sat up in a hurry and reached into Melissa's pocket. She gasped in surprise.

"Jack, what the hell are you—"

Jack took out the tiny device he and Michael had stolen.

"*Michael!*" he screamed, panic and desperation in his voice. "There are like, five Psychs outside, and three more coming from a few miles away. They want to kill Melissa and my mother and take me away, all of them!"

"Sweetie," Alana said, rubbing his face. "You're just having a bad reaction to 'the draw', and it's making you delusional. It happens sometimes, just relax. No one is outside. You're a Telekinetic, remember?"

"*Are you serious, Jack? Are you one hundred percent sure?*" Michael sounded worried, and he too seemed to have a note of panic in his voice.

"Yeah, Michael, I don't know how I know, but I just know that I know!"

Alana tapped Melissa on the shoulder. "Melissa, why do you look so worried? Don't let Jack alarm Paro over nothing. He's just having a bad reaction to—"

"Your son is an Unrestricted," Melissa interrupted. Tears streaked down her face as she told Alana what she had sworn to Paro she would keep secret. "I am so very sorry."

Alana looked crushed, like a car had run her over and left her to die. Her face puckered, and her eyes grew moist with dread.

"So you're saying that Jack just used Telepathy? And that there *are* people outside my home who want to kill us? Do you expect me to believe that?"

Melissa pulled her hair in frustration. "Yes, I know this is a huge shocker, and I know you need time to think about things, but if what Jack just said is true—and I promise you that it at least has the possibility of being so—then we need to do something right now."

In an instant, Alana pulled herself together. "Michael!" she called out, loud enough to be received by the device in Jack's hand. "Can you get in touch with Paro?"

"I'm going to try right now, Alana, let me see if I can find out where they are."

Another voice chimed in, causing Jack to reel in surprise. *"We're right here."* It was Sarah's voice, but how?

"Sarah, I don't understand," Michael said. It was Paro that answered next.

"Do you really think you're smart enough to steal a piece of my equipment without me knowing? I let you guys get away with it because I had a feeling something like this might happen. It made my life a lot easier, to be honest. I knew there was no way I could convince Jack to voluntarily walk around with something like this. You two did my job for me."

Jack didn't care that he had yet again been outsmarted. All he wanted to do was to make sure they were safe. "Paro, what did I just do? I tried to grab a bowl of popcorn, but instead I just blacked out and saw a whole bunch of people."

"What you did, Jack," he responded. *"Was save the lives of your mother and Melissa. Hang tight, and keep this device on you at all times. We're only a few miles away. Jack, do you have any idea who these eight Psychs are?"*

"No clue, Paro. I only know that the five outside my house are not with the three. But they seem to want the same thing. I have no idea how I know that, either."

"The three must be the ones we're after. This is just how we expected it to happen. Now's our chance."

As if by an invisible force, the device flew out of Jack's hands and landed into Alana's. A tremendous, dark fury covered her face.

"The *three* you're after, Paro? Is there something you're not telling me? God help you if I find out you put my son's life in danger for a case."

There was a hesitation on the other end, before the voice responded. *"Alana, I'm sorry, but you may as well know the truth now. I planned to tell you soon anyway. Those murders, the ones you must have no doubt heard about on the news—two young Psychs with incredible power carried those out. We don't know why, but they seem to want your son to join them. In fact they're dead set on the notion, and I don't think they'll take no for an answer. The people responsible are believed to be eighteen years of age, with a recently acquired accomplice."*

"Andy!" Jack called out. "But how? I thought you guys had him."

"I'm afraid to say that the prisoner transport was ambushed by our suspects, and they killed everyone on board. They now have

him back in their possession, but for the first time we know exactly where they are, thanks to you, Jack. We're heading over to your home now. And Alana, please forgive me, if you have any room left in your heart to forgive an animal like me."

Alana growled at Paro. "You were never an animal, Paro, just a boy in need of a good whipping. And I promise you when this is over you're getting another one."

She turned to Jack, barely restrained tears moistening her soft eyes. "Jack, I'm so sorry. You're an Unrestricted. Why did it have to be you born with such a curse? We'll talk about this later, for now I need you two to go upstairs. Go to your room with Melissa, and don't open the door for anything."

Jack felt a rush of pride for his mother so powerful that it almost moved him to tears. After everything that had just happened, she was pulling herself together, fighting through the confusion and planning on how to take action.

"Mom, I won't leave you by yourself. Those guys are gonna be here before my team is."

"Your team?"

Ah, crap, I just can't keep my mouth shut.

"That doesn't matter right now, Mom. I won't let them kill you."

"Melissa," Alana said.

"I know, Mrs. Harris, I know." Before Jack could raise a questioning eyebrow, Melissa grabbed him by his neck and dragged him up the stairs.

"Melissa, no! What are you doing? You can't leave my mom alone down there! Damn it, Melissa, what if she dies? *Let me go!*"

"I'm sorry, Jack. I can't."

Jack struggled, but to no avail.

Mom!

Chapter 27: You've Made a Big Mistake

"Melissa, please, you've got to let me go. *Get out of the way!*"

Melissa wasn't budging, no matter how much Jack pleaded. It wasn't just because she was doing her job—the reason she was even there in the first place—but more, she had made a silent promise to Alana. If she had to knock Jack over the head, she would, but so long as he stayed on the other end of the room, he could beg and plead as much as he wanted.

She stood with her back to the door, her arms spread out in a wordless refusal of passage. Jack paced back and forth between his bed and the dresser, running tense fingers through his messy black hair and over his eyes. His boyish features covered with worry.

"Everything will be fine, Jack. Paro and everyone will be here soon. You just have to believe in them."

She hoped that was the truth, she really did. It would break her heart to see anything happen to Jack's mom. Since meeting the woman, Melissa had really taken a liking to her. From the bottom of her heart, she didn't want to see any harm befall Alana, but she would be willing to do anything to keep Jack safe.

Paro's voice came through the device in her ear, which she'd snatched from Jack after dragging him upstairs. She never would've expected Jack and Michael's stupidity to turn into something that could save their lives, as without the device they'd be forced to use cell-phones, unreliable in a life or death situations. They were able to speak with the team in real time.

"Just hang tight, you two. We're coming as fast as we can."

Alana was not willing to be insulted. She watched from a small opening in the window above her front door as five people attempted to approach her home in silence. Alana didn't like snakes or people that acted like snakes. If they wanted to start trouble, they'd have to meet her face to face. She had to admit, though—without her son's warning, she'd never have noticed them. Things were easier to spot when forewarned.

Jack.

Why did her only child have to be an Unrestricted? They would never leave him alone now. Was there anything in this world she could do for him? Alana clenched her fists and took deep, relaxing breaths, forcing the worry and sadness from her mind. To live, she'd need to remain focused.

She threw open the front door and shouted at the five dark silhouettes across the street. "I know you're there! You want to talk? Come here then. Don't sulk in the darkness like cowards."

The five shadows ceased moving. What Alana assumed was the leader turned to her and walked towards the nearest streetlamp, revealing her face in the scant light amid the darkness. She was around Alana's age but she looked hardened, brutal, and a great deal sadistic. Under normal conditions, she'd be an attractive woman, but with a gaze like hers, even the dirtiest-minded would stand clear.

"I've never been one to appreciate being called a coward, Mrs. Harris. Very well, I'll oblige."

Alana led the woman into her home then asked her to take a seat at the kitchen table, where just hours before she'd been enjoying small talk with Melissa. She grabbed a pot from under the kitchen sink and boiled water, preparing tea.

Four men entered the home, following behind the woman in the same gear that Alana knew was used by recon officers. The woman was the only one dressed in casual clothing, with blue-jeans and a black-knitted sweater. The men were Psychs, no doubt. Their recon gear fooled no one.

"My name is Cemmera Wilson. I am both a team-leader and Captain of the Operations Department. Your son, Jack Harris, age sixteen, Telekinetic—we are here for him. Please stand aside and let us do our job."

An Op. team? An Op. team is in my house for Jack! Alana's thoughts turned frantic.

She had no idea why an Op. team would be after her son and probably neither did Paro, or he'd have warned her. Something like this shouldn't even be possible. From what Jack had let slip, it sounded like he had already been signed up to a team, which meant he wasn't suspected of any criminal activity.

Alana forced herself to smile, adding cheer and merriment to her voice. "Ah, you want to see my son? Okay then, no problem at all! Just show me the signed kill-order, and I'll bring you to him myself."

Cemmera snarled and bit her lip. Oddly, two of the men behind her gave each other worried, acknowledging looks, almost as if they'd expected Alana to respond the way she had. One was a muscular, middle-aged man, also around Alana's age. The other was a short and stocky man, appearing to be of Spanish descent.

"You'll be happy to know, Mrs. Harris, that we do not have a kill-order. We are just going to take him and ask him some questions."

Alana grinned. "You are, are you? I'm sorry, which department did you say you were from again?"

Cemmera slammed her fist down on the table and stood up, pointing a threatening finger at her. "Do not make a fool out of me, Mrs. Harris. I have an abundance of evidence linking your son to a series of murders."

Alana pretended to be captivated by her words, and with obvious mockery, she nodded like a child listening to a fairytale. "Whoa, that sounds awful. You should go and tell that to an Investigative team right away!"

The woman trembled with what was obviously rage. In two quick strides, she crossed the distance from the table to the stove where Alana was making tea and came to stand nose to nose with her.

"You're going to learn I don't like to be mocked, Mrs. Harris. Now, I tried to be civil, I really did. So here's how this is going to work. You can either *A*, lead me to Jack, *B*, sit here and do nothing, or *C*, you can run away screaming and flailing your arms. I will accept any of these options, but get in my way, and I will turn you into something that can slide down a sewer grate. Do we have an understanding, tramp?"

Well, Alana thought, *no one can say I didn't at least try to keep my cool.*

Alana kept her cheerful smile on her face and even paused to pour herself a small cup of tea, sipping at it with delighted ease. It was underneath this appearance of nonchalance that burned inside her a fiery pit of rage so massive that even the surface of the sun could not compare to the heat of it.

"You know, Mrs. Cemmera, umm, Wilson—was it? Before you go and retrieve my son, I was wondering, do you know anything about me? His mother?"

Cemmera scoffed at her. "I know you're some kind of lowly Psych, probably worse trash than the Carebears you seem to revere so much."

"Did you know that I used to go by another name? Besides Mrs. Harris, that is. It was a name I heard the most when I was asking someone a question."

Cemmera crossed her arms and laughed. "I suppose you're going to tell me something that will impress me? Please, then, by all means, what oh what did they call you?"

Alana's grin became wider, almost maniacal. "They used to look at me and say, '*As you command, General Harris.*'"

Cemmera wasn't given enough time to let Alana's words dawn on her. She got as far as raising a single eyebrow before Alana grabbed at her with a tremendous Kinetic force, lifting her into the air and sending her crashing through the kitchen window. For a moment, all that could be heard was the sound of the glass shattering, followed by the sound of a crash outside as the woman landed on—and probably broke—most of Alana's flowering pots. From beyond the window came a scream of agony and rage.

For almost ten full seconds, the four men looked at each other with their mouths hanging open before snapping out of their disbelief and surrounding her. Alana knew then that she was probably going to die.

She understood right away that the real problem, the nail in her coffin, was going to be the Reinforcer. As soon as the four men snapped to attention and launched their assault, Alana realized just how messed up of a situation she was in.

To call it dire would be an understatement—it was catastrophic. For one, the two Telekinetics were already after her with what could only be called a fanatic desperation as they attempted to grab, push, or otherwise cripple her. Alana had to draw on every last bit of power she could, down to the smallest drop, just to fight off their grabs. If a single one made contact, it was over.

This led to the second problem, the Telepath. The short and stocky man disrupted her. His head was face down, looking at the kitchen table. He was seated, his entire concentration bent on breaking hers. She could do nothing to stop him, because to divert even a single moment of attention from fighting off the two Kinetic's grabs would spell out instant death. She was doing everything she could just to hold them off.

It was for these reasons that the Reinforcer was the icing on the cake, but there was nothing she could do about him. To make matters worse, Alana could already hear the groans from outside the window as the Cemmera-woman recovered. She would be rejoining the fight soon.

Alana ripped open her topmost cabinet drawer and grabbed the sharpest knife she could find. Her chances of survival were almost zero, but there was still one possible way she could make it out alive. It was close to impossible, yet Alana wouldn't die without at least trying.

She needed to kill the Telepath—it was as simple as that. If she could stick the knife in his throat, she could handle the other three. Alana was a powerful woman, counted at one point among the greatest of her affinity. She was almost as good as her husband.

She lived Telekinesis, she breathed Telekinesis, and it was more to her than just her affinity—telekinesis was her life. It wasn't her power that had once caused her to be considered among the best. There had been Kinetics far more powerful than she, who'd never made it to the rank of Captain, let alone team-leader. Power could only bring you so far. Even a Psych with a fraction of another's power could emerge the victor in a fight, if the power was well used.

Much like the way a locked door can be opened if you have the proper key, or a gigantic knot can be undone by simply tugging at the proper string, there were always vulnerabilities in the affinities, and there was always *technique*. Alana wasn't the strongest, but she was the embodiment of skill. Even with the Path weakening her to such a large extent, she could still brush aside the grabbing attempts made by the two Telekinetics, regardless of their overwhelming force. It was almost a matter of pride with Alana. No Telekinetic, especially not ones that were Op. team animals, would bring this gal down.

The Reinforcer rushed her, trying to decapitate her with a down-handed swing. She leaped to the side, rolling on the white-tiled kitchen floor. The man's fist exploded through the sink, ripping all the way through to the cabinet underneath, spraying water and debris in every direction. The odds were so stacked against her that it was almost comical.

She charged forward, knife-end pointed downward, ready to kill the Telepath. The Reinforcer was faster, as she expected he would be. He jumped off the back of his heels and tried to tackle her. Alana kicked out her legs and threw herself to the ground as the man flew just an inch over her head. He landed on his stomach, and in an instant was back on his feet, only now he was in front of her. He knew what she had intended—it was obvious. He wasn't going to let her get to his Path.

Time was running out. It had only been a few seconds, yet it in another few the Cemmera-woman would return. Whatever affinity Cemmera was, it would be too much for Alana to handle. In fact, what she was already facing was too much for her to handle.

"Nice try," the Reinforcer said. "But you're not going near our Path."

He charged at her again, and this time Alana had nowhere to run—he was just too fast. If he collided with her, she would die. It would be like getting hit in the chest by a speeding bus. She had no choice. She had to divert all of her power towards stopping the large man.

The two Kinetics looked confused for a moment as they no doubt felt her resistance fade. Taking advantage of their momentary surprise, Alana poured her rage into the Reinforcer, throwing her Kinetic energies at him. Alana flung him in the opposite direction at an even faster speed than he was charging at her with. The Reinforcer was sent soaring just overhead of the concentrating Path. He crashed through the wall behind him and landed with a groan on the living room floor. Dust and paint chips were scattered on impact as Alana watched her house get destroyed. The home, however, was the very least of her concerns at the moment.

The Kinetics grinned. Now that they had an opening, they were able to grab at her. Alana cried out as she found herself slammed to the floor with a thud, only to be picked up yet again and tossed around like a child, skimming along the counter-tops, knocking plates, napkin-holders, and glass cups to the ground, breaking just about everything in her kitchen.

The pain was intense, and she struggled to once again regain control. They threw her all around the room. Each intense collision weakened her, causing her to shout out in pain. She screamed as she desperately tried to regain her focus and fight off the two. It wasn't easy, and the Kinetics managed to toss her two more times before she was once again able to reassert her dominance. She landed on her back against the hard, tiled-floor. The attacks had stopped, but they had done their damage.

"Damn you all." She coughed, and trickles of blood fell out of her mouth, landing on the floor beside her.

The Reinforcer was back on his feet. Alana didn't know if she was crazy or simply dazed from the beating she'd received, but when the Reinforcer returned to the room, he didn't use the door, choosing instead to enter back through the wall she'd sent him crashing through. This caused Alana to burst out laughing.

In what was Alana's biggest surprise of the night, each one of the men began laughing along with her.

"It is kind of funny," the Reinforcer said, covered in dust. "But hey, at least you get to die smiling, Mrs. Harris. I think everyone should know the name of the man who killed them. My name is Neil, and it was nice meeting you."

Alana was still lying on the ground and struggling to keep the Kinetics off her. As the man towered over her with his left hand gripped into a fist, Alana knew it was going to be the last thing she'd ever see.

"What's everyone laughing about? Can I get in on the joke too?" asked a voice.

The man, Neil, turned his head to face the voice. He only faced it for a moment, though, because an instant later his head snapped in the opposite direction. With a crackling, crunching sound a fist collided with his jaw, sending him soaring with a *bang* into another set of cabinets next to the sink, rendering more of Alana's kitchen destroyed and useless.

"They say when two of us fight, one of us dies. I've never killed a man, so I guess you're going to be my first."

Alana couldn't believe what she was seeing. Melissa, with a look of tremendous fury, hovered over Alana with her arm still extended from where she'd decked Neil.

"Melissa, why did you come down here? It's dangerous. You could die."

"Because," she said. "If I let his mom die, Jack will never forgive me. I can't live with that."

The two Kinetics gaped at the girl who'd just sent their Reinforcer scrambling face first into kitchen furniture. It was just the opportunity Alana had been waiting for. It was finally her chance to fight back. She was exhausted, badly injured, and at the very least had a few broken ribs, if not other bones.

Telekinetics could only move what they were able to see. Lying down, Alana tilted her head as far back as it would go, almost until it hurt. In the corner of her eyes, she spotted it—the two utensil drawers left of the now broken sink, which was shooting up water like a fire hydrant.

The two drawers sprang open, and in an overwhelming display of Alana's fullest, unhindered power, every last knife, fork, and even spoon zipped across the room, flying at tremendous speed towards the Telepath.

Melissa stood frozen in terror as almost thirty knives threatened to skewer her. Alana coughed a victorious laugh, and the knives changed direction in mid-air. They swerved and flew above Melissa's head without causing the girl any harm. The Telepath only had time to look up in confusion, as he was turned into a human dartboard, pierced from head to toe by knives, forks, and the reverse end of spoons. His death was instant.

Cemmera burst into the room, wearing a broken flowering pot as a hat. She looked like an enraged demon out of hell. Alana didn't think she'd ever seen anger on someone quite like Cemmera was wearing at that moment.

Her hands were shaking. Her tongue hung from her mouth. She craned her neck sideways and moaned.

"Kill you ... gonna kill you all ... *Gonna make it hurt!*"

Alana was too exhausted to even respond. She had done her best, and now she had to trust that Paro would arrive on time. She laughed at the foolish-looking woman with the flower-pot-hat before she passed out. She prayed that when ... if she woke up again, all would be fine.

Chapter 28: Prelude to Madness

Melissa watched in disgust as the woman, Cemmera, alternated between livid outrage and terrible sadness. Her expressions were changing back and forth so quickly that her face looked like it was going through a seizure.

To say she looked ridiculous would be an understatement. Dirt covered her face, and unbeknownst to her, she was wearing a flowering-pot as a hat. She walked over to the corpse of her fallen team-member. Despite Melissa's desire to remain neutral, she felt a small amount of pity. No team-leader wanted to see their members die, not even Cemmera.

The man, who said his name was Neil, also wore a look of disgust. He watched his team-leader crouch down beside the lifeless corpse. Dust still enveloped him from when Alana had tossed him through a wall. Mrs. Harris was lying unconscious nearby.

"Y-you did this, Cemmera." Neil looked to be on the verge of tears. He too wore the expressions of both anger and sadness, only, unlike Cemmera's, his did not alternate. They blended together to form a cocktail of desperation and sickness.

Cemmera, remaining crouched, turned her head to face Neil. Her voice was a whisper, but at the same time it was intense, commanding, and filled with a growing bitterness.

"No, I didn't! It was that woman, Alana Harris, *she did this*. I'll kill her for this. I'll kill all of them." Cemmera turned to face Melissa, as if finally realizing she was there. "*You*," she growled, meeting Melissa's eyes. "You think you can harbor criminals and live? I'm invoking my power as a Captain of the Operations Division and sentencing you to death for your crimes."

Melissa didn't even blink. She stood her ground. "Me? Let me tell you something—there's a reason we call you guys 'Op. team animals.' First of all, what makes you think that Jack Harris has any involvement in what's been happening? Please, tell me."

Cemmera stood up from her crouch and came to stare closely into Melissa's face. "You don't deserve for me to dignify that with a response, but being the better person I'll answer you. If you bothered to take even the most rudimentary glance at the evidence, you'd see that there must be a third killer. The two *must* have recruited an accomplice. It can be no other than Jack Harris. It is for this reason that my Telepath had to die. Santos died doing what was right!"

Melissa cast her eyes down, sadness filling each word as she spoke. "I'm sure you've heard the saying about making assumptions, and yet time and time again it's proven true. Cemmera, that is your name, right? There is an accomplice, but we already know who he is. His name is Andy Leonell, age sixteen, Manipulator."

Neil twitched upon hearing Melissa's words, pushing his way through the Kinetics and grabbing the front of Melissa's shirt. He screamed at her, but rather than anger, only a deep sadness came through. "What do you mean, girl? Tell me!"

Melissa kept her cool. "The information should already be updated by now. It should've been posted a few minutes ago, actually. The boy, Andy, escaped along with the two suspects we were originally after. If you don't believe me, then check for yourself."

Neil reached into his pocket and retrieved his P.D.A with trembling fingers. Melissa could see in his eyes that he prayed for her to be wrong—he wanted her to be lying.

"No ..." he said. "No!"

"I'm sorry," Melissa whispered. "But your friend died for nothing. His death was in vain, for no purpose other than to satisfy your desire to kill. There's more, though. The three that *are* your targets, well, they're on their way here."

Cemmera slapped her across the face, causing Melissa to once again calm her rising anger.

"She's lying, Neil! It must be Jack Harris. It *has* to be Jack Harris. Santos did not die for nothing. He can't be allowed to die for nothing!"

"Look," Neil said, tears streaking down his coarse face. He showed Cemmera the P.D.A and she shrieked. It was a loud, disgusting sound.

"We have to leave," he said. "We have to make this right. If we stop now, we might be allowed to keep our lives."

Cemmera howled at him, ripping the device from his fingers and throwing it to the ground. In a blind fury, she stomped on it, over and over, until it was smashed. Eventually the screen fell off, and the circuitry inside got entangled her boot.

"Girl," she said to Melissa. "Are you certain there are three more on the way? How can you know that?"

"Because," Melissa said, "Jack Harris is not a Telekinetic like you've been led to believe. He's an Unrestricted."

Even the Kinetics, who had yet to make a sound since entering the home, shifted on their feet and moaned. "Cemmera, you were wrong about everything," one said.

"Quiet, Joseph, you fool. Disrespect me again and so help me God I will punish you *and* your brother, I'll bring you within an inch of your worthless lives!"

Melissa watched as Cemmera backed away and paced around the room, almost tripping over the unconscious form of Alana Harris while muttering nonsense to herself. After a few moments she paused, and a dangerous glint entered her eyes.

"Here's what we'll do. We know that our three targets are coming. We'll kill them, and then we'll kill this girl and the boy's mother—and the boy too, of course—and then we'll report that the three targets were responsible. Yes, yes, it all makes sense now. We showed up too late, we tried to save them, but we just didn't make it in time. We got here, saw the three of them laughing over their murderous deeds, and we put a stop to them. We'll cry, so that they know how terrible we feel. If only we'd arrived here in time to save them. It's perfect!"

Melissa balled her hands into fists. "You," she said to their Reinforcer, the man known as Neil. "If you go along with this, you're just as bad as she is. Same goes for you two guys." The Kinetics looked at her but said nothing.

"Do not listen to this child," Cemmera growled. "You can either do what I say or spend your lives in one of those facilities. Neil, I already know you spent a few years there. Care to go back?"

Neil appeared to be deep in thought. Sweat trickled down his face, in what Melissa assumed was him considering his options.

"She's right," the Telekinetic, the one called Joseph, said. "This woman." He kicked the unconscious form of Alana Harris. "She's killed a member of our team. We need to kill every last one of them for this."

Joseph's brother nodded in agreement, and Cemmera smiled with pride at the Kinetic twins.

Melissa felt the tension in the room rise as they all shifted on their feet and faced her. She was furious at these people, these *animals*. Not only did they kick an unconscious woman, but now they were going to murder her and Jack, and for what? To cover up a stupid mistake that cost them the life of a friend? She knew what she said next was foolish, irresponsible even, but in her growing fury, she spoke out of impulse.

"You guys seem to value yourselves hunters, is that true?"

Cemmera grinned. "Of course, girl. There is none better."

She pointed to Neil. "If you have even the smallest shred of honor, if you are not a complete coward, unworthy of the very air you breathe, then fight me alone, Neil. I don't think I've ever been as pissed off as I am right now. Why don't we step outside, and I'll show you why you're nothing but an Op. team animal, all *brute* and no brains."

Neil howled at the derogatory term, smashing his fist through the fridge, breaking yet another part of the kitchen. It hurt Melissa to use the word on one of her own kind, but if she didn't start punching something soon, she'd lose it. The Reinforcer didn't look happy—made worse by the two Kinetics and Cemmera laughing in his face.

Melissa smiled. "You look angry, chump." She pointed. "How about we step outside? Maybe I'll dip my fist in paint and decorate your hideous face."

Neil turned to Cemmera and a pleading, desperate look crossed his eyes. Cemmera nodded and said, "Go ahead, have at her." Neil seemed so relieved that he actually whimpered.

At first, Melissa had no idea why she hated the man so much. She struggled to understand what it was about him that had her so filled with rage. It was only then as the man sighed with relief that she finally understood. Unlike the other three living members of Neil's team, he alone was not an animal. Cemmera and the Kinetics might be bloodthirsty hounds, but this man—and this man alone—knew in his heart that what he was doing was wrong. Melissa could see it in his face. He knew their actions were immoral and reprehensible, yet he did them anyway. It was for this reason that Melissa despised him the most in the bunch. There was nothing in this world quite like a person who knew they were committing evil yet continued to do so.

For a long moment, a quiet settled upon the room while the reality of the situation finally dawned on Melissa. The only sounds were of the water shooting from the broken sink, the occasional crumbling from the broken wall, and the sound of a snack being munched on too loudly.

Wait, what?

"This is getting so awesome," Jack said, sinking his teeth into another pretzel. "I liked the part where you said you were going to paint his face. I thought that was funny."

"I did too, Darling," said another voice, grabbing the bag of pretzels away from Jack.

"Hey, when did you get here?" Jack asked the girl, apparently oblivious to the three people standing to the side of him.

Melissa, Cemmera, the Kinetics, and even Neil—none of them spoke a word. Melissa tried to, she really did, but it felt like a concussion grenade had just been detonated in her skull as she watched Jack carry on a casual conversation with the three most dangerous people she had ever set eyes on.

"We've been here for a while, Darling, watching the fun same as you. Oh, Ruin, who do you think will win?" Requiem asked, munching on a pretzel.

"I don't know, Dearest Sister," Ruin said, "but I know who you're rooting for."

Requiem's face seemed to darken at the words. "I do hope that large man rips the Pig-woman's face off."

Jack spun around. "Hey, Andy, I didn't know you were coming over! Umm, I know you're like, evil now and stuff, but I still want to show you this new comic book I got. Basically, in a nutshell, well, how do I say this without any spoilers? Alright, so you know how spider-man has—"

"*Jack, Shut up!*" Melissa shouted. She shook her head. There were no words to describe the stupidity of the situation. It was like she had left America and moved into loony-land.

Cemmera was the first to recover from her lapse of disbelief. "You three!" she screamed at them. "My name is Cemmera Wilson, team-leader of Op. team four-H. I have a signed kill—"

"Oh, Ruin, Darling," Requiem interrupted her. "Why is that woman wearing a bucket on her head? Is today bucket-head day?"

Requiem casually walked through the broken kitchen and bent over to pick up a pan that had been knocked over during Alana's fight. She positioned it on her head with a cheerful sigh, imitating Cemmera. "Is this the fashion, woman? Did I do it right?"

Cemmera raised her hands and felt around the top of her own head, discovering the flowering-pot resting on top of it. She hissed with anger, throwing it to the ground and shattering it.

"Talk ends now! Joseph, Daniel, you're with me. We'll take on the three targets. Neil, kill the Harris-boy and his mother when you finish up with the girl."

"I understand, Cem—"

Melissa did not give him a chance to finish his sentence. With all the power she could draw, she charged into him, tackling him and sending them both soaring through the kitchen. With a tremendous crash, they broke through the side of the house. Neil landed on the grass, and Melissa fell on top of him. She still had the element of surprise. Before Neil could gather his surroundings, she repeatedly slammed her fist into his face.

Once, twice, thrice, a fourth, she lifted her hand into the air, crashing it down on the man's nose, blood covering her knuckles as she did as much damage as she could. With a wail, Neil grabbed her throat, picking her up and throwing her on the ground a few feet away.

Melissa hit the floor hard, and she felt the wind knocked out of her. She managed to jump out of the way just in time. The Reinforcer struck his fist where her head had been only moments ago, causing grass and dirt to scatter in the air.

"You're a third my age and a third my power, you stupid, stupid, little girl. I'm going to enjoy killing you."

Melissa laughed and spat at the man. "I think I'm glad that one of us is going to die. Because I know it's not going to be me."

Behind her, there were loud sounds of commotion. Melissa heard the banging of various objects crashing and colliding into others. She hoped Jack would be able to handle himself for the moment. Cemmera and her boys were only interested in the three targets for the time being, and Melissa was fairly certain that the three young Psychs wanted Jack alive, so right now he would be the last thing any of them cared about.

Melissa slammed her fists together and let her aggression run wild. She was going to win.

Chapter 29: Whoops

Melissa looked at the Reinforcer and smirked. The odds didn't matter, stacked against her as they were. Melissa was going to beat this man, and if not for her own sake, then for Jack's. For a brief moment she felt bad about destroying Alana's lawn, but with a peek behind her at the hole torn in the side of the house, she realized that at this point it hardly mattered. She was startled when she heard Michael's voice shouting in her mind.

"Don't even think about it!" Michael screamed in her head. With all the chaos going on around her, she had forgotten about the device in her ear, which in addition to audio also allowed them to see a visual of the situation.

"Melissa, this is Paro. Just hang tight. We're almost there. You are not to engage this man, do you understand me? I'm already on the phone with General Deven Moore, and he's furious. Let him handle these Op. team animals, it's his job, not yours. Do not make any attempt to engage Neil Witherson, age forty-four, Reinforcer. We are almost there. I repeat, do not engage."

"Forgive me, Paro." Melissa cracked her knuckles.

"Hmm?" Neil gave Melissa a questioning look. "So, you're wearing one of those devices, are you? Let me guess, we're in quite a bit of trouble—so much for all that false bravado, girl."

Melissa grinned. "You've got nothing to lose now, do you? Don't worry yourself. I'd never pick a fight I couldn't finish." To prove her point, she removed the device from her ear and crushed it between her powerful hands. "Let's see what'cha got, big-boy."

The man wasted no time, charging at her and taking a swing aimed at her head. Melissa ducked under the blow and attempted to return one of her own. Despite the man's massive size, he evaded the return-swing with ease, throwing yet another jab directed towards the center of Melissa's face. She stepped back just in time, feeling the wind from his punch on her forehead.

What the man had said was true. He had about triple her experience. However, he'd been wrong about one thing—he was *not* more powerful than she was. Everyone was born with a certain amount of power. It was unchangeable. Melissa estimated that she might even be the stronger of the two, although in the end it didn't really matter. To a Psych, experience and skill accounted for eighty-percent of the fight. Power had very little bearing in the long run. As if to prove this theory, Neil dashed forward and swung at her yet again.

Melissa reached deep and pulled out everything she could draw. She assaulted the man with a jab-cross, pivoting off her back foot and throwing her weight behind the punch. Their two fists connected with a loud crunch, and pain shot through Melissa's arm, cascading from her knuckles all the way up into her shoulder. Still, she held her ground.

Their two fists remained connected, struggling against the force of the other. In the end, the man's experience won out, as he started to push her fist back, following it up with an unexpected hook from his free hand.

Melissa's head was snapped back as the man's fist collided with her cheek, forcing her to retreat a few steps. She tasted blood in her mouth and spat it onto the grass. She swished her tongue around her mouth, checking for any loose teeth. It was only her cheek that had been damaged.

Neil advanced on her yet again, and Melissa began to worry. Already people were turning on their porch lights to see what all the commotion was about. In a risky move, she charged to meet the older Psych head-on. He braced himself, ready for her assault.

Before the two met for another round of attacks, Melissa stopped short and jumped into the air, well over the man's head.

"Huh?" he said in surprise as she came to land behind him. He turned to meet her, but found only her fist to greet him. He was knocked off his feet as fist hit bone. There was a disgusting crackling sound. She'd caught him off guard and he landed on his back.

Melissa blew on her first like it was a smoking gun. The man, Neil, screamed as he jumped back to his feet and once again rushed at her. Now, there was murder in his eyes.

His attacks were a great deal faster than before, swinging one-two combinations with his full strength. If even a single one hit Melissa, she'd probably close her eyes and never again wake up. She ducked, sidestepped, and even spun her way around his fists, narrowly avoiding each attack. The man was in a rage. He threw one punch after the other, each one almost close enough to graze Melissa's face.

If things kept on going the way they were, then it was only a matter of time before he managed to actually hit her, and when that happened the man was sure to knock her head off. She waited for the perfect moment, a chance to counter. She needed him to aim straight for her nose—an opportunity for her to win. If he threw even a single straight-punch, she'd be able to use something Kazou once taught her.

For another few heart-wrenching moments, she backed away from him as he pushed her towards the street, ducking and side-stepping his deadly fists powered by his massive arms. Finally, when she was almost against the curb, with the street just a foot behind her, he went for it. With a grunt, he sent his right fist soaring at her, a blow that if connected, would probably crush her nose and kill her.

She kicked off her right foot while at the same time she grabbed his wrist with her left hand and his shoulder with her right. With all the strength she could muster she continued along with his own motion, pushing him in the same direction he was punching, and positioning herself to the side of him. Using his own force against him, he was hurled to the ground at a speed that made him look like a homing-missile. He threw out his hands to defend his face, landing on the ground in a pushup position, smashing the concrete with his open palms.

It's now or never, Melissa thought.

This was her only chance—there wouldn't be another. Neil, for the shortest moment, was unable to defend himself. His palms were sunken into the concrete, and he was attempting to push himself back up.

Melissa ran at him, and at the risk of her own safety, she gave up all her own defenses. Even a weak Reinforcer could put their fist through her head as her tough-as-steel body softened to normal human flesh. She diverted all of her power into her right foot, every last drop, and then she launched it at the face of the Reinforcer, who was still in a crawling-position.

For a moment he met her gaze. He locked eyes with Melissa and he actually trembled. Her front-kick connected with his jaw, and the impact was so powerful that it sent him airborne. There was a terrible crunching sound, as teeth and blood parted his mouth, causing him to once again fall on his back in the middle of the street. He cried out in agony, rolling on the ground and holding his face. Blood dripped from his open mouth like a leaky faucet.

All at once, Melissa returned to reality. The adrenaline was gone, the hatred was gone, and now she looked on with pity at the man she had just harmed. She'd never hurt anyone as bad as she'd just hurt the whimpering Reinforcer.

Neil looked up at her. His expression was one of disbelief. His mouth was completely red, and the extent of the damage she'd done disturbed Melissa. Even for a man like Neil, she felt guilty. Melissa was no Telepath, but at that moment she knew what the man was thinking.

Did that just happen?

"K ... kill ... m ... me," he begged, tears in his eyes, his voice raspy and pained. Melissa must have knocked at least half the man's teeth out. "S ... Santos," he murmured.

Melissa didn't know who Santos was, but she suspected it was the Telepath Alana had killed. She felt a new kind of anger grow in her. Not the raging, murderous hatred she'd felt earlier. This time it was a disappointed, saddened anger.

"Everything that has happened," she said to wounded man. "All of it. These are the consequences of your actions."

Melissa looked down at her bloodied hands, and even through her pity, she had a sense of empowerment. She had just beaten a forty-four year old man, humiliating him in a way he'd probably never recover from.

The commotion from the house was becoming louder, and she realized with a gasp she had forgotten all about Jack and the unconscious Alana. She took the time to grab Neil's foot and drag him back across the street, or at least far enough so that a car wouldn't hit him, before dashing back towards the home.

Jack watched as Cemmera and the two men she was with— Telekinetics, if he'd overheard correctly—positioned themselves side-by-side, ready to take on Andy and the two others he was with.

Jack struggled to remember their names, close to moaning with the frustration. He hated it when a name was on the tip of his tongue and he just couldn't remember it.

Damn, he thought. *Was it Rupert and Roberta? No, that wasn't it. Was it Rambo and Rhonda? No, that's not right either.*

"Cemmera," one of the two Telekinetics said, "we should not fight this battle, you know. We don't have a Telepath, and they do. One-on-one I can understand, but to fight as a group without a Path among us, well, that's suicide. Their Manipulator is going to tear through us."

Cemmera snarled at the man. "I know that, you fool. But they're just children. I don't care how powerful they are. Hey, you," she said, pointing to Jack.

"Me?"

"Yeah, you need to help us here, and maybe, just maybe, I'll let you live. I need you to focus on keeping their Telepath occupied, so we can take down the other two brats."

Jack didn't like the woman, and from everything he'd seen she looked to be pretty evil herself, even if she was on the same side or whatever. Looking over, Jack saw Andy and his two creepy friends grinning at Cemmera. No matter how wrong Cemmera was for destroying his home and hurting his mom, Jack knew that he'd have to back her up. He made a promise to Paro to help stop the murderers for everything they'd done, for everything they'd still do.

Andy and his two partners in crime listened to their conversation, looking unworried and carefree. They remained motionless.

"Now, listen to me very, very carefully, Harris. What I'm about to tell you is both complicated and deeply important. You must heed every word of it to have even the smallest chance at surviving this. Their Telepath is going to stop my Manipulation, which normally would be no problem except for the fact that they've got a Manipulator too. I'm going to use all my power to neutralize their Manipulator's attacks, and as a result, I won't be able to deal any in return. Both of my Kinetics will do their best to stop their one Kinetic, but they too will be dealing with fending off the Path's attempts to weaken them. You see, there is a reason every team needs a Path, and if your tramp of a mother hadn't killed mine, those three would be dead already. Do you understand?"

A sudden, gripping panic entered Jack's mind.

I did it again! he thought. *I stopped paying attention when someone was trying to teach me something, because it was boring. It's okay. I'll just do what I always do. Pretend I understand.*

Jack narrowed his eyes on Cemmera and forced himself to wear his most confident grin. "I understand," he said, keeping his voice cool and confident. A glimmer of hope entered Cemmera's otherwise dark and desperate expression.

Jack walked in front the three Op. team members, positioning himself directly in the middle between Andy's group and Cemmera's. Jack knew what he would do. He'd use a burst, and send the three of them packing, just like when he'd fought against Melissa.

He allowed a very small drop of power to trickle in, groaning at the agonizing feeling of discomfort and nausea.

"Gah!" he called out. "It's like the worst thing ever."

The power rushed into him, and he extended his arm, holding out his open palm to the three murderous Psychs. Andy met Jack's eyes and retreated several steps, petrified of him for some reason. Requiem only smiled. It was a twisted, disfigured smile, lighting up her maddened face. There was a single strand of her smooth-flowing red hair dangling across her eyes, adding menace to her psychotic delight. Ruin looked as he always did, carefree, languid, and sincere.

Jack searched for that trigger—that familiar feeling, and using all the power he had drawn out he threw it at them, attempting to send them flying with his Kinetic might.

All at once there were screams, followed soon after by the sound of banging and collision, erupting from somewhere behind him. Several loud clangs rang throughout the kitchen. Jack looked over his shoulder ... and felt a wave of embarrassment and shame, as he saw the three members of Cemmera's team crash and break the few remaining kitchen cabinets. The Kinetics were unconscious, and Cemmera looked livid.

"Whoops," Jack said to the group with Andy. "I meant to do that to you three, not sure what I did wrong. Hold still, okay? Let me try this again. Not sure why it went backwards."

Requiem clapped her hands together and cheered. "Oh! Brother, Jack, Darling! That was wonderful! Well, well, done."

Cemmera screamed at him, shaking her fist in the air. A look of depression replaced the previous fire in her eyes. She had been sent crashing into the broken refrigerator, and now, in addition to the water from the broken sink showering her head, cracked containers of milk and orange juice were leaking on top of her as well. Between the dirt from the garden, the juice, the milk, and the water mixing it all over her, Jack thought she kind of resembled an alien monster.

"HARRIS!" she roared at him. "What kind of a man can't aim straight? You buffoon, you idiot!"

Jack felt guilty. He sort of had an idea of what he'd done wrong, and he was certain that next time he could correct it. "Sorry about that, guys, I made an oopsie. My bad."

One of the Telekinetic brothers fell forward onto his face as the cabinet he was leaning on gave out, while the other simply closed his eyes and drooled. Cemmera tried to stand, and made it halfway too, before the slippery floor got the better of her, and she tripped, landing painfully on her rump. Jack wasn't sure if it was the water and juice in her eyes, but it looked to him like she was crying.

Ruin gave Andy a pat on the back. "Do you see, brother? And you said it was going to be hard to get Jack Harris to join our side. Look, he's only taken one glance at us and he's already betrayed his friends. He knew we were family at first sight."

Andy did not meet Jack's gaze, once again making Jack wonder if he'd done something horrible to him, but for the life of him, he couldn't remember. Andy retreated a few more steps, to stand behind Requiem.

Jack scratched his head. "Umm, I think you guys might be a little confused. That was an accid—"

Requiem cut him off and grabbed his hands. "Darling, I have a present for you! You're going to love this. Come, come, come!" Before Jack could protest, he found himself dragged away by the deranged girl. She led him out of the house and started off at a run, pulling him with her. Jack ran alongside her, more than just a little confused. Ruin and Andy followed close behind, though Andy just a bit farther away than Ruin.

They led him to the back of a large, beaten-up van. The front window was missing, and blood was everywhere, some in very odd places. There were splotches on the dashboard, steering wheel, and even some on the tires.

Requiem hopped in the back, and Jack turned to Andy. The boy shivered just by having Jack look at him.

"Andy, did I do something?"

Andy fell on his knees with tears in his eyes as he backed away from Jack at a crawl. His hands scraped the concrete while he back-crawled into Ruin. The young man held Andy in place, preventing him from going any farther.

"S-stay away from me, you monster!" Andy looked horrified, so much so that he was unable to stand.

"What did you do to our Brother?" Ruin asked Jack.

"I don't know. I don't remember. I feel like I did something bad, but it's just not ringing a bell. Oh, by the way, you three are like, under arrest and stuff."

Ruin laughed. He helped Andy get back to his feet. Requiem emerged from the back of the beaten-down vehicle with a small, fluffy animal. Jack's eyes lit up. He remembered having one very similar a long time ago.

"Is that a rabbit?" he asked.

"Yes, it is, and I got it for you, Darling."

Requiem passed the creature to Jack. It was a small, white little thing, with tiny blue eyes and a round nose. He held it in his arms, and for a moment Jack remembered the one he had lost so long ago.

"Thank you," Jack whispered. He didn't understand why such a horrible person would do something so nice for him. The little rabbit didn't struggle, it even started to fall asleep in Jack's arms. Requiem blushed, and while Jack had not known her for long, he had the feeling that it was an expression she seldom displayed. Even Andy and Ruin seemed surprised by it.

"It was ... nothing, Darling," she said, crossing her left foot over her right and averting her eyes. For a moment, some of the madness in her eyes seemed to fade, only to be replaced in an instant. "Now, our newest and dearest brother, you must come with us. We're working on getting a home for everyone—for you, me, and your two brothers. Mr. Wellington and the rabbit too, of course. You're going to love him, Darling."

Jack didn't understand why, but he felt no anger or hatred towards Requiem or her brother. There was something about them, something off. He couldn't place it, but there was a look in her eyes as if there were more to her buried beneath the madness. They'd committed such terrible and despicable crimes, they had ruined lives and crushed people's dreams, and yet, Jack could not bring himself to hate them.

"Can I ask you something, Requiem? Requiem *is* your name, right?"

She smiled. "Ask away, Darling."

"How come you guys kill people? When I'm alone with you guys, you don't seem like such bad people, so why? Don't you feel bad that you take away other people's lives? I don't understand why all those people you killed had to die."

Requiem turned away from Jack and said nothing. Ruin spoke in her place. "Brother Jack, my sister and I learned at a young age that regardless of what you do in this world, as long as you're strong enough to get away with it then it can't be wrong."

Jack tried not to let sadness fill his voice, but some of it seeped through. "But how can you say that, guys? You seem to really care about each other. Are you saying that if someone really powerful came along and killed one of you that ... that it's okay because they were strong enough to do it?"

Requiem spun around and grabbed Jack's shirt. *"No!"* she yelled. "No one can ever take away my family. No, that can never be right."

Jack put an arm on her shoulder, and she blushed yet again. "Then how?" he asked, looking deep into her maddened gaze, trying to see past it. "Then how can you make other people feel that pain?"

She released his shirt and walked away, mumbling words to herself that Jack couldn't make out. There was more to her—he was sure of it. Ruin sighed and walked over to Jack.

"You'll understand in time, Brother. For now, we should be on our way."

"No."

"No?" Ruin asked. "What do you mean, 'no'?"

"I mean, no way. I'm not joining you guys. What you three do is wrong, and awful. No one has the right to do what you've done. May I ask you a question? You're Ruin, right?"

He nodded. "Go right ahead."

"You killed a boy named Jonathan Herbert, right? He was my age. In fact, he was in my class. Do you remember?"

Ruin crossed his arms and rested his chin on his left fist, deep in thought. After a moment he looked at Jack. "I don't remember the names, but I think I know the one you're talking about. What about it?"

"Did you know that our solar system was formed by something called a nebula?"

Ruin looked taken aback. "What does that have to do with anything, Brother?"

Jack ignored the reply. "Just answer me. Did you know that?"

Ruin laughed. "No, Brother, I didn't."

"Well, Jonathan did. He told me that once. It's amazing what you can remember about people after you find out that they're no longer alive. He wasn't like other people. Then again, nobody in this world is truly like anybody else. Ya see, Jonathan wanted to be an astronomer."

Jack had to struggle to continue speaking. Requiem had returned, and now both her, her brother, and even Andy looked at Jack with confusion as tears began to fall down his face. A deep sadness entered Jack, but he wiped away his tears and continued to speak. His voice occasionally broke into a whimper.

"When we went to that space-camp thing on a field trip, I don't think I've ever seen a person so happy. All he wanted was to work for NASA. He had so much that he wanted to do and a whole life ahead of him to do it. Every day he would come to class wearing those t-shirts, with the stars and stuff. Adam used to talk to him about it, because Adam knows a lot of things. He and Jonathan would go at it for hours, and I'd listen. I didn't understand most of it, but I understood that it was his dream. I wasn't really his friend, but I always hoped that one day he made his dreams come true. And he was doing it, too! At least, he was until he met you two. I read the file, you know?"

It was becoming very hard to continue, but Jack forced out the words. "They say he was walking home one night from the astronomy club, and it was dark because he'd stayed late at school. You two held him down. You." He pointed to Ruin. "You pinned him down kinetically, and you." He pointed to Requiem. "You allowed Ruin to see his heart. It was the same heart that filled him with wonder when he looked at the stars, the place that made him chase his dreams. And for no reason other than 'fun' you decided that his hopes, his dreams, his life. You decided to take all of that away from him. All I want to know is why? What did he do wrong that he didn't deserve to live? Was it because you didn't like him? Or did you even know him? Tell me, you two. Tell me!"

Ruin's smile did not fade, but his eyes did seem to take on a more serious gaze. "We chose, that's why," he said. "There is no reason, don't you get it? We don't kill because we hate the people we're killing. We do it to prove that we can."

Jack felt the beginnings of anger. *"Is that all?"* he shouted. "Just for that? You're willing to take away everything from people, just to show that you can?"

"We don't expect you to understand right away, Brother. But until you—"

Jack roared at the two. *"I am not your damn brother! I will never be your brother!"* He forced calm into his voice. "I don't know what happened to you two, but I wish I did, really, I do. Whatever the reason though, you two can't be allowed to walk free anymore, same goes for Andy."

He gently put the rabbit on the ground and allowed himself to draw from the disgusting, vile source of power he had come to hate. He did not close the 'door' right away, he allowed it to pour into him a moment longer.

He was almost unable to close it off as the torrent of wild power rushed into him.

"Ruin, Darling, the Harris-boy is drawing quite a bit of power, almost as much as *you're* capable of."

Ruin spat on the ground. "I guess you were right, Brother Andy, we can't make Jack Harris our family after all."

"Please," Andy begged, "let me kill him."

Ruin and Requiem answered at the same time.

"No!" Requiem shouted.

"Go ahead, Andy," Ruin said. He looked to his sister. "We must face the facts, dearest Sister. The Harris-boy will never be ours."

She turned around to face away from them. "I will not watch this."

Jack saw Andy raise his arms, a look of hatred and disgust shining through his once youthful-looking eyes. Now they were hardened, and the twisted man who stood before him replaced any trace of the boy Jack knew.

Jack began to sweat, and his face began to heat up. He wasn't sure how he knew, but somehow he realized what Andy intended to do. Fear bubbled in his heart, as he realized he was going to meet the same fate as Richard and his family.

The heat grew, and in an instant it went from being a mild discomfort into a burning sensation. In another second it would become agony, and Jack had no idea how to stop it. "Andy, please," Jack begged.

Andy ignored him, a sadistic smile on his face. There was no breaking through to him, the time for that had passed. He was going to kill Jack.

Jack closed his eyes and prepared for the worst. After a few moments, when the pain didn't increase, he opened them again. Not only had the pain not increased, but now, about a foot in front of him he saw a puff of smoke. All three of the Psychs seemed confused.

"Sister, why is our brother's ability failing?" Ruin asked.

Requiem turned back around to face them, and of all things, she held a look of relief. "There is a Telepath somewhere around here, and he ... no she, is interfering."

Jack's eyes widened. He was being saved, but by who? Andy and Ruin frowned at something in the distance and Jack spun around. Walking toward them were the five people in the world Jack had come to trust implicitly.

"Jack, are you okay?" Sarah asked, sprinting towards him. She ran in an odd, off-balance way. Her head was staring at the ground. "I got to you just in time," she panted. She was out of breath.

Michael, Paro, and Kazou came close behind her. To Jack's left, he could see Melissa charging from the side of his house with worry on her face. *"Jack!"* she called. For some reason Paro frowned at her, and Melissa returned a guilty look. Ruin grabbed Requiem by the arm and backed up, followed closely by Andy.

"I don't reckon I'll let you get away this time," Michael spat. Two lampposts ripped free of the ground, which cast darkness on the area they'd once lit, and sped towards the three fleeing Psychs. Ruin made a chopping gesture in the air, swinging his stiffened hand downward. Another two lampposts ripped free, colliding with the first two and causing all four to fall to the ground with a tremendous crash. Every neighbor on the street opened their doors, each looking to find out what had been causing the commotion all night.

"Not here," Paro growled. "Definitely not here. Besides, we couldn't pursue these three even if we wanted to. We've got everything from serious, to critically injured in Alana's home, including Alana herself."

"Not this again," Michael moaned. "I'm not letting these fellas get away a second time just cause of some protocol or another."

The three Psychs broke into a sprint, darting away from Paro and his team. Jack didn't care much for protocol either. This had gone on for far too long. He was damned if he was going to allow there to be another Jonathan, or Richard, or whoever else lost their lives to the three Psychs.

Jack was still filled with the power he'd drawn. It began to hurt—he knew he'd need to either let it go or use it, and he had no idea how to let it go. He stepped forward away from the team. Paro gave him a warning glance.

"What do you think you're doing, Jack?" Paro said.

Jack looked at him. "What you signed me up to do."

In what was perhaps one of the riskiest things Jack had ever attempted, he once again tried to find a trigger. Only, this time it was one he didn't have a clue how to find. If he thought about what he wanted to do, many of them felt right, but even narrowing it down there were still so many possibilities. Once again, Jack guessed.

"Paro, I think Jack's using Reinforcement," Sarah said. Both concern and amazement filled her voice.

As the power rushed into Jack's legs, he couldn't help but feel elated. Never had he felt so much strength within himself.

So, this is what it feels like to be like Kazou or Melissa.

Jack squeezed and wiggled his toes then looked ahead of him. He crouched to the ground like an Olympian at the start of a race, and with warning shouts and threats coming from Paro behind him, he ran off.

"That's my boy!" Michael shouted, running after him.

"Foolish children!" Kazou yelled, following behind Michael.

"You have just earned eight slaps!" Melissa added, running swiftly on her feet, faster than all of them.

"Damn everyone with a Telekinetic affinity, Unrestricted or not!" came the voice of Paro from behind them, as he too took up the charge.

"Wait up, you guys!" Sarah laughed.

Chapter 30: Fight or Flight

"Alright, rest time," Jack called out, panting and struggling not to double over. They'd run almost three miles, and now they were making their way through a shopping district, with stores on both sides of the street. It was just before ten p.m. so activity was dying down. There were still quite a few parked cars pulled up to various Delis, video stores, and laundromats, though far less than there would've been an hour earlier.

"M-maybe this ... maybe, maybe this was a bad ... bad idea," Jack panted. He gasped for breath. "You know what? It totally was." He stopped running and leaned over, sucking in air through giant breaths. Jack hoped they'd catch the criminals within a few blocks, yet here they were, three miles away and still in pursuit.

Jack yelped as Melissa unexpectedly kicked him in his butt. "This was *your* idea, Jack, *you* made *us* chase after you, and now you just want to give up? No way—you picked your poison, now drink it."

Paro nodded in approval. "We've already broken protocol by leaving the scene of a crime with injured to pursue hostile Psychs, so now we're making the best of it. Jack, we're here because of you, got it? *Now move it, Harris!*"

Jack inhaled one more giant lungful of air, enjoying his brief respite, before he forced himself to charge forward yet again. At first, he had outrun all of them except Melissa, his legs fueled by his use of Reinforcement. It lasted for a good mile, but when the power ran out, he found that he couldn't draw more of it while running, like everyone else seemed to be able to do. Also, unless it was an emergency death situation, Jack needed to "work" himself up to the draw. It was because of that awful feeling, forcing him to mentally prepare himself for the inevitable discomfort. The team wasn't giving him the time to work up to it, and so now they were practically dragging him along.

They ran through the shopping district, making an echoing, clicking sound as six sets of feet kicked down on the concrete. It was now the only thing that could be heard besides the occasional passing of a car. Sarah claimed to be following the trail of the three Psychs, but Jack could see no sign of them. She was sweating profusely with her face turned downward to stare at the ground.

"Left," she breathed.

Paro had once again taken charge, now in the lead of all of them. He directed them to the left, across a narrow one-way street. The rest followed close behind. Jack wasn't the sharpest tool in the shed, but seeing the way Paro was so quick to take command, Jack was coming to realize that Paro had intended this all along.

A team-leader, or captain, or whatever Paro was, wouldn't be able to order his team to pursue fleeing criminals, not when there were injured around, that much Jack had gathered from listening to their conversations. But when Jack had started running away, Paro had more than enough power to stop him in his tracks. However, when Jack ran off he had only sighed and followed along. Paro needed an excuse, a reason to disobey protocol, and Jack had given it to him. Once again, Paro had outsmarted Jack, and now he couldn't even complain about the exhausting run. He had basically asked for it.

Down the narrow street, Paro led them through yet another narrow street with three-story apartment complexes on both sides. The street was empty, save for an old homeless man wheeling a cart. He stopped wheeling for a moment and looked at them, before deciding that Paro and the gang were of no interest to him, returning to once again wheel along.

"Wait!" Sarah yelled. "Down there."

Paro stopped short, causing Jack to almost bump into him. "Down where, Sarah?"

She pointed to a manhole cover that Paro was standing on. "They went into the sewers."

Jack looked at the manhole cover under Paro's foot. Even from where he was standing, he could smell the stench of raw sewage seeping out of it.

"Well," Jack began, "I guess we'll just have to let them get away this time."

Melissa glared at him. "Don't even start, Jack. You know damned well we're going after them."

Jack tensed. "Melissa, don't be ridiculous. There's peepee and poopoo and bacteria, and God knows what else flowing down there. I'd rather die than have to walk through that."

She rolled up her sleeve and made a fist. "Well, you're in luck, because I might just take you up on that offer."

Kazou shook his head. "Jack, do you remember why we're doing this? Keep that in the front of your mind at all times and the sewage will not bother you. Try and remember the faces of all the people those three have killed."

Jack thought on it and found that in some way, Kazou was right. Thinking of Jonathan's ruined dreams, the slaughter of an entire family, even the children ... it was almost enough to make Jack leap down there ahead of everyone—almost.

Paro backed up. Michael made a squeezing gesture with his hand, and the manhole cover was ripped off, flying into the air and landing several feet away from them.

"Do all Psychs have their own like, thing they do?" Jack asked. "Like, Michael squeezes his hand into a fist, Sarah looks down, and that one guy ... *damn!* I just knew his name like, two minutes go. Was it Rembrant? Whatever, that guy makes it look like he's karate chopping the air. Do a lot of Psychs do this?"

Paro answered, "I never thought I'd say this to you, Jack, but you truly are very astute. In fact, it's almost hard to believe, considering how ... lacking you are in other areas. Yes, many Psychs, myself included—but not all—have their own little quirks. It helps them focus."

Jack didn't seem to have any quirks, but he knew he wanted one. His mind raced with ideas. Maybe he would do a back flip before using Telekinesis?

No, he thought. *I know what would be so totally awesome! I should call out my attacks like in an anime. But wait, then they would know what I was gonna do. Oh, I know! I'll clap my hands together and slam them into the ground, like on that show 'Full Metal Alchemist'. But wait, that takes too long. Ah well, I'll figure it out later.*

Michael winked at Jack. "Bud, I reckon you should cover your nose," he said, tipping his cowboy hat. He was the first to leap down.

Paro followed, but not before he turned to look at Melissa. "You go last, Melissa. Make sure Jack actually follows along. This'll teach him not to volunteer himself on cases."

She nodded. "Got it, Paro." Paro leaped down, followed by Sarah, and then lastly Kazou.

"Remember, Harris," Kazou said, placing one hand on the ladder leading into the sewer. "Keep your mind on why we're here." He let go of the ladder and dropped down.

Jack walked over to the sewer entrance—and tried not to vomit. Looking down into the darkness, he felt the first pinch of fear. Even from above ground, the stench was too much to handle. Jack thought of something funny, and being the impulsive person he was, he said it without thinking. It was something that, if given even another moment's thought, he wouldn't dare say.

"Hey, Melissa," he joked. "It smells like *you* down in that—"

She pushed him, and he screamed, flailing his arms as he barely had time to catch onto the slippery ladder. He slid down to land with a thud on the moist sewer floor. The smell was horrible. *"Pee-yew!"*

Melissa didn't bother to use the ladder, and much like Kazou, she jumped down landing softly on her feet. Jack wondered if anything could hurt a Reinforcer.

It was dark, almost blindingly so. It looked like an underground maze to Jack. The sewers connected and ran for miles, twisting and turning, occasionally leading into other sewers. He really hoped the team knew what they were doing.

"Hey, did you guys ever notice that just about *every* Final-Fantasy game had a part where you had to go through sewers? I always got lost on those parts and had to fight a million random encounters, I can't tell you guys how many times I used to call Adam over for help." No one responded to him, making Jack feel sad and unappreciated.

"How far, Sarah?" Paro asked.

Sarah pointed. "They're about a half-mile ahead of us. They know we're still chasing."

Paro tilted his head in acknowledgement. "Alright, let's go." Paro ran into the distance, taking out his phone while he sped through the sewers.

Jack was exhausted. He didn't think he'd make it another half-mile, especially not in this disgusting place. Michael turned to him. "Jack, you need to draw some more power, and quick. You don't want to get left behind down here."

Jack moaned. "Just go without me. I'm exhausted. I've got nothing left to give."

"Nonsense, bud. Go on, I know you don't like it, but give it one more go. I promise ya there'll be no more running afterwards."

Jack closed his eyes and prepared himself for the sickening feeling. He hesitated and realized after a moment that if he didn't do it soon, he'd never work up the will again. He drew the power into himself, feeling the nauseating, uncomfortable sensation. It was worse than the feeling of a thousand spiders crawling on your face.

Once again he searched for the trigger. He'd been lucky the first time, but now he remembered where to find it. It seemed that some things were easier to locate than others. Some Telekinetic stuff was easy, like pushing things, but grabbing was harder to find. The thing that let him draw power into his legs was the easiest thing Jack had discovered so far. For a moment, it almost seemed worth the disgusting draw, as the wonderful feeling of empowerment went through his legs.

"Michael, how do you keep yourself going? You're not a Reinforcer."

"There's a reason they send us to boot-camp, Jack. There are things we need to be able to do without using our natural Psych affinities. I can only do very basic stuff in the other affinities, which is usually the case for most Psychs, excluding only you and Paro that I know of. I'll never be able to run as fast or for as long as Kazou or Melissa, but I reckon I can still keep myself going longer than the average human."

"What's boot-camp? Actually, you know what? I don't even care. Let's just get out of this yucky place."

They caught up to Melissa, Kazou, and Paro. It was now so dark that Jack couldn't see more than a foot or two in front of him. They were following Paro based on sound alone and listening for the audible splashes as feet smashed into what Jack prayed was only water.

There was a squeak, and Jack knew that there were rats around. He hoped they'd reach wherever they were going soon. Somewhere in front of him, Jack heard Paro mumble into his phone, but he couldn't make out what was being said.

He felt something touch his shoulder, and he came close to screaming.

"Jack," said Melissa. "How are you holding up? I never thought I'd see you use Reinforcement. If you've got any questions just ask me."

"I thought you were a rat, Melissa. No, wait! Don't slap me—that's not what I meant. I'm just kinda afraid of rats, and I felt you touch my shoulder."

She laughed. "Oh, is that what it was?"

Even having run for miles, Melissa didn't seem to be breathing heavily. There was not a single bead of sweat on her face, which Jack could barely make out in the scant light as she ran beside him in the dark sewer. Jack was no longer sweating either, now that his legs were wrapped with the power of Reinforcement.

"Jack, there's something I want to ask you, and I want you to tell me the truth," Melissa said. She lowered her voice to a whisper. "I really need to know."

Jack turned to Melissa and looked into her eyes. There was something different about her. She looked worried, like she was bringing up something painful. She even slowed down, holding Jack's arm so he'd slow down with her. Whatever it was that was bothering her, she was taking it seriously.

"What's wrong?" Jack answered in a whisper. He kept his voice low, just loud enough for her to hear it. She clearly didn't want them to be overheard. Melissa looked both ahead of her and over her shoulder before continuing.

"Do you remember when we fought back in H.Q?"

Jack smiled, and he almost regretted it, because he kicked on the ground too hard and a splash of murky sewage water rose almost to the level of his mouth.

"Yeah," he whispered back. "Don't think I forgot about that date, either."

She smiled for a moment before her expression turned solemn. "How much ... of your power were you using?" she asked.

"Towards the end, I mean, before Paro told us to tone it down. Was it close to half?"

Jack tried to remember. He recalled that he'd allowed just a drop more power in than he usually did, and with a shudder, he remembered feeling like it would kill him.

"Hmm," Jack whispered. "I'm not sure how to answer."

Melissa glanced around once again to make sure they were far enough away not to be overheard. Then she spoke, but in an even quieter whisper, and Jack had to strain to hear her.

"I'm pretty powerful among Psychs, Jack. For the average Psych, they draw power from a source that's something that's like a cup of water. For me, it's more like a bowl. For someone like Paro, I'd be willing to bet it's almost as large as a puddle. How much did you draw, Jack?

Jack thought about the question and realized that it made a lot of sense to think about it in those terms. "I see what you're asking. I'd say it was only small drop, like what comes out of dripping faucet. Just a tiny amount and even that felt terrible."

There was a long pause before Melissa spoke again, during which she and Jack ran side-by-side in the darkness. For the first time, she was breathing heavier and sweat was finally beginning to show on her forehead. Somehow, Jack didn't think it was because of the run.

"Jack," she said in a nervous whisper. "A small drop, but out of how much? Tell me, please."

Jack decided there was no reason to lie. "I don't know how Psychs normally measure these things, but I guess, hmm, maybe the ocean?"

"*What!*" Paro's voice shouted from ahead of them. He had stopped and within a few moments, Melissa and Jack had caught up to him. There was an awkward silence as they stood in the darkness, but through the occasional shadows cast from the streetlights above, Jack could see a look of disbelief on Paro's face. Michael and Sarah seemed as if they were about to faint, while Kazou kept his usual stern, stone-faced expression.

Paro grabbed Jack's shoulders. "Are you serious, Jack? About what you just told Melissa, I mean."

Jack frowned at him. "I don't know how you did it, but eavesdropping isn't polite, Paro." Upon hearing this, Sarah turned away with a look of guilt, glancing at something in the distance. "You're going to learn that everything is my business, Jack, especially when it comes to Psychs on my team. Now, answer me, was what you just said the truth?"

Jack shrugged. "I guess."

Kazou walked between them. "Is now the time for this conversation?" he asked.

Paro flinched and shook his head. "You're right, Kazou," he said, releasing Jack's shoulders. "Sarah, how far?"

"Just ahead, make a right here and head up the next ladder."

Paro led them down one last stretch of sewer, until finally they arrived at the ladder that would lead them out of it. Never in Jack's life had he been so glad to see a ladder. Before any of them could make a move, Jack was already charging at it, scrambling up. As the distance between him and the sewer grew, he felt more and more at ease.

They emerged into another part of town, about a mile away. It took Jack a moment to get his bearings, but he realized they were in Anker town, not far from where Jonathan had died.

Jonathan, Jack thought. *I'm sorry you didn't get to be what you wanted. I'll try to make things right.*

Paro looked at his watch and then turned to Sarah. "Now how far?"

"They're moving much faster than before, so they're definitely not on foot anymore, but if we don't hurry up we'll lose them."

As if in answer to their desperation, bright headlights approached in the distance, almost blinding Jack. Pulling up alongside them was a van very similar to the one Requiem had gone inside of to fetch him the rabbit.

The Rabbit! We left it on the side of the road.

The side door to the van slid open, and Paro rushed everyone inside. Nineteen recon officers in full T.A.C gear, armed with assault rifles and bulletproof vests were waiting for them. Each one gave Jack a dirty look for some reason. He recognized quite a few of them. They had been there the day Andy was captured.

The van only remained motionless for about fifteen seconds, as Paro threw everyone inside and ordered the driver to get a move-on. "Hurry!" he yelled. "Sarah is going to lose the trace—drive as fast as you can."

The sudden lurch of acceleration was far more than Jack had expected. He tripped and fell then braced himself for a rough fall on his back. When he didn't hit the ground, he smiled up into the face of Melissa, almost carrying him in her arms.

"Thanks, Melissa." She pushed him off, and he sat down to fasten his seatbelt. The vehicle picked up even more speed, and Jack prayed they didn't get into an accident along the way.

"Where did they go?" Deven asked Alana while the medics patched her up and placed an icepack on her forehead. The Harris residence was now teeming with activity, over twenty emergency personnel, all 'normal' men who worked for the Psych-organization. They did their best to help collect evidence, care for the wounded, and clean the place up. They were the General's own personal men.

Alana grabbed Deven's shoulder, gripping him by the tattooed general's insignia and pulling herself up into a sitting position. Deven had to admit, she was one tough woman.

"I didn't mean to kill him," she said with remorse. "But it was life or death."

Deven looked over to the massacred Op. team member, Julian Santos, once a powerful Telepath, now nothing more than a dead body.

"Alana, where did the rest of Cemmera's team go? They aren't here."

She shook her head. "I don't know. Hopefully, they went to hell."

Deven laughed uproariously. "Still with the dark humor I see, Alana."

She grabbed his other shoulder and lifted herself back to her feet. Deven watched as anger replaced her sadness. She looked around at her ruined home.

"What's going to happen to me now? They'll kill me for what I've done. I'll be sentenced to death for sure. For a civilian to attack and kill a member of a Psych team ... what crime could be worse?"

Deven tried to remain straight-faced, but he couldn't help but grin. "How do you figure, Alana? It was him who committed the serious crime of attacking a general."

Alana made a sour face. "General? I quit ten years ago. What are you on about, Deven?"

Deven's grin widened. "Yes, you did quit ten years ago, and a wonderful retirement you had. I still wonder why you gave it all up, coming into my office yesterday and reenlisting. But who can tell?"

Alana gave him a reproachful look. "Deven, tell me you didn't."

He reached into his pocket and revealed the document, showing her the blood-seal. "But I did, General Alana Harris, welcome back."

Alana's face contorted, going from anger, to confusion, finally settling on unfiltered amusement. "It's this or death, isn't it?"

Deven shrugged. "Do you really want to find out?"

He braced himself. What he had to say next was going to sting. Most of the Psych Generals were serious, uptight people, lacking any sense of humor whatsoever. Alana and Deven had been the only two generals back in the day willing to mingle, and on occasion even party with those who'd served under them. He was glad to have the woman back—even if it was against her wishes—her playfulness and humor made her the only general he'd ever really liked—the only general that was similar to him.

When she saw his expression, she definitely knew what he had to say was going to be bad. "Out with it," she demanded.

"Rose has had another vision, Alana. It was about your son."

As he spoke the words to her, she fell to her knees and looked at him with pleading eyes. "That's not the life I want for him," she begged.

Deven spoke with genuine sympathy. "But it's the one the world is going to need. Without him ... God help us all."

.

Chapter 31: Forgiveness is a luxury

Jack squeezed his fingers around the seatbelt across his chest. He closed his eyes, struggling to remain calm as the large van accelerated and sped along The Outerbridge Crossing leading into Staten Island.

Andy had killed yet again. Several miles back they'd come across a dead family lying on the side of the road, all showing signs of death by Manipulation. Despite the need for haste, Paro had taken the time to at least cover what remained of their bodies—it wasn't much—before they continued along and resumed the chase. From what the team could piece together, the three were only interested in the family's vehicle, a silver Lexus ES.

One thing was clear though—their deaths were unnecessary. Jack still didn't know much about Psychs, but he knew that the one called Ruin, the Telekinetic, could have easily pulled them from the vehicle and left them on the road. Instead, Andy had decided to slaughter even more people.

Jack cried out as the vehicle made a sharp left. The van tilted slightly and pulled into the wrong lane, cutting off slower moving automobiles in front of them. Cars honked and drivers screamed while the van raced over the bridge. Jack looked out of the rear window and noticed that some cars had even come to a stop. Furious drivers exited their vehicles and shook fists, probably wondering why on earth someone would drive like such a maniac.

The nineteen recon officers didn't appear bothered by the reckless driving—neither the insane speed nor the angry shouts from civilian vehicles. Jack didn't see any fear on their faces, except for the times when they looked over at him. Why did he, out of all people, intimidate the tough-looking men and women of the recon teams? Jack shook his head. He supposed that now wasn't the time to find out. The recon officers sat with assault rifles held over their laps, hands gripping the weapons in a tight squeeze.

The rest of Paro's team showed no trace of fear, either. Paro was up front, shouting orders at the driver while Sarah remained deep in concentration looking at the ground. The only time she looked up was to shout information at Paro, and then she'd return soon after to continue her Telepathy. Michael and Kazou were making small talk, and Melissa was sitting with her (gorgeous) legs folded while she read a fashion magazine.

Would now be a good time to make another move? Damn, I'm not good when it comes to women so I don't know all the rules. Is a high-speed chase a good or bad time to turn up the heat? Michael would know.

Jack looked over to Michael. The blond-haired rogue met his eyes and tipped his cowboy hat. Jack didn't know anything about Telepathy, but when it came to Michael, he didn't need to. Lately, it seemed like the two could exchange feelings just by glancing at each other.

Jack winked, and for a fleeting moment, he shifted an eye over to Melissa. Then he returned to meet Michael's gaze and raised a questioning eyebrow. *"What do I do?"* he thought with a shrug.

Michael had no issue picking up on Jack's message. In return, he twirled his finger in the air then made a fist, slamming it into his palm. Jack understood the meaning perfectly. *"Tell her she has nice hair."*

Jack summoned all of the courage he could muster and cleared his throat. "Hey, Melissa, I love your golden hair. You really are the most beautiful thing in the world."

Melissa ignored the response and turned another page in her magazine. "Paro," she said after a moment. "Jack and Michael are up to their nonsense again. Do something about it please."

Paro glared at the two of them. "Cut it out, guys."

Michael gave Paro a look of outrage. "I haven't said a word to Jack, or Melissa for that matter, in like, ten minutes! She's got no proof or nothin'."

"I don't care," Paro growled. "I believe everything Melissa says, especially when it comes to you two damn Kinetics. Whatever it is you're doing, cut it out and be serious."

Unrestricted or not, Jack was being treated like the affinity he was born with. Paro had told Jack that his own natural affinity was Reinforcement, like Kazou or Melissa. Jack wondered if that was why Reinforcement was so much easier for Paro, or if that was why he used it more than anything else.

Jack didn't think it was possible, but the van managed to pick up even more speed. It left the bridge and entered Staten Island. Jack watched in horror as they approached a tollbooth. The vehicle showed no signs of slowing down.

"Paro, aren't we going to stop?" Jack asked.

"Like hell," he said. He shouted an order to the driver and the van continued forward, crashing into the lowered gate and ripping it off the booth. The teller shouted through the window at them as they sped past. He picked up a phone, probably calling the police or something.

Not even a minute later, Paro's phone rang, and he snatched it from his pocket. "Yeah ... yeah, don't worry. Yeah, that was us. Send the police away and tell them to stay clear. That's right, yeah." His eyes widened. "Please don't tell me that. She's a general again? My life is going to be even more miserable now."

Jack didn't know what he was talking about, but he suspected that Paro had called off the police. It was amazing what they could get away with.

"I think we're close!" Sarah called out. She stood up and pointed to something in the distance.

Jack turned to look out of the front window. He'd never been to Staten Island before, but he was surprised by just how open it was. Unlike Manhattan, Staten Island looked like a slightly more enclosed area than his own town. There were small to large houses, stores and small shopping centers, followed again by more homes. It was hard to see in the dark of night, but speeding past a red-light in the distance, he could just make out the silver car.

The driver shouted at Paro, but Paro shouted back even louder. "I don't care, slam your foot down!"

Jack moaned as the engine screamed at them, picking up so much speed that Jack had to struggle not to cover his eyes like a child. The van rocketed into a narrow street. A pedestrian removing a grocery bag out of his Honda jumped out of the way. With a loud crunch his passenger-side door was ripped off the vehicle, smashing into—and denting—a parked car just ahead of him.

"*We're all going to die!*" Jack shouted, undoing his buckle and standing up. He didn't know where he was going, but his first instinct was to flee. He realized just a moment too late, how stupid of an idea it was to take off his seatbelt.

The van, with no apparent warning, took a sharp left, and Jack was sent flying to the front. Paro shouted curses as Jack slammed into him, sending both he and his team-leader banging into the radio system. Music blasted at a volume so loud that even if the collision with the car door didn't wake up the residents on the street, then the booming voice of Lady Gaga surely would.

"*I'm on the edge, of glory.*"

Jack tried to get off Paro and failed, unable to regain his balance. Before he could try again, Melissa grabbed him by the neck and pulled him back to his seat. Her fingers were squeezing way harder than they needed to be. "*Ouch, stop, it was an accident!*"

"Don't get out of your seat again, Jack. Are you nuts? Don't force me to sit on your lap and buckle myself in with you. Act like an adult."

The word "*myself*" hadn't even fully left her lips, and already Michael was giving Jack a massive thumbs-up.

"*Get out of your seat!*" his expression shouted. Jack thought the better of it and strapped himself back in as Melissa returned to her own seat.

They were gaining on the car, faster than Jack had believed they'd be able to given the large size of the van and the speediness of the silver car, which was only a block ahead of them now. The car sped past a stop sign and almost impacted with an oncoming minivan. Even from where Jack was sitting, he could see the outlines of the three murderous Psychs.

"Can you stop it, Michael?" Paro asked.

"No, their Path is protecting the vehicle. I can't do anything to it."

Paro nodded and didn't hesitate, revising his plans in an instant.

"Michael, we're going loud! Break it." Paro ordered.

Jack wondered what the words meant, but he didn't wonder for long. Michael squeezed his fist and the front window of the van shattered outward, spraying sharp chunks of glass to both sides of the street, far enough away that the van didn't risk running over them and getting a flat.

Four of the recon officers rushed to the front of the vehicle, weapons in hand. Paro stepped out of the way, and Jack watched in bewilderment as the four guns flashed, the sound of gunfire overshadowing even the tremendous roar of the engine.

"Back-left tire hit," the leftmost officer called. She was the youngest-looking of all the recon officers, perhaps only a year or two older than Jack.

"Back-right hit," she called yet again.

The silver Lexus swerved on the road, losing control and skidding. The vehicle came to a stop, and Jack, without even realizing he was doing so, howled in victory. "Hell yeah! You go, girl!"

The recon officer turned to him and smiled—it was the first time one of them had looked at him with anything other than disgust. "My name is Rebecca, Mr. Harris. And yeah, I am kind of awesome." She winked.

"You're more than awesome," he cheered. For some reason, Melissa snarled. Rebecca returned to her seat, but not before stopping to ruffle Jack's hair. Even with the heavy dark-blue T.A.C gear, she was gorgeous. She had bright red hair, smooth green eyes, and freckle just above her nose that only made her look cuter.

Melissa didn't seem to like the exchange for some reason and leaned over to kick Jack in the shin. He cried out in pain and shot Melissa a look of hurt.

What is her problem? Jack thought bitterly.

The van sped towards the now immobile car. They were on a busy intersection across the street from a train terminal, not unlike the one Jack had brought Andy to back at home. The three Psychs jumped out of the car and made a run for the station. The driver slammed on the brakes, and Jack prepared himself. This time, they weren't getting away.

Chapter 32: Crushed

Before the van had fully stopped moving, Jack, followed by the rest of the team, leapt out of the side door and hit the ground running. Jack charged for all he was worth, unwilling to let Andy get any farther or allow him to kill even more people. Melissa grabbed the back of Jack's shirt while he was still mid-run, causing him to fall backwards.

"Jack, are you out of your mind?" Cars flew by on the other end of the intersection. The roar of their passing left a ringing sound in Jack's ears. "Wait for the red-light. What good will it do if you go after them and get yourself killed by a car?"

It only took a few moments for the light to turn red and the passing cars to stop, but to Jack it felt like an eternity. People watched in fascination as the nineteen heavily armed recon officers ran across the intersection with Jack and the team, assault rifles cradled in their arms. One man stuck his head out of his car and shouted at them.

"Hey!" he yelled. "Is there something going on? Is there a terrorist attack or something?"

Other people stared wide-eyed and added their own voices. Jack followed Paro and the recon officers, ignoring the shouts from behind him. The fact that it was night only added to the suspense.

"Won't they become suspicious?" Jack asked while he ran. They raced into the train terminal and through a crowd of terrified onlookers, most of who were probably wondering why a gigantic police force—what they probably assumed were SWAT officers—were storming their location.

"Of course," Paro said, "but as long as we refrain from using any Psych abilities, anything that happens can be explained. People already know about the series of murders in Elms New Jersey, and if we succeed here—which we must—then they'll also learn that the murderers were apprehended at a train station in Staten Island. Only a few people will ever know the full details."

Jack followed Paro to the head of the stairs leading down to the tracks. It was a wide area with no roof, and the ceiling consisted of only rusty metallic beams with large windowless openings along the top, supported by old, dirty beams running from the ground up.

Paro spoke to the men behind him. "Recon teams, listen carefully. Secure the area, surround the complex, and evacuate all civilians. Don't follow us down. My team will handle it from here."

The officers saluted Paro then eighteen of them broke formation to evacuate the citizens in the terminal. There were no protests, or even questions from the people who were attempting to travel by train that night. Most had already left the moment they saw the recon officers rushing inside, and the few that didn't were more than happy to walk, if not sprint away.

One recon officer remained behind, Rebecca, the one who'd shot the tires out the Lexus Andy had fled in. "Mr. Harris," she said. "Be careful." She turned and with haste rejoined her squad members.

Jack didn't know what that was all about, but for some reason Melissa had a dangerous glint in her eyes upon witnessing it. Jack followed Paro down the steps and looked around the station for any sight of Andy and the other Psychs.

"They should be surrounded," Sarah said. "They are in this room somewhere. I'm sure of it, yet ... I can't pinpoint their exact location. They're probably hiding."

Paro grinned. "They probably think they'll sneak onboard a train, but little do they know none are coming—I've taken care of that. Michal, Kazou, keep your guard up. If their Kinetic tries to throw anything at us, you two need to either knock it out with Telekinesis, or beat it down with fists. Melissa and Jack, I want you two to stay close and keep your eyes peeled. If you see them, make sure to tell me. Let me go in first. And Melissa," he added in a lowered voice. "If you see the eyes ... you know what to do."

A look of worry crossed her for a moment, replaced soon after with a bold determination. "I do," she answered.

Jack had no idea what they were talking about, but at that moment he didn't care. All he wanted was to put a stop to the murders and to find Andy.

Andy, why do I still feel like I did something terrible to you? And why can't I remember?

Michael and Kazou spread out to both sides of the group, and Jack appreciated the well thought out formations Paro used. With one of them covering each side, they'd be able to protect the team regardless of where an attack came from.

Paro motioned for the rest of the team to follow, and together they crept along the station. There were benches on both sides, as well as stairs on both ends that led to and from the terminal. Jack was certain they'd arrived early enough, at least so that if Andy or the other Psychs tried to escape through either set of stairs, then the recon officers would've radioed it in. That meant they were in the station somewhere.

"Let's check the other end of the tracks," Sarah said. "They're in here for sure, but where are they hiding?"

Melissa once again grabbed Jack's shirt. "Now what, Melissa?" Jack grumbled. "I'm not even moving."

"Yeah," she said, "but in a second or two you and I both know that you'd try to run across those train tracks—and don't even give me that look. Quit acting like you wouldn't."

They walked down the narrow path leading to the other end of the room and crossed over the ramp that allowed passage from one side of the tracks to the other. Jack looked around the room and realized that for a train station, there were quite a few places to hide.

The place was filthy and filled with discarded newspapers, plastic—and sometimes glass—cups and bottles everywhere, old wrinkled potato chip bags and discarded shoes. There were even half-eaten rotten sandwiches and other types of stuff that looked like at one time it might've been food.

They moved at a slow pace. Every few feet there was a ridge in the beams behind them, a place where a few people might've been able to hide in the dark of the night. They were careful to check each one, making sure it was empty. In the daytime, there'd have been no place for the three to hide, but at night, finding them was a daunting task.

"They must have broken all the lights," Kazou said. "It shouldn't be this dark in here. Sarah, are you positive they're still in this area? We've checked everywhere. I think we should retrace our steps."

She stomped her foot to the ground like a child and gave Kazou a defiant look. "I am!" she insisted. She turned around to face away and lowered her head in disappointment. Jack wondered why she had such a moody reaction.

Melissa whispered in his ear, *"She's very sensitive when it comes to people doubting her, Jack. Sarah is one of the weakest Telepaths in our organization. Actually, she's one of the weakest Psychs altogether. It really, really, really upsets her. She always doubts and hates herself whenever she makes a mistake. She thinks she's not good enough for us."*

Jack nodded. "Hey, Kazou," he called out.

Kazou turned around and faced Jack. "Yes?"

"We better keep looking because if someone as good as Sarah is saying they're still in here, well, I'd bet my own life that they're just under our noses."

It was hard to make out with her face turned away from them, combined with the darkness of the terminal, but Jack was sure he saw the left side of Sarah's face raise into a smile. She even seemed to blush. Michael and Paro too, seemed to be wearing genuine smiles, and Michael even winked.

"Jack's right, Kazou," Michael said. "I trust Sarah with my life. If she says they're here, then they are."

Kazou only shrugged and moved with them along the narrow path while they continued their search. They reached the other end of the room, across the side of the tracks opposite from where they'd entered. The team peered around in confusion. Jack was getting desperate.

"We've checked everywhere," Jack said. "I don't get it. Where could they have gone?"

Sarah shifted uneasily on her feet. "Maybe I was wrong after all," she said doubtfully. "I'm really not all that good." She twirled her fingers and tried not to meet their eyes.

Paro put a hand on her shoulder. "Sarah," he said. "I tell you this all the time, but you're too hard on yourself. You're one of the—"

"Are you crazy?" Jack yelled at her. "You're amazing, Sarah. You brought us here. Without you we wouldn't have even gotten this far. You're totally cool, and I know I'm new to the team and all, but I don't think there's anyone else than you that I'd rather be on the same side as. Now tell us, because I know that you know. Are they still in here?"

Sarah scrambled forward and hugged Jack, kissing his forehead. "Thank you." With a new strength in her eyes, she glanced down to the floor. "Yes. They are definitely here." Her voice left no hint of doubt or question.

Paro gave Jack a pat on the back. "Just this once," Paro whispered, "I'll let you off the hook for interrupting me."

Jack broke away from them. He walked forward towards the tip of the narrow pathway. It was a bit of a steep drop to the tracks below—not enough to cause damage but enough to make a person grunt in pain. He was careful not to fall off as he scanned the area. Something had been bothering him since they'd entered the terminal.

"Something wrong, Jack?" Paro asked.

"Nah, it's nothing. I mean. It's making me a little nervous, but you guys didn't say anything about it so I'm sure it's fine."

Michael scratched his head and looked around, receiving blank stares from the rest of the team. "Does anyone know what he's talking about? Jack, what's making you nervous?"

"Well, the beams that are holding up that roof-thing. I mean, if you look closely they look like they've been crumbling and getting weaker, but you guys didn't say anything, so I figured it must be normal."

Michael and Sarah regarded each other in confusion, while Kazou, Paro and Melissa twitched as if struggling to remain calm. "Paro, please tell me Jack's just seeing things." Melissa begged.

Paro walked to the nearest support-beam, and ran a hand over it. Panic sprung up almost immediately on his face. It spread outward, and like a chain reaction, caused the rest of the team become panicked one by one, until even Kazou appeared dismayed.

"Damnit, Jack, why didn't you say anything before?" Paro yelled. "Why did you wait until now?"

Jack, a little annoyed, frowned—he did *not* like when people shouted at him. He pointed a finger at Paro and gave a dirty look. "Well, you guys are supposed to be all like, amazing and stuff, right? I just thought that you or one of the other guys would say something if anything was wrong. What are the chances of someone like me noticing it and no one else?"

Paro closed his eyes and his voice dulled to a whisper. "Sarah, quit tracing them for a moment. Divert your attention to sensing Psych ability. Are there any Psychs currently drawing or using power?"

She blinked, and once again returned to look downward. She only remained in the position a moment, before whipping her head towards the team. Her face brightened with alarm.

"Yes! Manipulation, Telekinesis, and ... and there's more. It feels like it's been going on for a while. Paro, oh, oh God! They're going to rip this place down around us. They're going to crush us!"

Michael and Kazou stood dazed. Melissa grabbed Jack's arm for dear life, clinging to him. Jack felt his own rising terror, but he forced himself to remain calm. Paro seemed to be doing the same, and one at a time, the team went from frantic to a reluctant calm.

"We're going to leave right now. If they're going to bring this place down, they'll only be killing themselves. We'll be up there." Paro pointed to the nearest staircase. "We'll be waiting for them."

Jack noticed movement in the corner of his eye. "Paro, look!"

On the side of the tracks they'd entered, three forms crawled out from beneath a bench. There was no doubt that what Jack was seeing were the forms of Andy, Ruin, and the maddened Requiem. Requiem was the first to her feet. She licked her lips and looked at them from across the tracks.

"Darling," she spoke directly to Jack, "I'd leave if I were you."

Ruin peered daggers at her, but he was quick to return to his normal, carefree visage. "We've been waiting for you," he said. "Andy and I have been working up a little surprise for our good friends."

Paro spat on the floor and looked apologetically at his team. "Damn," he muttered. "How did we not look under the benches? I didn't think three people could fit under a single bench."

Andy focused his attention on Jack, with an intensity that felt like he was trying to burn a hole through his head with only his eyes.

"I wish I could stay to see you die, Jack." There was still a great deal of fear and terror in the boy, apparent in his shaky voice.

"Andy," Jack breathed. Before anyone—especially Melissa—could attempt to stop him, Jack drew on his disgusting, vile source of power. Once again, he poured it into his legs, and with all of his strength he leapt across the tracks, clearing fifty feet of air in a single leap. There was a loud bang as he landed on the other side. Now he stood only a few feet from the three Psychs. Andy backed up and ran behind Requiem, shivering and shaking.

"*Jack!*" Melissa cried.

"No, don't!" Paro yelled—but not in time to stop Melissa from doing the same. Only a Reinforcer could make a jump from such a distance. She landed next to Jack with her usual smooth gracefulness.

There was a rumbling sound as the beams crumbled and shook. The roof-supported metallic rods rang with a deafening sound, painful to Jack's ears.

Paro turned to Sarah and Michael. "There's no time!" he shouted. "We need to go—now!"

"I don't think so," Ruin laughed. "Andy, weaken that for me, please. Thank you." He made a gesture of chopping air, and the stairway behind Paro imploded, collapsing and barring their escape.

"We, on the other hand, really need to go," Ruin said. Requiem and Andy followed him as he walked casually up the stairs just to the left of the narrow walkway where Jack and Melissa were huddled together. They didn't even glance at the two on their way out—they walked so close that their clothing brushed against Jack's.

Jack was torn, and he suspected that Melissa was too. Were they supposed to chase or stay and try and help their team?

"Paro, please," Michael begged. "You and Kazou can make that jump. You can use Reinforcement. Grab Sarah and go. These roof-beams are going to collapse any second. Look, there's no point in all of us dying, and I'm doing everything I can to hold them in place. I can't stop for even a second. Just go!"

"You're right," Paro said. His voice lowered to a barely audible whisper. "There's no point in all of us dying." He turned to Melissa and shouted, "Catch!"

Michael and Sarah screamed in surprise as they were telekinetically flung at Melissa, soaring across the train-tracks. She braced herself and caught the two with a grunt then set them down beside Jack. A large, thick beam fell from above, crashing with a tremendous clang on top of the tracks with a force that would crush a car as easily as it would a person.

Kazou was mid-jump at the time and narrowly managed to survive being smashed by it. He cleared the object by an inch and came to land with a thud next to the four of them.

"Paro, hurry!" Sarah called. "Jump across, please, hurry."

Paro looked as if he were about to jump but stopped and instead glanced upwards. All at once, the beams gave out, and fifty deadly pieces of metal began to fall, moments from ending the lives of all six of them. They would all be dead within seconds.

Jack felt a foreign presence wrap around his waist, and by the gasps from around him, he could tell that the rest of the team did too. He realized what was happening. He tried to shout, but it was too late. An invisible grip picked up Jack and his four team-members and then threw them back towards the stairs. Even as he hurled through the air, Jack could see Paro grunting and sweating with exertion.

He tried to run forward to help, but Melissa grabbed him and pulled him up the steps, while Michael dragged Sarah who was attempting the same. Kazou assisted where he could, and within a few seconds, the overwhelming sound hit them.

One after the other, they heard the terrible ringing-clash as beam after beam collided with the train-tracks. It was so loud that Jack had to drop to the floor and cover his ears, as the metal screeched at them.

"No!" Sarah cried. "Did ... did Paro just die?"

When the sound quieted, Jack tried to run back down, but the crashed roof-beams completely sealed off the entrance. The sickening feeling of anger entered Jack, the one that he despised almost as much as the draw of power. He forced any thoughts of Paro out of his mind. Andy and his friends had done it yet again—they'd taken what they had no right to.

Jack marched up the stairs. He wasn't going to let them get away. Melissa once again grabbed him by his shoulders and pulled him back.

"No," she said. "Don't go after them. We need to call for help. We don't even know where they went or where our recon officers are."

"I can't reach them on the radio," Kazou said. He was showing little emotion, but a small amount of paranoia did creep into his voice.

Sarah fell to her knees and wept openly. Tears streaked down her face and splashed on the ground. "He couldn't have survived that," she cried. "Paro's dead, Michael."

Michael tried to comfort her, but he too grew red in the eyes. Jack had seen enough. He brushed off Melissa, and before she could respond he dashed up the stairs, back into the terminal. The three were still there, walking with a slow confidence and chatting with each other.

"*Andy!*" Jack thundered. "Where the hell do you think you're going?"

Andy turned around and almost fell to the floor in shock. "You're alive?" he shouted. "But how?"

Jack gritted his teeth and drew again from that vile part of him, almost howling in discomfort as the cringe-worthy nausea overwhelmed his senses. He let the power enter him for a second longer than he knew he should, but Jack needed it now more than ever. He felt it rush in, a maddening, overwhelming stampede of pure energy. After a moment it began to hurt, and he realized he'd drawn enough. He tried to cut off the flow of power.

I can't stop! he realized with a start.

Jack screamed, loud and pained, as Melissa, Sarah, Kazou and Michael rushed to join his side. "I can't stop!" he yelled at the top of his lungs.

"Can't stop what? What is he talking about?" Sarah asked. Andy and the two twisted siblings watched in fascination instead of fleeing, observing Jack's odd behavior.

Jack grabbed the sides of his head with his hands, and with every bit of willpower he possessed, he forced himself to close that door, that part of him overflowing with power. He stood back to his feet and eyed the three Psychs with a growing rage that burned even more than the draw of the power.

"Andy," he growled. The boy shrieked as Jack spoke. "You and your friends aren't leaving."

Jack searched for that familiar trigger, the one that he knew better than all others. With a massive burst, Jack hurled his growing hate at the three of them. Ruin's face changed instantly from relaxed to surprised.

"I don't know if I can stop this!" Ruin called out. He gestured at the air. Jack could see what he was doing, in a way he hadn't been able to before. Jack's projection of energy was a whirling force of might, and with what Jack supposed was all the strength the other Telekinetic could muster, Ruin threw an equally powerful one back at him. The two forces rippled across air with a buzzing hiss as they traveled then collided together in the space halfway between Paro's team and Andy's.

There was a massive explosion, one even louder than the previous sound of collapsing beams. Every window in the terminal exploded and shattered. The sliding entrance-door was ripped from its hinges and flew through the air, before crashing into a wall behind them and breaking into pieces. Trash cans, litter, and even vending machines—all were ripped free from where they sat and were sent scattering in every direction. The noise was maddening. In the middle of the room, at the point where the two forces collided, the marble floor began to crack, and after a moment, it too ripped free and was sent reeling to every corner.

Michael and Kazou bolted in front of Jack, Sarah, and Melissa, and did their best to keep stray objects from knocking into them. Michael squeezed his fist and a sharpened piece of glass was sent in the opposite direction. Kazou charged forward—a vending machine only a moment from crashing into and killing Michael smashed against Kazou's fist, falling harmlessly to the ground.

Melissa didn't move. She held her palm to her mouth and gasped as the terminal became a scene of complete and utter destruction. When the noise had finally quieted and objects around the room finally ceased moving, no one said a word—they only looked upon the destruction with a quiet disbelief.

Even Ruin, the Telekinetic, seemed to be shaken up. He didn't have that overconfident and carefree grin he enjoyed wearing. Instead, he was leaning over and panting. Somehow, by a means which Jack didn't understand, he knew that what Ruin had used to counter his burst was the pinnacle of his ability, and now he was exhausted, struggling to regain his breath. Jack, on the other hand, didn't feel tired at all. He still burned with anger towards the three Psychs.

"Brother, Darling," Requiem said. "That Harris-boy just used a power greater than your own. Can this be possible?"

Ruin looked at her. His carefree, cheerful expression was gone in its entirety. Now, there was a grim ferocity and a madness that almost rivaled his sister's.

"We need to kill these five and we need to kill them now!" Ruin exclaimed. "Andy!" He grabbed the boy's shoulder. "Get over your fears or you'll be forced to experience them again! I don't know what the Harris-boy did to you, but after using that much energy, he can't have much left to draw from. You want revenge? *Then take it, damnit!*"

Jack felt his arm brush against something and realized that Melissa had come to stand close to him. She stiffened and cleared her throat.

"Jack and I will handle Andy. Michael, you and Kazou need to take on those two."

Jack felt pride well in his heart while he watched Melissa take charge. He knew she was just as devastated over Paro as the rest of the team, but she wasn't letting that get to her, not when there was still something that needed to be dealt with in front of them.

Michael and Kazou picked Sarah up off the floor and nodded at Melissa, accepting her leadership.

"I reckon this has gone on for too long," Michael said. "Jack, when all this is over with, I think I'm gonna ask you to teach *me* what you just did."

Jack grinned. "I can't, because when all this is over I need to get home and watch the new episode of Breaking Bad."

Chapter 33: One last question

Melissa felt the agony in her heart. She felt the tears that were begging for release, but she ignored all of it. With the three murderous Psychs standing a few feet in front of her, the situation had become kill or be killed.

"Sarah," Melissa called back over her shoulder, "get yourself together, girl. Without you we're as good as dead."

Sarah was devastated, her face contorted in misery. A grimace replaced her usual smile. "I can't feel him. Oh, Melissa, I can't feel him."

Melissa tried to show sympathy. She wanted to comfort Sarah. But if Paro had in fact died, then the loss would be great to them all—it would be something they'd never recover from. Yet, Melissa was not ready to join him. It was for this reason that she felt a growing annoyance towards the sobbing Telepath.

"You're about to not feel any of *us*, either!" Melissa snapped. "Are you *trying* to get us killed?"

Sarah peered up at her, and Melissa immediately regretted her sharp tone. She could see in Sarah's eyes that her words had stung. Sarah opened her mouth to speak but instead shook her head and took a breath.

She wiped her eyes with her sleeve and nodded. "You're right. I'm sorry, Melissa, everyone."

Sarah walked away from Kazou and Michael and came to stand with Melissa and Jack. She didn't stop when she reached the two of them. She continued to walk and Michael shouted after her.

There was a large hole in the floor from where the two humongous Kinetic forces had collided, leading to what seemed like a maintenance tunnel below. Sarah walked carefully around it, pausing to glance at the destruction. She shook her head—it was the same reaction Melissa had when she'd first glimpsed the destruction.

What is Sarah doing? Melissa wondered.

Melissa tried to grab Sarah and pull her back. Jack surprised her and tugged at her own arm. "No, Melissa. Let her go."

"But Jack," she protested. Jack was not one to make demands of anyone, yet he seemed intent on allowing Sarah to walk right up to the three Psychs. None of the three appeared alarmed by her approach. If anything, they seemed amused as she stood before them.

Sarah was in her mid-twenties, but Melissa wondered if emotionally she was the youngest on the team. Despite being almost a decade younger than Sarah, Melissa was the one protective of Sarah, usually acting the role of bigger sister. Sarah tried to hide it, but everyone on the team knew she held a deep self-loathing and a complete lack of confidence. She was a beautiful woman, but if asked, she'd say she was hideous. Sarah was brilliant, but she thought herself an idiot.

When Melissa had first joined the team, Sarah had been the first person she'd connected with. She was kind beyond what most people were capable of, and never tried to be anything but helpful. Sarah hated confrontation, and she was tolerant of everyone. When Melissa was new and still struggling to come to grips with her life as a member of the Investigative team, Sarah guided her through it every step of the way.

Sarah did not have the frame of mind to confront people like Requiem or Ruin, so Melissa didn't understand what could've possessed her to approach them. The possibility of violence usually terrified her.

"My name is Sarah Blighter," she said in greeting to the three of them.

Requiem stepped forward and ran a hand over Sarah's face, causing Michael to leap forward. Kazou grabbed Michael and held him in place. Melissa was tempted to charge in as well.

You've got to be kidding me. Just what in God's name is Sarah trying to do?

"Darling, you're like me, aren't you?" Requiem asked. "You can do some of what I can, yes?"

Sarah neither flinched nor moved while Requiem ran her smooth fingers across her face and along her lips and chin. Melissa held her breath as she watched the exchange. She was curious to understand Sarah's motives.

"I'm not like you at all," Sarah said. "But we are both Telepaths, yes."

Requiem removed her hand and shrugged. "When you walked over here, Darling, you were staring at me and only me. Why me? What is it that you want?"

"If we let things continue in the direction they've been heading, then more of us will die. And ... it's crazy when you really think about it, you know? Because when the smoke clears, all that's left is the memory of the people we care about. Why do we have to do this to each other? It hurts me, don't you get it? To see people die, to see them close their eyes and never wake up—I hate all of it. So, you asked me what I want, right? Well, I want you three to just give up. Please, just give up and end this. I don't want to kill any of you, and I don't want to see you die, either. Why can't we just stop this?"

Sarah paused for a moment. Her features darkened and her breathing slowed. "You killed someone today, someone I really cared about. He was a person that believed in helping people, people like you, actually, and not just for the sake of saving others, but even to save you from your own selves. It's for his sake that I don't want to see you three end up in the ground. So please, I'm begging you, just surrender and let's finally put an end to all of this pointless killing."

Melissa felt a newfound sense of appreciation for Sarah. Even now, the Telepath only wanted what was best for everyone. Sarah didn't show any trace of fear while she defiantly peered into the eyes of the three people that wanted her dead.

Requiem's expression didn't change, except that now her eyes held a small glimmer of interest. "And why, Darling, would we just give up? Why, when we could simply kill the last of you and be on our way?"

Sarah breathed a sigh. "There's more here that you don't know. Let me tell you a little something about the way that things work and then maybe you'll understand. You see, people like me and the ones standing behind me, we believe that when someone does something wrong, they need to be stopped. We go after them and we do just that. But there are others like us, and they exist for the people that we *can't* stop. Now, these men and women I'm talking about—they won't speak to you the way we do because they don't want you to surrender."

Sarah paused for a moment then continued, "Their only job is to kill you and everyone like you. And with the scene you've caused here, they're sure to be on their way as we speak. Now look, I know you're probably thinking to yourselves, 'We'll just kill them too.' Well, there are many, many more like them, and if you don't turn yourselves in then for the rest of your lives you will be hunted with no chance of ever negotiating surrender. I know the three of you think you're powerful, but trust me—there are people out there who could kill you with a single thought. They *will* find you, and whether the people that hunt you are powerful or weak, whether they are tall or short, or even old or young. They will all have one thing in common—they hunger, they *lust* to see you die."

Andy's knees crumpled beneath him upon hearing this, while Ruin's usual grin turned into a mask of outrage. "She's lying!" Ruin said.

Requiem, keeping her eyes on Sarah, spoke to her brother behind her. "No," she whispered. "Don't you remember that ridiculous woman back at the Harris-boy's house? She said something about killing us."

Sarah nodded. "Yes, those are the people I'm referring to. There are many of them around the world, and no place you go will ever be safe from them."

Requiem appeared to think for a moment before nodding her head. "I will make you a deal, Darling. Give us the Harris-boy and allow us our freedom, and I give you my word that none of us will ever kill again. Does that seem fair?"

Ruin glared at his sister. "Requiem, are you nuts? Don't go making promises without—"

"*Silence, you fool!*" Requiem hissed. "Did you not hear what this goat-like woman has said to us? It's this or a lifetime of nonsense."

Sarah's face took on a saddened look. "I don't have the power to give you your freedom, or to give you Jack. Tell me, why do you want him so badly anyway?"

Requiem's maddened expression softened for just a moment while she shot a passing glance at Jack, causing Melissa to feel an unexpected, burning anger.

"Because," Requiem answered, "he has taken something from me that I want back." She pointed to Jack. "He has taken my eyes and I want to know why."

Melissa heard Jack shift on his feet, and she turned to look at him. He peeled his eyes back in surprise, then followed it soon after with a look of disgust.

"Nah-uh!" he said. "I didn't take anyone's eyes. That's like, gross. Besides, I've never even been to med school."

Requiem tilted back her head and laughed wildly into the air. "Oh, Harris-boy, Darling, you are a funny one!"

Sarah waited for her to finish her laughing fit before continuing to speak. "What do you mean he's taken your eyes?"

Requiem opened her mouth to answer but stopped as she glanced over at Jack, who stomped his foot into the ground and wore a very stubborn look.

"Who cares what she means, Sarah? She's obviously lying. I never took away anyone's eyeball—that's the weirdest and grossest thing anyone's ever accused me of. And one time, someone accused me of eating a peanut butter and lettuce sandwich—also not true! She's trying to get me into trouble, just like Melissa when she farted on the way over here and pointed a finger—"

Melissa dove at him, closing his annoying mouth shut. "You don't know what you're talking about, Jack!" she yelled at him.

As far as Melissa could tell, Jack didn't even realize that she was covering his mouth, as he was continuing to ramble, the vibrations tickling her palm.

"*UUmmmph, ummumzm, sumpzmz ummp.*"

"So you're saying it's either a lifetime of imprisonment or death?" Andy asked. He stood back to his feet, and his face held a twisted combination of relentless fury and pained sadness.

"I don't know for sure what the punishment will be, but I can promise you that you won't be killed. Can't you see I'm only trying to help you?"

"Help us?" Ruin whispered. *"Help us!"* he screamed.

Ruin walked forward to join his sister, and for the first time that Melissa had seen, he entirely lost his casual, carefree look. Instead, he wore a visage of lunacy, of a terrifying madness. His sister's paled in comparison to the growing mania spreading across his face. His lips peeled back, his eyebrows rose, and his nose curled as his entire body trembled. His hands began to shake too. Since the night she'd first seen him in the park with Jack, Melissa knew there was a deep darkness to him, one not displayed as openly as his sister's. But never would she have expected this. No, this was beyond anything she could imagine.

"Help us!" he screamed in something that was halfway between a laugh and a cry. "You want to help us? Where were you when ...?" He stopped speaking and his eyes filled with a lustful hatred.

Sarah gasped as she was lifted into the air. "Sister, show me her heart—now!"

Melissa, as well as the rest of the team, didn't need to hear any more than that. They charged forward. Melissa and Kazou leaped over the wide gap where the floor had been destroyed, while Michael and Jack dashed around it.

"Melissa!" Kazou shouted, running beside her. "Attack the Kinetic to kill. Take no chances!"

Melissa didn't need to be told—she was ready. Feelings, emotions, consequences, these were all things that could be dealt with later. For now, there was only Ruin and the woman he was trying to kill. Kazou and Melissa were the first to reach the lanky Kinetic. As one, they threw their powerful fists down towards him, an attack that would kill any Psych, no matter how powerful.

Melissa attacked from the left, Kazou from the right. Sarah let out another gasp as she was dropped to the floor, released from whatever Kinetic binds held her. Ruin leaped backward, a maneuver that barely saved his life. The two Reinforcers of Paro's team brought their full strength down on the spot he'd occupied just a second before, crashing into the floor and breaking completely through it.

Andy and Requiem were quick to assist their "brother." Andy shouted something that Melissa couldn't make out, and Kazou clutched at his face. "Sarah!" he screamed. A spot on his forehead, just below his vicious scar, turned red, and small plumes of smoke drifted out of it.

Sarah pushed herself off the floor and extended a hand to Kazou as if trying to grab him. Immediately, the smoke vanished, only to reappear about a foot away from the large Japanese man, which struggled to break through Sarah's shielding.

"Melissa, duck!" called Michael. Melissa dropped to the ground just in time to avoid a two-hundred pound vending machine soaring overhead, aimed to kill the now frenzied Ruin. He did not try to avoid it. Instead, he made his typical gesture of chopping air, and the machine fell to the ground. It shattered, spilling out snacks and change. Bags of potato chips as well as Hershey and Snicker bars rolled along the floor while the sound of a thousand dropped quarters echoed in the destroyed terminal.

A thought came to Melissa. It was among the most inappropriate things a person could think during a life or death situation, yet it was beyond her control—a single penetrating idea rang out in Melissa's brain, one that she felt deeply ashamed of.

If Jack stops to pick up any of those snacks, I'm going to kill him.

Ruin telekinetically picked up everything and anything, gesturing so fast he resembled a composer of a musical orchestra. Loose pieces of floor, broken glass, and even some of the snacks—they all flew towards Sarah.

"They're trying to take out our Path!" Melissa yelled.

If a Telepath died during a battle between Psychs and there was no second Path, it was game over. If for even a moment Sarah stopped fighting off Andy's Manipulation, he'd kill them one at a time with the same agonizing methods he'd used against Richard and his family.

Melissa needed to separate him from the fight. It was the best chance they had of survival. "Jack!" she called. "Get over here!"

Jack, who at the time was treading carefully around the chasm in the floor, was for some odd reason laughing. What was he on about now?

"Haha, Melissa. Scorpion from Mortal Kombat says, 'get over here' too."

Melissa was going to kick his butt for that when they made it through this, of that she was sure. They *would* make it out alive, and he would receive a plethora of slaps for his outrageous comments amid a fight for their lives.

Jack ran to the side of her. Michael and Ruin were sparring to keep control of the various hazards flung around the room, while Sarah struggled to keep Andy from killing Kazou, who was still pinned down from the Manipulation trying to melt his face. Requiem was deep in concentration, and Melissa wasn't certain, but she suspected the girl was weakening all of them. They were in a deadlock—and losing.

Melissa charged at Ruin, who turned to meet her. He was a Telekinetic of incredible power. Melissa knew he would be able to repel her attacks while still fending off Michael. He raised a hand to impede her, but before he could so much as draw an inkling of power, Melissa dashed off her right foot and leaped to the side of him and then ran in a straight line towards Andy.

Jack followed after her. Andy backed up as he saw her charge at him, and with all her strength, Melissa attacked again in a downward smash, one that was easy to avoid. Only this time, she wasn't aiming to connect with Andy.

The ground below them cracked, giving way under the power of her monstrous strength. Jack screamed as the three of them plunged into the dark tunnel below.

Chapter 34: Sometimes Things Don't Work

Jack didn't understand what Melissa was attempting until it was too late. Chunks of the marble floor were sent scattering, and a moment later Jack had the uncomfortable sense of losing balance. An instant after that, when Jack felt the first sensation of tumbling downward, the realization entered his mind. Melissa was plunging the three of them into whatever nightmare awaited below.

It didn't occur to Jack that he was falling until he felt the bubbly, acidic burn deep in his lower stomach. To Jack, the worst part was not knowing how far he would fall. It also didn't help that he didn't know where they were falling to in the first place. Luckily, they only descended for a few seconds before Jack landed with a painful squish onto gravel and then stumbled forward. For a brief instant, he believed that the ride was over, and then once again Jack felt the sensation of dropping. Only this time it was like rolling down a hill.

Jack yelped as his arms scraped against the gravel while he forward-rolled down a steep hill into the darkness below. The only sounds were grunts and cries of pain, as Jack, Melissa, and Andy plummeted and rolled down, occasionally bumping into each other. They would all be scraped up, the sharp gravel leaving something in their skin to remember it by. The dizziness was nauseating. The world flipped up and around. Jack went from his stomach to his back, picking up speed like a bicycle down a steep hill.

"Melissa!" he yelled, tumbling into the shadowy depths. "Was this really necessary?"

Between the pitch-black darkness, the scraping of gravel, and the nauseating rolling-front flips, Jack was in unrelenting misery. There was a confusing moment where Jack no longer felt the gravel under him, and he wondered if the torture had finally ended. It was then that he felt the return of the falling sensation. With a groan, he landed on another strip of gravel. He hacked and coughed up the icky stuff. But he was finally still.

He sat up and shook the gravel and dirt from his messy black-hair then looked around. There were strip-lights lining the floor, small circular objects that were just bright enough to cast a bit of light a few feet around them, but otherwise it was complete darkness. The lights extended far into the distance, with no visible end. Jack figured it was some sort of underground maintenance tunnel that ran along the path of the train tracks.

"Melissa, are you okay?" She was dusting herself off and standing to her feet.

"I was going to ask you the same, Jack." She looked around at the darkness, her eyes scanning along the floor. For a moment Jack didn't know what she was looking for, until he remembered the reason for their descent in the first place.

"Andy!" Jack yelled. The boy was also getting to his feet. Andy looked at them. Terror and panic spread along his features. There was more, though. Just behind his shaken exterior, Jack could see fatigue in his former friend's eyes. Andy must've been weary—tired of everything that had been happening to him.

"Please," Andy croaked, "just let me go."

Small scrapes and gashes covered Andy's arms and legs. Jack was wearing black jeans and Melissa wore tight-fitting black leggings, so their lower-bodies had been protected from the rough gravel, although both of their pants had small tears and holes from the rough fall. Jack's arms were pretty scraped up, and he wondered why Melissa had remained completely unscathed, until he remembered that Reinforcers could be as hard as steel if they wanted.

Jack forced himself to ignore Andy's pleas, but it wasn't easy. There was a part of Jack, a feeling that still hammered at his heart that desired to save his friend. It covered Jack with guilt, washing over him and filling him with uncertainty.

No, Jack reminded himself. *The only way to save Andy is to bring him down. After what he did to Richard, after what he did to those two little girls—no, I can't let him leave.*

Melissa put a reassuring arm on his shoulder. "I know this is hard, Jack. But it's time we ended this."

Jack nodded. "Andy, I really don't wanna hurt you. Please don't put up a fight. Let's get out of this place."

Andy glared at Jack with an icy rage. "You don't want to hurt me? How can you say that? How can you tell me that after everything you did to me, Jack! I'll never get those faces out of my head. I'll never be able to forget. The moment I let down my guard you'll do it again!"

Jack inhaled and steadied his hands, fostering calm into his voice. "Andy, I don't know what I did to you. Sometimes I feel like I did something but then later I don't remember. Look, I just ... I'm sorry if I hurt you, but you really gotta listen to me. I know everything seems like it sucks right now, but things can suck so much worse. Please, you have to listen to me. You're gonna die if you don't come with me. I know you've never really thought of me as a close friend, even if I always thought of you as one. But if you've ever thought of me as a friend at all or at the very least trusted me, then please, believe me now. If you don't give up, you're dead."

Andy's face darkened and a single tear fell from his eye. His voice was a whisper. "I know ... I know, and I don't care anymore. I've done what needed to be done, and I did it for *us*, Jack, for everyone *like* us. And I don't just mean people that can do what we can do—I mean everyone who's ever been afraid to go to school, for everyone who's ever been forced to feel pain just to make others laugh, for everyone who's ever cried themselves to sleep because the abuse was too much to handle. Why can't I kill them, Jack? Why can't *we* kill them? I don't care if I die anymore—I'm done with life, anyway."

Jack felt a mixture of disgust and disappointment. "So you're just gonna give up? After everything that happened you're just gonna throw in the towel? What gives you the right? Do you think you can just die after all the people you've hurt or killed? Look, Andy, I'm sorry how the other kids treated us at school, I really am. If anyone understands, it's me. But that doesn't give you the right to go on a killing spree. To kill children!"

"The two little girls were an accident."

"That doesn't matter!" Jack roared. He leveled an accusing finger at Andy, one that carried the full weight of his emotions. "Take responsibility for what you did! You killed them, not me, not Melissa, and not the bullies at school. *You* did that, Andy. And even if it was just Richard and no one else, it would still be wrong."

Jack felt the disgusting anger build. He poured his emotions into his words. Jack wasn't a bully or a tough-guy, but as he dug into his heart for the words he needed to say, he felt the anger grow stronger, along with a desire to cause pain. "Do you know what hurts me the most, Andy? It's that you think you were doing this all for me. Don't ever put that on me, Andy. Do you hear me?"

Jack's voice turned cold and he poured every last drop of his rage into a thundering shout. *"DON'T EVER PUT THAT ON ME!"*

Andy opened his mouth to speak but said nothing. He turned over his hands and glanced down on them. His eyes filled with confusion. With a sudden jerk he twisted around, making a crunching sound as his foot slid across the gravel and he ran into the distance.

So he won't surrender, Jack thought with a disappointed sigh.

Melissa bolted after him, and Jack ran for all he was worth to catch up. Andy wouldn't be able to outrun a Reinforcer, but that didn't stop Jack from feeling a burning disappointment towards his former friend. Jack had offered him one final chance to redeem himself, to show remorse for what he'd done. Even after everything that happened, Jack had still considered Andy a friend, but that was over now. By fleeing, Andy was now nothing to Jack. There was a small pain as Jack felt the fleeting passing in his heart for the boy he once knew as Andy. The boy whose home he had invaded to force him into round after round of Street Fighter. The boy he dragged to the movies on rainy days, despite his muttered protests.

Andy was a loner, and Jack had tried to be there for him, because he knew that deep down, Andy had always been grateful for the company, even if he'd never admit it. But all that was over now. Andy was nothing more than murderous scum. Jack was determined to do all he could to bring Andy in alive, and when it was all over he'd wash his hands clean of him. It would be his final offering of goodwill to a person he once called friend.

Andy, you're not getting away again.

It wouldn't take Melissa long to catch up to the boy. Jack was panting to catch up, still a few yards behind. He pumped his arms and ran. All he could see were the lights moving towards him as he sprinted through the criminally dark tunnel. The sight of the slow moving lights approaching was mesmerizing—the sounds of crunching gravel added balance to the sensory-depriving dark tunnel.

Jack heard Melissa scream, and in an instant went from determined to terror-stricken. He felt his concern for Melissa as real as he felt the breath in his lungs. He could make the two of them out only a few feet in the distance. Melissa was kneeling, sweating and gritting her teeth. Andy was beside her with his palm extended towards her face.

Jack knew what he was doing—he'd tried the same on Jack back at home. "Andy, no!" he cried.

Andy ignored him, focusing intently on killing Melissa. Jack didn't know how long she could hold out for, or how long her Reinforcement would prevent Andy from turning her into the same bloodied mess as he'd done to Richard's family.

Jack didn't have time to draw any power. Each millisecond was another leap towards the death of the girl he loved. Jack charged at Andy, empty of the power that Psychs used, but filled to the brim with the one in his heart. He balled his right hand into a fist and with all of his might, Jack crashed it into Andy's unaware face, causing the boy to stumble backwards then fall to the ground.

Melissa took a deep breath and rubbed the spot above her right eye where Andy had tried to burn her. "Thanks," she breathed. "We need to stop him before he can try that again."

Andy was already regaining his footing. His lower lip trickled with a small amount of blood. Melissa ran at him with her fist drawn back, ready to let loose. Andy backed away from her in terror. Melissa swung at him, her fist homing in on his face.

Andy didn't have a chance. Melissa's fist smashed into him and the result was brutal. Andy's lower-lip pulled back and he was thrown off his feet. Blood spewed from his mouth as he landed with a rough crash on the floor. Jack knew that Melissa had only hit him with a small portion of her power, or Andy's head would no longer be attached to his body.

Melissa grinned. "I think he's down for the count."

Andy lay on his back with his eyes closed and his mouth leaking blood. His injuries looked severe, but the blood made it appear far worse than it actually was, or at least Jack hoped that was the case.

He walked over to Andy and scowled down in disgust at his unconscious form. It was hard to believe that the small blond-haired boy had caused so much death and pain. Jack shook his head at the complex emotions boiling within him.

"You did this to yourself. This is your own fault."

The boy's eyes popped open, and a maddened grin formed on his bloodied lips, leading up to his bloodshot eyes. Melissa gasped, and Jack was stunned for a moment.

"Melissa should have hit me to kill," Andy said with a laugh. "This is what happens when you lack conviction."

Jack felt the burning sensation on his face. He knew what was to come, and it paralyzed him with fear. Before Jack could so much as blink, Melissa clutched his shoulders in a death grip, so painful that he wondered if having his face melted off would actually hurt less. Melissa picked him up and threw him backwards, sending Jack flying nearly ten feet behind her, landing on the gravel floor then skidding a few paces. Jack tried to get back to his feet, but Melissa jumped on top of him and covered his body.

"What are you doing?" Jack yelled. He couldn't see or hear a thing while she covered him. All he could feel was her weight.

"Shut up," she groaned. There was a sound of incredible pain in her voice. "He can't manipulate what he—" She stopped speaking and cried out in pain. "He can't manipulate what he can't s-see. Just s-shut up."

"I don't want you!" Andy's voice screeched. "I want Jack! Hurry up and die already." Jack struggled, but Melissa was using her full strength to keep him pinned down. The scent of burning flesh filled Jack's nose, and he grew alarmed.

"No!" Jack cried, struggling against Melissa. "What's he doing to you? Get off of me!" Jack tried to break free but he couldn't push her off. "Don't let him kill you. Please, let me help. Please."

Melissa cried out in pain and the scent of burned flesh grew stronger. Jack's heart beat faster, and he was overwhelmed by a torrent of rage and terror, a sickening combination that made him flail his arms and kick his legs, panic and desperation mixing together to create a frenzy of emotion.

"*Melissaaaaa!*" Jack's shout was a bloodcurdling scream. "What is he doing to you? Melissa!"

"If you want to know so badly then I'll tell you, Jack." It was Andy's voice. Jack couldn't see him with Melissa blocking his vision.

"I'm burning a hole through your girlfriend's back, and it's already broken the skin. I wish you could see it. It's red and bubbling. Oh, it looks like it hurts, too. Pretty soon she'll be dead, and then you'll feel the same pain you've caused me."

Melissa screamed in agony. Tears fell from her eyes and landed into Jack's. "It hurts, Jack," she cried.

"Then get off of me!"

"No," she whimpered. "He'll kill you in a ..." She howled in pain. "He'll kill you in a second."

Jack did the only thing left to him, the only thing he still could. He opened himself up to the draw of that disgusting power, the source of his greatest discomfort. He needed more than just a little—he needed enough to save the girl of his dreams, the person he both looked up to and loved, even if she would never feel the same about him.

It entered him in a flood, and within a few seconds, Jack knew that he was approaching the point of no return. He could still seal it off, but if he didn't draw enough, Melissa would die. Jack resisted the urge to flee, the urge to close himself off from the power and stick to what he'd drawn. Instead, he allowed it to continue. All at once Jack felt a burning sensation. It was an inferno of heat and power so vast that with each second Jack felt he'd be swept away by it.

Jack screamed louder than Melissa as the ocean of power tried to occupy him. It was only a few drops, yet it felt as if the world were spinning faster. His head fogged up as his heart beat faster and faster, to the point where he couldn't breathe.

Jack realized he'd made a mistake. He tried to close it off, but it was no longer possible, as he knew would end up the case. All he could do was allow himself to be bombarded by the massive rush of energy, until it eventually overwhelmed and killed him. There was only one small hope for him, one last thing he could try. If it failed, he'd be dead along with Melissa. There was no longer any time for caution.

The power slammed into him, filling him to the point of bursting. He'd never before tried to use any of the power while it was still being drawn, but if he didn't at least try then his death would be assured. He closed his eyes and scrambled around for a particular trigger, for a feeling or sense. Everything was shifting so fast, changing before he could do anything with it. There was a small spark of recognition, and Jack thought for a moment he saw what he wanted. He no longer had the luxury of making sure. Putting Melissa and his life on the line, he grabbed at it.

Sarah kept her head to the ground, glancing up every few moments to keep track of the battle. The rogue Psychs were just too powerful, and the Telepath, Requiem, was far stronger than she.

I'm no good, Sarah whimpered in her mind. *I'm just not good enough. I'm going to get Michael and Kazou killed.*

Kazou pushed Michael out of the way as yet another piece of sharpened glass came within an inch of piercing his body and possibly his heart. Kazou ran forward at Ruin and missed yet another attack. The Kinetic slowed him down just enough to leap out of the way. Kazou's fist smashed through the terminal wall.

Sarah tried to weaken the Telekinetic, but his sister had complete control of the situation. Every time Sarah tried to do anything, she was counteracted. Not only was Requiem able to keep her at bay, but she had no problem weakening Michael or Kazou.

Sarah wept, knowing that her team was going to die because she was too weak to be useful. As her confidence faded, so did her ability. She found her control over her power slipping, only moments from the point where the other Path could enter her mind and switch off her brain, killing her then killing her team.

Kazou removed his fist from the wall, but Ruin was already gesturing. Like a pitch being hit by a baseball bat, Kazou was sent flying across the room at a speed that would have killed him, had Michael not been able to slow him and set him down gently on the floor.

Michael and Kazou were sweating, exhausted, and losing what was clearly a battle of attrition.

"Damn," Michael said. His cowboy hat was lost on the floor somewhere, and now his curly blond hair was hanging freely off his face. Kazou too, seemed to be on the verge of collapse.

"Just keep fighting," Kazou ordered. "Sarah!" he called to her. "Don't give up."

Sarah nodded, but she knew it was only a matter of time before she'd be overpowered by Requiem, and once that happened her team had no chance. They'd die as surely as night turns to day.

Ruin lifted a bench off the ground and sent it hurling at Kazou, who smashed his fist through it. Michael sent his own bench in return, but Ruin simply gestured in the air, causing it to fall back towards the ground.

"How in the hell can they be this powerful?" Michael asked. "Ya'd think that by now we'd have gotten the edge on them. It's three of us and two of them. Fellas, I think we're in some serious trouble here."

Kazou laughed in defiance. "They're not so tough. Paro could've taken these two down with the blink of an eye." A brief look of sadness crossed his expression.

Sarah tried to ignore the name. If her resolve broke any more than it already had, she'd lose the mental battle and get herself killed. Requiem was fighting like an enraged beast, pounding on her skull to the point where a splitting headache was now ringing through Sarah's ears.

Michael and Kazou stood beside each other and seemed to be deep in thought, as if searching for some way of turning the tables.

"Gentlemen," Ruin taunted, "what's the matter? Had enough? Why don't you save me some time and cut your own hearts out."

Michael spat on the ground. "I reckon this fella needs a beating."

Michael squeezed his fist, and all around the room, the three remaining benches that hadn't been destroyed lifted off the ground and soared at the carefree Kinetic. The young man only grinned, and without even moving, he gestured three quick times in succession. A bench fell back to the floor with each gesture.

During this, Kazou was already running directly towards him with a fist pulled back to strike. Once again the Telekinetic proved too powerful. He was able to slow Kazou down—almost to a complete halt—while taking his time to move out of the way. Kazou's fist broke through yet another wall, and Requiem cheered at her brother's victory.

Sarah felt yet another stab at her mind, and she knew that this time the girl would break through. Requiem was immensely powerful, and Sarah was done for.

I am nothing. I am not even worth the grave they're going to bury me in.

Sarah closed her eyes and waited for her death—then snapped them open when she heard the booming voice resounding throughout the entire terminal. It seemed to come from every direction at once. It was so loud that it drowned out all other sound.

"CAN ANYONE HEAR ME?"

Michael and Kazou stopped in their tracks. Even Ruin and Requiem halted their assault and looked around them, searching for the source of the voice.

"What in the hell was that?" Michael asked.

"No clue," Kazou said.

"Darling, did you just hear a voice?"

"I did, sister."

Sarah looked around the room, positive that no one else had entered. It was still just the five of them. "Did you all just hear that voice? Who was that?"

"I don't know," answered Michael and Kazou at the same time.

"Hmm, we don't know either, Darling," answered Requiem.

"I DON'T KNOW EITHER," answered the voice. *"WHO COULD IT HAVE BEEN? I ONCE HEARD A VOICE WHEN I WAS EIGHT, AND I THOUGHT IT WAS A GHOST. IT TURNED OUT THAT IT WAS JUST A RADIO THAT HAD FALLEN UNDER THE—"*

"Jack!" Michael, Kazou and Sarah exclaimed in unison.

"How are we hearing you?" Sarah asked. She scanned the room for the Harris-boy but he was nowhere to be seen.

"SARAH, I NEED YOUR HELP! BUT FIRST, I WANNA KNOW WHO THIS VOICE IS. I THINK I HEARD IT TOO."

"You're the damned voice!" Michael yelled back. "Jeeze, Jack, even as an omnipotent, unexplainable booming voice from the sky you're an idiot."

"OHHHHH, AND I SUPPOSE YOU'RE JUST SO MUCH BETTER THAN ME, MICHAEL. YOU KNOW WHAT? YOU'RE NOT MY FRIEND ANYMORE."

Sarah cleared her mind. "Jack, can you speak directly to me?"

"Maybe," said a voice in her head. *"Is this better?"*

Jack, Sarah thought. *How is this possible? Person to person communication is not supposed to be possible. Not even with Telepathy.*

"Don't know," Jack said. *"But listen, Sarah. Melissa and I are dying, and you're the only one who can save us."*

Panic entered Sarah immediately. *You're dying? Jack, please, you have to save Melissa and come back to us. We need you. You can't die!*

"I don't plan on it. That's why I need you. Listen to me, Sarah. As we speak, I'm drawing so much damned power that I'm gonna die from it long before Andy manages to kill us. I need you to seal it off, or I'm done for. It's ripping me apart."

Michael and Kazou looked at Sarah with questioning eyes, but she ignored them. She had all her attention focused on Jack.

I'm not good enough! she cried in her mind. *I don't have the power to do any of that. We're about to die ourselves.*

"Paro told me you're one of the most brilliant Psychs, Sarah. If all you're lacking is power, then here, take this."

Sarah put confusion into her mentally spoken words. *Take what? Jack, you should know that it's totally impossible to—*

Kazou and Michael shouted in alarm as she grabbed the sides of her head and screamed into the air.

"What's wrong?" they shouted.

Sarah wriggled on the ground. "This shouldn't be possible! Good God, it's so much. How can a single person even hold this much power?"

Sarah fell to her knees, and yelled in her mind, *That's enough! I don't know how you're doing this, but it shouldn't be within the realm of possibility. That's enough, Jack. That's enough! I can feel your mind. Hold tight.*

Jack pushed the screaming Melissa off him. Andy watched in confusion as Jack began tap-dancing on his feet. He jumped on one foot then the other like a man in desperate need of using the bathroom.

"Gah!" he yelled out. "It burns, too much power, gah! It burns like battery acid."

Jack looked down at Melissa and the nasty bloodied wound on her back. He didn't think it had reached the critical point, but he could tell it was very painful.

"Jack," Melissa croaked, unable to get to her feet. "What's going on?"

Jack didn't stop his jumping. He spun in circles and flailed his arms. He knew he looked like an idiot, but he didn't really care.

"Gotta use it, gotta use it. Gahhhh! This is too much."

Jack didn't know how to use such a tremendous power, and so he began throwing massive Telekinetic bursts in random places, in an attempt to get rid of some of it. All around the room, sections of wall detonated as if struck by a bomb, spraying gravel and chunks of wood in every conceivable direction. The ground shook, and the ceiling leaked chips of stone.

"Jack, you're going to kill us! Stop that right now. No more Telekinesis, damnit." Melissa got to her feet, and put a comforting arm on Jack's shoulder while Andy watched with his mouth agape.

"It's too much, Melissa. It hurts like hell. I need to get rid of it."

"Then use it on him," Melissa said. She pointed to Andy.

Jack nodded, and Andy backed away, tripping over his own feet. He fell on his rump and eyed Jack with a look of both amazement and horror. Jack would end this here and now—he was literally overflowing with power.

Andy held out his palm, extended towards Jack. Melissa's eyes widened and she once again tried to position herself in front. This time, it was Jack who did the grabbing. He stopped her in her tracks and gave her arms a confident shake. "Just watch, Melissa."

A puff of smoke appeared almost three feet from Jack, locked down behind an impenetrable barrier. Andy's eyes welled with tears, and he shook his head in disbelief.

"How?" Melissa asked. She seemed just as astonished as Andy.

"It's Sarah," Jack said with a smile.

"But that's not possible. Sarah's too far from us."

"I found her, Melissa. I don't know how, but I found her. She's with us now."

Jack felt Melissa's arms around his neck as she pulled him into a hug. His heart warmed and he returned the embrace. Melissa had tears in her eyes, and she winced from the pain in her back. Jack tried to remove his arms, which were probably worsening the pain, but she didn't let him go.

"Jack, I ..."

"Not now," Jack said. He turned to look at Andy, and he gently pushed Melissa away. "Gah! I gotta get rid of this. Andy, hold still. I don't know how to do too many things, or how all this stuff works, but I think I've got an idea."

Andy tried to crawl away, but his arms gave out and he sat on the floor, immobile.

Jack cupped his right wrist over his left then lowered it to the side of his waist. He interlocked his fingers before crouching down and then extending his arms.

"*Kaaaa-meeeee-haaa-meeee-HAAA!*"

Jack blinked in confusion when nothing happened. "Are you serious? That does *nothing*? Wow, that's lame."

Melissa looked at him like he was insane for a moment then smiled. "You're a real goofball, you know that? Here, I'll show you something that actually does work. It's lights out for you, Andy."

"But I—" It was the last words the boy spoke. Melissa charged at him, and protected by Sarah, no longer had any reason to fear death. This time, when her fist collided with Andy's nose, he really did go unconscious.

Chapter 35: The distance between reality and dream.

Michael tried to ignore his fatigue, but even he couldn't deny that his body was screaming in protest, begging him for a moment's rest. Ruin, however, showed no signs of exhaustion. In fact, the only time Michael had seen the Kinetic come close to sweating, was when he and Jack did that monstrous exchange of Kinetic energies.

"K-Kazou," Michael panted. He looked to his left to see the large Japanese Reinforcer dripping sweat, breathing even heavier than he. Kazou was not a weak man, far from it, yet not even he could continue at this intensity for much longer.

Everything in the terminal had been so thoroughly destroyed that now Ruin was attacking them using nothing more than bursts— there was nothing left to throw at them. He gestured with his hand, an exaggerated motion of chopping air, and Michael could feel the energy rushing at him. It would be enough to send Michael slamming into the wall almost fifteen feet behind him, probably ending his life, too.

Michael's body tensed and constricted, filling with pain as he forced himself to draw out yet another bit of energy, just enough to throw his own burst back towards the one Ruin tossed at them. The two collided, and unlike Jack's, which had created a massive detonation, Michael's was overpowered, weakening Ruin's just enough so that Michael was only thrown a foot backward, landing with a painful crash on his right shoulder blade.

Lying on his back, dazed and staring at the ceiling, Michael craned his neck to the right and looked at Sarah, who also seemed only moments away from collapse. A few minutes earlier she had yelled something about helping Jack, and while Michael no longer doubted anything the boy was capable of, it didn't make it any easier to grasp.

Sarah had yelled at the top of her lungs, screaming about sealing something off that she'd claimed weighed more than a mountain, or something. At the time she seemed to be overflowing with power, but when she'd finished doing whatever it was she was doing for Jack, she too became just as exhausted and weakened as the rest of them.

"Oh, Ruin, Darling!" Requiem shouted out. "The woman is almost mine. Finish up, Darling. Kill these three so we can find our brothers and leave."

Ruin paused, only moments from sending a burst into Kazou, and he turned to face his sister. "Forget those two," he said. "I'm sick of Brother Andy, he's pathetic. And Jack, well, you've almost killed us several times because of your insistence on taking the boy."

Requiem's eyes flared in outrage, and she marched over to her brother. "Did you just say what I think you did? We will *not* abandon our brothers! How dare you, Ruin?"

Michael watched Ruin's lips twitch. It seemed he was trying to force himself to smile but struggled at it. "Dearest sister, you know I care about you more than anything in this world, don't you? Sometimes plans have to change. I know in the beginning it seemed like we needed more family, but things have changed. We don't need Brothers Jack and Andy. We have only ever needed each other. It has gotten us this far, hasn't it?"

Requiem grabbed the front of his shirt and forced him to meet her maddened gaze. "They are our family now! I won't let them be left behind. I won't let anyone we love be left behind."

Michael didn't understand the exchange, but he was grateful that he was being given just a short moment to rest. Still lying on his back, he rolled his head and looked around the room. Without realizing he was doing so he began to laugh, a sound that resembled a hysterical grunting cough.

Just an hour earlier, the train terminal had been a neat and organized place, with people coming to and from, flowers and pictures hanging in every corner. There had even been a man playing guitar with a tip-cup. Now, it looked like an abandoned warehouse from the late-twenties. There were holes in so many parts of the floor that moving around was now a very risky endeavor. Every light had been broken, all the windows shattered, and broken soda cans were still spraying misty cola around the darkened terminal.

Vending machines roared with their built-in alarms, broken potato chips and other snacks were still being knocked around, some even falling into the dark tunnel below. Even the ceiling had been broken, or at least the glass part of it on top of the dome-shaped structure. It must have been shattered when Jack and Ruin unleashed their full powers against each other. Well, Ruin's full power, Michael reminded himself. God only knew what Jack could do if he ever dug deep enough.

"Can......hear me," said a broken, static-filled voice from Michael's left pocket. He felt the first welling of hope. He reached into his pocket with a shaking, unsteady hand.

"It's Mic—" he tried to speak, but his voice was tired, and exhaustion was washing over him. "Michael here, do you copy?" he forced out at last.

"This is Rebecca Alvarado, officer of Recon Team B. We're still waiting outside as instructed, awaiting your orders, over."

There was a shadow of movement from above Michael, and it took him a moment to realize it was the form of Kazou being tossed to the other end of the room. Somehow, Michael knew he wouldn't be able to get back up again either. Looking once again to his right, he could see that now Sarah too, was lying on her back, breathing heavily. The two Psychs would start their killing soon.

"Rebecca," Michael croaked. "We're down."

The voice from the other end sounded surprised, but determined nonetheless. "All of you?" she asked.

"Yes, even Paro. They don't know I'm speaking with you. Listen to me. I don't think you guys, not even all nineteen of you, will be able to handle these two. There's no need for you to die with us. Just leave."

"Negative," the voice replied.

Michael coughed a laugh. "You can't refuse an order from a Psych Operative," he said.

"We just did. Hang tight."

Michael groaned as his body was lifted telekinetically, hovering in the air for a moment before he was thrown in a direction he couldn't discern. He was too exhausted to register the motion, and only realized he was thrown to the right when he landed next to Sarah with a grunt. Kazou was also sent piling on top of them as he hit the ground with a roll, coughing and moaning.

Ruin and Requiem came to hover over them, both wearing their fashionable madness to the fullest. Ruin had by far surpassed his sister's menace, his face so contorted in lunacy that Michael felt tears come unbidden to his eyes just glancing at him.

"Who should we kill first?" Ruin asked.

"Darling, let's start with the woman. I didn't get to have any fun because of her meddling."

Sarah cried out in disgust at hearing the two speak of her fate. Michael heard her screams and added his own. Not for fear of his life, but for fear of seeing the woman who he loved above all put through the grueling torture that these two had perfected.

"Come on now," Michael begged. "Can't ya start with me? Leave Sarah alone and I promise I'll scream nice and loud fur ya. You like that, don't you?"

Requiem cast her eyes down on Michael, but only for a moment. It was Ruin who spoke.

"No," he said. "It's personal now. You people have caused us a great deal of misery. I will start with the woman, because I know it will hurt more than anything I could ever do to you."

Michael screamed at him, empty sounds devoid of words. He was too exhausted to make coherent speech—he was too worn to think, either. He simply shouted his rage at them, a bellowing sound that promised vengeance.

Sarah lifted off her back, floating up to hang limply in the air. Her eyes were unfocused and her whimpering stopped. Michael wondered if she still had the energy to scream, or even look at the two that would end her life.

"Show me, Sister. Show me the heart that keeps this one breathing."

Michael tried to stand. He tried to draw power. But there was nothing he could do. Everything that could be done, had been, and so now, lying on his back and gazing up at the limp form of Sarah, he would witness the unspeakable—an atrocity so great that Michael promised himself that even if he somehow lived through the night, he'd take his own life to make up for Sarah's.

"Do you see it, Darling?"

"I do. What a wonderful heart it is. I wonder what would happen if I—"

Requiem tugged on her brother's arm and shook him. "Ruin! Guns! They're coming from behind, shield us—now!"

Ruin spun around and Sarah fell back to the floor, unharmed for the moment. One of the few sections of the wall that had yet to be damaged detonated with military grade explosives, blowing the western section inward and sending large, rocky chunks rolling on the floor.

Before the smoke had finished rising, the thunderous sound of nineteen firing rifles filled the terminal. The flashing of the barrels casted the most light the place had seen in an hour. Ruin held out his hand, and Michael could see the exertion on the young Psych's face. The bullets were pounding into his barrier, some almost breaking it while others bounced off and fell to the ground without much trouble.

Ruin began to sweat with the daunting task of fending off such a large quantity of bullets all at once. They poured into him, and each time they hit the barrier, there was a small spark of light in front of him. Then the bullets ricocheted in the opposite direction.

The recon officers wasted no time. When their clips emptied, the terminal quieted but for the sound of the shell casings clattering against the ground while the officers reloaded, ready soon after for another volley of fire.

Never in Michael's life had he been so glad to hear the deep crackle of gunfire.

"Brother, Darling!" Requiem cried. "Can you hold them off?"

Ruin grunted. "I'm trying, Sister."

The bullets assaulted the two Psychs, and Ruin fended them off as they came. For a Kinetic, it was one of the hardest things to do. Michael shook his head in disbelief while he watched the young Psych maintain his defenses for such a long period of time.

Any Telekinetic could make a decent burst if they were trained, something that would send just about anyone or anything packing. With bullets, they were too fast to see. You never knew when a bullet was about to strike, so when someone held a gun to a Kinetic, there were really only two options.

If it was just one or two gunman, then you could try ripping the weapons out of their hands, but if it was several, the only thing you could do was maintain a continuous stationary burst. It was an exhausting—and sometimes crippling—exertion of power, one that required you to literally pour energy into one location and maintain it until the men who were firing at you, well, stopped firing.

"Is there anything you can do here, Sister?" Ruin asked. "I don't know how much longer I can hold them off for."

The bullets continued to fly at them, the sound of gunshots filling the air. The brightness of nineteen automatic weapons created an almost blinding display of flashing lights. Ruin took one step back, then two, before he was shuffling backwards with his sister, sweating and struggling to maintain his defenses. If only Michael or Kazou could still move, now would be the perfect time to finally put an end to the two. It was nothing more than a wish, however. Michael couldn't bring himself to speak let alone stand.

"Buy me some time, and I will handle them, Darling."

Several moments passed before yet again the recon officers reloaded, intent on beating Ruin down until their bullets finally penetrated his defenses. This time, Ruin did not seem content to allow them a third round of fire. He gestured with his hand and threw a burst of kinetic energy in their direction. His stamina amazed Michael. Ruin had yet again been brought to the point of exhaustion, and he was already recovering and building back up his momentum.

The officers were thrown back, not hard enough to be fatal, but hard enough to knock all nineteen men and women off their feet.

Requiem grinned. The officers were quick to get back to their feet. Before the first officer came to a full stand, he collapsed back down again, followed soon after by the rest of the officers. Some were still rising to their feet when they fell back down, others had not yet begun to stand. Michael knew she wasn't killing them. She was putting them into a shallow sleep, an extraordinary feat for a single Path to knockout that many people at once.

"There's no time to toy around anymore," Ruin said with a disappointed sigh. He removed a small knife from the back pocket of his dark jeans. "I'm ending this now."

He spun around and knelt down, placing his knee on Sarah's throat. She coughed, and Ruin slowly brought the knife down on her neck. "I really wanted to play with this one," he said. "But I guess we'll have to settle for this."

The knife closed in on Sarah's throat, and Michael struggled for all he was worth to save Sarah, whimpering but unable to move. This was it. They were going to die after all. Closer and closer, the knife approached her throat. A sadistic glee spread on Ruin's face as the knife drew nearer.

There was a whooshing sound, like that of a sword cutting through air. A sharp looking rock raced across the terminal, smacking with an audible crunch into Ruin's forehead. Instinctively, Ruin dropped the knife, clutching at the trickle of blood falling over his eyes. He looked enraged, livid, and he howled in pain as he scanned the room for the source of his misery.

There was a loud crash, and another section of wall was blown out, admitting a limping, bruised man. Blood was falling from his mouth, his arms, and almost every part of his body. But he was far from dead—his eyes burned with the intensity of a collapsing star. His hands were balled into fists, each knuckle smothered in dark red blood.

"You know ..." he said to no one in particular. "There are a lot of things in this world I don't like. I don't like being yelled at. I don't like when Jack makes stupid comments. I don't like long lines, or people that snore too loudly. But now there's a new thing, something I hate more than anything. *I don't like people who drop freaking buildings on top of me!*"

Michael cried, as unmanly as it was, joined in by Sarah. "Paro!" he called, finding his voice.

Paro looked beaten to a pulp. He was bruised, limping, and not a single part of him appeared to be in good condition. Ruin and Requiem walked over to him.

"This one lived?" Ruin asked.

"It seems that way, Darling, though it doesn't look to be by much. We should kill him first, I think, yes? He's the only one still a threat to us."

Ruin gestured with his hand ... and let out a sound resembling a squawk when nothing happened.

"I'm sorry," Paro said to Michael, Sarah, and Kazou. "I never intended on letting you guys fight them. You're not quite ready for these types of Psychs. Someday, but not yet."

"Darling—do something! Throw another burst at him."

Ruin was sweating, his eyes widening in fear and confusion. "I'm trying, Sister! I have been."

Looking closely, Michael could see that dust and empty wrappers were moving as if by an invisible wind, yet it was only slight, and in no way resembled the massive power Ruin had been displaying all along.

You've gotta be kidding me. Michael thought to himself. *Paro's not even being moved an inch? Not even with all that force?*

"Sit," Paro commanded.

Ruin and Requiem shouted in surprise. One moment they were standing up straight, and the next they were thrown to the ground, slamming face-first into the marble floor.

"Or, you can lie down," he added with a wry grin.

Paro walked over to Michael and knelt down before him. There was concern on his face. "Did ... did anyone die?" he asked.

Michael struggled to form words but forced them out. "No, we're all still alive—ah! It hurts. We're alive, Paro. Everyone is still alive."

Paro nodded. "Good, because I'd have killed them both if you told me any differently."

Michael trembled. He'd never seen Paro use this much force before, never, not once in the years he'd known him.

"You guys did great. I'm so proud of all of you, and I'm sorry I let you guys get hurt this much. I should've known they'd do something crazy."

Sarah tried to embrace Paro, but her arms were shaking. Paro walked over to her, bent down and completed the hug. Michael felt a pang of jealously—it was a shameful emotion. He forced it from his mind.

"I'm so happy you're not dead," Sarah said.

"That makes two of us."

Michael brought himself into a sitting position. "Shouldn't you be keeping an eye on those two?" he asked.

Paro waved a hand at Michael. "Don't worry, those two aren't going anywhere. I've got them locked down. Right now, it's you three I'm worried about. Speaking of which, where's Jack and Melissa?"

"I'm not sure. They were off chasing Andy, but we haven't seen them since," Michael answered.

"You guys really tore up the place," Paro said. His face lit up with astonishment. "I mean, how did you guys manage to do this much damage? Between the train tracks and now the upper terminal, this station will probably be out of service for a year."

"A lot of it was Jack," Kazou said with a grunt, clutching at his sides. He seemed to be in more pain than all of them.

"That, I can believe."

There was an ear piercing shout from behind them, and Michael felt the return of fear. Even Sarah sat up to see what new trouble was heading their way.

"No!" screamed a voice. "I wanna!"

"Don't even think about it," answered another voice in a high-pitched yell. "You're not running out there looking like that."

"Too late, I'm already there."

Scrambling into the terminal from the street-side entrance came Jack, Melissa, and an unconscious and shirtless Andy. Jack was wearing what appeared to be a cape made out of Andy's shirt.

"You look ridiculous." Melissa snarled at him.

"I'm here, everyone!" Jack shouted to the room, flinging his cape over his shoulder.

"I'm not doing it," Melissa said, folding her arms in a position of defiance.

"But Melissa, you promised," Jack insisted. Michael had no idea what they were talking about. "Are you someone to go back on your promises, Melissa?"

Melissa frowned at Jack. "Fine, whatever, just make it quick. This is going to be humiliating."

Jack cleared his throat and addressed the room. "Prepare for trouble!" He shot Melissa an expecting glance.

Melissa sighed. "Make that double."

"To protect the world from devastation!"

Melissa seemed to be forcing the words out. "To unite all peoples within our nation."

"To denounce the evils of truth and love!"

"Okay, that's it. This is ridiculous. Get inside, Jack!"

Jack scratched his head when he looked around the room, pausing a second to glance at each one of them. He shouted in surprise when Melissa ripped off his 'cape.'

"Whoa, what happened to you guys?" Jack said. "You look terrible. Wow, Paro, you're alive! I'm so glad you're not dead or dying a slow painful death crushed between fallen beams!"

"Jeeze, thanks," Paro mumbled in reply.

Andy was lying on his back with his hands bound beneath him, and Melissa dragged him by his left leg. She pulled on him without care, his head occasionally bumping into things as he scraped along the floor.

"Wow," Jack said. He pointed at the subdued forms of Ruin and Requiem. "You guys already took down those two? Damn, I need to use some of this power. It's killing me."

Michael had no idea what Jack was talking about, and from the looks of things nobody did, except Sarah, who nodded at his words. Jack extended a hand toward the street-side entrance. There was a bang, and even more of the terminal was destroyed, chunks ripping apart.

"What did I say, Jack? Stop with that nonsense."

"I can't help it. I need to get rid of some of this power. It burns!"

Paro limped over to Jack and looked down at the unconscious form of Andy. "I'm too wounded or exhausted to care about any of this right now, Jack, and I'm even willing to let that unauthorized use of destructive force slide. Just don't let me see it again, okay?"

Jack looked worried. "Fine, I won't use any more bursts, I promise ... after this next one." Jack once again sent another burst, creating another large bang, causing more sections of wall to be blown out. Pretty soon, there'd be no walls left. It was a miracle the building was still standing at all.

Melissa slapped him. "Cut it out, Jack! I'm serious. You almost killed us like, five times on the way out of that tunnel. Using power isn't like going to the bathroom. You don't just 'get rid of it.'"

Jack shook his head. "I'm telling you, it's different for me. It burns, it really does. Okay, just let me use a little more, and then I promise—"

"No," Paro interrupted. "We've done enough damage here. Let's just grab these three and head back to H.Q. This time, no less than ten Psychs will stay with them at all times. I'm done leaving things to chance."

The recon officers were getting back to their feet, and they rushed to once again secure the perimeter. Michael felt gratitude towards them. If not for their actions, the Psychs of Paro's team would have died.

"Alright, I'm going to call for medical personnel immediately. We're also going to need an emergency transport for the prisoners," Paro said, regaining control of the situation.

"That won't be necessary."

Michael turned and felt a return of his previous terror. Approaching were the last four people in the world he wished to see.

"Cemmera," he growled.

Jack, Kazou, Sarah, Paro, and Melissa, all turned their heads to see the four Op. team members glide confidently into destroyed terminal, watching their step and taking care not to fall through the several holes in the floor created during the battle.

They were all bloody, worn, and still injured from the incident at Alana's home. Cemmera looked just as twisted as Ruin or Requiem, only her face was pulled back in an expression of delight. "*Finally*," she hissed. "Finally, I will have my kills. I've been waiting for this. I need this."

"No," Sarah moaned, "after all of this, after everything we've been through, for them to just show up like this? No, I can't accept this."

Ruin and Requiem, still pinned to the floor, each let out a moan as well, remembering Sarah's words and hearing the pitied ones she spoke now. Paro walked to meet them.

"You look like hell," Cemmera said with a laugh. "Out of my way, Carebear."

"Hold a minute," Paro demanded. "I am the team-leader here, and I am personally declaring Jack Harris, Melissa Sayre, and all members of my team not-guilty of any illegal acts. I know you tried to murder Jack earlier, but I am here now, and I forbid it. Are we going to have a problem here?"

Cemmera laughed. "No, no, of course not, my dear, there is no problem at all. Consider that awful situation all cleared up, an accident if you will. We are not here for any members of your team, and as they say, let bygones be bygones, yes? No, we are here for those three. We have a signed kill order for each of them."

Paro did not move. "Well, as I'm sure you can tell, we've already apprehended them. There's no need for any killing, Cemmera."

Cemmera grabbed his bloodied shirt and leaned her face into his. Her voice was a whispered hiss, spoken in an enraged, maniacal tone. *"No,"* she said. *"No, I need this kill. I'm not leaving here until I've killed something, do you understand me? Get the hell out of my way."*

Michael felt the hopelessness of the situation. They had gone through so much to apprehend the Psychs, and now in the end they'd end up dead anyway, the Op. teams arriving just in time to make the kill. Michael had no doubt that they'd been watching the entire ordeal, waiting to see if Paro's team got killed, definitely hoping for it. When that didn't pan out, they made their move.

Paro closed his eyes, opening them a moment later with a saddened look. "You can't have Andy," he said. "By law, we were able to bind and secure him for a period of longer than ten minutes. He has been subdued, and you have no right to kill him while he remains in our custody."

Cemmera growled but then nodded a moment later. "Fine, fine, I'll settle for those two," she said pointing at Ruin and Requiem. "If I don't kill something soon, I'm going to lose it."

Neil laughed—it was a disgusting sight. The Reinforcer was missing half his teeth. From what Michael understood, Melissa had ruined his face.

The two Kinetics followed Neil and Cemmera.

"Hey, Melissa, what are you doing?" Jack yelled. "Why are you covering my eyes? What's happening?"

"Don't watch, Jack," she whispered. "Don't watch."

Chapter 36: What is, what was, what will be.

Jack's vision was as dark as night. Melissa's hand covered his eyes. "What's going on?" he asked again.

Jack tried to pry her fingers loose, but she clutched his face with a force that only a Reinforcer could manage, almost to the point of pain. Jack tried to remove her hand, using both of his own in an attempt to lift her one, but all he did was make her grab at him tighter. He even tried to duck and squirm, but she followed along with his motion, handling him like a child.

"I've been waiting for this," the voice of Cemmera said. Jack could hear her just fine though, and from the sounds of things, she was walking towards where Andy was secured with the other two Psychs.

"Paro!" Jack yelled. "If you really want me to be part of this team, then stop trying to baby me. Tell Melissa to let me go."

There was a moment of silence, and all Jack could hear was the occasional shifting of feet, his vision still covered in darkness.

"Let go of him, Melissa," Paro commanded.

The hand on Jack's face pressed tighter. "Jack's not ready to see this, we can't let him—"

"That's an order," Paro interrupted. All at once Melissa removed her hand and let go of him. She didn't look happy, but neither did the rest of the team for that matter. Sarah was once again sitting on the floor, weeping quietly into her sleeve.

"At least we saved one," she said with a resigned sigh.

Cemmera, Neil, and the Kinetics were hovering over the pinned Ruin and Requiem. The two Psychs had a look of fear, though overshadowed by a tremendous glare of defiance. They did not avert their eyes while the four peered down at them.

"I won't hold them in place," Paro said. "If you're going to do this, you do it alone."

One of the Kinetics, Joseph, if Jack recalled correctly, seemed to grow excited upon hearing this. "Good," he said. "It looks like my brother and I get a small taste of the kill after all." He licked his lips, kneeling down with his brother, carrying a look of hunger mixed with lust.

"Melissa," Jack said. "What do they mean by that? He said he's gonna get a 'taste of the kill'."

"Do you remember what we told you about the Op. teams, Jack?"

"Well, yeah, but we captured the three of them. They're not really going to kill them, right? They were too late, so now we gotta take them back to H.Q, just like we said we would."

Michael walked over to Jack on unsteady feet. He wasn't limping as bad as Paro, but he was definitely not at ease. He put a reassuring arm on Jack's shoulder. "This is the way it works sometimes, bud. Are you sure you wanna watch this?"

Jack shook his head, trying to clear his mind of the growing confusion. "Wait, we're going to *allow* this? This is just a joke to scare them, yeah? We'd never actually let these creeps kill them, right?"

Sarah stood to her feet and joined Michael in embracing Jack. She rested her chin on the back of his neck and hugged him with tears moist in her eyes. "I'm sorry," she whispered. "We saved Andy, but we were too late for the other two. They've got signed kill orders. There's nothing we can do at this point. The only reason we're still here is to ensure they aren't tortured. It's against the law, but Op. teams do it anyway."

Jack felt a tremor of nausea travel the distance from his feet to his eyes, creeping along his body in a cascading wave. It had nothing to do with the power he still held—it was a sickening feeling of realization, as he allowed Sarah's words to dawn on him.

"I still don't understand, Sarah. We captured them. How can they be killing them right in front of us? You told me that if we captured them then they wouldn't have to die!"

Jack felt the back of his neck grow moist from Sarah's tears. "I'm so sorry," she said. "There's nothing we can do anymore. It's the law, and it's one that we don't have the power or authority to change. We can't stop these four now. The fate of their lives is up to the discretion of the Op. team now."

"So you're saying it's *their* choice?"

"Yes, Jack. It's their choice, and they're intent on killing those two."

Jack gently leaned away from Sarah and looked at the four Psychs of the Op. team. They were smiling while they prepared to slaughter their two captured victims.

"Hey!" Jack called to them. "You, Cemmera, answer me!"

Cemmera turned to Jack with a look of annoyance. "What do you want now, Harris? I'm not sharing the kill with you—you can forget it. If you want a piece of this you need to join our Op. team. We've got a spot open for a Path, and seeing as how you can technically be anything, I'd take ya. Hell, if you'd sign a contract right now, I'd even give you the kill of your choice. One's still mine, though, hopefully the boy."

It took Jack a moment to take in her words. He wasn't sure if she was being serious. Realizing that her words were genuine, Jack filled with disgust.

"These are people we're talking about, Cemmera. They're not animals. Why are you going to kill them? They can't hurt anybody anymore, we've captured them."

Cemmera looked at him as if his question was among the dumbest ever asked, which was almost funny to Jack, because in his life he'd asked quite a few of those.

"I'm sorry, what?" Cemmera asked. "I don't get the question. You're saying why we *shouldn't* kill them, or why we *should*?"

Jack tried to hold his temper. "I'm asking you why you're going to kill them. I don't understand it. They've already been stopped."

Cemmera scratched her head. "Well, because if I don't kill them, then I'm going to have to go yet another day without a kill ... Did you hit your head or something, Harris?"

Only then did it dawn on Jack. Standing before the four members of the Op. team, he came to understand the truth of what these people were. "You ... you enjoy this?"

Cemmera tilted her head to the sky and laughed. "Of course! We live for the hunt. We would even die for the hunt. Get with the program, kid. Now, my offer still stands—do you want in on this or not?"

Jack's only response was to raise an extended palm and ready himself for yet another attack on Cemmera. Before he could so much as lift his arm above his waist, Melissa was already standing beside him with a firm grasp on his opened hand.

"Don't even think about it," she hissed. "You'll be sentenced to death for something like that."

"You attacked them earlier," Jack argued. "All of a sudden they're good guys now?"

"That was different, Jack," Sarah said. "What happened back at your house will probably turn into an unresolved dispute, one that will carry on into our higher courts for years before being chalked up to error on both ends and discarded. If you attack them here and now, while in the middle of an operation in progress, with targets only inches from them, then you'll be in more trouble than we can get you out of."

Jack moaned with the emotion building inside of him. "So we have to just stand here and watch? We're going to let them just kill people for no damn reason!"

"No one said it was going to be easy," Paro said. His eyes were downcast and he had a look of defeat on his face, one that had nothing to do with the beating he'd received from the roof-beams collapsing on him.

"Alright, I can't wait any longer. You got em pinned, boys?" Cemmera beamed delight when the two Telekinetics nodded.

The change happened in an instant. One moment, Ruin and Requiem were gazing at Cemmera in defiance, their eyes declaring a wordless challenge. An instant later, with almost no transition, the reality of the situation finally dawned on them. In the time it takes for a balloon to pop when pierced or the light to fade after flicking a switch, their eyes changed from defiant to terrified, knowing their lives were only moments from ending.

"Ruin, Darling, they are serious, aren't they?" Requiem asked.

Ruin did not answer. His maddened and twisted expression faded in its entirety, leaving like it had never been there. Jack had only ever seen two looks on the young Kinetic. He'd seen his carefree and cheerful side, and more recently, he'd seen a madness that rivaled his sister's. Now, there was none of either. There was only the face of a young man, likely only a year or two older than Jack, coming to realize that his life was about to be snuffed out of him.

Requiem struggled against the force of the two Telekinetics holding her down, unable to so much as wiggle a finger.

"I see what she's trying to do," Cemmera said. She laughed. "Jason, Daniel, let her, please. It will make this so much more fun."

The Kinetics grinned and Jack thought he could see the way their Telekinesis shifted, allowing Requiem to move her arm. Reaching out, she grasped her brother's hand, holding it deep into her own, gripping it tightly.

She looked past the four members of the Op. team, past Paro, past Melissa, past Jack and Michael, to land her eyes on Sarah's. Her madness was not gone, but it did seem to fade a little, making room for her own terror.

"Darling," she said with a shaking, fear-ridden voice. She even seemed to be panting as she spoke, her words coming out in small shivers. "D-Darling, didn't you s-say that we could surrender, yes? Please, I am s-sorry, th-that I did not listen earlier. We can go now, yes? Please, yes? We can go, Darling, yes? You will take us home, yes?"

Sarah shook and turned away from the girl, grabbing Michael and weeping. "Don't look, sweetie," he said holding her tight. "Don't look." It was almost the exact same words Melissa had said to Jack earlier.

Jack did not move or speak. He was too shocked to do either. The sounds of Requiem's pleas grabbed at him, tugging on his heart far more tightly than Melissa's grip on his hand.

Is this really happening? Jack thought. *Are we really allowing this?*

"Flip him," Cemmera commanded. Ruin was lifted into the air, spinning over, and coming to land on his back.

"Sister," he whispered. "Sister!" he yelled. "SISTER!" he screamed.

Cemmera sat on his chest and Jack realized that at that moment, she looked far more mad and twisted than the two Psychs ever could. Her grin spread across her entire face, enveloping her. Cemmera's pleasure was evident in her moaning sighs, while she removed a knife of her own from her pocket. "I'm getting personal with this one." She let out another laugh.

Requiem cried as her face was kinetically turned and she was forced to watch. The sound she made was sickening. Jack felt, more than he heard her cries. It pierced his heart, stabbed at his soul. "Ah! Ah!" Requiem cried, and Jack assumed she was no longer able to form words. Tears began to fall from her face.

"AH! AHH! No, p-p-please!" Requiem begged. "I'll stop, we'll stop, I promise. Please, we're sorry. Sarah!" she called. "Sarah, we're sorry!"

"Aww," Cemmera teased. "I wonder how many people asked you the same thing. Stupid kids, thinking you're so powerful just cause you're Psychs. Now look at ya, sucks don't it?"

With that, clutching the knife in both hands, she brought it down on Ruin's chest. Blood splattered out of his open wound. The man—no, the boy—gurgled a cry. He kicked once, then twice, and then stopped moving. Just like that, he was dead. There were no last words—there was no last anything. In the blink of an eye, his life was extinguished.

"NO!" Requiem howled, "No, No, Oh no!"

"Let her go," Cemmera said, still straddling the lifeless Ruin. Requiem stood to her feet and jumped on top of her brother as Cemmera got off him. "Good work, boys." Cemmera said, licking the blood off her knife. She sang and danced. "We got him, we got him, oh yeah, yeah, we got him. Go team!"

Requiem grabbed her brother by the shoulders. She spoke fast, almost too fast to understand her frantic words. "Oh, you're just pretending, right, Darling?" She patted her brother's head. "Of course you are, stop sleeping, Darling. Open your eyes now, okay? I'm here, that's it, that's it, that's it, yes now, yes, okay yes, okay, Darling, open your eyes. Ruin ... My brother! My friend! Oh, please, Ruin, please, open your eyes! Stop sleeping now, Daddy's going to be home and he won't want to see us. Please, Ruin, please just open your eyes one more time for me, Darling. Oh, Ruin, oh please!"

There was a shriek, an inhuman wail of the purest agony and pain, so loud that not even a bomb could overpower its massive sound. She rolled over on her back, and for a moment Jack thought the Kinetics were pinning her down again, but looking into her eyes, Jack could see he was wrong. They were watching her like she was some kind of circus animal, enjoying every moment.

"NO!" Requiem howled, "MY BROTHER! YOU KILLED HIM!"

She trembled, rolling around, back and forth, clutching at her heart, flailing her arms, and then grabbing at her sides, "NO! NO! NO! NO! NO! I LOVED HIM! GIVE ME BACK MY BROTHER!"

Tears escaped from her eyes, so many and so fast, that her shirt became soaked and her eyes grew red with misery. She tried to stand, but she tripped over her own feet. She began to crawl, screaming with such intensity that both of the Kinetics had to cover their ears.

"MY BROTHER! MY FRIEND!"

Cemmera stopped her dancing. "Will you shut up already, tramp?" Cemmera placed a boot on her back, and Requiem was pinned to the ground, water falling from her eyes like an overturned glass.

She looked around the room until her eyes settled on Jack. There was something off about them, something odd. It was something that Jack should have seen sooner.

How could I not have known? All this time, and I didn't see it.

"Jaaaaaaaaaaackk," Requiem cried. "Please, don't let them kill me! My brother! Jack, they killed him!"

Those are my eyes, Jack realized with an almost heart-stopping epiphany. *At one time, her eyes were the same as mine. At one time, she was just like me. What happened to her? Why has she become what she is now?*

"Alright pin her down again, boys. This one's becoming an issue. It's like fishing, ya know? Gutting them is my favorite part."

Melissa's grip tightened on Jack's hand. Now she too began to cry. Jack, Paro, and Kazou, were the only in the room dry-eyed, watching the scene with a horrified fascination. "Melissa," Jack whispered. "This is ... awful."

"Jaaaaaaaaackkk!" Requiem cried, being flipped over. "Jaaaaaaaaackk!" She held out a hand, unable to move, trying to reach for him.

He couldn't take it anymore. This was the last straw. "*Cemmera!*" Jack shouted. "Get your hands off of her—now!"

Before Melissa could react, Jack pushed her off him and charged at Requiem, diving to the ground and grabbing her hand. The moment their fingers intertwined Jack's mind exploded. It felt like a million volts were shooting through his brain. The room spun and shook, the terminal revolving around him.

Faster and faster it spun, until the dizziness was too much to bear. Then came the darkness.

It took Jack a moment to realize he still existed. He took in the scene. It was snowing, and all around were the signs of a beautiful Christmas Eve. Houses lined the wide street on both sides, with decorations and snowmen, Christmas lights bloomed in the otherwise dark night. There was cheer in the air, surrounding him, the very spirit of Christmas. It wove around him, thick in the air, from one house to the next. Happiness filled the world, everywhere except one place. In front of Jack there was a home. It was different from the others. There was darkness around it, an intensity that Jack could sense, separating it from all the others.

Where are we? It was a voice in Jack's mind. It was her voice. It was the voice of the one who once held his eyes.

"I don't know," Jack said aloud.

Can we go home?

"I don't know how to take us there," Jack answered.

The darkness returned, casting them into a void, only to reappear a moment later, this time inside of a home. Jack suspected it was the one carrying the feeling of darkness, the one he'd seen from the street.

I don't want to be here, Requiem said.

"I don't either. I don't know how to go back."

The home was rundown and filthy. There was trash everywhere and a stench of alcohol. Dust and grime were as much residents of the home as the people that lived there. It was a small place with two bedrooms, a kitchen, and a den. There were pictures on the wall with faces of a woman scratched out.

Our mother, Requiem said. *She left us.*

There was a whimpering sound, and Jack reeled in surprise at the sight of the two small children huddled together behind him. They were tiny, perhaps no older than five or six years of age. They were sitting against a wall, almost hidden behind the thick layers of dust that covered them. Their clothing was torn, nothing more than scraps on unwashed bodies.

"Let me go," one of them begged.

"Never, Sandra," answered the other.

"But why does it always have to be you? Anthony, please, I don't wanna let you do it again. I can do it too."

"He doesn't like you," Anthony answered. "I'd never let him hurt you the way he hurts me, Sandra. Never, ever, ever. I promise you."

"Who are you two?" Jack asked them.

I don't think they can hear you, Jack.

"That girl, is she you?"

Once upon a time.

Jack knelt before the small child and looked into her eyes. There wasn't much madness in her face, just deep dark eyes, filled with life and wonder. They were strikingly similar to Jack's, but they were not his own. No, they were already changing. In them he could see the beginnings of madness, spreading along the corners of her pupils.

From outside the home Jack could hear the sound of keys being dangled, and the two siblings embraced each other in a hug.

"Not again," Sandra begged. "Please, don't let him do it anymore, Anthony. Let me go, let me take some of the pain."

"Never," Anthony said, kissing his sister on the forehead. "I'd never let that happen to you."

The door opened and a large, hairy man entered. His face was wrinkled, his breath reeking of alcohol. Jack could smell it from across the room. Though, even without the scent it was obvious. In the man's hand, he clutched a bottle of whiskey for dear life, some of the liquid still falling down his mouth like drool. He had a sickening grin, and he allowed himself a hearty laugh.

"I'm home, Darlings," he announced. "Where's my special boy?"

Ruin—no, Anthony—tensed, grabbing his sister tighter. "He looks like he's had a lot tonight," he whimpered.

The man knew exactly where to look. Somehow, Jack knew that they'd always hugged the same wall.

I don't want to see this, Requiem said. *Please.*

"I can't make it stop."

The man walked up to the two shivering children and bent down, his disgusting alcohol-breath bearing down on top of them. "Anthony, daddy's home. I've been waiting all day to see my boy."

"No!" Sandra shouted. "Let me go."

The man looked at her in disgust and slapped her across her small face, making the child bleed. Jack forced himself to watch. He needed to understand.

"Don't hurt her! I won't fight you, Dad." Anthony held out his hand, and the father grabbed it. Pulling him into the nearest room and slamming the door behind him, all the while humming to himself.

No more, please!

It wasn't long before the screams started, and Jack wanted to be gone as badly as Requiem.

Again there was darkness, and again it faded. This time, the children were older. Already, Jack could see the madness in Requiem's eyes taking form, growing, and a prelude to what she'd become. They were in a park, with jungle gyms, slides, and see-saws. They were sitting at a table together, and across from them sat a man.

Redemption, Requiem said. *Our only true father.*

"Do you two understand?" the man asked. He was covered from head to toe in brown garb. Only his eyes were visible, and Jack was taken aback by them. They were the most powerful and commanding eyes he'd ever seen.

"Yes," Anthony answered. "Everything that's happened to us, it happened because we weren't strong enough to make it stop. Things are only right and wrong because the people in power make them so."

"And what will you do?" the man asked.

"We are going to rip out our father's still beating heart and show it to him. What else would we do?"

"Your choices are your own," the man said. "Make them wisely."

Yet again darkness enveloped Jack, only to fade and again Jack reappeared inside the home. This time, it was different There was blood everywhere—on the walls, on the floor, even on the ceiling. Lying on the ground, covered in a pool of blood, was their father. He had been tortured, to the point of absurdity. His eyes absent from their sockets, his skin flayed, and his heart removed. Jack tried to feel pity for the man, but he couldn't bring himself to feel even a drop of it.

There was a splash on the blood-stained floor—it was a single tear from Sandra. Anthony turned to her. "Let this be the last tear you ever have to shed, Sister."

The sadness left her eyes immediately, replaced with the madness Jack had come to know as her current self. "Never again, Darling. I'll never cry again."

She laughed, and so did her brother. The two stood in a puddle of blood, and for close to ten minutes poured out years' worth of missed laughter. The only tears they shed were ones of joy. "Anthony, such a pitiful name. Call me Ruin from now on, Sister."

"Sure, if you call me Requiem, Darling!"

They held hands, and they laughed. "We are amazing," Ruin said. "Look at the things we can do. Sister, what say you and me change the world together? We can do things no one else can. Why don't we tear this world down and rebuild it from scratch?"

"Sounds lovely, Darling."

"Don't ever forget our promise," Ruin said.

"I won't, Anth—Ruin. Never again. We will never cry again."

Jack opened his eyes, his hands still clutching Requiem's in a tight grip. Only a moment had passed, and it was a moment that felt like hours. Requiem cupped Jack's face and looked at him with pleading eyes. "How? How did you do that?"

"I don't know," Jack said. "But I understand now. I'm so sorry, Sandra."

Everyone in the room turned to give Jack a confused stare. "Sandra?" Paro asked. "What are you talking about, Jack?"

Cemmera shrugged. "I don't even care. I don't know what just happened between you two, but it's killing time. Out of my way, Harris."

Jack looked down at the dead form of Ruin—Anthony—and into the maddened gaze of Cemmera. Much in the way that Sandra once shared the same eyes as Jack, Cemmera held the same eyes as their father. It was a look Jack would never forget. It was the look of a predator, the look of evil.

Jack let the anger take hold of him. He let it grow, allowed it to seep into every fiber of his being. When it was too much to handle, Jack felt his emotions fade, he felt them recede within himself. It was fine. There were things in this world Jack didn't want to feel.

"What's with the Harris-boy's eyes?" Cemmera asked.

All at once the members of Paro's team, still situated behind Jack, rushed over. "What did you just say?" Michael yelled out. "Cemmera, did you just say that there's something wrong with his eyes? God help us all."

Jack stood and turned to face the members of his team. Michael stopped mid-run and fell back on his rump. Sarah paused and eyed Jack with fear. Kazou stopped moving and took a step back. Only Melissa and Paro came closer. Jack walked across the room to meet them.

"Jack, are you okay?" Paro asked. "Please, talk to me."

"I am fine," Jack said. "And you?"

"J-Jack," Melissa said. "What are you feeling?"

Jack thought about the question for a moment. Just what was he feeling? Jack wasn't certain he felt anything. He remembered being this way before.

Ah, Jack remembered. *So that's what I did to Andy. I wonder why I can't seem to remember these things later on? I suppose I should feel disappointed in myself, but I'm not sure I know what disappointment feels like.*

When Jack spoke to them, his voice was plain, robotic, lacking of any emotion. "I don't feel anything, Melissa."

"What do you mean? Jack, what's going on?"

Jack shrugged. "I'm supposed to save Requiem. I think I wanted to do that. Though, now I'm no longer sure I care. When I'm like this, I don't understand why human life is so important. Guilt, sadness, these things have no meaning to me anymore."

Michael and Kazou backed up even farther, but Paro and Melissa went towards him. "Jack, tell us, what's happened to you?"

"I'm not really sure. I remember this happening to me before. I don't know, I guess I'm on autopilot. I mean, I'm still me, I'm just a better me, I guess. I don't feel anything. Yet, I know that I can't stay like this. It's weird, you know? I know there's something I really want to do, but at the same time I wonder if I should still do it. It doesn't matter to me either way, but I know that it will later on. I guess I only have two choices. Do what I wanted, or don't. I might as well, I mean, from what I can see, it's the only logical choice. I know that if I don't do what I wanted, I'll feel disappointment later on, even if I'm unable to feel any right now."

Neil whispered something into Cemmera's ears and she nodded. "Look, Harris, I don't know what in the hell is going on with you, but you can take your Carebear drama somewhere else—you're killing the mood. As for you, sweetie," she said, looking down at Requiem. "I'm going to have fun with you. Did ya like the way I killed dear old brother?"

Jack kicked off his back foot, and in a single leap, he crossed the distance of the terminal and landed between Cemmera and Requiem. "We never got to be properly introduced, did we Cemmera?"

"Kid's eyes are freaking me the hell out," Joseph murmured.

Cemmera ignored the remark. "What are you playing at, Harris?"

Jack spoke. His voice was robotic. There was neither inflection nor emphasis on any of his words. "Well, let me introduce myself. My name is Jack Harris, and I'm sixteen years old. I love popcorn, and my favorite movie is 'Back to the Future.' Oh, yeah, and can you please do me a huge favor and die?"

Cemmera chuckled at his words. "Wait, what? Harris, get lost, before I add you to my kill-list on the grounds of interference. Damned kids these days." She knelt down with the knife, intent on ending Requiem's life. Jack grabbed her arm, hard enough to break bone. Cemmera howled in pain.

"Ouch!" Cemmera screamed out. "Help, I'm being attacked by a rogue Psych! Neil, he's using reinforcement."

Paro and the rest of the team remained motionless as Neil charged at Jack. "Harris!" the man yelled. "How dare you attack our team-leader?"

Neil drew back his arm, an attack meant to take Jack's head off. Jack knew he would be amazed—if he were capable of such a feeling—at just how weak the Reinforcer was.

Did I really think these people were powerful? They're like little insects.

Melissa cried out to Jack in warning. Neil's fist crashed down on Jack's face with all the power he was capable of using. Jack didn't move—he didn't even raise an arm to defend himself. He allowed Neil to attack him with every bit of power the man had.

Neil's eyes widened and his arm trembled. Jack was not moved by his punch. He didn't even feel it. Using a sense he didn't know he had, Jack saw the bones in Neil's wrist explode. It was the result of a fist colliding with an unbreakable object.

Neil dropped to his knees and let out a bloodcurdling howl. "*Ahh!* Cemmera, my arm, my bones have been shattered!"

Jack knew that the man was done for, no longer a threat to him. There was no longer a reason for him to attack the Reinforcer. Had he been his normal self, he'd know that it'd be wrong to continue to attack the man. Yet, he was not his normal self. Jack gave the man a punch of his own, for no other reason than it seemed an interesting thing to do at the time.

The man's cries were silenced as Jack's fist knocked out the other half of the teeth that Melissa had missed. Neil was sent flying across the room, landing in front of Paro. Jack turned, ready to finish him off and end his life.

Melissa blocked his path. "No!" she yelled. "Jack, he's down for the count. Listen to me, please. You don't want to do what you're about to."

Jack shrugged. "I don't really want to do anything," he said. "I guess I'll just do what I think I wanted."

"Be careful," Melissa warned. "It looks like Cemmera and the Kinetics are getting ready to attack you."

"Who? Those three?" Jack asked, pointing. "They've been trying for a while now, look closely." The three of them were sweating, panting, and exerting a great deal of force against Jack.

Requiem was looking at him like he was some kind of God, her eyes sparkling in wonder. Jack bent down and picked her up, cradling her in his arms like she was a small child. Jack drew power into himself. He erected a barrier around them. No one would be able to pass, he was certain of it.

I shouldn't stay like this, Jack realized. *But I can't forget everything, either. I need to make sure I remember just enough to understand my situation. It's dangerous, but I think I know how.*

Jack closed his eyes for a moment, and when he opened them, he looked around in confusion. All at once he felt the weight in his arms, and he peered down at the face of Requiem, looking back up at him. She was worn, tired, but she seemed to understand her situation.

"You saved me, Darling," she said.

Melissa turned around and called out to Sarah. "He's back!" she said with cheer. All at once they came running, every member of the team.

"Wait!" Jack shouted. "I've put up some kind of barrier, and I don't think anyone can get through. Not sure how I did it."

Cemmera was getting back to her feet, her face covered in a blinding fury. "Harris," she hissed. "For assaulting an Op, team during the removal of targets, I now exercise my right as a Captain and Team-leader of the Operations Department to execute you for treason."

Cemmera charged at Jack and screamed out in pain as she was thrown back almost ten feet then sent rolling across the ground. She stood back up. Blood dripped from her lips. She charged again, only to meet the same result.

"You two!" she screamed at her Kinetics. "Knock down whatever barrier he has and kill him!"

"We don't know how," answered Joseph. "I don't even know what he's done."

Jack ignored the commotion going on around him, knowing somehow instinctually that he was safe. He felt the warmth of the girl in his arms, her face red from the tears that were still falling.

"He was my everything, Jack," she said. "Ruin ... Anthony was my everything."

"Can you do something for me, Sandra?"

"What is it, Darling?"

"Just for once, just for me, I want to see you."

"But you're looking at me right now."

"Without the mask, Sandra. I want to see the real you. Please, just this once."

She nodded, and for a moment, however brief, the madness left her face. She looked up at him, with her fiery red hair and the most beautiful blue eyes Jack had ever seen. For a moment, she was an angel, a thing of beauty, a Goddess.

Jack pulled her in, still cradling her in his arms, and he kissed her. He knew Melissa was watching, and he knew he'd feel guilty later on, but for the moment it was only him and the girl that could have been like him, had the world not turned its back on her.

The kiss lasted a lifetime, a perfect moment between Jack and the misunderstood girl. He heard screams from his team, screams from the Op. team, and screams from what sounded like a thousand recon officers surrounding the two with weapons drawn. None of that mattered. There was only him, and Sandra. Never again would he call her by another name.

She gripped him tighter, pulling him in from his shoulders. Jack knew she felt secure in his arms. He had taken her away from those disgusting animals that hunted her, the animals that were no different than the one who had destroyed her life.

When they finally separated, Sandra looked into his eyes, and Jack was relieved to see that the madness did not return. "If you live, Jack, I promise that I will too. Darling, I love you."

Jack felt his heart beat faster at the words. No one had ever told him that before. "How can you love me? You don't even know me?"

"I knew you the moment I saw you, Jack. I was passing by the day you made the fire, and I knew it was you, I knew the moment I saw your beautiful eyes, the ones that I used to have."

"They can be yours again, I promise."

"How? Look around you. Your friends are surrounding us. By the way, Darling, why is that woman grinning?"

With great effort he tore his eyes away from the beautiful Sandra. Standing at the edge of the barrier, four feet away from him, with one of the most amused, devilish grins he'd ever seen, was his mother.

"Sweetie, show a little modesty. You've been kissing that girl for over twenty minutes."

Jack blushed, embarrassment spreading over him. "Is that you, Mom? Gah! What are you doing here?"

Paro's team—his team—stood around the barrier. There were now over two-hundred men swarming the room, and outside there were sirens and police cars surrounding the building. Standing closest to him, Jack saw his mother with a man he didn't recognize. He was a tall, muscular black man, with a kind face, and a look of deep, complex intelligence.

"Mr. Harris, my name is General Deven Moore." The man wore a white uniform with the emblem of a crow on the left shoulder. Come to think of it, his mother was wearing the same thing.

"This is quite the barrier you've put up, hmm, I'd say one part Manipulation, one part Telekinesis, but ..." He reached out a hand, and Jack tried to scream a warning. Nothing happened, and the General was able to put first his hand, then his entire body inside of it. "Two parts Telepathy," he finished.

Jack backed away from him. Sandra held him tighter, shaking with fear. "I won't let you kill her," Jack growled.

Deven smiled. "I'll do no such thing, Jack."

"How do I know I can trust you?"

"Just look into my eyes and see for yourself."

Jack did as he was asked, and looking into the older man's face, he could see the kindness that was within, the sincerity, and the hope. Jack did not know who this man was, but at once he trusted him implicitly. Jack set Sandra down, and she ran behind him, hugging his waist.

"Darling, I don't want to go," she said.

Jack spun around and made her meet his gaze. "You have to, Sandra. I promise you, I won't let anyone hurt you, ever again."

Deven held out his hand, but did not make any attempt to approach the girl. "Your name is Sandra, yes? If Jack likes you, then I like you. Come on, why don't I take you to a nicer place?"

Sandra took one step, and then two, before crossing the third step, and holding the General's hand. "That's a good girl," he said.

Alana took a step forward. "Did you take down my son's barrier? Wow, that's a weird thing to ask. I never thought I'd ask that in my lifetime."

Deven laughed. "It's down," he said.

Alana took Sandra's hand and led her away.

"So, what do we do now?" Jack asked. "How much trouble am I in? And why is my mom wearing the same clothing as you? Also, what time is it? I think I might have missed Dancing with the Stars."

Deven's face filled with mirth. "I'll tell you about your mother later, but for now just know that she's a General. And as for you being in trouble, well, consider yourself lucky this time. The moment that Op. team attacked your mother, they were no longer operating under an official capacity. All you did was beat up a bunch of rogue Psychs."

"Umm, General, sir, can I ask you a question?" Jack had no idea why he was about to ask this to a complete stranger, yet something felt right. Something told Jack that if he didn't say what he was only moments away from saying, then something horrible would happen.

"Why of course, Jack, go ahead. What is it?"

"Does the name Redemption mean anything to you?"

Deven's lips quivered, and he seemed to twitch, but those were the only indications he gave that he was troubled. "It might. Let's get you home."

Epilogue: Rose

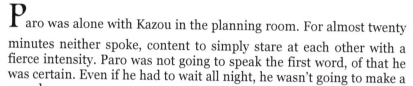

Paro was alone with Kazou in the planning room. For almost twenty minutes neither spoke, content to simply stare at each other with a fierce intensity. Paro was not going to speak the first word, of that he was certain. Even if he had to wait all night, he wasn't going to make a sound.

It hurt to sit up straight, and in all honesty, he should still be in the med center. He'd broken quite a few ribs. Thankfully, he'd make a full recovery. Even breathing hurt, and Paro's body begged him to lie down. Paro knew he couldn't, though. He would show no weakness in the face of his Reinforcer.

Kazou tried to hide his emotion, but Paro knew him too well. There was worry in his eyes—a great deal of it, and as the twenty-minutes turned to twenty-five, sweat began to drip down the Japanese man's forehead. By a half-hour, his face was drenched. Finally, after close to an hour, he opened his mouth to speak.

"Paro," he whispered, "I know what you're thinking, but there's more to it."

"You know what I'm thinking, do you?" Paro said. It still hurt to speak. "Choose your words carefully, Kazou, because if you tell me anything that isn't true, I'm throwing you out of a window. And no, that isn't a joke. So help me God, I am serious."

Kazou looked down at the glass table, refusing to meet Paro's eyes. "I ..." he said. "I was the one who called the Op. teams, and I was the one who gave them the files."

Paro forced his face to remain free of emotion, and he succeeded. What Kazou couldn't see was Paro biting down on his inner lip until he tasted blood. It wasn't nearly as painful as the wounds to his body.

Paro stood up from the chair and paced around the room. "Kazou," he said. "Do you realize that by doing so, you brought upon us a problem even greater than the two Psychs we were after? You almost got Alana Harris, Jack Harris, and Melissa Sayre killed. Cemmera Wilson, as you've no doubt seen for yourself, was an even bigger basket-case than the murderers we were chasing."

Paro watched as Kazou swished his mouth, struggling to gain the moisture to form words.

"They'd killed so many people, Paro. I never wanted to hurt the team, I swear it. It's just that every time I saw another person die, I felt like there was more I could be doing. Please, I'm so, so sorry. I swear to you, upon my life, my honor, and everything that I am worth, that I only acted in what I believed was the team's best interests."

Paro sighed and tried not to feel pity for the well-meaning Kazou. "I know you did, Kazou. If I thought you acted for any other reason, I really would have thrown you out of a window. But, I can no longer trust you. Kazou. You're off my team."

In one of his rare moments, Kazou's emotions came through, and they were powerful. At first his eyes grew moist, and then his lips quivered, until the man who almost never cried, bawled like a newborn.

"Please," he begged, "I have no one else. I don't have any friends, and my brother is the only family I have, and he's on an Op. team—I never get to see him. Without this team I have nothing. No reason to live, no reason to go on. I don't do this job just because of the importance of it. I do it because of the people I get to be with. I ... I love all of you, even the annoying Harris-kid. *Onegai shimasu!* Do not make me leave, Paro. Please, I can't be alone again."

Paro had to bite his tongue to stop himself from forgiving him. Paro needed to be strong. He needed to act like a team-leader. As a friend, Paro would take him back no matter what he did, but as a Captain and team-leader, there was only one choice left to be made.

"Get out of here," Paro commanded. "Get out of here!"

Kazou went to his knees and continued to beg, the biggest display of emotion Paro had ever seen from the man. "Please, I beg of you. Don't make me be alone again! Without the team I have nothing."

Paro forced his last bit of willpower into his voice and eyes, narrowing them on Kazou. "I said get the hell out of here—now!"

Kazou trembled as he stood, walking out of the room with his head held low. Paro knew he'd feel the guilt of his actions later, but for the time being he had to put them aside. There was a meeting he needed to attend, and he had to be focused.

The ride to the top floor was a quiet one. Paro was alone in the H.Q elevator. When the elevator beeped and the doors opened to the General's wing, Paro almost forgot about his ordeal with Kazou. It was a magnificent place.

So, this is what it looks like? Paro thought.

There were windows everywhere, providing three-sixty degree views of all of Manhattan. It was beautiful. Buildings shorter, and some taller, could be seen in every direction. Paro didn't have time to take in the sights. It was only a short walk to the first room on the left, where he'd make his meeting. He knocked.

"Come in."

Paro walked into the room. Sitting at a large glass desk was General Deven Moore. Standing beside him was a woman Paro did not recognize. She was of average height, but dressed in an extravagant red kimono, and Paro realized it must be General Rose. It was said that the woman wore the clothing of a different culture every day.

Her eyes weren't visible. They were hidden behind a book she held in front of her face with a steady hand.

"Have a seat, or stand if you like," the General said. "I'm not much one for formality."

"I'd like to stand, if possible. Thank you, General Moore."

"Please, call me Deven."

It was a massive breach of protocol, but Paro nodded and smiled. "Okay then, Deven."

"Normally I'd make small talk, but I don't have much time. There's a flight I need to catch. So, Paro, there's two things we need to talk about. First, I want to know what happened between Jack Harris and Andy Leonell at the terminal in Anker. Don't look surprised, did you really think all those recon officers would remain quiet about something like that? I'll forgive you this time, but if it happens again, I'll sic Rose here on ya."

Paro shuddered at the thought of the memory, yet he did as commanded. For this he took a seat. Over the next ten minutes Paro told them all about the incident. He even admitted how it was the single most frightening thing Paro had ever been through, in a life filled with horrors. General Deven's face tilted with interest during some of the darker parts, but Rose seemed content to continue reading her book.

"May I ask you a question, sir?"

"Deven."

"Ah. May I ask you a question, Deven? It's something that I doubt I'd be privy to. So, if you're unable to answer in the interest of security, I understand."

"Go ahead."

"Could you do what that boy did? Using Telepathy, I mean. One of the things a member of my team suggested was that perhaps we only thought what Jack did was impossible because none of us had ever seen it done before. We were wondering if perhaps he's not a freak, and just really powerful, like a General."

Deven grinned and nodded with approval. "A very smart team you have. Well, I'm really not supposed to answer that question, but I trust you, Paro. I think if it was life-or-death, I could do what the Harris-boy did, maybe even for as long as he did it. But," he said with a pause. "It would kill me."

Paro shivered, hearing his words. "So then Jack—"

"Is a freak," Rose interrupted, turning yet another page in her book. "He's a freak that will either destroy our world or save it."

The words hit Paro like a truck. "I'm sorry, what was that? Did you just say that Jack is someone who will ... I don't even know if I can repeat that."

"You heard her correctly," Deven said. "Her visions are almost always true. When Rose sees two paths, the world almost always travels one of them."

Paro shook his head. He knew there were certain Telepaths who could see beyond the ordinary, but this was absurd. Jack might be the most powerful person Paro had ever encountered, but saying the fate of the world rested on his shoulders was beyond ridiculous. "Excuse me, General Rose, may I ask you a question?"

There was an almost five minute pause, during which Rose turned the page of her book four times, before putting it down for a moment to meet Paro's gaze. She was a striking woman, with an almost omniscient set of eyes. Paro felt as if a single glance from her would reveal his entire life. It was unsettling.

"Yes, go ahead," she answered.

"Are you quite certain about what you just said? That something as big as the world could be destroyed by Jack, of all people? Or saved, for that matter?"

She didn't respond. Instead, she held the book back to her eyes and continued to read. Paro looked at Deven in confusion.

"You'll get used to it," Deven said. "Whenever someone asks Rose a question, she considers her words very carefully. I've never once heard her say something she later regrets. There are many people in this world that speak without thinking. Rose is on the opposite end of that. It can be frustrating, but you learn to deal with it. Once, I had to wait forty-five minutes for a response when I asked her to pass me the salt at a dinner-party. You get used to it."

Paro wanted to ask why he didn't just get up and get it himself, but he thought the better of it.

Rose remained silent for almost ten minutes, flipping through pages in what Paro figured was probably an entire chapter. He was caught off guard when she finally spoke. At the time, Paro was counting the number of words he could think of that started with the letter 'A.'

"I am certain," she said finally. "Though in what capacity, I am not at liberty to say. One errant word from me and disaster could befall us all. Just proceed as normal for the time being. There are very bad things to come, and you'll know what to do well before they're on their way."

"What bad things?" Paro asked

Rose brought the book to her face and continued to read. Deven laughed. "You're not going to get an answer to that one, Paro.

Come on, I've got a flight to catch but I can buy you a beer on the way there."

Paro grunted. "I'm not supposed to leave H.Q. I'm pretty badly injured. I'd need a release."

"Here ya go," Deven answered, already removing a signed document from his white General's coat.

"You have a document for everything, don't you? Can you even do that?" Paro asked.

For a moment he regretted it, he was speaking to the General like he was a friend, an equal.

Deven only laughed. "That I do. And yes, I can do whatever I want, I'm a freaking General!"

Paro shook his head and followed the man out of the room. A bit of alcohol would do him some good after the nightmare that had been his last few weeks.

"Mr. Harris, I'm going to ask you one more time—do you have your assignment or not?"

"Yup, I do, Mr. Trinchard! It's right here somewhere. I'm just trying to find it."

The teacher sighed, and rubbed his eyes. "Do you mean that piece of paper that you're writing on right now? For five minutes you've been telling me, 'I've got the assignment' all the while you've been writing like a madman on that paper. Mr. Harris, are you trying to do your homework in front of me and claim you've done it at home?"

The students in the class laughed, but Jack ignored them. "Nah-uh, I'm just trying to exercise my wrist muscles."

"Mr. Harris, you've got until the count of three to hand in your assignment, or you're getting a Z-"

Jack groaned. "Wait, isn't F the lowest thing you can get?"

"It used to be, until I got *you* as a student."

Jack cried out loud, "Why is everyone so mean?"

The End

21548512R00169

Printed in Poland
by Amazon Fulfillment
Poland Sp. z o.o., Wrocław